FAULT LINES

FAULT LINES

Stories of Punishment and Rectitude

Illustrated Edition

Colin Heston

READ-ME.ORG INC.
PUBLISHERS

Australia, New York & Philadelphia

Library of Congress Control Number: 2023932522

ISBN: 978-0-911577-66-2 (paperback)
ISBN: 978-0-911577-68-6 (digital)

Contents

1. Pardon My Tutu 1
President Biden's attendants seek to rehabilitate him.

2. Nothing to Declare 20
Happiness unappreciated.

3. Deliverance 29
Teacher, student, and strap.

4. Spilled Milk 34
Spilled milk reveals many years of silence.

5. Dishonorable Discharge 40
A duel compounds the vicissitudes of honor.

6. Matchmaker 45
A matchmaker applies her craft to crime and punishment.

7. For France 62
A psychiatrist grapples with torture.

8. Fault Lines 71
A boy is punished for his misadventure.

9. Road Rage 82
A child is saved by punishment.

10. Size Matters 85
A bully gets his comeuppance. 85

11. Crowd Pleaser 90
Little kid wins big. 90

12. Cleanliness 94
A child is punished for swearing.

13. Imperial Blunder 98
A famous cricketer breaks the rules, with dire consequences.

14. Disposal 117
A dysfunctional family meets its logical end.

15. Truth in Sentencing 123
A Self Inflicted Punishment?

Contents (cont.)

16. Bullies 130
Like water, punishment finds its way.
17. A Matter of Honor 135
The reward of punishment.
18. Finding Fault 142
The mini monstrosities of a classroom
19. Parallel Lives 152
The monstrosities of mass punishment
20. Pardon my President 160
Why JFK was assassinated.
21. Unforgiven 175
Donald Trump wins by losing, maybe.
22. Greatness 191
Of winners and losers.
23. A Notice of Infraction 199
The punishments of everyday life.
24. Felony Media 209
A new off-the-wall TV series breaks all records.
25. Felony Media Episode 2 230
Audience participation at its Best.
26. The Hungry Priest 243
A hermit feeds on the sins of others.
27. The Punishment Game 253
A law professor is convicted of evil intent.
28. Punishment Therapy 260
A restauranteur seeks counsel during COVID lockdown.
29. Discipline 275
Parallel fathers discipline their sons.

1. Pardon My Tutu

President Biden's attendants seek to rehabilitate him.

"Come on, man!"

Georgie yelled back, "come on man your fucking self!" and threw his biodegradable coffee cup, half full of a four shot flat white, right at the TV. It had no effect of course. President Biden continued to speak, informing his fellow Americans of the coming roll-out of the Corona virus vaccine. Georgie's long suffering partner Fiona lay on the couch, groaning.

"Georgie, you better get the car ready," said Fiona with a faint smile.

"Already?" asked Georgie, "so soon?"

"I know. But there may be something wrong. Better sure than sorry."

Georgie drove Fiona to Bethesda Hospital where she would give birth to their twelfth child. He did not wait for the arrival, though, because he had other matters of State to attend to. President Biden's speech infractions had to stop. It was a terrible example for all Americans, and undermined his committee's work. He punched "Clinton Cleaners, Pennsylvania Avenue, Baltimore" into the GPS. He would raise this issue at the weekly meeting. They met in secret because of the many threats they had received from extremist republicans. Of course, there were no republicans on his committee.

Georgie looked around quickly at the interior of his old Toyota Prius to make sure all the doors were locked. He had chosen this place in Baltimore because he wanted the committee to meet far away from the Capitol building, but also on the assumption that the press would never look for them in one of the worst places of Baltimore. Besides, members of the "unofficial" undercover squad of "genderamerie," basically hate-speech spies, always attended his meetings and they were paranoid of having their covers blown.

If you are as prejudiced as most people who are not good democrats, you are no doubt wondering how come a life-time democrat has a partner, wife, that is, in old terminology, and eleven going on twelve kids. The answer is a bit complicated, but the simple one is that he was born a catholic and remains a good catholic, and in spite of the modern catholic doctrine of turning a blind eye to birth control, he does not believe in it, obviously, though he is of course in favor of abortion and all the rest. That's the short answer, the official one that he tells when asked by prying individuals and other friends so-called.

The real answer is quite different. It goes way back to the time at high school when he was changing in the locker room for gym. He was a teenager as were all the others, some a little more advanced, one might say. There were bullies and the usual fools mucking about, flicking towels at each other. Then one of the kids spied him trying to cover himself up, so he pulled Georgie's towel away from him and pointed, laughing, "look, he's hardly got one! It's so small!" The kids danced around and made fun of him. All Georgie could think to say was, "you wait, it might be little but it's a good squirter!"

Now on Pennsylvania Avenue, Georgie stopped at the lights, checked again that all the car doors were locked, then perused with some detachment the continuous rows of boarded up houses or shops that lined each side of the street, and the frequent vacant blocks where there was once a house. As the lights turned green, he saw the sign "Clinton Cleaners" painted in black letters on a dull yellow board that covered where there was once a window. Who would have anything cleaned in this neighborhood? It would be all they could do to buy food at the local store, let alone dry cleaning. The answer was that locals did not use it. Rather, people from the suburbs or from downtown places of work, the university being one of them, found it a convenient drop-off place, and easy parking. Mind you, they all looked over their shoulders when they got out of their cars.

Georgie pulled into the vacant block next door. The meeting house was the boarded up place right next to the dry cleaners. He had made sure it was comfortable, though. Fitted out with standard issue office chairs, two multi gender toilets, basic kitchen for making coffee and reheating take-out meals that many brought with them, and of course the essential refrigerator. He had, after special request, installed a refrigerator with a very large freezer compartment, because one of the genderamerie hate unit had a fetish for stracciatella gelato.

There were about a dozen members of the committee, including the few from the gender and hate police who sat in on discussions. To be honest, it was not his first choice of committee assignments. Georgie was a bit embarrassed when he had to admit it to himself. A loyal democrat all his adult life, working his way up the ladder, first a council man, then chair of the school board, then assistant to the state congressman that represented his county in Bethesda. There he had remained locked in and unable to move up, until after some twelve years and the birth of his eighth kid, an opening came up to assist the congressman representing his district in the congress of the United States. This, he thought, would at last provide him with a way up, though he was not quite sure where "up" would take him.

The trouble was that, after four years of Trump, his unexpected rise to power, and the incredible rallies he conducted, one memorable one in Virginia, Georgie and most of his committee members had come to the conclusion that Biden had no hope of winning the presidential election. So they mostly, for the year leading up to the election, fooled around a lot of the time. They did draft the incredible document that Speaker Pelosi would sanctify, the one that erased all mention of gender in official documents of the United States Congress. When they drafted it, many of them did so after quite a few drinks, combined with a few whiffs of weed. So they were all amazed when Biden won, and of course invigorated by the upset. Now, Georgie had banned liquor or weed for the entire session of their meetings, and allowed them to imbibe only after they had finished their business.

These meetings were now ones of great excitement. The real possibility to make a difference. A President who thought what they thought. Or so Georgie thought until that morning when President Biden had begun his TV speech with the well-known favorite opening words, "Come on man!" He would, on this very morning, raise this issue that had bugged him from the very first day he was appointed chair of this now very powerful committee. Indeed, its power was unfettered. It could publicly accuse anyone of hateful, gender-biased speech, on Twitter or anywhere else, and it would automatically result in the character destruction of that individual. He had the power to destroy people's lives, without actually killing them. What more power could one want? But should he do it to the president? Surely he did not want to destroy him, the president of his own party?

The answer to his quandary came from an unexpected source, the genderamerie, gender police.

Now at the risk of revealing classified information, the genderamerie was the brainchild of none other than Hillary Clinton. It was she who gave it the French sounding name, telling Georgie, her hand covering her mouth, that it would be enough to confuse the far right Russian spies. At first, Hillary resisted Georgie's appointment as chair of the committee, because he had more than one child. But his unmasking of many of her enemies as gender offenders, especially, well, we should not list their names for fear that the information is classified and stamped as "FOR HER EYES ONLY," that she reserved the right as the only one who had permission to reveal the names, which she did so at the most opportune moments. It was she who ordered the committee to go on a rampage of unmasking many greats of old. She had commanded Georgie to begin the committee's work by ferreting out all the salacious details of J. Edgar Hoover's cross-dressing, which Georgie found when Hillary told him the file was in the hands of Edward Kennedy's grandson, Owen Kennedy. Actually, this proved to be not quite true, but did lead to an amazing revelation. The file, actually the manuscript of an unpublished book written by Woodward the Watergate hero, according to Owen Kennedy, lay hidden in the President's oval office, sat on by every president since JFK's reign. Each had promised that they would release it for publication, but once in office, none did.

Would Biden do the same?

That was the question that Hillary had put to Georgie, one that he promised he would investigate. He had been trying to get an interview with President Biden for several weeks, in fact since the very day of his inauguration, in order to follow up this lead. And now, with that insulting and unempathetic opening line of "Come on man," it was time to call him out on it. He had asked Hillary if she could get him a meeting with the president, but she had cut him off in her well known crabby manner. He was annoyed with himself for asking her. Should have realized that Biden had the job that she coveted. Fair enough.

Georgie called the meeting to order. We need not go into all the boring procedures and silly addresses and questions to "Mister Chairperson." Georgie insisted on as much congressional double-talk as possible to maintain the decorum of the meeting, also demanding that all the gender permutations of Mister chairperson be used throughout the entire meeting. This required a recorder, usually appointed by him at the beginning of the meeting, to keep track of each permutation, to inform the person who spoke, which permutation to use, and at the end of the meeting if not all permutations were used, the recorder for reasons of equity, was to address them all to the chair before Georgie would declare the meeting closed.

Georgie called the meeting to order. We need not go into all the boring procedures and silly addresses and questions to "Mister Chairperson." Georgie insisted on as much congressional double-talk as possible to maintain the decorum of the meeting, also demanding that all the gender permutations of "Mister chairperson" be used throughout the entire meeting. This required a recorder, usually appointed by him at the beginning of the meeting, to keep track of each permutation, to inform the person who spoke, which permutation to use, and at the end of the meeting if not all permutations were used, the recorder for reasons of equity, was to address them all to the chair before Georgie would declare the meeting closed.

At this meeting, an important piece of information was unmasked by the genderamerie. One of the gender police operatives had a close relationship with the FBI liaison to the White House. He had observed Biden reading the secret manuscript during one of the weekly briefings with the FBI. Why not ask Woodward what's in the manuscript that every president finds so interesting and that the public must never know about? After all, everyone knows about Hoover's cross dressing.

Woodward was famous and revered because he always made sure that he had three independent sources for any salubrious piece of dirt he dug up on his quarry, usually a president. Thus, anything he wrote and published was absolutely true. The operatives of the genderamerie had pressed Woodward on this secret manuscript, even threatened him with leaking false information, and claim that it was in his manuscript. This thoroughly annoyed Woodward, but he would not give in. Speculation had it that whatever was in the manuscript was the reason why every president since JFK, allowed Woodward access to the Whitehouse and was able to write a revelatory book about each president. Why did he have such access? It had to be what was in that secret manuscript.

Georgie had an idea. He turned to a genderamerie spy. "Can you get me into the weekly meeting of the FBI with the President?"

The operative shifted uncomfortably in his seat. "I could try," he said looking sideways.

"Good. Then you can pick me up and we will go there together," said Georgie with a big smile that reminded the operative of Georgie's close relationship to Hillary.

*

President Biden was enamored with the Oval Office. He treasured the few times he had sat opposite President Obama chatting and waiting for Hilary to show up (she always did). And on the day of his inauguration, President Obama had sidled up to him and slipped something into his pocket.

"I don't smoke," joked President Biden, "if that's what you're sneaking to me."

"Neither do I," grinned President Obama. "I've just given you the key to the long kept secret of every president going back to the time the Whitehouse was built."

The President felt in his pocket and discovered a small, round disk, smooth to the touch. "Feels like a poker chip," smiled Biden muttering through his PPE mask that was decorated with a likeness of Hillary.

President Obama looked around to make sure there was no hidden camera or person eavesdropping. "Every president hands it down to the next occupant of the oval office. But given, well you know, Trump, I decided to hang on to it until someone respectable was back in the Whitehouse."

"That's very kind and wise of you, Mr. President, if I may say so," said the President.

President Obama continued. "And I replaced what was a big key and tag with a remote ID chip. All you need do is wave it near the inset bookcase with the semicircular top to the left of your presidential desk, and it will open up."

President Biden looked at President Obama, incredulous. "You mean, it's a secret door? To where?"

"A small basement, kind of like a man's cave, you know? When things get to you, and they will, I can tell you that, you can sneak away down there and do your own thing, have a nap, or whatever."

"Could come in handy," mused President Biden, "I'm surprised that Clinton didn't use it."

President Obama grinned. "Yeh, you'd think so. But he loved the limelight, and besides you know what he was like. He just couldn't wait."

"But even to get away from…"

"Yeh. Hillary. Maybe he did. Anyway, Bush passed it on to me and I'm grateful for it. It's why we're such good friends."

"Well, thanks, and stay safe," said President Biden, in a most presidential way.

It was no small basement. When President Biden sneaked into it after he had dismissed all his entourage of secretaries, interns, assistants and advisers, he waved the disk just like Obama said, and the bookcase responded accordingly. It opened into a large room, not really a basement, though the stairs did go down somewhat. It was crammed with all kinds of mementoes and souvenirs, much of which he had no idea of its significance. But of great interest was a dart board set up in one corner of the room, on which was pinned a black and white photograph of J. Edgar Hoover standing in a hallway, his legs crossed, naked except for a tutu. It reminded him of a painting he had been forced to admire at an art gallery in Los Angeles Museum of Contemporary Art, that featured a special exhibition of Lucian Freud's paintings. He was there for a charitable opening of some kind, and part of his duties were to visit the gallery's special showings. There, he was confronted by Freud's giant painting of an overweight man, legs crossed in a kind of pirouette posture, and every part of his body showing. It was gross, but he grinned to himself, thinking that it would have been a very funny painting if the man were wearing a tutu.

He picked up a couple of darts and threw them at Hoover. They both missed the board. Then he spied something else lying on the rather dirty floor to the right of the dartboard. It was an actual tutu, tinged with blue. For reasons he still could not explain, he leaned down and picked it up, shook the dust off it, then pinned it to the dart board, and went back to have another throw. He missed again. Then he did a three sixty of the entire room noticing something else that he should have noticed before. There were mirrors all round. That caused him, without even thinking, to start a careful search for hidden cameras. He found none. And why would there be if past presidents had kept this secret for so long? He turned, listened for any noise in the office, and, hearing none, squeezed his key and the door opened for him to return and automatically closed upon his exit.

He was back just in time. There was a knock at the door and Tom Pain, White House chief of staff entered. "Your weekly FBI briefing, Mr. President."

Deputy director of the FBI, Saul Butt, entered followed by an entourage of notetakers and assistants, including Georgie. They were all introduced carefully in order of their seniority, and finally Georgie, to whom the President turned.

"You're new, I think?" asked the President.

"Georgie, sir, chair of the Congressional Committee on Gender Eradication."

"Yes of course. Excellent work you guys are doing. Keep it up. And why are you here at today's briefing?"

"Our committee is working closely with the FBI, sir, to ferret out and unmask miscreant abusers of gender identity and hate speech, sir."

"And why are you here?" persisted the President pressing Georgie.

"Sir, it has come to our notice that there is, in the Whitehouse library, or possibly on a shelf in this office, a manuscript authored by the famed Woodward of Woodward and Bernstein, and that it includes a number of hate speech and gender infractions," said Georgie in his most formal manner.

"That's serious. In this office you say?"

"Yes sir. Would you mind looking around for it?"

"I don't have to. It's in the bottom right drawer where I keep my, err, never mind."

The President leaned down and withdrew a large manuscript, the edges of its pages torn and grubby. "This what you're looking for?" he grinned. "The former, er, President told me about it. Said he couldn't see anything wrong with it and it might as well be released for publication. Said he felt sorry for Woodward, the pathetic little guy. Of course, if that President said there was nothing wrong with it, that was a red flag to me. So I decided to keep it close to me for safe keeping. I have not looked at it myself, though by the look of it, many presidents before me have."

"Sir, I respectfully request that my committee be permitted to examine it for gender unmasking and hate speech analysis," requested Georgie, most officiously.

"All for a good cause!" quipped the President. "Here you are, you can have it for one week and one week only, and it must not be taken out of the Whitehouse. An intern will hold it for you."

"Thank you Mr. President." Georgie leaned forward and

took the manuscript.

"Now what does the FBI have to tell me this morning?" asked The President.

*

It was, indeed, a remarkable manuscript. The title was "Secrets of the Oval Office: From Taft to Trump." A large portion of the book was devoted to the so-called secret basement. Georgie easily smuggled it out of the Whitehouse by promising an intern a significant place on his gender eradication committee if she brought it with her to their next meeting. He even picked her up outside the Whitehouse and drove her to their Baltimore meeting place. She was a little nervous when they came to the rundown parts of Baltimore, asking where were they going, did the committee really meet in such a terrible place, fearing that he had designs on her. To which he answered, as he always did, that it was necessary to remind ourselves of how the poorer half lived. He then, out of the blue, made an offhand comment, "by the way, my wife Fiona is giving birth to our twelfth child probably as we speak."

The intern tried to hide a gasp and her cheeks turned red. But completely out of nowhere she blurted, "oh, my goodness! Poor thing!" Shocked at her own words, she covered her mouth with both hands. "Oh, I'm sorry. I mean, I meant, that's wonderful! Congratulations!"

Georgie grinned. "Don't worry. I'm used to it. I'm proud of it too. Fiona's fine too. She'll be a bit sad for a few days, because she loves being pregnant. We both love children. I just hope this time it will not be a false alarm like it was the last time I dropped her off at the hospital on my way to our last meeting ."

He pulled into the vacant lot next to Clinton Dry Cleaners. His Toyota Prius looked a little pathetic beside all the smartly polished black SUVs and Hummers. The comparison made him feel extra good. But he knew that he would face, this morning, a challenge of immense proportions. He would make a proposal to censure President Biden for using gender insensitive language, specifically "Come on man." Simply arguing that it was a common manner of speech was no excuse. Many of those old words and expressions had been eradicated from all speech and dictionaries. "Come on Man" had to be eradicated or at least reworded so that it was no longer offensive.

Without thinking, Georgie held open the door for his intern who looked at him with a mixture of fear and disdain. How dare he do that? Opening the door for her was an infraction of the gender eradication code, was it not? The intern gave him a disapproving look. He extended his hand and said, "hand me the manuscript if you will." And she did, making sure that their hands did not in any way touch when she gave it up. She wanted no skin contact with this guy. She did not trust him. He took the manuscript and walked quickly to the entrance. She scrambled out of the car (from the back seat mind you where he had insisted that she sit) and ran to catch him up. "If there's anything I can do, take notes of something?" She pleaded.

"Thanks, but no. Notes of this meeting are the last thing we want." Georgie pulled the door open and walked in, leaving her to catch the door as it closed.

Georgie immediately swung into action. "Good morning members and visitors if there are any. Please place your phones on the table in front of you. I request that you switch them off for the duration of the meeting. No notes or recording permitted. The members sat at a large oval table, at one end of which was a very large office chair that would be his as chairperson. The rest of the chairs were standard prison-made chairs, square metal frame, hard wooden seat.

Now, one must understand, that, when a group of more than three or four people comes together to deliberate on a plan of action when faced with a difficult problem, the odds are that it will reach an illogical, strange or unpredictable conclusion. What was about to happen would prove that to be true.

Georgie called the meeting to order, then produced his own phone, fiddled with it until YouTube came up, and then started a video, turning the phone so that all present could see it. He had made a composite video of the opening remarks of the last several speeches Biden had made over a few weeks. This resulted in a video that repeated many times over "Come on man!" All members of the committee stirred uncomfortably in their uncomfortable seats. Georgie began his well-rehearsed speech.

"I regret that I must broach this very difficult problem of President Biden's favorite opening remarks to almost all his speeches that implore the viewers to do or agree with a particular policy or action he is promoting. Is he not speaking also to women, I mean those other than men – my apologies? The expression is incredibly gender insensitive, and violates the common sense of inclusiveness and diversity."

One of the genderamerie interrupted. "Then tell him to stop! Problem solved!"

"It's not that simple," put in an unmasking gender eradication expert. "Our work requires us to uncover all past infractions and make perpetrators pay for their past mistakes. None can be allowed to get away with their lack of empathy. And that includes the president. I applaud Georgie for having uncovered this blatant infraction that has occurred hidden in plain sight on a daily basis."

"Then what would you suggest be done? Impeach the President?" put in another.

"That's a bit of overkill. Censure would be more appropriate," put in yet another.

And so it went.

Until finally, Georgie produced the secret manuscript. "We have heard many good suggestions. Let us break off to talk informally, then come together to make a resolution. During the break I am passing around a bit of a bombshell. It is the secret manuscript by Woodward that many of you have no doubt heard about. Look through it and see if you find anything that might be applied to solve our problem with our miscreant president."

With money and equipment donated from Farbucks Coffee, Georgie had set up an espresso bar, complete with a barrista (the gender of that term he was not sure of) to serve the best coffee in town, as everyone had heard. The secret of the coffee was simply that the barrista routinely served double the shots customers asked for, and they predictably responded with "wow what great tasing coffee." The caffeine therefore did its job, and had everyone talking animatedly, though there was some jostling around the single copy of the secret manuscript. However, always thinking one step ahead, Georgie had installed a small office copy machine so they were able to make copies of the more interesting and relevant pages. Those pages turned out to be those that described the dart board and J. Edgar Hoover in a tutu.

As a favor, Georgie had his intern call the meeting to order. "Before we get down to the business of the day I would like to make one personal announcement," said Georgie. He put his phone down carefully on the table. "My dear wife Fiona has just given birth to our twelfth child. They are both doing well."

The intern smiled excitedly and blurted out, "boy or girl?" She immediately put her hand to her mouth when she realized her mistake. A hushed silence descended on everyone around the table. A gender spy took notes.

Georgie forced a grim smile. "I'm sure we can overlook that offensive remark," he said, "they are both doing well regardless."

The intern abruptly got up and left, crying on the way out.

Georgie continued. "Now, what ideas do we have for the Come-on-man fiasco?"

"Before we get to that," interceded a gender spy, "what does this manuscript have to do with it? Besides, I wouldn't be surprised if Woodward made it all up."

"Very perceptive," countered Georgie. "It has nothing to do with Come-on-Man directly. But therein lies the idea for how we may get compliance from President Biden."

The group stirred, feet shuffled.

"Do tell us," said the head of the genderamerie, with a heavy dose of sarcasm.

"I thought that, in order for the President to demonstrate how sorry he is for using vile gender epithets, he should go on national television, dressed in a tutu like J. Edgar, and apologize, promise he will never use that manner of speech again."

"You're mad!" exclaimed a small spy who sat in the corner.

The room erupted with everyone talking at once. Exactly what Georgie wanted.

Another gender spy stood up to make his point. "I will repeat what I said right at the beginning. Just tell the President to stop saying it. That's all that is needed."

Another interjected. "No, it's not enough. He must make up for this egregious error. He must apologize. He's the great example to all citizens and especially children. He must show everyone that he understands his error and convince the viewers that he is really sorry for what he has done. After all, it must amount to several hundred, even thousands of infractions of the gender code."

Yet another spoke up. "Yes, it's not enough to simply say you are sorry. He's on TV. He must truly show that he is sorry. The question is, how does he do that convincingly?"

Everyone looked each way and that, waiting for a bright idea.

The intern returned and quietly took its seat.

"I still say, just tell him to stop it. That's enough," insisted the gender spy.

The intern spoke up in a querulous little voice, "I did tell him to stop it. Well, not exactly, I just mentioned once that maybe the Man part wasn't appropriate."

"And what did he say?" asked the gender spy.

"Nothing. I don't know if he heard me. I'm only an intern, you know. I probably shouldn't have said anything."

The group murmured as one. Shoes scraped the floor.

"Then it's clear that we must educate him," responded Georgie. Then he held up the manuscript, turned to the page on J. Edgar and the tutu. "Here is a way out suggestion, but I think it would do the trick. We have him dressed in a tutu just like J. Edgar, while he gives his sorry speech."

Shuffles and silence. Georgie looked around the table, challenging each one to look him in the eye. None did. They all looked down to the table.

Except the intern who blurted, "great idea! He'll look just like that Lucian Freud painting, except he's not quite fat enough."

It's doubtful whether any of the group, except the gays whose numbers were unknown, knew what painting the intern was talking about. But Georgie did, and responded with a loud laugh and all followed. It was done. Now it remained who would convey this demand for the punishment of a sitting President?

The Director of the genderamerie decided that it was about time he asserted her authority. "I hate to say it, but isn't this unconstitutional? The only way a punishment can be delivered to a sitting president is to impeach or censure him-her-it."

"We are not punishing, just asking for an apology and correction of past wrongs. It's a bit like a confession," answered Georgie quickly.

"Is there a second for Georgie's proposal?" asked the intern.

"I'll second," answered the genderamerie director, "though I want it noted that I still think it's unconstitutional."

"Any more discussion?" asked the intern very businesslike and not waiting for any response. "Then all those in favor, say, aye."

Of course, the ayes had it, unanimously.

"Who should convey this demand, I mean request or sugg- estion, to the President?" asked Georgie.

Silence. All eyes turned to the intern.

Georgie checked his phone. "I have to run. My wife is giving birth to our twelfth child, as some of you know. I have to run. I'll leave it to you all to decide who conveys the message." He shoved the manuscript in the direction of the intern and left.

*

Predictably, the gender eradication and hate speech comm- ittee failed to appoint the messenger, though it was pretty clear that they wanted the intern to do it. It was the logical solution. It had nothing to lose, whereas the futures of all others were at stake. They were not prepared to stick their necks out.

The Intern, however, would have been overjoyed to do It, anything to get close to the President, the most powerful gender-thing in the world. But he-she-it did not speak up. Instead, gathered up the manuscript and hitched a ride back to the Whitehouse with some gender spy who spoke not a word to it-her-him.

*

When Georgie finally arrived at the Whitehouse VIP gate,

he was fearful of how the President may respond. While he sat at the gate awaiting the security guard to clear him, he thought of poor Fiona, who had let out her last gasp, truly the last, the baby born with all, and we mean all, the necessary equipment to become a thoroughly successful gender addition to diverse America. A truly fitting replacement for Fiona.

The security guard informed him that he was not on the list for today, but made the mistake of addressing him as "sir" to which Georgie quickly pointed out his hate speech error, so the guard let him through. He quickly made his way to the outer office adjoining the west wing lobby, where all the interns were kept in voluntary captivity. His gender eradication intern sat immediately outside the door to the oval office.

"Do you have the manuscript?" he asked.

"It's in my desk. The President has been in here twice asking for it. I didn't want to give it up without you saying so. He…sorry… I mean the President, was quite angry."

"Give it to me," ordered Georgie crossly. He marched straight into the oval office only to find that the office was empty. He stopped, embarrassed and returned to the intern room. "He's not there. I have to go. My wife Fiona…" He held out the manuscript and just as the intern was about to take it, it was snatched away. And there stood the President, an angry smile on his face, all those teeth, his eyes reduced to little horizontal cracks in his forehead.

"Give me that," growled the president.

"Your Presidential Self," addressed Georgie, "my apologies for keeping the manuscript for so long. But my committee on gender eradication and hate speech met this morning and it took quite some time to come up with a solution to the Presidential problem that I must now urgently inform you of."

The President looked at him, trying to process the jumble of words that Georgie had just tossed his way. "Step into my office. I have just five minutes. It better be good."

Georgie beckoned to the intern to follow. The President sat at his desk, looking all business-like. "Come on man!" he said. "Out with it."

The intern put hand to mouth to cover the shock of hearing this abomination yet again. "Your Highness, I mean President, that's hate speech! You can't say that!" Sobbing loudly, she-her-it turned and ran out of the office, slamming the door behind her-she-it.

All those white, gleaming teeth burst into yet another grin, this time not angry but empathetic. "You better go and console her," said the President to Georgie.

Georgie ignored the advice. "I have to inform you that the gender eradication and hate speech committee resolved unanimously this morning that you must make a public apology for using your most used offensive expression, 'Come On Man,' further, that you must make amends for having spoken such hate so many times. One of our interns has counted several hundred occurrences in the last six months."

The teeth remained in their smiling position, this time surrounded by disbelief. "You mean I have to go on TV and make an apology?" asked the President.

"Yes, First Citizen, if I may call you that."

"You may. Indeed I quite like it," answered the President still smiling.

"And there's one more requirement," said Georgie, a little nervously, "it comes from the secret manuscript." He pointed to the dog-eared pile of papers sitting on the president's desk.

The First Citizen looked down, and flipped through the manuscript pages with his thumb. "Let me guess, you sons of bitches…"

"Please! First Citizen! No more hate speech. That's shocking. I don't want to have to go through this all over again with yet another infraction of the gender code."

"My apologies, what's your name again?"

"Georgie, sir, I mean First Citizen."

"Well, Georgie, out with it. What's the committee's recommendation?"

"It's not a recommendation. It's an order."

"I don't think you understand, No one can order me to do anything. I'm the President, First Citizen."

"Yes, First Citizen. But in this case, we are dealing with thousands of infractions against the gender code. If you don't get out in front of this, your opponent will slaughter you in the next election. You will be a one term president."

"That's not too bad a thought," quipped the President, First Citizen.

"First citizen!" cried Georgie, demanding attention.

"All right then. What do they want me to do?"

"That picture of J. Edgar Hoover, dressed in a tutu..." murmured Georgie.

"You mean the one pinned to the dart board?" said with a very large presidential smile.

"Yes, First Citizen. We know about the secret basement."

"You know more than I do. I assure you there is no such basement. That manuscript is all crap."

"Whatever, First Citizen. It is the committee's unanimous verdict that you must dress in a tutu, a tutu only, and apologize for your past gender infractions and hate speech, on live TV, or we are prepared to allow it to be done on You Tube."

"But they'll think I'm..." The President managed not to say what would normally have come naturally.

"Indeed they might. But then, is this not very much in your favor? You will be the President of all the people, all diversities, all genders. It will be a magnificent triumph of unity!" Georgie couldn't believe he had come up with such a fantastic proposition.

"What's your name again? Georgie, of course. Georgie my boy, I mean my premium citizen, I thank you for this great opportunity to empathize with my people." As if it could not get larger, his smile truly reached from ear to ear, and those teeth gleamed as the sun's rays penetrated the oval office window that looked out on to the lawn. "Let's get to it!" he shouted. He picked up the phone and shouted, "send in the media people. I am going to speak one-on-one with all my citizens!"

Georgie remained rooted to the spot. He thought briefly of how proud Fiona would be of him at this moment.

The President turned to Georgie, now with an affectionate smile. "You know, maybe you should come and work for me. Your talent is wasted out there with the gender spies and hate speech researchers.

"First Citizen! I would be honored! When do I start?"

"What about right now?"

"First Citizen?" Georgie asked in an inappropriately intimate manner.

"Yes, Georgie?"

"Have you ever seen the painting by Lucian Freud? The one with a naked individual showing all its equipment?

Moral: The masking of truth is its revelation.

2. Nothing to Declare

Happiness unappreciated.

Little Rita eagerly looked forward to the day, promised by her mamma for as long as she could remember, that she would make her confession. Actually, it was even before she could remember, because mamma had said, as her proud pappa (now departed for other temptations) held her in his arms, "our little darling, wait until you can go and make your confessions!"

So on Rita's eighth birthday mamma met her after school, and they walked together to the little church of San Clemente, just a few streets away from where they lived on Via del Colosseo. Rita skipped along excitedly, down the steep steps to the Colosseo, then to Via Labicana. Mamma squeezed her hand and took her into the church. It was small, as Roman churches and basilicas go, nevertheless to a ten year old it was massive and whelming. The confession box was tucked away in the far corner on the first level of the church, behind the altar. Not that Rita had never been there before. It was the church in which she was christened, according to mamma, and Rita accompanied her almost every day and watched while she knelt at the altar and thumbed her rosaries and mumbled things under her breath. In fact after her dad departed, they went there even more than once a day.

"Now be sure to tell everything to the Father when he asks you. Just like I told you. OK?" said her mom as she leaned down and gave Rita a little kiss on her forehead.

"I will mamma."

Her mother knocked lightly on the confessional door and there was a faint rustle of clothing. She opened the door and saw movement through the finely carved confessional window. "In you go. Make sure you kneel nice and straight."

Rita stepped in, the door closed behind her, and she knelt down, curious to see who was behind the window.

"And what can you tell me this afternoon, my child?" purred the priest.

"My mamma said I have to confess my sins today."

"Then tell me dear child of Mary mother of God."

"My mother's name isn't Mary. It's Christina."

"Yes, of course. What sins do you have to tell me today, my child?"

"I don't have any, Father. I haven't done anything bad or anything. I don't think so."

"You know that you must always tell the truth to your parents and to your priest, do you not?"

"Yes, Father. My mamma always tells me that. But I can't think of anything I have done that was bad. I always have a happy time and my mamma has never spanked me. So I can't have done anything bad, can I?"

"My dear child. Everyone, children included, commits sin. You must have done something bad."

"You mean my mamma has done something bad?"

"In confession, my child, we can't talk about your mother. Only your sins."

"I really don't have anything to confess, Father. I'm sorry for that."

"No bad thoughts, even?" asked the priest, slightly annoyed.

"I'm always happy, and I don't have anything to think about that's bad."

"No one is always happy, my child. Are you sure that you are telling the truth?"

"Oh! Father! I would never lie. And now I think I have just committed a sin. I have got upset with you."

"Do you get upset with your mother?" asked the priest, feeling he was making progress.

"Oh No! Mamma is the sweetest kindest person I know. I love her so much. She couldn't do anything that would make me have bad thoughts."

The priest responded, trying to hide his disbelief. "She hasn't once had to discipline you?"

"I don't know what that means, Father."

"I mean, did she say you've done something wrong, and punish you for it?"

"No, Father. I told you. I haven't done anything wrong, ever."

"No bad thoughts? Jealous of someone perhaps?"

"I don't think so, Father. What does jealous mean?"

Frustrated, the priest responded. "My child, this confession is over. Please say one Hail Mary twice a day, just to be on the safe side, in case you have not been telling me the truth."

"But I haven't confessed to any sins, Father. Why do I have to say a Hail Mary?"

"It is not for a child to question a priest, my dear." The priest closed the window. There was a scuffle of clothing and shoes scraping the wooden floor, and he was gone. Rita stood up and left. Her mother was waiting by the altar.

"How did it go?" she asked.

"I said I didn't have any sins to confess and he got angry with me, I think. But I couldn't see him."

"What did he say?"

"You said I'm not allowed to tell what we talk about in the confession, didn't you?"

"Yes, you are right."

*

On her eleventh birthday, Rita asked her mother if she would be going to confession like last year.

"I think we will wait until you are twelve," she said. "The Father told me he didn't think you were old enough."

Rita didn't question that. Just gave a happy shrug and said, "OK mamma."

And so, a year went by and at last, her twelfth birthday arrived, celebrated with her friends and cousins. And after they had left, Rita asked, "am I going to confession today?"

"I have made an appointment for you tomorrow. I'm not sure if it will be the same priest. But it shouldn't matter. They all work for Jesus and Mary."

"Do they get paid?" asked Rita innocently.

"Of course, but not by Jesus and Mary, silly! The Pope pays

them, I guess."

"That's very good of the Pope. He must be a very kind man."

"He is."

"And very rich too. There are so many Fathers to pay."

"I have booked you in for tomorrow after school, at San Clemente. Do you think you can go there on your own?"

"I've been there so often, mamma. I'm sure I can go there. I just knock on the confessional door when I get there, *è vero*?"

"Yes. And it's the same confessional as before, down behind the altar, in the corner. Don't be late."

*

Right on time, Rita knocked gently on the confessional door. She heard the rustle of clothing and stepped in. She had tried to prepare herself this time. Read some stories about people going to confession. How they were supposed to think hard about what bad things they had done, read the ten commandments and go through each one to see if they had broken any of them. This she did very carefully. She read every commandment and decided that she had not broken any of them. Even the one about honoring your parents. She wasn't quite sure what the word "honoring" meant, but if it meant did she do what her mother told her, she had, every time and always. Of course, she couldn't say anything about her father because he had departed a long time ago, when she was a baby. She wished that one day she might get to meet him. But wishing for that wasn't a sin was it? Maybe it was honoring him in his absence?"

"Good afternoon my child," said the priest. It was the same voice that she remembered from two years ago.

"Bless me Father, for I have not sinned or anything as far as I can remember," said Rita, shifting a little on her knees.

"But my child, that is not possible. When did you confess last?"

"Two years ago, Father. It was my first confession."

"And you have not made one since then?"

"No. Mamma said I wasn't old enough, but now I am. I think the Father told her that."

"Then I will ask Jesus and Mary to overlook that, only this

one time. But my child, remember you must confess every week, more if necessary.”

“I will Father. But it’s the same this time.”

“What do you mean?”

“I read all the ten commandments. And I haven’t broken any of them.”

“Have you not even disobeyed your parents?”

“Never would I do that to my mamma. My dad left and I never knew him.”

“Bad thoughts?”

“I don’t think so. But I really don’t know what bad thoughts are. I’ve always been a happy kid. Never a dull moment, my cousins say.”

“My child, it is a grave sin to lie to your priest in confession. Of course, lying is a sin at any time and for any reason.”

“I don’t lie, Father, I would never do that. I am always happy. I have nothing to lie about.”

“Are you not lying to me now?” asked the priest with a touch of belligerence.

“Oh no! Father! I would never do that! I love Jesus and Mary so much, how could I do that to you?”

The priest took a deep breath. He had never experienced anything like this. He should have spoken more to the girl’s mother after her first confession, but did not because of the sacred bond between confessor and priest that their exchanges should never be revealed.

He had another go at it.

“Have you never wished for something that another girl had, maybe one of your playmates?” he asked, this time he would surely trap her.

“Oh no Father, I would never covet my playmate’s toys.”

The Father was taken aback. “You know what covet means?” he asked incredulously.

“Oh yes, Father I read it in the ten commandments. Thou shalt not covet thy neighbor’s wife.”

“Not even one of your playmate’s dolls?”

“Oh, Father, I think I made a mistake. I had this really pretty

Barbie doll."

"Go on."

"And I was playing with Tina, my cousin, and she started to cry."

"And?"

"She said my doll was prettier than hers, and she wished she had it."

"Are you sure it was not the other way around?"

"Oh no, Father. But then I was feeling so sorry for her, I gave her my doll. And that made her very happy, and made me very happy too. Was it selfish of me to feel sorry for her?"

"I don't think so," answered the Father, again crushed by this child's unmitigated happiness. He was on the verge of giving up, but then, against his better judgement, decided to have one more try. He coughed a nervous cough. The child was twelve. There was one way in which he could catch her, no, that was not a good way to think about it, help her discover the sins that hovered deep inside the body.

"Touching?" he asked in a thin voice.

"Touching, Father? I don't know what. It's not a sin to touch something, is it?"

"Sometimes it is."

"I mean, once I touched mamma's hot iron and burned my finger. Was that a sin?"

"Well, if your mother told you not to touch the iron, then yes, it was a sin because you disobeyed her. You violated the fifth commandment."

"I don't remember her telling me not to. But I suppose she might have when I was really little."

"There, you see. You did have a sin to report."

"I have always tried very hard to obey my mamma. I never disobeyed her on purpose. So I don't think that's a sin."

The priest, in spite of himself, coughed a nervous cough again, and said, "have you ever touched yourself?"

"Don't be silly, Father, of course I have. I do it every day when I wash my hands and face. That's not a sin is it?"

"Mostly, not. But there are places on your body that you

should not touch."

"You mean my…" Rita put her hands to her face covering her eyes, "I can't even imagine it."

"Perhaps I should speak with your mother."

"About touching myself? But everyone has to go to the toilet, don't they? How can you not?"

"It isn't what I was thinking," said the Father, immediately regretting having said it. Fortunately, Rita did not follow the thread.

"Father, when you think, do you think bad thoughts?" asked Rita innocently.

"We all do, my dear, even priests," he answered, relieved. "That's why I also go to confession every few days."

"I'm glad you do. Hey! One day I could hear your confession after you've heard mine," said Rita with a giggle.

"You have to be a priest to hear a confession. It's the work of Jesus and Mary."

"Mom said you get paid for your work by the Pope."

"On earth that is so," boasted the priest.

"So who pays the Pope then? Jesus and Mary?"

"Of course not. They are in Heaven. But my child, let's get back to your confession."

"Sorry Father. Thank you for listening to me. I'm a bit of a chatterbox when I get started, my mamma is always saying. Do I have to say any Hail Marys?"

"It's always a good idea to say some, even if you haven't committed any sins. So I will leave it to you to decide how many you want to say."

"Thank you, Father."

"May the peace of God be with you, my child." The priest gave a sigh of relief and left the confessional.

Rita's mother waited for her in front of the basilica. As you may have guessed, she was a devout catholic, very careful to follow all the requirements of ritual and practice of the catholic church. "She is such a perfect child," she muttered to herself. But as soon as she said it, she crossed herself and looked up saying, "forgive me Jesus for I have sinned the sin of pride." There had never been a time when she had to scold her little girl, even raise her voice. The child was so happy. Yet it seemed that her happiness caused much trouble for others, especially the priest who had heard her first confession. The priest had in fact broken the sacramental seal and hinted to her what had happened in the first confession. She was very grateful for the priest's concern and his sharing it with her, but at the same time, the Father had been forced by Rita's happiness to break one of the most sacred rules of the church.

Rita, her innocence radiating like a halo, knew nothing of this. She simply enjoyed life and found not the slightest speck of badness even in situations that were awful, her absent father for example, or the day she tripped on a cobblestone near the Colosseo and broke her arm. She did not cry at all. Just said she was sorry for slipping over and causing such fuss. Why was she so happy? Was there something wrong with her? She looked up and saw Rita skipping happily towards her. Everything must have gone well. Too well, perhaps?

"How was confession?" she asked.

"The Father was very nice."

"How many Hail Marys do you have to say?"

"Mamma. You told me I'm not allowed to tell what happened in confession."

"Children are allowed to tell their mothers. Didn't the Father tell you that?"

"No. He just said I can say as many Hail Marys as I want."

"Nothing more?"

"Lots more. We talked a lot, or, maybe I talked a lot."

"You had a lot to tell him?"

"Well, he said some silly things."

"Like what?"

"I don't think I should say, should I?"

"It's different between mothers and daughters."

"So would you tell me what you say in your confession?"

"Well no. It's not like that. I'm not allowed."

"That doesn't seem fair." Rita gave a little giggle, then looked up, "but I don't mind. I can tell you the silly things that the Father said. I'm sure he wouldn't mind that."

"Go on."

"Well, he asked me whether I touch myself..."

Moral: The innocence of youth feeds the guilt of adulthood.

3. Deliverance

Teacher, student, and strap.

The tiniest teacher in the school was also its most senior. Every day without exception she came to school dressed in grays and browns, sometimes a black beret sitting precariously on a head of grayish brown hair, cut short, though still covering her ears. And for a dash of color she wore a beige scarf tied loosely around her neck. The boys most likely paid little attention to Miss Brown's dressing habits though they had good reason to, since she stood out to the boys in the school—hard to believe—as its giant disciplinarian, (and girls too, probably, though they were spared the specific punishment designed to make a man out of its recipients).

No matter what the problem was, if there was any altercation or kids' complaints of any kind, they went to the door of the staff room that opened out into the quadrangle, where Monday morning's assemblies occurred (lorded over by the alcoholic school principal), knocked timidly and waited. Inevitably, Miss Brown would come to the door.

"Yes? What is it?" Miss Brown would bark, usually munching, or seemingly so, on a biscuit, the crumbs falling on her beige scarf.

"There's a boy spying on us through the fence, Miss," complains the sixth form girl, her school jumper pulled tightly over her slightly bulging breast, her navy blue school dress reaching just below her knees. Miss Brown looked up at her face, then down at her knees.

"I'm not surprised. Look at your dress! School rules require that it be no more than four inches from the ground. Yours is at least six inches!" barked Miss Brown in her grating almost man's voice, so gruff for such a tiny person, or any woman for that matter.

"They was looking through the fence, Miss Brown,"

persisted the girl, looking down.

"They were, young lady, do you not pay any attention to your English classes?"

"Sorry Miss."

"Who is this boy? Where was he?"

"I'm not sure who it was, Miss. I think it was Geoff Peterson."

"And where are your manners? It's Miss Brown, I'll thank you very much!"

The girl stepped back from the step upon which the tiny Miss Brown stood, now on her tippy toes trying to make herself feared all the more.

Miss Brown waved her hand as if the girl were a fly. "Get away, now, and mind your own business, you hear me?"

The girl backed away as Miss Brown came down from the doorstep and called out to a boy who was crossing the quadrangle. "You there!" she barked, "come here, boy!" She stepped back up to the doorstep and the boy, probably a fourth former, approached her. "Do you know a boy called Geoff Peterson?"

"Yes Miss."

"Yes what?"

"Yes Miss Brown."

"Go find him and tell him he is wanted at the staffroom right away. Tell him to hurry as the bell for classes will be going in five minutes."

"Yes Miss."

"Yes what? You want the strap too?"

"Yes Miss Brown, I mean, No Miss Brown."

The boy ran off. Miss brown retreated behind the door of the staffroom and set up her step stool. She knew Geoff Peterson. He was the tallest kid in the school. Long and lanky, and took great pleasure in looking down at her.

Within minutes he arrived, knocking at the staffroom door. The diminutive Miss Brown opened it and straightened her scarf as she did so. Peterson noticed this and knew immediately he was in for it. She straightened her scarf every time she was about to use the strap, and looked straight ahead, which meant more or less looking at his belly button. She unfurled the strap, a yard of thick brown leather with a wooden handle bound to one end. She made the handle herself because the width of the strap was too big for her little hand to grasp the strap firmly. There was nothing more embarrassing than the strap flying out of one's hand at the top of a swing. Peterson looked down at it. She had a way of jiggling it so that it looked a little like a snake hanging by her side.

Peterson pleaded, knowingly full well, that it was useless, "I haven't done nothin' Miss!"

"You were spying on the girls through the fence. I know it was you!"

"No Miss Brown," he complained carefully, "it couldn't be me. If I wanted to look at them I could just get up on my tippy-toes and look over the fence." Peterson was putting on his usual tough defense.

"Put out your hand," demanded Miss Brown, ignoring his plea.

"But Miss Brown, Oh Miss Brown!" he cried, now with a big grin, "you wouldn't strap a poor little boy like me, would you? Especially when there's no evidence."

"You are such an insolent boy!" snarled Miss Brown. She stepped up on her stool, at which Peterson put his hand to his mouth to cover his grin. He (and she) remembered the last time she strapped him (only yesterday). He had moved his arm this way and that and she ended up almost chasing him around the staffroom unable to land the strap on his open hand. And when he did stop and put out his hand, she was so short she could not manage to raise the strap high enough above his hand in order to bring it down with any kind of hard blow. So this time, she had brought in a stepping stool to give her more height.

Up she stepped, one hand on her hip, the other brandishing the strap. "Come on, then, out with it young man!" she demanded.

Peterson burst out laughing. He almost said, "out with what?" but managed to hold it back, instead laughed uncontrollably,

which of course incensed Miss Brown even more.

He moved his hand this way and that, Miss Brown lunging forward and sideways, hampered by her having to remain on her stool. He laughed and jiggled around.

"Stand still!" she yelled.

But Peterson was by this time out of control. He waved his lanky arms around so that Miss Brown managed to lay a few strokes here and there, though not with the satisfying smack of leather on a bare hand that she liked.

"The left, now. Come on! You're getting six of the best for your insolence. Out with it!" she snarled, her face wrinkled with anger.

But then, the bell rang for classes, and almost relieved, Miss Brown stopped and stepped down from her stool. But she was very frustrated and, completely losing control of herself, she swiped with her little, though quite strong arm when she was able to do a full swing, at Peterson's legs. The strap wrapped around his legs, and though they were protected by his gray school pants, it was nevertheless a shock of the unexpected, and Peterson let out a wail you would never believe.

Miss Brown immediately stood back, her hands on her hips, the strap dangling beside her body, no longer taut, relaxed, one could almost say as though after a bristling climax.

Peterson, for his part, backed off and fled to class. He had a story to tell that would amuse and delight all his mates.

Moral: Effective punishment requires the full cooperation of its recipient.

4. Spilled Milk

Spilled milk reveals many years of silence.

This story is based on true events, as is all fiction. In 1950s Australia, in a small and rapidly growing suburb of Geelong, a place called Norlane, there was a little old pub, built of bluestone, now painted a dirty cream, red corrugated iron roof, a couple of red brick chimneys, and a very old public bar, complete with a pock-marked linoleum bar counter and vintage old taps. The bar room was about the size of a two car garage, which appeared big early in the morning at opening, but by 6 o'clock at closing time, patrons were packed in like sardines, elbow to elbow. As you might guess, there was no shortage of brawls when the men jostled each other to order drinks for themselves and their mates. The din of men talking and chortling was huge.

Hidden away at the far corner of the bar was the only man sitting in this bar made for standing. This was the special stool that the pub's owner had put aside for good old Joe Smith, the painter. The noise of the bar made no difference to him. He sat on his stool, stared straight ahead across the bar counter, eyes dreamy, maybe focused on the only picture in the bar of the young Queen Elizabeth, hanging above the refrigerator that kept the beer cold.

Joe was a special kind of painter, crucial to the Ford Motor company that stood across the road from the pub. Every day, now going on fifteen years, Joe showed up there for work, dressed in paint spattered overalls, nothing except underwear underneath (so one supposed), because it was so hot when he donned the plastic coated outer garment that covered him head to toe. It was his job, as was one other who worked with him, to spray-paint the bodies of the cars as they passed along the production line. The paint in full spray was of course toxic so he breathed through a contraption that was most likely an adaptation of the old gas masks they used in World War I.

Joe and his mate (to whom he spoke rarely) painted from eight in the morning, ten minutes smoke-o and a cup of tea at ten, then paint again until lunch at twelve, a sandwich his wife made him every morning, and a quick run across the Melbourne road to the pub for a couple of beers then back to work at twelve-thirty. Then they painted until four, knocked off and sprinted across to the pub to drink the rest of the day until closing at six. This had been Joe's routine for the last fifteen years. He was very proud of his work, drove his painter mate almost crazy because of his insistence on attending to every small detail. He would not allow any blemish to go down the line. Every car, he said— that is when he spoke which was rare—must be perfect. Would you want a new car that had a paint blemish on it? He would ask. Not that he himself ever had a car. He couldn't afford it. And anyway he was happy enough sitting at home, doing his garden and coming in and having a beer by the telly.

Because the paint fumes were so toxic, even when you wore all the protective clothing and masks, Ford had a rule that a painter could only work at that particular job for fifteen years, and that was it. They were then reassigned to some other part of the production line. Of that, though, Joe would have none of it. He was a painter and that was all he was. No standing at a production line doing the same thing over and over again, having to listen to all the gossip of the other men.

So Joe retired when his fifteen years were up. He always said he would. This meant that he had lots of time to spend in his garden, and that was what he did every day. After breakfast at eight he went out, rain or shine and worked on his garden. The front full of rose bushes and geraniums and the back full of seasonal veggies. Usually, he worked at the front in the mornings, broke off for morning tea at ten, returned to the front, hoping there would be no people walking past that he would have to talk to. At midday, off he went to the pub, just ten minutes' walk down North Shore road, sat in the corner on his stool and socked down a few beers, in the winter often a few glasses of Abbotsford stout to keep him warm in the garden when he returned home, always at about one. He allowed this small change in his routine, and indeed, sometimes even made it one-thirty.

Missus Joe as she was known to all up and down the street, did not drink. They could not afford for both of them to spend money on drink, she announced ceremoniously every day, or at least to Joe is seemed like every day. She especially upbraided him when he came home after lunch and she could smell (so she said) the stout on him.

"You're not a bloody invalid, are you? So what are you doing drinking that muck?"

Joe simply ignored her, or seemingly so, though he did grunt, a small grunt, one that she would not detect, since she was too busy rummaging around in the kitchen cupboards, complaining that she could not find what she wanted.

"Why don't you build me some new shelves for the kitchen instead of buggering around in the garden and drinking your beer?"

"And why don't you go fuck yourself" Joe muttered to himself.

"Did you say something dear?" said Missus Joe, a sarcastic smile and tilt of her head.

Joe turned away. He could not bear to look at her. Compared to the cars he painted, she was truly ugly. And away he went to the garden. Afternoon was veggie time, where he spent a lot of time laying out the garden in very straight rows, nice little paths between each bed, each bed bordered by rows of empty beer bottles pushed into the soft dirt, bottoms up.

Missus Joe, for her part, labored over the kitchen sink that looked out over the back yard. She sang to herself, happy that Joe was out of her kitchen. "If only..." she mused to herself, but forced herself to stop. She washed the dishes over a second time. She had wanted children badly. But it was not to be. They tried, and finally gave up. Joe wasn't up to it anyway. She blamed it on his drinking. Makes men sterile, that's what her friends at church said. She had thought of leaving him, but truth be said, where would she go? What would she do for money? Get a job, maybe? Not that anyone would employ her so old, and a woman and all. She had pleaded with Joe not to retire. But he would not listen. Once he got an idea into his head, there was no shifting it.

"Stubborn old bugger" she grumbled to herself.

And so their gritty life ground on, a grit that seemed to hold them together, yet made a life as two individuals never truly to meet.

One day, it could have been any day, or any year of their marriage, but on this day, Joe came in from the garden, a little earlier than usual because he had pricked his finger while pruning his roses.

"Time for a cuppa," he mumbled to Missus Joe as he trudged past her into the bathroom.

"It's not ready yet. You don't come in this early do you?" She did not expect an answer of course. But she hurried and put the kettle on and got out the cups and saucers and placed a small plate of yo-yo's, as she always did, at the center of the table. And he always complained, though did not say anything, just made an obvious wince when he got up from his chair and leaned across to get the yo-yo.

"What are you doing in there?" yelled Missus Joe, her voice a rough crackling voice, one that penetrated silence like a bull-dozer.

Joe finished sucking his thumb when the bleeding stopped. He wiped his hands on the towel, noticing that it was smudged and had not been washed properly. He walked steadily to the kitchen and sat down on his usual chair. Missus Joe stood at the stove waiting for the kettle to boil.

Joe sat motionless, elbows on the table, propping up his chin. "Come on! Where's the bloody tea?" he complained.

On cue, the kettle whistled and Missus Joe made the tea. Her routine was also messed up. She went to the cutlery drawer to retrieve knives and forks and placed them on the table at their respective places. She had to reach around Joe in order to place the knife and fork exactly in the right place. If they were not straight, he would notice. Wouldn't say anything, mind, but she knew he would be annoyed. Immediately, he sat back in his chair, a heavy wicker chair, and stared ahead. "What's this for?" he asked, then licked his lips and pushed his tongue against his teeth as though the words were stuck in there. "Don't need a bloody knife and fork to eat a yo-yo, you silly bitch."

Missus Joe tried to ignore him and reached over to take the knife and fork back.

"Steak knives too, they are, you silly bugger!" He grabbed his knife, banged the handle on the table, and reached for the fork, pushing Missus Joe's hands away. She turned to pour the tea in the cups and pushed his towards him. Joe leaned back in his chair, his eyes seemingly out of focus. He now held one of the steak knives in his clenched fist. Missus Joe, struggling to remain calm, went to the refrigerator and retrieved the small bottle of milk. She leaned over him and went to pour a small amount into his cup, just a tiny amount. She had to hold the bottle steady and be very careful, because if she poured too much, he would be furious and would demand another cup of tea. Holding a bottle of milk, mostly full, poised above a small teacup was a challenge, even though she had done it a thousand times. "In my defense," she thought, "the bottle is slippery from the condensation on the bottle." Perhaps it was that thought that tilted the bottle forward, the hand of her aching arm letting go. The milk splashed out into the cup with such force that the teacup overflowed, and tipped over. Missus Joe dropped the bottle of milk on the table where its contents gurgled out and flowed slowly to the edge and on to the lap of Joe's old gardening overalls.

Joe was a man of few words, everyone knew that, especially Missus Joe. He gulped and his eyes grew wide, pushing at his red cheeks swollen from years of alcohol, his lips pursed tightly shut. His nostrils expanded like those of a Spanish bull about to charge. His fist tightened even more on the steak knife and his eyes, no longer dreamy, quickly focused on its serrated blade reflecting the florescent light of the kitchen. His thumb moved down to the blade and tightened. It was an awkward grip. But no matter. He rose from his chair as though thrust by a canon, and lunged wildly with a wide slashing movement, as though pulling open the curtain of a large window. And just as quickly, he dropped down on his chair, exhausted. Missus Joe was standing, pale and rigid with fright and shock, one hand to her bleeding throat, the other leaning on the table to keep her balance. For the first time in a long time, Joe looked at her right in her face, stared into her eyes. From where he sat, she looked like something from Madam Tussaud's wax museum. But only for a moment.

Her body sagged, then fell to the floor, Joe's eyes still staring where her eyes had been. She fell with a plop, blood spraying all over the place, a couple of spasms, and she was plainly dead. Joe looked at the floor and was upset for a moment that she had got blood all over the floor. Then he realized of course, that it was none of her doing. No, correction, her end was all her doing, it was just him who finished the job.

Moral: Punishment delayed, is punishment unleashed.

5. Dishonorable Discharge

A duel compounds the vicissitudes of honor.

There is honor, and there is honor, if you will forgive the repetition. A couple of hundred years ago, the western world was overtaken by what could only be called a neurosis of honor which beset only males, and males of a particular class, so-called. When a man's honor was attacked or questioned, usually by some kind of verbal abuse or a physical slight, intentional or not, it was incumbent upon him to challenge the aggressor to a duel; in the 1800s, usually a duel in which each party brandished a pistol. The reason for this unwritten law of behavior was that if any man's honor, that is, his standing as a gentleman was questioned, he had no recourse but to demand a duel to "clear his name."

So it was in Sydney in 1827 that a certain Henry Fodsworth challenged a Dr. Pisston to a duel in an isolated field in Home-bush. It should be added that these names have been changed in order to protect their forbears, who may be innocent. These two gentlemen were, in the eyes of Sydney society and of course in their own eyes, men of good standing, deserving of the respect of their stations. Henry Fodsworth was, after all, the brother-in-law of Governor Darling, which was as close to high society as could be. And Dr. Pisston was editor and part owner of *The Australian*, a paper whose name remains today Australia's shining light of national media, and certainly owned by a gentleman of that class.

The severe breech of honor was instigated by Dr. Pisston. It should be added that he was also a pal of Charles Wantsworth a serial litigator and dueller, who met his end when one of his enslaved convicts murdered him on his Petersham estate in 1834. Dr. Pisston accused Fodsworth of taking information from *The Australian* and leaking it to the *Sydney Gazette*. This was a false-hood, claimed Fodsworth, and promptly challenged Pisston to a duel.

According to the rules of dueling predominant at the time,

each party of the duel could appoint a second, or assistant. In some cases, they could even pay a representative who could fight the duel for him. But on this occasion, Fodsworth accepted the challenge and they both showed up at Homebush field to face off. Fodsworth appointed Wantsworth as his second who, upon presiding over the duel, urged Pisston to accept a verbal apology from Fodsworth. Fodsworth offered the apology, but Pisston declined it. Wantsworth retired, no stranger to duels himself, and prepared the dueling pistol for his friend.

Now it is important to understand that, although the outcome of such a duel was by no means certain, there was plenty of room for error, and indeed luck. Not to mention that neither of the parties was handy with a pistol and from twenty paces (or whatever it was they agreed upon), it was pretty hard to hit the target, and besides, if you aimed at the head, and missed, you were an open target yourself. Or, if you aimed at the chest or widest part of the body giving yourself a higher chance of hitting the target, chances were that you would not be lucky enough, unless a really good shooter, to hit somewhere that would incapacitate your quarry so that he would not have time to get in a shot.

Wantsworth stood by the two men who first faced each other then about faced and stood back-to-back.

"Gentlemen!" called Wantsworth. "You will take twenty steps to my count, but before I begin, you to turn to your opponent and offer a verbal apology, should you be so inclined to do."

The duelists remained silent, or if they didn't they muttered something so that they could not be heard. Later, Wantsworth claimed that Pisston said he would rather die than to accept an apology from that excuse-for-a-gentleman. And Fodsworth opened his mouth as though to speak, but coughed instead, putting his hand up to his mouth, the one holding the gun. He jiggled his arm as though it needed to be loosened up. Then he took the gun out of his firing hand and exercised his fingers, opening and closing his fist, again taking hold of the pistol and waving his arm around.

"Pistols pointing to the ground, please!" ordered Wantsworth.

Fodsworth coughed nervously, and his finger tightened on the trigger.

Wantsworth stepped back and announced in a ceremonious voice as the duelers walked: "One, two, three, four, five, six, seven, eight, nine, ten, eleven, twelve, thirteen, fourteen, fifteen, sixteen, seventeen, eighteen, nineteen, twenty!"

The two men turned, eager to get in the first shot. Fodsworth, a comparative novice, pulled the trigger before he was fully facing his quarry. The bullet zoomed off somewhere into the eucalyptus bushes. Dr. Pisston, a practiced cool hand, now faced Fodsworth squarely on. He raised his arm slowly, his handlebar mustache twitching as he squinted to get Fodsworth in his sights. He pulled the trigger and a very loud bang followed, the gun recoiling so much that he dropped it. Fodsworth fell to his knees in fright as the bullet whizzed by where his left ear might have been. Pisston scrambled to retrieve his gun that had landed in what looked like a rabbit burrow.

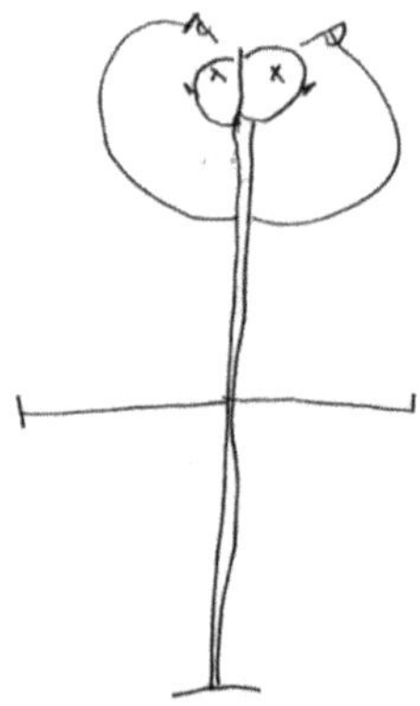

Fodsworth now had him in his sights. He was not sure whether it was allowed to hit a moving target, but he wasn't going to wait for Wantsworth to make any kind of judgement. He had four shots left (these were antique duelling pistols that were custom five shooters rather than the usual six; no one in Sydney wanted to copy the Americans after all). Pisston, caught without his gun, scrambled up from his knees, and, doubled over, ran for the bushes. Fodsworth aimed in the general direction and squeezed the trigger five times, his wrist hurting from the recoil, and the bullets flying who knows where.

Wantsworth ran forward, making sure he was out of the crazy Fodsworth lines of fire. He waved his arms, holding his rare copy of the Kanun duelling rules. "Halt! I say! No firing when the other is down! No firing!"

Fodsworth threw down his pistol and announced himself the winner. Wantsworth ran forward to retrieve the gun, one of a pair of a very expensive collector's item. "Hey Dr. Pisston!" he called, concerned about the pistol.

Dr. Pisston rose up from behind the bushes. He limped forward, his face twisted in pain. "I'm hit!" he cried, "I'm hit!"

"Where's your gun?" asked Wantsworth, most concerned to retrieve the pistol.

"I don't know. I lost it. It disappeared!"

Fodsworth reached out to Dr. Pisston to shake hands as gentlemen. The insult had been corrected.

Dr. Pisston looked at Wantsworth. "I'll not shake hands with that filth who claims to be a gentleman," he snarled.

Both Wantsworth and Fodsworth were aghast. This was an ungentlemanly flagrant breaking of the rules!

"You can't do that!" cried Wantsworth.

"At least I am a gentleman," announced, Fodsworth. his mouth full of false pride.

This was a most unhappy ending. A duel was designed to overcome such nasty outcomes. The winner of the duel, no matter what had happened before it, was clearly the right and proper gentleman. The prior differences that the two gentlemen had were erased by the outcome of the duel. That was why there were duels. Otherwise the resentments between two gentlemen, whose honor was very much at stake, could never be resolved, and the fight, as it would become, could go on forever, each one inflicting damage on the other only to be hurt himself when the other responded. Dr. Pisston's refusal to accept the duel outcome would now unquestionably become the cause of vengeance. And such vengeance would eventually lead to feuds that could last over generations. Every sensible gentleman understood that. The very course of history had been sullied by Dr. Pisston's refusal.

Wantsworth was most embarrassed. He was, after all Dr.

Pisston's second. It was partly his responsibility to make sure the rules were followed right through to the end. He flipped through his copy of the Kanun Code. There was no mention of this unhappy outcome. No one had envisaged that one gentleman would behave in an ungentlemanly way.

"Dr. Pisston!" he cried as he reached inside the rabbit burrow and with considerable satisfaction retrieved the pistol. "You have broken the dueling code of honor. I don't know what I or anyone can do to fix it!"

Dr. Pisston ignored him. He was of course, in pain. Blood streamed from half way down his leg. He limped over to his horse and with great difficulty, managed to get himself up, then rode away.

Wantsworth offered his hand to Fodsworth, who took it gladly. "I pronounce you winner of this duel on this day!" he said in a thin and faltering voice.

"Thank you Wantsworth. I am amazed I managed to pull this off. Thank you for your understanding and professionalism. We are both fine upstanding gentlemen, are we not?"

"We are indeed," nodded Wantsworth, "we are indeed."

They both went to their horses and rode off. As far as they were concerned the matter was settled.

As for Dr. Pisston, although he was a doctor, he did not act like it, or at least maybe the state of medical knowledge was still developing. He was so upset over the outcome of the duel that he kept riding on into the bush then out and about until he finally, after some hours arrived at his residence. He had lost quite some blood, and the leg developed gangrene. Having removed the legs of many men in battles of yore, he did not wish to have some surgeon do the same to him. And so he died of gangrene within the week..

Moral: Deserved punishment is always a balancing act.

6. Matchmaker

A matchmaker applies her craft to crime and punishment.

Auntie Aasiya proudly put down her phone. She would be on the next plane to Philadelphia. To imagine, that Philadelphia's District Attorney had requested her services, offering a very high retainer, and an irresistible daily expenses rate, the job expected to last several months! And paid in cash! The DA's assistant, who spoke Hindi in a perfect Awadhi accent heaped praise on her, saying that he had several friends and relatives who had found each other thanks to her wonderful services. She was so flattered, she succumbed to the request, without even asking for any details of the type of match anticipated. The DA had simply said that her services would be required for a period of several months, possibly longer, to help in a major project for the city, designed to improve the DA's dedication to implementing a fair and just criminal justice system. All he would say was that she would be key to helping the poor and weak who were caught up in a criminal justice system that no longer worked.

"How soon can you come?" asked the DA's assistant.

"I have one case almost tied up. I should say in one week," answered Aasiya (let's call her Auntie for short as everyone else did). "I will have to speak with my husband of 35 years first."

"That's no problem. We will pay for him to come with you, if that is necessary."

"Oh, thank you. That will make it much easier for me to get away, especially if it is for a long time."

Auntie had no inkling of what she would be getting into. The idea was the brainchild of Deputy District Attorney Ace Hole, a recent graduate of the influential University of Pennsylvania Law School, whose job it was to work with prosecutors and defense attorneys to hammer out sentences of a range of felons, usually through the practice of plea bargaining. As most know, plea bargaining, an informal practice re-discovered and incorporated into the criminal justice system in the 1970s, is used to short-circuit trials, to get the prosecution and the defense to agree ahead of an expected trial, for the offender to "plea" (a word rich in meaning, that's for sure) guilty to usually a lesser offense for which he was charged, thus avoiding the expense of a lengthy trial. Unfortunately, there are many distasteful side effects of this practice. There is the temptation for prosecutors to over-charge the defendant, to make sure he gets a punishment that matches the crime for which he is charged. But in these situations the defendant is often forced to plead guilty to a crime he did not commit. The resultant sentence (the punishment pronounced) is thus an abstract assessment of his guilt, only indirectly, of the crime he is supposed to have committed. Even worse, it increases the possibility that the offender will plead guilty even if he has committed no crime at all, in instances where prosecutors and their collaborators, the police, know he is innocent of the crime, or forced a false confession from the defendant.

But that is only the half of it. The actual range of punishment that is available is minimal, especially for "serious crimes" (generally referred to as "felonies") for which fines or probation are considered no match. Prison is the central and only punishment available, and the bargaining can go on for weeks or more over how much prison the offender should plead to, via the DA manipulating the crime for which the offended will plead guilty, regardless of the supposed original offense. For example, a DA may reduce the charge of first degree murder (intentional killing) to one of manslaughter (less intentional killing) if the offender agrees to plead guilty to the latter, usually in the circumstances where the DA is not sure she has a good enough case to get a guilty verdict on the first degree murder.

This system of make-believe justice has been criticized by experts for many years, but the fact that it is so functional, and makes it possible to process many offenders more quickly. Most important, it dispenses with the need of expensive and lengthy jury trials. Probably over ninety per cent of cases in the USA and elsewhere in the Western world, are decided in this way. One is not found guilty by a jury of one's peers. Rather, one is found guilty by a bargain reached between the prosecutor and defense, with a helpless client stuck in the middle.

How would Auntie Aasiya fit into this rigid system that nobody in theory wants, but with which all comply? Auntie's expertise lies in matching two people, often strangers to each other, even until the day of the marriage. The expectation (and the statistics bear this out) that the two, once married will stay together for a lifetime, their personalities and preferences and hopes a perfect match, as they say. Auntie was proud of her record of matches. The majority of them stayed together for at least ten years, many for a lifetime, or close to it.

*

Auntie was whisked away from Philadelphia airport in the DA's personal limousine, and deposited at the apartment reserved for her in Society Hill, not far from center city, and just around the corner to the original site of American Justice, Independence Hall.

Now before we get into the complexities of matching crime and punishment under the newly conceived idea of Ace Hole, a little background is necessary concerning how punishments have been matched to their crimes in recent history. In a duel, for example, the punisher is the victim of a dishonorable insult, and the offender is the one who offends. This is a perfect case of matching the punisher to the offender. The match is, however, one that runs the risk of an awful injustice. If one of the duelists is a crack shot, the other not so good, and if the crack shot is the offender, then there is a good chance that a serious injustice may be done: the offender may shoot, even kill, the punisher (i.e., victim). The victim of the insult is victimized twice over. And of course, being punished by shooting for a mere insult is obviously a failure to match the offense to the punishment. The serious flaw in the duel is that there is no dispassionate third party who has any authority at all to make sure that everything matches: the offender and his offense to the victim and his suffering, and finally to the choice of a punishment that matches the seriousness of the offense.

That's why we have a modern system of criminal justice,

you are no doubt thinking. Unfortunately, although superficially it looks as though that is the answer to this difficult problem, today it falls a long way short. For serious crimes (felonies, let's say, though that is also an overly simple term), there is only one punishment that is made to fit all crimes: prison. The third party, the judge, dreams up, guided roughly by a criminal code, what amount of prison, months, days, years, is equal to what kind of serious offense. To give you an example of the impossibility of matching carefully a punishment to a crime; if an offender commits two murders, he obviously cannot in actual fact serve two life sentences—though judges routinely deliver such impossibly matching sentences. You see the point.

An alternative, sometimes allowed in Islamic systems, is when the victim may approve or even carry out the punishment (including the death penalty), or forgive the offender completely, or settle for a monetary amount. But again, if it is left totally to the victim to match the punishment to the crime, forgiving a murder, that is, letting the offender go scot free, fails to match the crime to the punishment.

These and many other very difficult problems of matching punishment to crime are the reasons why Ace Hole and his collaborators have embarked on this history making solution: to focus entirely on matching the punisher, via a third party who is likely more dispassionate, as is a matchmaker of marriages, to the criminal and his crime. The focus is on the criminal as the primary ingredient of determining the punishment, and the seriousness of the crime only secondarily. And it was deputy DA Ace Hole, recently appointed by the new woke progressive DA of Philadelphia, who, having followed all instructions of the DA never to prosecute burglaries or any thefts; the argument being that it is unjust for some people to be richer than others, so it is only right that those who have not, take from those who have. This principle, of course, does not apply to crimes of violence (though there are some extremists who would indeed apply the injustice rule to these crimes as well). In any case, without the necessity to prosecute "property crimes" as they used to be called, the DA office found itself with lots of time on its hands. Hence, at a three martini lunch, as they called it many years ago when corporate executives had that luxury, Ace Hole came up with his idea of using a matchmaker from India to establish a system of matching punishers to offenders. It started out as a joke, but the next day it appeared on the morning's agenda meeting as a serious project.

Auntie Aasiya insisted on bringing her husband to her first meeting with the DA. She had heard so many stories of men in government preying on women in America, she was taking no chances. The limo picked them up at 10 am, and whisked them the to the DA's office, passing Independence Square, the Liberty Bell and the rest. "This is a very important place," said her husband. "It is where America gained its independence, and they did it much before India. It is a very great country." The driver smiled and nodded his assent.

Auntie Aasiya clutched her satchel to her breast. She was a little nervous. This was something entirely new. Why would they want a matchmaker, no matter how good she was? Maybe the DA's son or daughter was looking for a match? She leaned forward and called to the driver, "is the DA Indian, perhaps? Mr. Hole, certainly does not sound like an Indian name."

"No Ma'am. He born and bred in America. White as they come, you know." Auntie leaned further forward. She saw that the driver was African American and couldn't help turning up her nose just a little. The driver, fortunately, was watching the traffic, so did not see. The traffic was jammed up, road work on one of the side streets. They were on Twelfth Street, just below Market Street, and her husband shouted, "look! There's an Irish pub." The limo pulled up right outside it.

Auntie and hubby sat still.

"This is your stop. They're all waiting for you in there," said the limo driver with a smirk.

"This is 3 Penn Square?" asked Auntie.

"Not likely, Ma'am. But it's where Holey likes to have his early morning meetings, away from the media, you know."

"Holey? That's how you pronounce his name?" asked Auntie.

"Ah, no. I've known him for a long time, so I call him that

'cos we're friends, you know," the driver answered with a hint of mystery. "You better get out on the curb side. You'll get run down if you get out on the road side." He made no effort to open the door for his puzzled passengers.

"Lucky I brought you with me," muttered Auntie to her husband as she slid out of the car and on to the sidewalk. Thankfully, Ace Hole emerged from the Irish Pub and held out his hand to assist her.

"Ace Hole at your service, Doctor Aasiya, I believe?" said Hole with a very large grin. His rather dark complexion, probably of southern Italian ancestors, though could be taken as Indian heritage somewhere in the distant past, pleased Auntie. He was close enough to be like her, that is, her light almost white complexion that was the envy of all her Indian friends. "So pleased to meet you, Doctor Hole, and this is my husband."

"Welcome to Philadelphia, the city of sibling love," announced Hole bowing a little. "We are very much looking forward to learning all your secrets of successful matchmaking."

"I will do my best."

Hole led the way into the gloom of the Irish pub, empty of customers this time of the morning, but with an attentive bar tender, and a few secretaries and hangers-on. Already, they all held a glass of Guinness in their hands. The pub manager had set up a large round table for them to sit at.

"Can I get you a Guinness?" asked Hole.

"It is fortunate that I am not a strictly practicing Hindu, or I would have been shocked at this venue. They don't drink alcohol, you know. It's the one thing that India refused to take on from the British invaders. However, it is too early in the day for me to take alcohol. I must keep my mind clear, for matchmaking is a demanding intellectual task."

"Be assured, Auntie—may I call you that?"

"Of course," answered Auntie, though a little offended by this presumption of intimacy.

"We did our homework, Auntie. We know all about you. And we are very impressed by your accomplishments and success in your business."

Auntie smiled politely and looked sideways to see that her husband already had a large glass of Guinness in his hand. He was very much at home, having done his Ph.D. in economics at Oxford.

"Then let's get down to business," continued Hole, raising his glass of Guinness. "To matchmaking."

Auntie lifted her bulging satchel on to the table and withdrew her wads of notes.

Ace Hole addressed the participants, many curious, some trying hard to hide a smirk.

"The DA claims to want a "woke" administration, and I am justifying this unusual approach to criminal sentencing as the logical outcome of that policy. It can't be achieved simply by not prosecuting crimes, as is now the policy for all property crimes and misdemeanors. Serious crimes must be punished. We all get that. There's no way around it. But how can we do it in a progressive manner, a way that replaces, hopefully completely, the shockingly complicated, unjust system of sentencing and punishment of criminals in this woke world?"

All around the table nodded seriously and took a swig of their glasses of Guinness. Hole continued.

"A few weeks ago we came up with what we think is a promising solution. Instead of matching punishments to crimes, the traditional method that we know is impossible in most cases, if not all cases, why not match the punishment to the criminal, rather than to his or her crime or crimes. Then we realized that we should, if we are to be consistent, match the punisher whoever that will be, to the criminal. Thus, the matching punishment should emerge from a perfectly matched coupling."

Hole looked around the table. "Are you all with me on that?" he asked.

Auntie shifted in her seat and flipped through a wad of notes.

"I see no problem in using my method," she said, " which is, simply, draw up a list of preferred characteristics of the one, and match them to the same or responsive characteristics to the other. Of course, there will be some disagreements and we rarely get a perfect match, but we should be able to get close. Of course, the list of characteristics would, I should think, be very different from those for marriage match making. The relationship between a criminal and his punisher is hardly a marriage, if you see what I mean. Though, I would want to know whether you see the punishment to be one that continues over a lifetime, or long period. If so, some of the characteristics of marriageability may carry over."

This was a rather long speech so early in the morning, and as well, Auntie's heavy Indian accent made understanding her difficult. And it didn't help that she spoke so quickly. Several of the assistants, just out of law school, had to shake their heads to keep themselves awake. Auntie's husband retired to the bar and sat on a stool, sipping his Guinness, chatting with the Irish bartender, or was she English?

"Could we see what your lists look like?" asked Hole.

Auntie rummaged around in her over-stuffed satchel, and finally withdrew a handful of dog-eared pages. "Here's one I used recently for a very successful match of a very shy little girl of eighteen and a large rotund man of thirty three, meek and cuddly. On the face of it you'd think they would not match from a physical point of view."

"How did you determine he was cuddly?" asked Hole.

"That is part of my personal magic. I have a gift to see through the characters of my clients," answered Auntie proudly.

"Yes, it's her special talent," called out her husband from the bar with a proud grin.

"I also found out about his character from his big sister," added Auntie.

"It sounds as though we would have to give this task to a social worker. We have lots of them anyway. I always wondered what they do, so it will be good to have them make themselves useful," observed Hole with authority. "And the lists, Dr. Aasiya?"

"I am getting to that," said Auntie.

Auntie laid out her lists on the table, then glanced around the room, a serious look on her face. "The list is very long, so I will only give general indications of what I consider to be the basic, or essential characteristics to be considered. First, and probably the most important, the caste must match. You do not have this here, I know, but you have something like it. I have friends and relatives in Philadelphia, so I can give some examples. In general, race must be considered as a primary characteristic. A black offender from West Philadelphia public housing should be matched to the same for the punisher."

Hole interrupted. "Even if the victim is white from the Main Line?"

"That is not for me to say. I am just showing how my methods might be applied to your situation. "Next, how big a dowry will the punisher put up?"

"But we don't do that here," complained Hole with a frown. "Besides, how could that apply to punishing the offender?" He looked around the table waiting for one of his assistants to contribute. A young fresh law graduate raised his finger.

"Instead of a dowry, the would-be punisher who is also the victim can be compensated by us, according to how much he or she has suffered," suggested the graduate with confidence.

"Worth considering," said Hole.

"I should have said," responded Auntie, "that the same principle applies to gender. If a male offender, it must be a female punisher. Of course, I do not do same sex matchmaking."

"And this applies even if the sex of the offender is the same as that of the victim?" asked Hole, tapping his fingers on the table.

"Again, that is up to you people to decide, though I would suggest that the same sex victim find a surrogate punisher of another sex. Now comes the next most important factor I consider, and I would think it is very relevant to your situation. When one gets into an argument, or feels wronged by someone (usually a relative but that's probably not relevant here), is she or he able to forgive? How caring are they? How spiteful are they? How vengeful? How resentful? Do they have nice happy thoughts most of the time, or do they think dark, unhappy thoughts?"

The law graduate who had spoken was now engaged. "So you would match opposites here, male-female, caring-uncaring, and so on."

"That is exactly what I advise," answered Auntie with a big smile.

"Excuse me," called a voice from the bar, "but you have talked about the offender and the punisher, but what does the punisher do, exactly, what is the punishment and how is it determined?" The room fell silent. The Irish bartender grinned. The voice was that of Auntie's husband, a clear, perfectly pitched voice, beautifully clipped, the wonderful sound of an Oxford accent. So clever, knowledgeable, and wise.

Auntie smiled and looked back at him, then around the table. "That's my husband. Isn't he marvelous? He has a doctorate in Economic Deprivation from Oxford, you know. I call him Hubby and you may do so too."

"Pleased to meet you all," said Hubby. "You should read my award winning dissertation on *How Deprivation Benefits the Poor*. Many of your offenders are poor, I presume."

"They certainly are," answered Hole, "but we are doing a lot to change all that. In fact, we no longer prosecute any crimes that are committed by those who have less than $100,000 in assets."

"That is a good beginning," said Auntie with enthusiasm.

Hole continued. "The trouble is that we have only prisons, amounts thereof, to use as a punishment for serious crimes. So the punisher does not have much to choose from. Only differing amounts of prison, essentially."

"Then you must balance this off with the contrasting characteristics of the punisher-offender relationship," said Auntie, "if you will excuse my rather clinical language."

"That's right," said Hole, "a rich punisher gets to prescribe a small prison sentence if the offender is poor and vice versa. We can construct a formula that adjusts the prison sentence to the difference between assets of the punisher and the offender."

The law graduate stirred excitedly. "This will revolutionize sentencing guidelines," he chirped.

The entire group erupted into engaged discussion. Auntie had no idea what sentencing guidelines were, but obviously they were something very important to her audience. She got up ready to leave and looked around for Hubby, but he was nowhere to be found. Nor was the bartender.

"He's fallen for her accent!" Auntie muttered to herself.

"What was that?" asked Hole. "We didn't quite get that."

"My apologies," said Auntie, forcing a smile, "I see that Hubby has left for better things, so now I can say what I want to say."

"But we are open to all suggestions and ideas," urged Hole. "We have open minds here." The rest of the group muttered their assent.

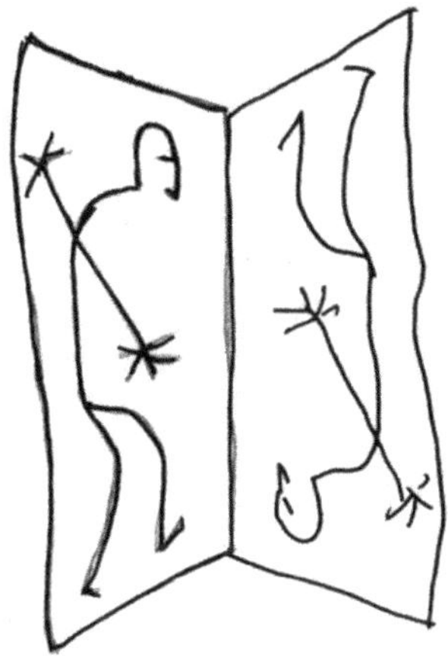

Auntie rummaged in her satchel once again, and finally pulled out a notebook that itself bulged with press clippings and notes scrawled on every page. "This is a case study that I have prepared to present to you. I was unsure whether to do so, but now that I am assured of your open mindedness, I will take the chance."

"Do tell us," said Hole.

Auntie passed out a bunch of press clippings. "No doubt you have all heard of Philadelphia's most infamous rapist, kidnapper and serial killer, Gary M. Heidnick. Apart from his long criminal career of violence, during the period 1986 through 1987, he kidnapped six women, held them chained in his basement raped and tortured them, and killed two of them through starvation or denial of medical care. They were all African American. Of course, he was white."

"The younger people here may not know of this case. I certainly do," said Hole. He was finally executed for his murders on July 6, 1999, by lethal injection."

"I ask you," said Auntie, "how would a matchmaker deal with this offender? All he did, the kidnapping, raping, torture and two murders. And all you have available to you in the present day is prison. And even the death penalty is not enough, don't you think, since he, apart from killing one person, killed another and tortured and kidnapped others. If you added up the legislated punishments for all those crimes they come to several life in prison terms and two death penalties. Yet he can only be killed once, and only serve one life sentence."

Suddenly, the group came to life. The group as one stirred uncomfortably in their chairs. The law graduate, proud of his legal knowledge of the Pennsylvania criminal code, said, "it is what it is. The Pennsylvania criminal code lists the possible punishments, the judge has discretion—depending on sentencing guidelines—and determines the most appropriate punishment."

"Who cares about sentencing guidelines? I have no idea what they are. But as the matchmaker, I do care about matching the punishment to the criminal. Note here: it is matching to the criminal, not the crimes," lectured Auntie with authority

"Yes, but who or what are you matching to the offender? " complained someone.

" Auntie, I think we are asking you, who does the match-maker represent?" responded Hole.

"Exactly the question," said Auntie with satisfaction. The big difference between match making in marriage and in punishing criminals is that in most cases, when I match husband to wife, they are strangers to each other. Often, they have not even met until the day of the wedding. It is therefore crucial that I have worked out the best match, because they will spend the rest of their lives together. Also, I only work with one side, usually the parents of either a son or daughter. In this case of Heidnick, I would represent all the victims as one."

Auntie hesitated, waiting for a response or disagreement.

"Go on," urged Hole.

"The fact is that once the criminal has attacked the victim, the victim is no longer a stranger. Her identity becomes entwined with her offender. It is up to the match maker to unravel this forced relationship. One that, you might say, dropped from the sky, like a huge stone from Hell."

"Oh, I see what you are getting at," said the law graduate. "It's another version of restorative justice. Where the identities of each, the offender and victim are brought together and they learn to understand the suffering of each other. They reach an accord, a mutual understanding."

Auntie stared at him and then saw a number of the younger individuals nodding with approval. "Bakavaas!" she cried, lapsing into her Hindi tongue, "Poppycock!" I never heard such nonsense!"

The room suddenly erupted, all talking at once.

"OK! Quiet down, now!" called Hole. "One at a time."

A middle aged woman, a sad and sorry face, heavily lined, probably serially divorced, raised her hand.

"Yes, Barbara, what is it?" Hole spoke as if she were going to ask if she could go to the bathroom.

"I have devoted my life to social work and will not sit here and listen to this drivel. There's no serious difference between offender and victim. They both are responsible for the crimes. They are an essential part of the crime. In fact the crime could not occur without a victim, willing or unwilling. That is why restorative justice makes sense. The offender and victim are treated as equals."

The room now became hushed. Auntie fingered her notes. "Well. as they say," she said sarcastically, "I will take that under advisement. In the meantime, let me finish, for I have only just begun."

Hole leaned forward over the table and looked around the room. All eyes were on him, expecting him to intervene and shut this dreadful matchmaker up. But he said nothing.

Just then, Hubby reappeared from behind the bar, his hair a little ruffled, the bartender stepping forward. "Anyone for another Guinness?" she asked. All raised their hands.

"Coming right up!"

Auntie continued. "As the victims' representative, here is what I would suggest as a procedure to match the needs of the victims and the unwanted reciprocal relationship they now have with the offender."

"We are all ears," countered the social worker.

"Let us list some of the things Heidnick did to his victims. One, he kidnapped them and chained them helpless, in his basement. Two, he administered electric shock to them in a bathtub, killing one of them. Three, he raped them at will. Four, he starved them, denied medical attention. Five, he tortured them in many ways."

"But why go into all this?" asked Hole, impatiently. "He got the death penalty which is what he deserved. Case closed."

"But that only accounts for one killing, does it not? Besides, he was put to death without pain. How does that match what he did to his victims?" countered Auntie.

"Auntie, if I may call you that," said a group member, this time the group's sociologist, a tall thin fellow with a tiny razor thin moustache, "I would like to go back to your original proposition, that victims are strangers to their offenders until they are victimized. We know that close to 70 percent of all assault victims know their assailants, usually family members, relatives or friends. So your basic premise does not hold."

"A mere detail, and I compliment you on your attempt to avert this embarrassing discussion away from its proper focus," countered Auntie. "It matters not whether the victim knew his or her offender. If they did, then I insist that the transformation works the other way around. Once formally victimized, that is, designated a victim by the criminal justice system, then the victim becomes a stranger to that offender even if he or she was known to the victim. In fact, it is important that the identity of stranger to offender be groomed and exalted, for without that distance, it becomes very difficult for the victim to comply with a match-maker's recommendations: that is, to match the pain of the punishment as closely as possible the pains that the victim has experienced at the hands of the offender."

The group fell silent. Auntie looked around the room, her eyes met quickly with Hubby's and moved on. Hubby for his part, sipped his Guinness and did his best to convey to Auntie his approval and support. Auntie continued.

"What I am going to say now," said Auntie, a very serious frown on her face, "is going to upset some of you. I simply ask that you bear with me, and try hard to put aside your prejudices that favor the so-called enlightened morality of Western civilization, of which I am sure all in this room believe the USA is the shining beacon."

Hole sat back in his chair and nodded approval. All eyes looked down at the table. What terrible thing could a matchmaker from India say that would upset this well-educated, progressive and tolerant group?

Auntie shuffled her papers some more then looked around at the group. She had prepared them well, and addressed them in her best Indian Oxford accent that she had learned from Hubby.

"Now, we have already acknowledged that one life in prison is nowhere near a match to the six kidnappings, tortures and two murders. But we can enrich the offender's experience of prison with a slow but methodical application of the pains that reflect what the victims felt and what the offender did. Here, now, is my list of recommended pains.

"One. He chained his victims to the wall of his basement. So he shall be chained to his prison cell for six years, one year for each victim chained.

"Two. He tortured all six with electric shock. So he shall receive severe electric shocks to his genitals once a month. That will give him something to look forward to. Of course, the applications will be supervised by both a qualified medical practitioner and electrician.

"Three, he will be fed tasteless mush every other day, and in between days the odor of grilled steak will be fanned into his cell.

"Four, and this is probably the most important and effective. Over the period of his first twenty years in prison, once a year, a piece of his body will be surgically removed. This will begin with the ten fingers followed by ten toes. The victim's family members will be invited to wield the chopping instrument. Of course, no sedation or anesthetic will be allowed."

Auntie glanced at Hubby who stood, his mouth open and eyes almost popping out. He could not believe what he heard. He nervously gulped down a big mouthful of Guinness, and his grip tightened on his Irish Bartender's pliable rump. She, for her part, thought it all a joke and ruffled his greying hair with her lily-white hand.

"Five…"

Auntie hesitated. It was time to let them interrupt. And she was not disappointed. Ace Hole cleared his throat loudly as he fingered his phone.

"I think we have heard enough," grumbled Hole. Then he made a very bad blunder. "I don't know what you people do back in India, but here in America, the bastion of civilization, we do not do such disgraceful things, or even think about them, no matter how awful the offender is."

Murmurs of agreement fluttered around the table.

But Hole's words had incensed Hubby. "I'll have you know that India's advanced civilization outdates anything you have here, and far surpasses it in its rich traditions and devotions to justice and caring for all people, including all life. In fact, it is a tragedy that the English came and disturbed the blissful tranquility of Indian life." All of this said in his very best clipped Oxford accent.

Hole was about to both apologize but also chastise Hubby, but Auntie cut him short. "Let us not get sidetracked with accusations and pontifications. I am presenting a case study, it is an example or outline only. I am opening your eyes to what is possible, and to the considerable parameters that are available to you when you allow yourself to think clearly, without prejudice or preconceptions, in order to determine how one may match the punisher's preferences with the parameters of the offender's character and his crimes."

The room fell silent once again. Hole went to speak, but decided against it. The social worker, incensed, got up quietly and left the room. Hubby grabbed some more of the Bartender and they quietly slipped away and out of sight.

Auntie continued. "Five — and this is where we really get to the question of reparations. During his twenty years in prison, he will donate various organs that he can live without, (an eye, a kidney, for example) to save the lives of at least two people, a deed that will make up somewhat for the lives that he brutally extinguished."

Hole cleared his throat once again. He stood up and leaned against the back of his chair. "Doctor Aasiya, you have certainly given us something to think about. You have given us a new way to look at the matching of punishment to crime. I am not sure that..."

"...it would be constitutional to carry out such punishments, even on the worst of the worst criminals." Auntie finished his sentence for him.

"Yes, precisely," responded Hole.

Auntie smiled a little and said in her wisest voice, one full of feeling and empathy, "one day, your great Congress will remove the prejudices and blinders built into your constitution by your founding fathers, who, having themselves suffered at the hands of tyrants, failed to confront the injustices of man against man and man against woman."

Moral: Though imprecise, punishment is
the essential measure of justice

7. For France

A psychiatrist grapples with torture.

Family is the most important thing in my life. Is it not so in every life? In the end, we are left with family. No one else really cares. Is this not why, regardless of every effort, neglect and even abuse are routinely uncovered in aged care homes and institutions?

Every morning before I leave for the office, I pause at the kitchen table, watch my two children, Pierre just twelve years old, and Mateo ten, munching on their cereal. I lean over and kiss each of them good-bye and call Marie who responds from the bathroom, a muffled "bye." She used to come out and we would hug, but for some time now, we have both felt somehow uncomfortable, distant. Strangely, our bedtime trysts have been incredibly physical, I suppose I mean, aggressive. You might even say violent. On my part that is. There is something there, I am sure. The boys don't sense it though, or at least I hope not. And Marie, I know she wants to talk, but I have avoided it. I suspect that she knows, and soon I will have to come clean.

When I say that I leave for the office, I don't really mean that. It's not an office, at least not any more. Not since I gave up my private practice and offered my services to the *Commandement de la Gendarmerie Nationale* in Algiers. I used to be a psychiatrist, a very good one, but patients were hard to come by in private practice. In the 1960s psychiatry was a specialty in its infancy and for people to admit that they went to a psychiatrist was to admit that they were stark raving mad.

Nor did I actually offer my services. They came knocking at my door. "I am here at the direction of General Massu," began the impeccably dressed man in civilian clothes, obviously a career bureaucrat of all bureaucrats. "The General respectfully requests that you attend an audience, with a view to taking charge of the D.O.P."

"Which is?" I asked. I had never heard of the D.O.P.

"The *Détachement Opérationnel de Protection.*"

"Which is?" I repeated, receiving no reply.

General Massu would later describe this operation as a division of "specialists in the interrogation of suspects who want to say nothing."

Mindful that the main mission of any psychiatrist is to get one's patient to talk, "the talking cure" as they say, I agreed to meet with the general, himself a famous military man, well known for solving the problems of terrorism facing French colonies around the world. And my wife and I were very much concerned about the political turmoil in Algiers, the bombings and riots. Right now, Algiers was not a safe place to live or to raise a family. So it was easy for me to agree. Although I diagnosed the general as a hard man, obviously an egotist of the first order, he was a patriot, and seemed honest and direct. General Massu was also a well-read man who had survived torture by the Nazis during World War II. He asked me to take on the job of director of intelligence. He thought that a professional, such as myself, would be able to conduct interrogations that did not require the use of torture, which he had experienced himself and of course abhorred, as would anybody. And as he said to me, he wanted to make sure that torture was not used unless absolutely necessary, to which I of course agreed. It was an easy choice to take on the job. In fact, I felt flattered. The money was good too, a great opportunity to earn some money for my young family. We had been struggling for some time. The hospital had no psychiatrist and did not see the need for one. I had tried doing general practice, but there was not much need for that either. People did not have the money to pay for doctors. They were grim economic times then, and still are, made worse by the economic turmoil. It's why, of course, so many Algerians are packing up their bags and migrating to France. We should do the same. But my wife does not want to leave her many relatives and friends.

My staff included a number of assistant interrogators who had police training, a couple of male nurses, a psychologist, and several male secretaries, perhaps the most important of all staff, to record the respondents' answers, describe their demeanor and so on. It took me many weeks to find secretaries of such caliber. It demanded much more than simply taking shorthand or typing. It required a level of sensitivity and perceptiveness on the part of the observer/recorder to set down in good prose everything that happened, being careful to avoid any slightly inflammatory wording, finding words that, one might say, neutralized such actions as hit, whip, drown, etc. "Pressure was applied," was a popular expression, as were "subject was persistently asked…" or "subject's answers were double checked by other inter-viewers." We never used the word interrogate or its derivatives.

I should have taken one thing that the General said more seriously. That my work was part of military intelligence. There-fore secrecy was absolutely necessary. Nothing we did or learned from our suspects was to be conveyed to the outside world. No talking to friends or relatives no matter how distant. Of course, never ever talk to the press, those cunning sneaks who wormed their ways into bureaucracies and organizations. "Information is power," pronounced General Massu. "If even the slightest inkling of our activities is leaked to the press, we lose. It's as simple as that."

I thought later that I should have asked, "and how will we know that we have won?" It was only later still, after I had become accustomed to my secret life as chief interrogator, that I answered my own question: "when all the terrorists are dead." I know now that this answer is also just as silly. For once the terrorists are dead, the journalists and politicians will mine the records of history to find out what really happened behind the secret walls of the imperial buildings of the *Commandement de la Gendarmerie Nationale* and its connected neighbor *Barber-ousse* prison. Though in some ways, there were no secrets. Or at least there was plenty of submerged knowledge of the happenings behind the walls of *Barberousse* prison. Convicted terrorists were guillotined behind its walls. Everyone knew that. What they didn't quite know, and I and my staff pretended not to know, was that many were probably convicted on the basis of the testimony offered up by our subjects.

My driver showed up as usual and we drove off, a ten minute

ride. The car can be any color or make, seems to be a different car each day. Security says they do that so terrorists can't learn what cars contain *Gendarmerie* personnel, so make it less likely to be bombed. I'm appreciative of that. But the car does show up the same time every morning, so I wonder if a terrorist out there —and believe me I know who many of them are, having interviewed them—knows where I live and could easily lie in wait. But praise Allah, it has so far not happened. Of course I say nothing to Marie about all this. She would go nuts if she knew what I do.

Well, what I do is psychiatry at the highest—and lowest— level. I know the theory of mind control. After all, isn't that what psychiatrists are supposed to aim at? To exercise enough control over the patient's mind to put him back in control of himself, to be able to live with himself. How many normal people have trouble living with themselves from day to day? Most, if you ask me. I spend just as much time helping my staff as I do helping our mostly unwilling subjects answer our questions, tell us what they know, get it off their chest. It's a burden to them, to keep information in and to be unable to share it. This is a basic principle of psychiatry, in my view. It is the aim of any good psychiatrist to help his patient to talk about his worries and cares, insufferable thoughts and impulses. Not only that. We clinicians also know that there are many thoughts and past traumatic events that lie beneath the patient's consciousness. We can help by getting them to vomit (excuse the unseemly word) up what lies deep inside their consciousness (or unconsciousness, if you are Freudian or one of his followers).

I have been doing this for almost a year. My staff have come and gone. There are only a couple upon whom I can rely and be sure are trustworthy. Those who have suddenly left, saying that the job was too stressful, I let go of course, but am required to notify my bureaucratic superiors of their whereabouts. I try not to worry about them. I trust that General Massu does not have them watched, that they will not talk to the press or anyone else about our work. After all, they have been willing participants. To speak out is also to admit that they too are complicit in our secret mission.

Since you are reading this, it is reasonable for me to assume that you know why you are reading this "story"—let's call it that. You are curious. You want to be let in on the Big Secret of interrogation. Especially by one who is trained in psychiatry, the science of mind control.

Interrogation of unwilling suspects has a very long history, from the slaves of Roman times, to the Spanish Inquisitors who catalogued and mastered the art, merging on science, though they did not know it. I should add that we do everything to avoid the use of any violent means to extract confessions. We French are a civilized people after all, with an impressive history of caring for those in countries who need and will prosper on our enlightenment. Government by the people, for the people. An idea that we French invented.

The first step, then, with those who will say nothing, is to scare our subject by demonstrating our omniscience of his past actions and collaborators. Embedded in this trick is something that may be obvious to you: if we know everything, why is it necessary to extract a confession out of this unwilling subject? I could answer that, but will not right now. There are many apparent illogicalities in the torture trade. We confront him with a *boukkaraor cagoulard*, a Muslim terrorist with his head covered in a bag with eye slits, who is one of our successes, and is now an informer. Some of these informers are very good at what they do or are made to do. Many will drop to their knees, their hands tied behind their backs, sobbing, wobbling back and forth, singing the names of accomplices, and whatever else we ask. Depending on our psychological assessment of our unwilling subject, we may use a female informer, instead of male. If we have concluded that our subject has a special relationship with a woman, this may be a very effective technique, especially if we strip her down a little, just enough to give him a taste of what we are capable of. I say "we" here, but I assure you, as a psychiatrist, I would never touch any subject or intentionally hurt them in any way. I leave that to my assistants provided from the military arm of D.O.P. Some appear to enjoy what they do a little too much. If

I see that, I quietly take them by the arm and usher them out of the interrogation room for a cooling-off period.

The majority of our suspects break down easily when confronted with these informers. I sit at the back of the room, often with a secretary and record the names of collaborators, their addresses, and so on.   And if pending attacks are indicated, I quickly convey this information to the D.O.P emergency personnel. May I remind you, we are doing this for France and her dominion Algeria. We have brought Algeria out of the dark ages. They will become civilized whether they like it or not. Their supposed independence for which they say they fight is nothing but a cry to go back to the barbarous ways of little tyrants in their little fiefdoms, dishing out a primitive justice to their enslaved people.

In the rare (though admittedly increasing) occasions when our subject does not "break" (he is hardly broken, this is violent language that we try to avoid), we move on to the necessary next step. No, wait. There is an intermediate step. After showing him our sobbing informer, we send our subject back to his cell, where we leave him for a day or so. We may even send a guard into his cell as though he is to be taken out and tortured, but then make up some excuse for not doing so. The guard may feign good will on his part, pretend that he is taking pity on him. We make the best of psychological manipulation. It is our aim to make our suspect completely dependent on us. We can do this by manipulating his environment: we provide drinks of nice or horrible taste, a little food, though this is not recommended because should he vomit in response to our interrogations, it makes a terrible mess, not to mention the smell. And of course, there is the danger of choking.

A few more sessions like this will usually get our suspect talking. And if this should fail—I repeat—we only do this as a last resort, our methods up to this point work with ninety percent of our patients, I mean, suspects, in the unlikely event that our subject does not open up, we move on to the next technique. Once again, we depend on psychological methods. We abhor violence, the essence of torture. I owe a debt of gratitude to my military associates who provided us with the necessary equipment. This was an army signals magneto that, when wound up, would produce enough alternating current to cause quite a jolt of electric shock. We called it the *gégène*, which proved to be very effective. It is very important to note that we did not adopt this without any research on its effectiveness. In fact General Massu told us that he had tried it out on himself and found it most effective and safe. This was applied to various parts of the body, from ears, fingers, mouth and teeth, and later, inevitably I suppose, the penis and testicles. We pioneered this technique which was later to be adopted by interrogation departments throughout the civilized world.

But the most valuable feature of this form of interrogation was that it left no marks on the body (if applied properly). And once this was fully realized, we then experimented with other types of torture that did not leave visible marks on the body. The most obvious was the one that has been used for centuries: water torture of various kinds, but mostly forcing water in the mouth, bringing the subject close to drowning, then saving him. From a psychological point of view, I preferred this method because it made it look like we were successively saving the subject's life. We were doing him a great service.

I could go on, but it is not my aim to scare or outrage you, the reader. I do want to remind you that our intentions were always noble and controlled. Anyone under my supervision who took too much pleasure in these proceedings was immediately moved to a different task. On the other hand, though, if anyone refused to carry out these tasks, for whatever reason, we insisted that he show clearly why this was so, to explain what other course of action was open to us? We did these things not because we wanted to, but for, quite frankly, the good of France, for the bright future of Algeria. We were saving a country that was under attack. We doubtless had the blessing of Allah!

This seemed all very well and good. But you have to understand that doing this day in and day out, takes its toll. They say that if you do not enjoy your work, you should quit. But how does this apply when one's job is torture? This is what it came down to. And besides, it was the very nature of torture that one must not enjoy doing it, otherwise if you do, you are some kind of sadistic creep, is that not so? I routinely managed to fire most of my interrogators who appeared to enjoy inflicting pain. I first tried moving them out of the interrogation room, but they resisted, even reported me to my superiors for not being fair, complaining that I was punishing them for doing their job with enthusiasm. This was an unsustainable logic.

I am a psychiatrist, I told myself. And psychiatry is a new science. I should keep my emotions out of it. But how does one do this without falling into other traps of logic? Is not the psychiatrist supposed to have empathy for his subject? But this was asking too much. I can't have empathy with my subject if at the same time I am inflicting horrible pain and suffering can I? Or is this the same as saying to a patient, "this will hurt" when giving him an injection?

My solution in the end was the good old psychological tricks of self-deception and denial. I justified my actions by arguing that this was the same as working in a slaughterhouse, killing and preparing animals so that eventually people would be able to enjoy eating them. It was all to the good.

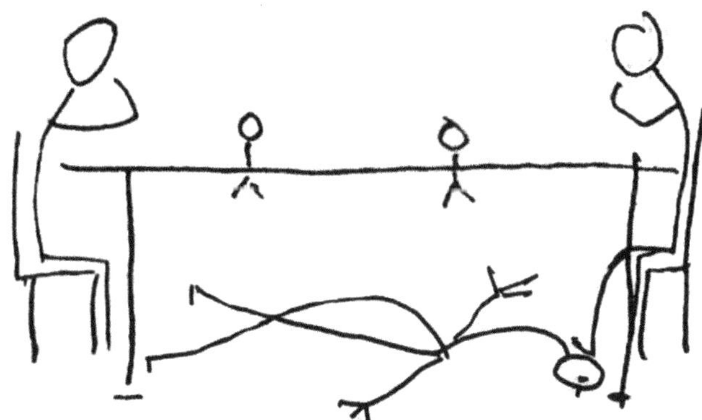

And so on this day, a day like every other day, my driver dropped me off at the office, I did my duty, then at the end of the day my driver picked me up. And on the journey home, I pondered, even worried, that this was a car that had probably picked up suspects late at night and brought them to my interrogation center. I also knew, but tried to dismiss it from my mind, that some such suspects never made it to my office.

"Hello my darlings," I called, "I'm home!" The children ran to me. I kissed them both. We ate a delicious supper of Moroccan lamb that Marie had cooked. She said nothing. Just a faint smile, I think. But the lamb reminded me of the slaughterhouse. I excused myself and went to the bathroom and had a long shower. I scrubbed every inch of my body. It was like I had fallen in a cesspool. My body smelled like armpits all over. I went straight to bed. Marie came to me. Or did she? I was in some kind of delirium.

Then she was shaking me. "Wake up! Wake up!"

It was morning. My driver was waiting downstairs. Would he take me to my office? What did he know? He never spoke. Just looked at me in the rear vision mirror. Or was it my turn to disappear?.

Moral: To punish another is to punish one's self.

8. Fault Lines

A boy is punished for his misadventure.

There were two boys, one big, one small. The big boy was big, a lot of meat on his bones as they would say, a solid eight year old. Everyone called him Butch. The small boy was a little six year old, skinny frame, a slightly protruding tummy. Everyone called him Tich. They were both in Grade 4. Butch had been kept back two years in a row.

On December 14, not long before school would break up for the holidays, an incident occurred in the playground that Tich would remember for the rest of his long life. It was the day after his sixth birthday and his Mom had made a birthday cake of sponge filled with jam and cream, followed by strawberries and homemade ice-cream, his favorite.

The school playground was large with tall eucalypts dotted throughout the grounds, and peppercorn trees lining the peri-meter. Tich and his friends played marbles among the exposed roots of the gum trees, games that they made up as they went along. There was a large shelter shed with the boys and girls lavatories next to it, about one hundred meters from the red brick, two story school building.

On this day, at lunch time, Tich and his friends were playing "follows," their made up game that required each to fire his marble to a series of spots hidden within the exposed roots of the trees, the first to get to the end the winner. Butch, as he usually did, stood apart, calling them babies for playing such a silly game. Tich was close to winning, he thought, when the bell rang and at the same time he realized that he had to run to the toilet, having held it back for quite some time, absorbed in the game as he was. He wasn't the only one. Many of his mates also ran to the toilet at the last minute. The trouble was that Tich had to do number two. All that cream the day before at his birthday party had caught up with him. And when he got inside the toilet, to his dismay, the one cubicle was taken up. He banged on the door, crying, "hurry up! Hurry up!" And to his horror, Butch's voice rang out full of glee, "you gotta wait, I got here first anyway!" The bell rang and rang, and Tich danced around, trying to hold it back. He cried out again, clutching his stomach, bent almost double, crossing his legs, anything that would stop the inevitable evacuation. "Please! Please! I gotta go!" he cried.

Then the bell stopped and Butch emerged from the cubicle, a big grin on his face, enjoying every minute of it. Tich darted forward, but Butch's thick body stood in the way. "Don't you piss on me ya little shit!" he growled.

Tich, one hand on his tummy, the other pushing at the door pleaded again, "please! Please!" But Butch held the door closed, just enough to make him wait a little longer. Then Butch suddenly let go, and Tich lurched forward as the door gave way.

Then everything was quiet. Butch was gone. And Tich to his horror felt a warm ooze push into his school pants, and a little trickle run down his legs. He stood there, unable to do anything, tears running down his face.

*

Miss Penny looked over her class, and glanced at her watch. The Nature Study broadcast from the ABC was about to start.

"Where's little Freddy?" she asked, looking at the vacant seat two rows from the front.

Butch raised his hand, a serious look on his face. "I saw him go into the toilet, Miss," he said innocently.

"What did you do to him?" demanded Miss Penny, always ready to jump on this nasty piece of work, as she always described him to her fellow teachers.

"I didn't do nothing, Miss," whined Butch.

"I bet you did," muttered Miss Penny. She turned to Freddy's desk mate. "Stewart, go down to the toilets and see if you can find him. And come straight back, do you hear?"

"Yes Miss."

"And the rest of you. Sit up straight, all hands on the tops of your desks. No fidgeting! Now go on! Do it now! The broadcast is about to begin."

Gentle music of a Mozart sonata wafted into the classroom, announcing the beginning of the broadcast.

"Now sit straight and listen!" commanded Miss Penny as she walked to the door of the classroom and peered down the passage looking for Freddy and Stewart. But only Stewart appeared, puffing a little having run as fast as he could down to the toilet and back again.

"He won't come out!" cried Stewart. He's howling something awful," he panted.

"What do you mean he won't come out? What's wrong with him.?"

Stewart looked away. "Miss, I think he's pooped his pants!" It was awful, Stewart couldn't believe it. But he had to try very hard not to grin.

Miss penny looked down at him, horrified. "Are you sure of this?" she asked in a measured tone.

"Yes, Miss. I'm pretty sure. He was crying that much I couldn't tell what he was saying, but I went in there and it smelled like...." Stewart put his hand to his mouth, trying to hold back his grin.

But Butch could not hold it back. "...shit!" he cried.

The entire class gasped and the noise of their feet scraping against the old wooden floor filled the room.

"My goodness!" exclaimed Miss Penny. "Butch you horrible dirty boy! Class, settle down, or you'll all be kept in and there'll be no playtime for two days!"

She turned to Stewart. "Go down and fetch the Principal this minute," ordered Miss Penny, "and be quick about it!" She grabbed Butch by the ear and pulled him to the front of the class. "Now children," she said, speaking sternly, her eyes narrowed under a deep frown, her lips pushed forward that, if it were not for the current circumstances, might have looked like the beginning of a kiss. She let go of Butch's ear, went to her table and opened the drawer. The children looked with wide eyes; they knew what was coming. Or at least they thought they did. But Miss Penny did not retrieve the familiar leather strap, but instead a small block of Palmolive soap and held it out to Butch who stood motionless, a silly look on his face, clearly enjoying the attention he was getting.

"Butch Smith, you have a filthy mouth," snarled Miss Penny "which is why you must now wash it out with soap and water. "

The class gasped as one.

"But Miss…!" cried Butch.

"No buts! Go on, take a bite then go down and wash out your mouth at the tap."

Butch stood fast, still a smirk, but nevertheless he took the soap. There was no bathroom in the building, except the one for the staff that was forbidden to children. He would have to go down the stairs and outside to the gully trap.

"Bite it! Now!" demanded Miss Penny, who then opened the table drawer and withdrew the coiled strap. "Do what you're told or else!"

Butch was no stranger to the strap. He stood there, holding the soap near his mouth. The class was goggle-eyed.

Miss Penny unfurled the strap. "You'll get it around the legs if you don't hurry up and do what you're told."

"Oh no! Oh no! Not the legs!" Butch cried, knowing from grim experience that it hurt much more when the leather curled around the legs.

Miss Penny stamped her foot loudly, causing the whole class to murmur and shift nervously in their seats, their leather shoes banging on the floorboards. The sudden bang did the trick. Butch took a small bite at the soap, dropped it on the floor and ran for the door, which suddenly opened before he got to it, and there stood the principal, Mr. Foster, Stewart standing sheepishly behind him. Miss Penny gave Butch a little shove that caused him to lunge past the principal and knock into Stewart as he entered the room.

"What is it, Miss Penny? Stewart would not tell me what had happened. Only that you had to see me at once," said the Headmaster, a little annoyed.

"It seems that young Freddy Brambles has, er, you know, is holed up in the toilet and has had an accident," said Miss Penny.

"You mean he hurt himself?" The Principal frowned.

"No, not that kind of accident. You know…" stuttered Miss

Penny.

"Good Heavens, Miss Penny, how awful. Here, I will take care of your class while you go down and see what's the matter."

Miss Penny grimaced. "Oh! But he's in the boys toilet, I would think," miss Penny answered quickly.

"He's just a boy, now Miss Penny. That doesn't matter. Now off you go and look into it. If it's what you say, I will have to contact his parents."

It was a good hundred yards out to the boys toilet. Miss Penny was not at all pleased. And it was not until she reached the bottom of the stairs that she thought of a solution. Of course, there was a student teacher in the building, assisting with grade 4, she thought, and the classroom was right at the bottom of the stairs. She walked straight into the classroom. The children were also listening to the Nature Study broadcast. She approached the teacher who sat at her desk, looking very busy.

"May I borrow your student teacher?" she asked. "There's been a small accident for which we need a little extra help."

The teacher looked up, smiled a little, and pointed to the student assistant who sat studiously taking notes, at the back of the class. "Of course, take her, but bring her back before the end of the broadcast. She has to teach the lesson."

"Thank you so much," smiled Miss Penny. "This is one I owe you, with all my heart."

"Miss Prendergast," the teacher beckoned," could you go with Miss Penny, please? She needs your assistance with a small emergency, is that right Miss Penny?"

"Yes, indeed. Miss Prendergast, please follow me."

Miss Penny left the classroom, followed by the reluctant student teacher.

"You may leave your notebook there. You will not need it," said Miss Penny.

Miss Prendergast followed Miss Penny out the door, down the corridor and out past the gully trap (Butch was nowhere in sight) where Miss Penny stood facing the playground and pointed. "Down there, in the boys toilet. One of my pupils, his name is Freddy, but all the kids call him Tich. I'm told he has had an accident of some sort. Could you go down there and see what's up?"

"An accident? I haven't done my St. John's first aid exam yet. If it's a serious accident…"

"It is serious, but not that kind of serious. Now off you go and get him. In the meantime I will try to find a place where we can take care of him."

"There's no sick room?" asked Miss Prendergast innocently.

"We've never needed one. There's the staffroom, but we couldn't use that for obvious reasons."

"Why not?"

"You'll see. Now off you go."

"But it's the boys. Shouldn't it be a male teacher who goes there?" complained Miss Prendergast.

"It doesn't matter. He's just a little boy. Now get going, if you want to get this over before the Nature broadcast is finished."

By this time, Tich was beside himself. He thought of taking off his pants, but then thought in horror what would come out and what it would reveal. He went to sit on the toilet seat, but was dismayed when he felt the squelch inside his pants when he sat, so he quickly jumped up again. He just jigged from one foot to the other. Waiting. No longer crying, but whimpering. Anticipating what was to come. And at last it did. It came in a high pitched voice.

"Is there someone in there? I'm Miss Prendergast. If there's someone in there, could you come out please? We are all worried about you." Miss Prendergast had already forgotten the name Miss Penny told her. "What's your name, young man?" called Miss Prendergast. All she could hear was whimpering and sniveling. "Now sniveling won't help any. Just come out and we'll see what we can do to help you. Are you hurt or something?"

"No Miss," came a pitiful voice, cut off by another whimper.

"Now it's no good crying. That won't help. Where are you hurt?"

Tich's crying all of a sudden turned into a wail. The words, if there were any, were garbled. It was no use. Miss Prendergast could not understand what was wrong. She would have to get up the courage to enter the boys toilet. Something that she, of course, had never ever done before. She entered, tried not to look at the open urinal, wanted to hold her nose, and almost turned around and ran back out. Tich's wails were so ear splitting, she had to force herself to keep going, pushed at the door to the cubicle, but it would not open. Titch was pushing against it.

"Don't come in! Don't come in! I've pooped myself!" he cried in between his wails.

Miss Prendergast stepped back in horror. "Oh My God!" she whispered to herself. She pushed harder at the door.

Finally, Tich gave in, and retreated to the back of the toilet, now shivering, knees clasped together, arms held across his small chest. A pitiful sight curled up in the corner.

"Come on now," said Miss Prendergast, "take my hand and we will go back up to the school and get you cleaned up." She offered her hand and waited. Admittedly, her hand was stretched out as far as she could in a silly effort to keep as much distance from him as she could. The pitiful little creature looked up, his dark brown eyes blurred by tears, and gingerly offered his hand. Miss Prendergast forced a smile. "That's right, come on then." She looked around the gloom of the rather filthy cubicle and took his hand, having no idea what she would do next, except take him to the principal's office. And who would want this smelly little crying bundle in his office? She led her reluctant little smelly boy up to the school and was met at the door by the principal who immediately put on a bright and brisk smile.

"Come now, young man, let's get you cleaned up," he said with a cheerful grin. But he made no attempt to hold Tich's hand. Simply walked, assuming he would be followed, down to the end of the hallway where there was an old table that the caretaker had retrieved from the storeroom, and a big dish of water set upon it.

Tich waddled along, holding Miss Prendergast's hand now quite strongly. And out of the principal's office emerged a buxom woman, a parent of one of Tich's classmates who lived nearby. She had come with a clean set of clothes, soap and washcloth.

"Let's get him on to the table," said the Principal, meaning of course, that Miss Prendergast must lift him up. "And then let's get those clothes off him and put in this bag here that Mrs. Foster has brought.

Miss Prendergast hesitated.

"Don't worry Miss Prendergast," said the Principal with soft reassurance, "you can teach your lesson tomorrow or whenever it suits your classroom teacher. This is more important for now."

Miss Prendergast tried to lift the shivering Tich by grabbing under his arms and lifting him at arm's length. This made him heavy and she struggled to lift him up, but finally managed, when she saw that no one was going to help her.

"Now Miss Prendergast," said the principal, "I have an old dust coat you can put on to protect your lovely dress. Then you better undo his clothes. There's going to be such a mess, there's nothing for it but to get him naked and wash him down thoroughly. Now I'll leave you two to it." He smiled and quickly retreated into his office.

Mrs. Foster laid out the fresh set of clothes at the end of the table. "He'll be all right once we get him cleaned and dry and into these fresh clothes, poor little thing." She handed the wash cloth to Miss Prendergast who took it, reluctantly.

"Freddy, can you undo your shirt and pull it off please? There's a boy," she asked.

Tich fiddled with his top button, but his shivering and whimpering got in the way.

Mrs. Foster took over. "Come on, I'll do it. We don't have all day! These young teachers," she muttered to herself.

She briskly unbuttoned Tich's shirt, tossed it into the bag, then proceeded to do the same for his shorts, trying not to look at the brown smudges that were now making their way down his legs.

"Better take off his shoes and socks first," suggested Miss Prendergast.

"Then please do it," said Mrs. Foster curtly.

Miss Prendergast carefully undid his shoes and managed to pull off each one without getting anything on her fingers. The socks were another matter. They were by now well soiled at their tops where Miss Prendergast would have to grab them.

"Freddy, lift your foot, now, come on. You can't expect us to do everything for you. You're not a baby, now, are you?" said Mrs. Foster.

The shoes and socks were off, the socks thrown into the bag, and now the shorts dropped to his ankles, followed by his underpants that Mrs. Foster, with the fingernail of her index finger and thumb, managed to pull down.

And there he stood, up high on the table, naked, his knees pressing together, his arms crossed tightly over his shivering little body.

Naturally, his underpants contained most of the nasty mess, and these were tossed into the rubbish bin. Now Mrs. Foster started to wipe him down, all the time rinsing the washcloth in the big tub of water, adding soap as she went. The water was cold, and Tich cried and cringed some more as Mrs. Foster splashed it over him then rubbed the cloth all over with her rough hands.

By the time they got him clean, and were putting the finishing touches to their good works, the bell signaling recess sounded, and the noise and rustle of kids' voices flowed into the corridor.

The table was right by the stairway where all the bigger kids from the upper grades came down.

The principal came out of his office to make his presence felt when the kids walked by, two by two, and to inspect the good works done with Freddy. The kids, including those from Tich's own class, walked by, pointing and giggling. Tich, of course, cried even more, especially when Butch pointed and laughed loudly. At which the principal called out, pointing at Butch with a stern finger, "this is nothing to laugh at, young man! Let it be a lesson to you all. And if you don't stop laughing this minute, I'll bring you into my office and strap the lot of you!"

The laughter reduced itself to chatter. And then the Principal, his hands on his hips beamed, "cleanliness is next to godliness, you know. Now move along, children. That's the spirit." And he returned to his office.

Mrs. Foster produced the clean clothes from her basket and handed Miss Prendergast a towel. Together they wiped Tich down and dressed him in dry clothes.

Miss Prendergast brought Tich back to his classroom just as the bell rang signaling the end of recess. He sat in his place, his head on the desk buried in his arms, as the class came in from recess. Sniggers and snickers passed over the classroom like leaves of autumn blown in the wind. Miss Penny stood in front of the class, her face very serious. She raised a finger, her lips pushed out a bit. The kids knew that they were going to be yelled at.

"Stand up, Freddy!" she ordered.

Tich sat, face buried, and did not move.

"Freddy! I said stand up!"

Butch started to laugh, and leaned over to prod Tich in the back.

"Butch!" cried Miss Penny. "This is no laughing matter! Come to the front this minute and stand over there in the corner." She then advanced to Tich and pulled him out of his desk, shook him so that he had to release his arms from his head, and stood limply in the aisle. She dragged him to the front and faced him to the class. "You have all seen what happened to Freddy. Let it be a lesson to you all. When the bell rings for you to come in from the yard, you come in immediately. You go to the toilet before the bell rings. Going to the toilet is never an excuse for getting in late for class. Is that clear?"

"Yes, Miss Penny," muttered the class in unison."

"But Miss Penny," came Tich's quivering little voice. "I would have had time but he wouldn't let me into the toilet." He pointed at Butch standing in the corner, a big grin on his face.

"How dare you speak back to me. I don't want to hear any more of this. There's no excuse. None at all." She shoved Tich forward, and pushed him into his desk.

"And as for you," she said looking at Butch, "you're getting what you deserve. She returned to her desk and opened the bottom right drawer. A faint sigh of anticipation rippled across the classroom. They all knew what was in that drawer. "Put out your hand," she demanded.

Butch, his well-known silly grin on his face, put out his hand and received one of the best.

Moral: Humiliation is the handmaiden of tyrants.

9. Road Rage

A child is saved by punishment.

The wistful, somber, unmitigated devotion, adoration, and of course all-embracing love of a mother for her child is universally depicted by the great artists of pre and post renaissance of Italy. In the Duccio Maestà of Siena, for example, there is a hint of the child's resistance to its mother, often interpreted as a foreboding of what is to come: the tragedy of crucifixion, the child will die before its mother. Hidden deep in every mother is such a fear. And every new day brings with it such a threat.

Iris was preoccupied with the challenges of her working day as she walked proudly along Philadelphia's Pine Street with her toddler, sometimes in his stroller, but often, toddling along on his own two feet. How proud she was when he took his first steps! And now, he wanted to run, out of his stroller then back again.

"Sammy! Not so fast! Keep my hand! Don't go onto the road! Watch for the big cars!"

It was just after eight in the morning and they were on their way to Day Care, the street busy with morning traffic of people going to work, and trucks stopping for deliveries. Sammy was being a little devil this morning. He wanted to run ahead. He had so much energy! Iris called out yet again. "Sammy! Sammy! Don't go on the road! You hear?"

But Sammy did not hear, or if he did, he took no notice. And on to the road he ran, right at the intersection of 11th and Pine.

Iris let go of the stroller and ran on to the road after him. Cars screeched to a halt. Sammy turned to her, laughing, then all of a sudden crying as Iris scooped him up roughly in her arms and ran back to the curb.

"You naughty little boy!" she screamed, tears in her eyes. "You must never do that again! Do you hear?"

Sammy looked at her, still not comprehending. He was part laughing and part crying, and probably thinking that he should scream like his mom too.

Iris had read somewhere in a child rearing book, maybe her mother's old worn Dr. Spock, never chastise a child in anger! Calm down and do it rationally, always with a quiet and sensible explanation.

So she set him down on the sidewalk. He went to climb into his stroller, but she grabbed him and pulled him to her and held him by his shoulders. But Sammy squirmed and wriggled. He managed to grab the stroller with one hand and pulled it and it fell sideways. Passersby were a little annoyed at having to walk around this rapidly evolving spectacle.

"Sammy!" cried Iris, "stop it!" She wrenched him away from the stroller and pulled both him and the stroller to her as she flopped down on the old marble steps that protruded on to the sidewalk. "Don't you understand?" she pleaded, knowing of course that he did not understand. She began to cry a little herself, and that was enough to have Sammy follow suit.

They sat for a while sniffing back their tears as Iris hugged Sammy to her. "I couldn't bear it if something happened to you, darling, don't you know?"

Maybe he did know. He hugged her and nestled his nose into her breast, perhaps a slight throwback to the days when he was still on the breast. It certainly was enough to calm Iris down as she looked out at the busy traffic and passersby.

"Now Sammy, I want you to listen to me very carefully," she said. She held him by both shoulders, held him out in front of her so she could look straight into his eyes. "You know I've told you many, many times not to run onto the road. Haven't I?"

Sammy did not answer. He just looked back at her and wriggled a bit. Her hands were hurting his shoulders because she held him so tightly. He wriggled some more and she let go. But then, she stood up, holding Sammy by the hand, pulling him up with her.

"I'm going to tell you again, and this will be the last time. And just to make sure you remember it, I'm going to give you a hard smack, to help you remember."

Iris twisted his arm a little and his tiny body turned around.

With her free hand she gave his bare legs a hard slap. Sammy was a little surprised, but one would not call it shocked. Rather, he simply took it as another thing of the many surprises of life that happened to him every day and every minute of his young life. Because there was no immediate response, Iris took it that she had not hit him hard enough. So she gave him another hard slap, and this evoked a loud wail, close to a scream, from Sammy, who now cried buckets of tears.

"Let that be a lesson to you!" said Iris, also crying. "You must never-- you hear me? Never run onto the road again. Is that clear?"

Sammy wailed some more and did not answer.

"Answer me, Sammy. Is that clear? You must never run on to the road again!" And she gave him another slap, this time rather half-heartedly.

Sammy whimpered and sniffed. He wanted to get into his stroller and she let him do so. He put his fingers in his mouth and sucked them as he sobbed.

Iris leaned down to tie him into his stroller. She kissed him on his red wet cheeks. "Mommy's sorry, darling! But she just couldn't bear it if you were killed by a car. You know?"

Did he know?

Moral: A smack is worth a thousand words.

10. Size Matters

A bully gets his comeuppance.

The school bus stopped a few houses away from Tich's house. It was the third week back at school, and there were new kids on the bus, one of them who already had a nickname. Steamer, it was. A name that expressed his looks, a round, roly-poly figure, big and heavy like a steamroller. He was easily twice the size of Tich, and pretty much his opposite. Tich was small for his age (hence his nickname), thin and runt-like, the nostrils of his nose showing from beneath a flattened nose, not unlike a pig's. Thankfully, though, the kids did not call him "piggy," a name that would be far worse than Tich. For his part, Steamer lumbered along as though he were pushing against a mountain of sand, his wide stumpy legs forcing his body to turn with each step. He ran with difficulty, gravity holding him upright, his arms pulling at the air as though he were swimming.

They stepped down from the bus and immediately Tich ran forward, but Steamer held him back, his big round face, eyes almost closed shut from his enormously fat cheeks, grinning with glee. "No you don't!" he warned.

"Let go of me!" cried Tich, trying to twist his arm out of Steamer's vice-like grip.

*

Three weeks earlier.

Now in grade 8, the new school year had got off to a rocky start for Tich, all because of the school bus, actually, not the bus, but the presence of the new kid, Steamer. At first he had almost liked him, because he seemed to be a jovial kid, his being fat and all, and laughing all the time, even when there was nothing to laugh at. So on that first day, when Steamer grabbed him as soon as they got off the bus and started pulling him along, laughing and calling out, "you're with me! You're with me! Let's have fun! Let's have fun!" Tich took it all in good humor, going along with it, not trying to twist his way free, allowing himself to be dragged along the street. But then, when they came to his house, Steamer did not let go, and pulled him along, his grip tightening until it hurt.

"Let go of me!"' cried Tich, "this is my house!"

"Come on! We're going to my house! Friends are friends!" laughed Steamer.

And so it went. Every day, they got off the bus, Steamer grabbed Tich, and dragged him past his house all the way to his own house, almost a block away. Tich even tried pretending he was happy to go along and then hope that Steamer would let go of him, but he never did. Steamer thought this was great fun. Tich had become his compliant slave.

*

Tich's dad was away at work every day until quite late. He had a well-equipped work bench in a shed at the back of his garage, and it was there that Tich hoped to find a solution. His mum was pleased that he was working away there and never asked what he was doing. It was enough for her that he was occupied and not whining or complaining that he had nothing to do. His first idea was to make a ring with a spike sticking out that he could plunge into Steamer when he grabbed him. He had found an old ring, a key ring maybe, to which he tried to affix an old gramophone needle. But it proved impossible, with no way to make the spike stay firm, and besides the electrical tape he found, stretched and did not do the job.

He then sneaked a knife from the kitchen, but this would not do either. It was a regular bread and butter knife, with a curved end, so it would not be easy to jab it into Steamer's fat hand, or anywhere on his body for that matter. And he could not take the carving knife, because that would be noticed immediately, and besides, how could he hide it in his school bag, and what if he were caught with it. No, that would not do either.

There were containers of nails, but Tich could not think of any way to use them to advantage. He did bang some nails through a thin piece of wood, but then the problem still remained, how could he explain the weapon, if a teacher found it in his bag, and probably worse, Steamer would quickly spy it in his bag anyway, and then he could imagine Steamer taking it off him and using it against him. Frustrated, he threw down the hammer and nails and retreated to the front of the house, and stood out front, bouncing a tennis ball on the newly laid concrete footpath. This he always enjoyed when he got fed up, especially as there were millions of ants scurrying about and he could aim his bouncing ball to kill as many of them as he could, though there seemed to be an endless supply of them. And there, slowly, each evening in the twilight, a solution to his problem came to him.

*

Today

The bus slowly passed the line of modest houses of the new suburb of Norlane, most of them "commission" houses, public housing that is, and drew to a stop at the corner of Melbourne and Sparks roads. Steamer with his big grin and fat cheeks, positioned himself on the step at the bus's door. Tich positioned himself behind a couple of other kids, one of them a girl, and managed to slip out without Steamer grabbing him. He ran a little forward, looking back to see whether Steamer would chase him. And chase him Steamer did.

Now Steamer, for all his weight, was not that strong a runner, but nevertheless, because he was twice Tich's size, could probably catch him in a short run, so long as Tich did not run out of breath, and could put on a spurt at the start. So on this day Tich got a little ahead, with Steamer already set to catch him. He looked back and taunted, "Ha! Ha! You can't catch me!" and ran as fast as he could, making sure he was just out of reach.

Now came the *coup de grâce.*

It was difficult for Tich to keep up a fast pace, at the same time looking back to see exactly where Steamer was. It was essential that they both were at their peak speeds. Timing was the essence. A miscalculation and Tich would be beaten to a pulp, or at least that was what he imagined. And now, Steamer was practically on top of him, Tich running as fast as he could. He took a quick glimpse back over his shoulder, then suddenly bobbed down, crouching into a ball, ducking his head into his arms, squatting head down on to the concrete footpath, feeling its hardness on his knuckles that shielded his face and head.

He felt a slight bump at his back, but nothing else. Then a scream and thump as Steamer sailed over Tich's crouching body, and fell straight ahead of him, arms sprawled out, unable to protect his landing, his fat face banging into the concrete, his legs kicking well past Tich, his knees deeply grazed by the rough concrete surface.

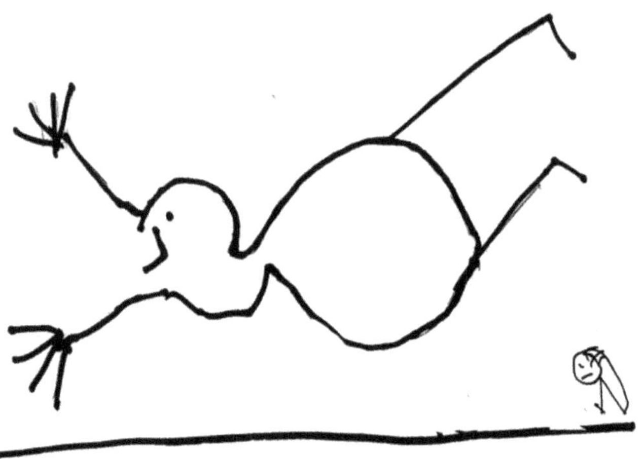

Tich rose up, and looked down at the prostrate body of his nemesis. "It serves you right! Leave me alone!" he cried, with some satisfaction, but mixed with fear, fear that Steamer might lose his temper and really come after him. He stood briefly looking down at Steamer, a moment that would remain with him forever. There sat Steamer examining his cuts and bruises, feeling the blood run down his face from a horrible graze on his forehead.

"You'll pay for this!!" growled Steamer. "You just wait!"

Tich rushed home, not looking back.

*

The next day, Tich tried to fake an illness so he wouldn't have to go to school and face up to Steamer. But his mum would have nothing of it. So he was prepared for the worst. Well, not really prepared. He had not thought much of what might happen after he pulled off his stunt. He had hardly slept last night, so pleased and excited that his solution had really done the trick. But now, what if Steamer came after him like he was sure he would? He had only glimpsed Steamer's agony, but it looked like he was pretty banged up.

On that day, he looked out for Steamer at school and on the bus coming home. But Steamer was not on the school bus, not for a whole week. And the day he showed up, Tich pursed his lips, looked with some fear at the scars on Steamer's face and elbows and knees, trying to hide his satisfaction. He was about to say he was sorry. But Steamer didn't look at him. They got off the bus together, and Tich expected the worst. But it did not come. Steamer never mentioned it, and they rarely spoke to each other. Each walked at their own pace, several steps apart, to their own house, Tich hanging back, preferring to follow rather than lead.

Moral: *Courage, though foolish, is the counter of tyranny.*

11. Crowd Pleaser

Little kid wins big.

Two kids, one 10, the other 8. The big kid, they called him Moons (he had a big round face like a moon) was top heavy, his body like an upside down pear. Being big, you would think he would be a bully. But it wasn't that simple. True, kids smaller than him, or even about the same size, kept away because he did look large, and he acted like he wasn't scared of anything. Always boasting how good a fighter he was, and telling stories of the last kid he had beaten up. No matter that nobody had ever seen him beat up anyone.

One day, down in the school yard, behind the shelter shed, a friend of mine (no longer a friend) dared me to go up to Moons and call him names, tease him and get him mad and see what he would do.

"Go on, betcha can't. Too scared," taunted my friend.

"If you're so smart, why don't you do it?" I say, feeling smart.

The other kids gathered around. "Scaredy-cat! Scaredy-cat," they chanted.

I looked over at Moons who was hacking away at the shelter shed trying to carve his name in the wood frame. "Hey Moons, you'll get into trouble doing that!" I cry.

"So are you gunna stop me?" He mutters with a big grin, his face more like a moon than you could imagine.

My friend nudged me, and the other kids pushed him into me. "Go on, I bet you can't," chided my friend. "Anyway, if he goes for you, we'll all join hands and keep him off you."

I took an unwanted step towards Moons. "You better stop doing that, or I'll report you, Pie-face."

Moons stopped his carving. "Whatdja call me?"

"You heard. Pie-face," I said cheekily.

"You wanna get bashed up?"

Moons took a step towards me, his pocket knife clenched in

his hand. This scared the shit out of me. But it was too late to step back, the bunch of kids behind me pushed me forward and I almost fell against Moons who now stood like a rock, his big tummy poking me in the chest.

I'm not quite sure what happened next. The bunch of kids behind me, and my friend, so called, pushed me a little off balance and I fell forward, my right leg stretched out, one big step behind Moons's thin legs, and my right arm thrust forward, thinking that I would save myself from falling down. Instead, it had the effect of banging Moons on the chest just as my leg hit against the back of his legs. You guessed it! It was the classic trip they teach you in self-defense school. Anyway, his top heavy body simply fell backwards over my leg and down he went with a plop!

All the other kids gasped as one. Here I was, the littlest kid in the grade, just dropped the biggest. Now they all gathered around in a circle and chanted, "go on! Do it Again! Doo - it! Doo - it!"

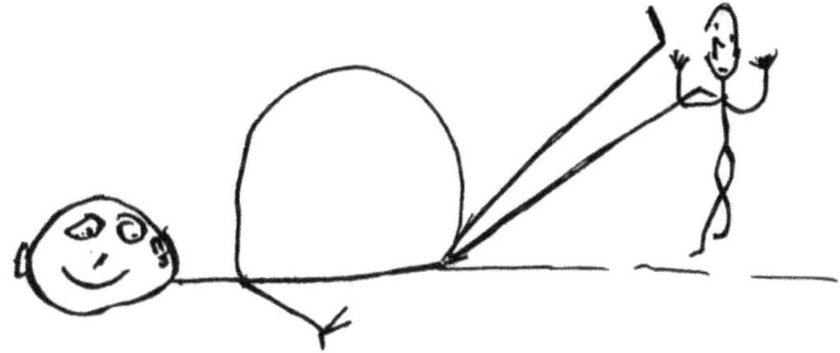

Moons got up, with some difficulty, because his body was so heavy and his legs long and thin. Yet, to my amazement, he showed no signs of anger, just grinned and patted himself down, brushing away the red dust of the playground. Then I understood that he wasn't a bully at all, not like we all reckoned just because he was so big. He just looked at me silly-like. And I stepped up and this time I put my leg out behind his, and with my left arm this time gave him a sharp push backwards over my leg, and tripped him again. Down he went, amidst the cheers of the other kids. I looked around at them and they were all looking at Moons, not me.

Then they taunted Moons. "Get up ya fat shit!" And everyone laughed, calling yet again for him to subject himself to humiliation.

And he did. And now we became an act. He stood up, and I tripped him, and we did it over and over until the bell rang and we all ran into class.

The next day, during morning recess, all the kids ran down behind the shelter shed and egged us on, and Moons just stood there, a big grin on his face. The circle of kids formed around us and I walked up to Moons, enjoying the chanting of the kids, "trip him! Trip him!"

But it didn't feel right. And besides he was much bigger than me, so why didn't he just push me away or even fall on top of me? If he did that it would squash me to death! So I looked up at him and he looked down at me, already preparing himself for the fall. I wanted to walk away, but the kids around us were jeering and swearing. How long could this go on until Moons flattened me? And if I walked away, what then? Would the kids start calling me names? Like Coward! Yella-belly!

I looked up into Moons's eyes, they were each about as big as my face, I reckoned. He seemed to be enjoying all this attention, even though the crowd's fun was at his expense. What if I pushed him down really hard and he hurt himself? Would that change things? Maybe he would get mad and flatten me? And what would the other kids say? "Do it again?" Surely they would not want to see him get hurt?

We got ready, my leg behind his, my arm forward of his chest. I tried to whisper to him from where my face was level with his tuberous chest. "This is the last one. I'm not doing this anymore. Sorry!" I whispered.

Down he went, and as he went down, I just walked away, pushing gently past my friend. I did not wait for them to call me back. I just kept walking fast towards the classroom, and was fortunately saved by the bell for classes to begin.

I ran home from school that day, avoiding any of the other kids. And I did not sleep that night, imagining how I would be made fun of the next day for walking away and not standing up to fat Moons.

But I had lost sleep over nothing. The next day it was as though the whole thing had not happened, and my friend did not even mention any of it. Moons did come up to me and asked if I wanted to play, and I said, no thanks, though I then wondered whether he wasn't really meaning that I should knock him over again to the crowd's enjoyment, but simply to play with him and be his friend.

> *Moral: The pleasure of a crowd is always*
> *at the expense of others*

12. Cleanliness

A child is punished for swearing.

In his classic, *Mirage of Health,* Renes Dubois convincingly demonstrated how the greatest gift of western civilization to humanity was cleanliness. It was not so much the great scientific discoveries of the late 19th and early 20th centuries, the discovery of penicillin, of anesthetics, vaccinations and so on, but rather the improvements of public health facilities: the engineering feats of sewerage systems, piping and storage of fresh water, the routine use of soaps, detergents and habits of cleanliness to keep bodies and living spaces clean. From all these great accomplishments of civilization, so came the modern epithet, "cleanliness if next to Godliness." To this day, parts of the world that do not have modern public health systems—crowded towns and cities where people live amongst open sewers and so on—are at much greater risk from "natural disasters," whether of plagues, floods, or earthquakes. If the basic infrastructure ordained by western civilizations—standards of public health, safe building regulations, urban planning, roads and bridges and so on—is not available or has not been built, then the health and safety of everyday life is constantly at risk.

It is against these circumstances of everyday life that most those who live in societies that have been touched by western civilization (probably nine-tenths of the world where even the remotest places have been reached by imperialism of one kind of another) that this story takes hold. Though before we can begin, we must also acknowledge that a basic tool of cleanliness of western civilization, the knife and fork, adds a serious dimension to health and safety, as do other eating implements such as chop sticks, and certainly discriminates against those societies whose eating habits do not conform to the western rule of cleanliness; that is the skill of eating stews and mushy meals with one's fingers and various breads that take over the function of a fork or spoon. Washing one's hands before and after eating thus becomes an essential rule of health. And in an era of pandemics as has overtaken the world in the 21st century, the washing of hands has become a prime focus of cleanliness and defense against health disasters.

There are, however, other kinds of cleanliness that have become a constant companion to hand washing in many civilized societies. Such is the focus of this story.

*

Thomas Randolph was the only child of Mr. and Mrs. Randolph who inhabited a prim little house at 36 Pakington Street, Geelong West. Mr. Randolph worked at Donaghy's rope factory as a foreman and rode his bike there and back each day, his lunch carefully made by Mrs. Randolph, and packed in a small tin container that was strapped on to the back of the bike. Thomas attended Geelong West primary school, a red brick schoolhouse, the schoolyard completely covered over with bitumen, a city school typical of those in cities and towns of Victoria in 1950s Australia.

On this Sunday morning, a morning that would remain fixed in Thomas's memory for the rest of his life, Thomas sat at the kitchen table eating his Rice Bubbles. A robust ten years old, just finishing sixth grade, he was more than ready to go off to Geelong High School next year. His mum hovered above him, watching his every move. Thomas for his part was doing what he did every Sunday morning, slurping every spoonful, trying to delay as much as possible, hoping that just maybe one Sunday he would not have to go to Sunday school. He reached across the table for the bottle of milk, but his mum grabbed his arm and said, "now that's enough milk, young man. Hurry on now or you'll be late for Sunday school." Annoyed, he pulled his arm away and to his and his Mum's horror, he knocked over the milk bottle and milk poured out all over the well-scrubbed table and started to drip off the edge on to his pants. Thomas pushed back his chair and cried out, "shit Mum! Look what you made me do!" He gulped and his cheeks went all red.

Mrs. Randolph stood back in horror, her hand to her mouth. "Thomas! How dare you speak to me like that! How dare you!"

She ran out of the kitchen and called for her husband who was working in his old shed. There was no answer, so she ran out to the shed to convey the terrible news.

Mr. Randolph emerged from his shed. "What's the matter?" he sighed.

"It's Thomas! He swore at me!"

"Well, it's only to be expected."

"What do you mean by that?" cried Mrs. Randolph.

Mr. Randolph coughed nervously. "You know what I mean. He's growing up. Going to high school next year, you know. It's only to be expected."

"Not in my house! Speak to him! I won't have a child in my kitchen who talks like that!"

Mr. Randolph sighed again. "All right. I'll speak to him." He turned to go back in his shed.

"Now! Talk to him now! He can't go off the Sunday school talking like that!"

"All right! All right!" Mr. Randolph emerged from the shed again, this time wiping his hands on an old oily rag. He had been working on the car.

Thomas stood at the table, wiping it down with a washcloth. There were a few streaks of milk on his good school pants that his mother insisted he wear to Sunday school. He edged back to the corner of the kitchen, getting ready for, he knew not what. The word had just slipped out. He didn't mean it, of course. Who knows what his father would do to him. He expected a belting, though he had never been smacked before, as far as he could remember. Maybe he would get to stay home from Sunday school. That wouldn't be too bad.

Mr. Randolph walked straight through the kitchen to the bathroom to wash his hands, without looking at his wayward son. Thomas looked down. He was on the verge of crying, but tried very hard not to. He was too old to cry. His mother stood at the table scrubbing it with a scrubbing brush. There were tears in her eyes. She wasn't too old to cry. He heard the tap run, then silence. And finally, his father emerged from the bathroom, a dripping bar of Palmolive soap in his hand.

"Take this!!" ordered Mr. Randolph.

"It's all wet and slimy!" complained Thomas.

"Take it or else!" threatened his dad.

"What's it for anyway? I didn't do nothing!"

"You swore at your mother!"

"I didn't! I mean. I didn't mean to. It just slipped out."

"You used a dirty word, Thomas," said his mother, trying to calm things down.

Mr. Randolph stepped towards his son, grabbed his hand and forced the slimy bar of Palmolive into it. "You have a filthy mouth," he said, "so now you must wash it out with soap and water."

"But dad!"

"No buts!"

Mr. Randolph grabbed Thomas's hand and the Palmolive soap and pushed it into his mouth. Thomas clenched his mouth shut. The soap hit his lips and hurt them.

"Don't! You're hurting me!" he cried.

Mr. Randolph had gone as far as he could. He pushed Thomas ahead of him and guided him into the bathroom. "Wash your mouth out with soap and water and don't come out until it's done." He gave him a little shove, then quickly retreated out the bathroom and pulled the door shut.

"He won't do it, will he?" asked Mrs. Randolph.

"Probably not. But he's learnt his lesson."

Mr. Randolph went back to his shed. Mrs. Randolph finished cleaning up the spilled milk from the table and the floor. She looked at the kitchen clock. Time to put in the roast to cook while they were all at church. Thomas would miss Sunday school this morning. The first time in many years

Moral: A perfect punishment reflects the crime it punishes.

13. Imperial Blunder

A famous cricketer breaks the rules, with dire consequences.

There was once a famous cricketer, Peter Vigna was his name, a batsman better even than Donald Bradman or Virat Kholi. At a very young age he was selected to open batting for the Australian Test side, and routinely made a century or two in each innings. It was not long before he was chosen as captain of the Australian cricket team in the great test matches that were the pinnacle of this imperial sport. But on February 21, 2019 there occurred an event at the Melbourne Cricket Ground that will go down in history as a huge turning point in the story of Western Civilization, and brought into stark relief just how important had been the imperial reach of Great British Culture in Australia and all former and current British colonies in every corner of the globe.

For those readers who do not have a background or did not grow up in a country where this imperial sport reigned, here is a very brief sketch of the classic qualities of cricket, that is to say, its sacred rules. Without this knowledge, it would be very difficult, if not impossible to appreciate the significance of that event in 2019, and the shattering aftershocks that followed it.

In general terms, one must understand that the game of cricket represents all that is good in an ordered society, especially one that has received it from its founding country, England, now part of the United Kingdom. In the heady days of imperialism, English and European countries expanded their reach to many countries around the world, driven initially by the search for riches. And in return for the riches they reaped, they gave those countries the essential elements of a civilized society, none better than the game of cricket.

Cricket is a game in which detailed rules are sacrosanct, demanding unquestioned respect for the order of the game, which, in the great test matches that last for up to five days, is supreme. The pitch is 20.12 meters long and 3.05 meters wide. At each end is a set of three stumps (three thin poles hammered into the ground spanning 22.86 cm wide). Or, to put it in simpler language before Napoleon imposed the metric system on Europe, the pitch is 22 yards long by 10 feet wide. The bowling crease (where the bowler's leading foot must not step over when he releases the ball) is five feet from the stumps at either end. The pitch is composed of carefully crafted tough turf, rolled down very hard.

The bowler is strictly limited to bowling the ball "over-arm" but he must not bend his elbow when tossing the ball. Throwing the ball like in baseball would be a foul and definitely cause for one of the two umpires at each end to discipline the bowler. The batter at the other end of the pitch has to hit the ball with his specially crafted wooden bat (usually a particular type of willow) that has a round narrow handle and a broad flat area for hitting the ball. The basic idea is for the bowler to bowl the ball and the batter to hit the ball away so that it does not hit the stumps, in which case he is called "out." There are eleven players on each team. Like in baseball, there are innings, in a "test" match two for each side. There are two batters batting at a time, one at each end. The bowler gets to bowl an "over" of six balls, then another bowler in his team bowls the next over. When all batsmen are called "out," the innings is over and the opposing side takes up the bat. The batsman strikes the ball and the batters then decide whether to run or not. If the ball goes far, they run to each end (1 run) and back (2 runs) and must make it to their respective creases before the fielders (all 11 of them) throw the ball to hit the stumps before the batter at either end makes it back. In this case he would be "out" and another batter come in. A batter may also be called "out" if the ball he hits is caught by a fielder before the ball has hit the ground. There are a myriad of other situations in which a batsman may be called out or make runs, but these are the basics and hopefully they give a reasonable picture of this game of rules.

In this story, however, we are concerned with one rule that applies to the ball, the composition and surface of which are crucial to the game. The ball is traditionally made of a cork core, bound tightly by string and covered by a red leather case with a slightly raised seam where the two halves of the cover are sewn together. The spin and swing of the ball can be managed by the bowler, but the surface of the ball, especially the seam, can affect its behavior considerably. There are therefore very strict rules as to what players may do to the surface of the ball. They may polish it on their clothes after each ball, but they may not pick at it in any way. Those who know baseball may wonder about this. In general, the idea of cricket is for the bowler to bowl a ball that bounces first before the batsman hits it. Thus, the extent to which the ball may both swing and bounce at an angle not expected by the batter is the crux of the game. If the ball is tampered with, its bounce can become less predictable by the batter.

*

Peter Vigna was a boy who grew up very quickly, mainly because of his natural talent with a bat. From the very first day he played cricket on the sand at Torquay (the one in Australia, not England), at the age of 3 or 4 or 5 (the pundits never got it quite right; it was as if he were born with a cricket ball in his mouth), his future as a world star of cricket was cast. Otherwise he had a normal upbringing. His mum and dad doted on him, gave him every opportunity to play cricket with bat and ball, but from the very start, it was the bat that he took to. The ball was simply a means to the bat. His father, a quiet man devoted to his family, taught mathematics at the local high school, and his mother was a recent immigrant from England. So it was an easy choice that, once his talent became obvious, he eventually went to England to play club cricket at the tender age of seventeen. And it was inevitable that one day he would be selected for the Australian Test team, and that happened in 2012, selected as a bowler, of all things (very important to our story, though). But his batting soon caught the eye of selectors as he made century after century. They loved him, and he soon took over as captain of team Australia. What more could a young and talented man want?

The answer is simple. He wanted to win, for that is what drives all those who play team sports, or any competitive sport for that matter. Ask them why they do it, what drives them. And they all answer without any hesitation: "I love to win, and I really hate to lose." This is commonly said with a deep emotional thrust. Would they do anything to win? By this one means, would they break the rules to gain an advantage over their opponent? Or maybe not exactly break the rules, but bend them a little? To do that, though would not be playing fair. The drug scandals in the Olympic games, and many if not all international sports (bicycle racing for example), are legion. But it is not just drugs. Consider what young gymnasts will do to their growing bodies in order to win. For such talented people, winning drives them with the same power as does any human instinct.

So now, we already understand why Peter Vigna was all set up to win at any cost. All it needs is the temptation and opportunity. One might say that cheating is an occupational hazard for highly talented athletes.

There is a considerable difference between cricket and other sports. Cricket has a grand and sacred history. And to repeat, English history. And to repeat again, imperial history. It is a game that was transported to all of the colonies of then Great Britain. All those countries (or nearly all, at least the most progressive of all) that were colonized by once Great Britain continued to play the game even after they were decolonized or gained a measure of independence. (There are some inexplicable exceptions, Canada being one of them, but we can put that down to its degradation by its neighbor, the United States.) If you doubt this assessment, just consider that, when Australia's Test Cricket team captain Steve Smith and his collaborators were accused of ball tampering, none other than the Australian Prime Minister, Malcolm Turnbul publicly denounced the cheating and demanded that something be done.

It was ball tampering in which Peter Vigna was involved. As captain of the Australian Test side against India in 2019, he was caught on camera along with a couple of his colleagues, rubbing the surface of the ball or picking at the seam with his fingernails that had been strengthened by a secret substance, or possibly attachment, that made them as sharp as a knife's edge. The investigation never did determine how the scratches to the surface of the ball and slight roughing of the seam were achieved. In fact, similar to the case of the notorious Bancroft scandal of 2018, the umpires did not detect any unusual scratches or damage to the ball, and did not prescribe the penalty of five runs against the offending team, as was their prerogative. Nevertheless, vigilant commentators examined and re-examined video of Vigna rubbing and scratching the ball in ways that looked like he was trying to scratch the surface, against the rules of cricket, according to these ever vigilant commentators, some of whom, of course, were themselves former cricket heroes.

The public outcry, more accurately the media frenzy, over the sin of Vigna's alleged violation of the rules, led to an inquiry by Cricket Australia and threats from various politicians that the Australian Government had a duty to step in and regulate the sport. But the search for Vigna's collaborators conducted for almost two years, found none. And it is now claimed that the collaborators will never be found because of a code of silence that has arisen within cricket teams around the world, a lesson learned from the Steve Smith scandal. In any event, Vigna was fined one year's salary (a few million dollars), demoted from the captaincy forever, and barred from playing top class cricket for two years. Further, he had to admit his wrongdoing in public on Australia's national radio and television the ABC, and to apologize to the nation for his wrongdoing. They wanted to call it "sin" but the government communications specialists thought that such language would violate the separation of church and state, a fiction in Australia, copied from the USA.

And so it happened. At the opening of the first Test match between Australia and England on December 26, 2021, both sides assembled as though they were to remember a famous colleague who had died. The teams lined up in two columns starting at the entrance. Vigna entered the oval and walked as though through a gauntlet. The crowd erupted in boos and hisses and many yelled awful derogatory remarks, some of them racist. Facing the stand that contained all the media people and the officials of the Cricket Australia Board, Vigna dropped to his knees, clenching his hands together in front of his breast. Cricket Australia had given strong instructions to the camera operator and his director to do as many close-ups of Vigna's face as possible, especially when he cried, which Vigna, after some arm-twisting, had promised to do.

This is what he said, in a clear, shaky voice, a special microphone set up to catch even the tiniest of whimpers:

"To the proud people of the Commonwealth of Nations, I express my deepest apologies for bringing our wonderful game

of cricket into disrepute. I accept full responsibility for my actions of tampering with the cricket ball at the MCG on February 21, 2019 in the test against India, I made foolish choices and I am ashamed, so ashamed…"

Vigna bowed his head and tears trickled down his face. The media were not pleased with this, as his bowed head hid the tears from the cameras. The director tried to signal to Vigna to hold up his head, but as it happened, this was not necessary. Suddenly, Vigna raised both hands and lifted his head, his eyes wide, staring at the dark clouds above. Still on his knees he cried:

"I ask forgiveness! I have given my life to cricket, and will not be able to live with myself ever again! I am so sorry, so sorry, sorry, sorry, sorry for breaking the sacred rules of cricket in such a careless manner! Please, I beg you, accept my deepest heart-felt apologies for this cricket crime of the century!"

The crowd once more erupted into boos and hisses. The camera quickly drew back from his face and scanned the crowd. It had turned into a huge angry mob, fists shaking, mouths twisted in hatred and disgust. This was a media sensation. Many millions, perhaps billions around the world witnessed this drama. And after the noise of the crowd died away, Vigna stood up slowly, and bowed to the crowd all around the stadium. His team mates, even the English took small steps toward him and then a few patted him on the back, trying to console him. He withdrew to the stand along with his team. He would not be opening as he used to. But he would be batting. Australia was to bat first. And Australia won that test match, Vigna making a total of 265 runs, over both innings. In fact, without his performance, Australia would have lost. The Cricket Board was jubilant. Vigna received many accolades. But it was not to last.

The media was not finished with Vigna yet. In the match reviews, various cricket greats from the past, some of them media personalities themselves, were brought before the public and asked what they thought of Vigna's return and especially his apology. There were mixed reactions. Of course, his fantastic batting could not be criticized. He was no doubt a genius of a batter. But a number of former captains and others expressed some concern that what Vigna had done was irreparable. He had besmirched the entire game. "Was there nothing he could do to repair that?" asked the media pundits. The answer seemed to be "no" and some insisted that the punishment was not severe enough. Though others, usually those not as old as the former greats, mused that maybe the punishment was too severe, especially as the umpires had not penalized Vigna's team when the offense was reported to them, and no damage could be discerned to the ball that might have affected the outcome of the game in any way.

The Australian Cricket Board was well aware of these views. Indeed, some members of the board thought that there should have been no punishment except a reprimand. But the chair of the board, Sir Douglas Pinster was adamant. The very basis of the game had been insulted and broken. Besides even the Prime Minister had expressed his concern on behalf of Australia. And the Queen woke from her afternoon nap and gave a brief public address to express her concern to all her subjects.

The saga might have ended there, the media growing tired

of it, always looking for something new, except that Australia almost lost the second Test Match, even though Vigna once again performed in a way that showed just what a talented and gifted player he was. He even made two fabulous catches that, combined with another two centuries, clearly demonstrated to the Board that he was an essential player to the team. Without him, the team would lose. And to lose to England was always the height of humiliation.

We have said very little about the coach. Let us just say that he was a kind of amateur psychologist, like most coaches of team sports in the 21st century. Of course he was a former test cricketer, an outstanding wicket keeper (the "catcher" who stands behind the wicket and fields the fast balls as they whiz by the batter). His name was Clive Brown and he was an incessant talker, again like most coaches. Almost all his conversations with the players were in the form of speeches derived from his notes taken in coach's class to which the Cricket Board demanded all coaching staff attend. But on what was about to occur he had no quick speech. He was dumbfounded at the insolence and sheer disregard for others, lack of respect for him, the coach. Yet that was not at all what Vigna intended. He simply wanted to be made whole again. He wanted true forgiveness for which he had groveled and pleaded in his public apology.

"Coach, can I have a quiet word?" asked Vigna after he stepped away from the practice net, bat still in hand.

Coach Brown, a short thin fellow, raised his head and looked him in the eye. "Of course. I am always available for any concerns or suggestions you may have," he answered with a big, patronizing smile.

"Coach that's always good to hear. I have been thinking about this since the day of my apology."

"Thinking? About what? I hope you have not been worrying or brooding. That's not good for one's mental health, you know. It can affect your game too."

"Yes and no. It hasn't affected me so far, has it?"

"That's for sure. But it's still important to be mindful of the dangers of too much thinking," advised coach Brown.

Vigna, not quite sure what the coach meant by the word "thinking" shifted on his feet and swallowed a little saliva. There was a brief silence, while the coach looked him up and down, a frown appearing, but then a big smile as well. This was enough encouragement for Vigna to continue. "I want to be captain again," he said.

Coach Brown's jaw dropped and the frown appeared again. His tongue made a nervous little dart out of his mouth and back again. "That's not going to happen," he said quietly, always like that when he said no to something his players wanted.

"Wait, I haven't finished what I wanted to say," Vigna quickly replied.

"The answer's still no. You heard the crowd. You copped the Cricket Board demand for punishment. Leave it alone, or it will get worse."

"But I did a full apology and I really meant it. And I asked for forgiveness. Isn't that enough? Shouldn't the punishment be ended?"

"Don't! Don't do this. You will only harm yourself. It's the whole game that needs to be rehabilitated, not just you." Coach was climbing on his high horse.

"And you're doing it through me," muttered Vigna.

"I suppose so, in a way. But you brought it all on yourself. You shouldn't have broken the rules. I thought you understood that," lectured the coach.

"I do. I do. Believe me I do. That's why I have another request to make, actually it's another way of asking for the captaincy back."

The coach looked around to see if anyone else was listening. Probably not. He leaned in closer to Vigna. He wasn't a bad fellow really. He felt sorry for him, but the Board had spoken. And there was the fact that no actual damage had been done to the ball and the umpires never announced a penalty during the match. "What is it then? If reasonable I will go back to the Board. But I can tell you. They're going to say no."

"My public apology I now know was not enough. But I truly want to be forgiven so I can start my life over. The only way I can see that I will be forgiven is to be punished really and truly in public, before the crowd in the stadium."

"But we already did that. You did a great job. The media loved it."

"Please coach. I don't want to suffer for the rest of my life with this burden of my apology not being accepted." Vigna wanted to grab his coach and give him a good shake. Of course he held back.

But the coach said, resisting the urge to put his arm around him, "there's nothing else you can do. You have to accept your guilt. I can arrange counseling, if you wish, to help you overcome it all,".

Immediately Vigna blurted it out. "I want to be whipped in public in the Melbourne Cricket Ground."

"What? This is no joking matter!" exclaimed the coach.

"It's no joke. I really mean it. Twenty lashes, more if they like. It's that, or I quit right now and the team will have to do without me."

Rarely lost for words, Coach Brown stepped back speechless. Vigna continued:

"And I want to be whipped by one of the media personalities of past cricket fame. Preferably a fast bowler who will have a big swinging arm and will be able to lay on the strokes."

"You're mad!" cried Coach Brown.

"Maybe. But I am convinced it's my only way to get back my life. Surely if the fans see me actually get punished, they will accept my apology. It's the only convincing way I can think of that shows absolutely that I have been punished, paid for my sins, and with every scream in pain as each stroke is laid on, that will be enough to show that I am so sorry for what I did."

"I can't go to the Board with this crazy request. I'll be a laughing stock, and they will probably fire me," complained the coach.

"Are you not prepared to take that risk? It will save the team from a big loss. I will quit, I tell you. I will quit if they will not do this. I want my life back at any cost."

*

Coach Brown called for an emergency session of the board. Sir Douglas was outraged to be called away from his annual coastal retreat and golf week. But coach did not want to go down in cricket history as having lost a test match to the pommies (English) by such a big margin, which is what would happen. And just in case, he brought Peter Vigna with him. They met in the MCG legends room, a huge room that looked like any modern hotel dining room, big round tables covered with blindingly white table cloths, a massive bar running all the way down one side, and on the other side facing the oval, huge windows giving a view of the entire pitch. But today, Sir Douglas had the curtains drawn across the windows. The lights were turned down, he wanted a somber atmosphere, no hint of celebrity. And no beer or anything else alcoholic. Just jugs of water spaced out around the table and glasses in each place. There were ten of them, representing the executive board. There was no need for a full board to meet on such a trivial matter as a disciplinary action. The board took their seats, leaving two vacant directly opposite Sir Douglas. Coach Brown took his, but Vigna held back. Coach tugged at his sleeve. They were both dressed in their Melbourne Cricket Club blazers of course.

Sir Douglas coughed loudly to bring the members to order. "I hereby announce the opening of a special session of the executive board of the Melbourne Cricket Club," he said.

There was a muffled noise of chairs being pulled into place. The large table seated twelve. However, immediately, there was a problem because Vigna refused to sit and insisted on standing behind the chair next to Coach Brown.

"Take your seat, young man," harrumphed Sir Douglas.

"I don't deserve to sit at the table with you illustrious gentlemen," mumbled Vigna, head bowed.

Coach pulled at his blazer sleeve. "Sit down you silly bugger," he whispered.

Vigna stepped back, head still bowed.

Sir Douglas coughed yet again and looked around the table. "All right then. Let's get down to business. Coach Brown, please explain the problem. We thought we had already dealt quickly and fairly with this embarrassing matter."

"Sir Douglas and honorable members, I am honored to speak to you today. Peter Vigna, who is our only hope of winning this test series against England, has requested that he be allowed to be made whole again."

"Made what?" asked Sir Douglas in consternation. The rest of the board wriggled in their seats, signaling their agreement.

"Made whole. He feels that his life has been ruined and that even though he has been punished for his offenses, and has publicly apologized for them, he has not been forgiven, people still boo and hiss at him when he comes onto the field."

Sir Douglas sat back in his chair and twiddled the pointy end of his mustache. "Coach Brown, what more can we do? Besides, if the fans will not forgive him, that's up to them, don't you think? We have done our part. We punished him fairly and reasonably."

Vigna looked up and took a step to stand against his chair. "That's just it, sir," said Vigna raising his voice, I need to be punished more, so they, and you too," he looked around the table, "will be convinced that I really am sorry for what I did."

"More? What else can we do? Stop you from playing forever? We could do that…"

Coach Brown interrupted, "but it would have dire consequences for our team, not to mention destroy Peter's life."

Leaning on the back of his chair, Vigna blurted out, "I want to be publicly whipped! Whipped till I cry, only that will convince the fans that I'm sorry. Only that will convince all of you that I have paid for my sins and can become captain again. Made whole."

The board members stirred in their chairs and muttered to each other.

"You are joking or course," said Sir Douglas with a frown, trying to keep a straight face.

"He's not joking, Sir Douglas, he's dead serious," put in the Coach.

At that moment the door opened behind them and a tall man entered the room, perfectly groomed, carefully shaven face and clipped hair. He looked like he had makeup on. It was none other than Ian Church, the all-time cricket great, Australian legendary spin bowler who bowled out the entire English side in the final Test match against England in the 1974 series for just 36 runs. He was now a media favourite and commentator. He was also followed by another individual, rather over weight, a full head of hair, a short, heavy-set young man of around forty. His presence made everyone stir, especially Peter Vigna. For he was Fred Cousins, Vigna's agent.

The two men, looking a bit like Laurel and Hardy, stood behind Vigna. Coach Brown didn't like anyone standing behind him, so he stood and offered his seat to Church, who gratefully took it. Fred the agent, started to walk around the table, one hand in his pocket jiggling his phone.

"This is most irregular," complained Sir Douglas.

Cousins, always the agent, took over. "I demand that you restore Peter's full privileges and status as a member of the cricket team of this important series, and appoint him back to his rightful place of Captain. Furthermore, since he committed no specific offense that actually affected the game as it played out— the ball was not damaged—you must declare him innocent."

The board erupted with angry complaints and epithets. Exactly what Cousins wanted of course.

"If I may?" asked Vigna. "I want to be publicly whipped, enough to make me feel the pain of the accusations against me. I accept the guilt. I want to be rid of it. I want all the fans to see me suffer."

"But you have already suffered," insisted Sir Douglas.

"Obviously, it's not enough," interjected Church. "What is needed is a public spectacle. I suggest that he be stripped naked and receive twenty lashes in front of a full crowd in the middle of the pitch at the Melbourne Cricket Ground!"

"That's OK with me," said Vigna, his head bowed once again.

Cousins the agent spoke up. "Ten lashes and nothing more, plus he gets his captaincy back immediately."

"And TV Channel 7 gets full exclusive rights," added Church.

Sir Douglas banged the table with his open hand. It stung.

"That's enough. This is beyond the pale of decency. I will not allow such degradation!"

"But it's exactly what I need," said Vigna in a soft voice, "don't you see? It's the only way I can convincingly pay for what I have done, or am supposed to have done."

"Now you're saying that you might be innocent? That you didn't necessarily do anything wrong?" complained a board member.

"This is disgusting," cried another.

"We found you guilty," said yet another.

Church looked around the table. "Not quite," he said in his golden voice, "the people, the fans, the media found him guilty. They judged him, found him guilty, and now they want his punishment carried out to the fullest extent. Peter Vigna's life must be restored to him. Only the public can do it."

"But to whip him naked is barbaric," said Sir Douglas, pushing back on his chair, then standing up tall, twirling his mustache.

"Eight strokes with a cat-o-nine tails," countered Church.

"Shocking!" cried another board member.

"A belting on the bare bottom with a one meter ruler," offered Cousins.

"That would be childish. I want to be whipped!" cried Vigna, now dropping to his knees. "If naked, so be it."

"But that would be pornographic," objected yet another board member, blushing as he said it.

Church smiled. "It certainly would," he said quietly to himself.

Sir Douglas looked around the table. "Order please!" he cried, then sat back in his seat. He beckoned to a bar tender who stood transfixed. "Bring us a few jugs of beer and a whisky for those who want it. This meeting has become too stressful. We need to settle down and talk this over like civilized adults."

The beer and whisky arrived. Most went for the whisky. Coach Brown allowed himself a beer, but forbade Vigna from having any alcohol at all. Cousins objected, but the coach held firm. Finally, Cousins bargained for a Red Bull. Sir Douglas, accustomed to being in charge, but now no longer was, downed a few more quick whiskies. In fact, media personality Church had taken over. "All those who agree on half a dozen strokes with a leather strap or belt, say aye." There were a few ayes and a few grunts. "Then the ayes have it," he proclaimed.

"Naked or not?" asked a board member, blushing.

"Those in favor of naked, say aye," said Church. More grunts and ayes in response. "Then the ayes have it.

"Full frontal or not?" asked Cousins.

"He will be whipped on the back, so no full frontal. Besides, that would be almost pornographic. Would it not?" said Church, feigning serious concern.

"That depends," put in Vigna, "doesn't it?"

"To hell with it, do what you like!" spluttered Sir Douglas who, like Pilate, had washed his hands of the whole business.

"Then let's say we will leave it up to the discretion of the video director and Peter Vigna himself," said Church with authority. He then went on to the next question.

"Should Vigna be restrained or not? He is a willing subject, so maybe restraint is not needed?"

The one member of the board who was a doctor raised his hand. "He should be restrained. When the body feels sudden pain the normal reflex is to withdraw and thrash about. If that happened, the strokes of the belt could hit vulnerable parts of the body."

"How should he be restrained, then?" asked Church.

"On a cross, of course," said Cousins, half joking.

This was too much for Sir Douglas, a good Christian man. "That is a blasphemy of the worst order!" He licked his mustache and downed another whisky.

"On our Chanel 7 weekly broadcast of the early history of the penal colony in New South Wales, the whipping triangle was used. The subject is lashed to the triangle, hands tied together at the top of the triangle, legs spread apart and tied to the respective bottom corners. All those in agreement?"

More ayes came this time.

"Then the ayes have it," proclaimed Church.

Now came the most difficult question. Who would wield the belt?

"This is our most difficult decision," announced Church, sounding more and more like a clergyman." I suggest that we break up into small groups of three to discuss this issue then come together in, say, fifteen minutes. All agreed?"

Mutters of agreement.

Church continued. "Then look to the right and left of you, those will be your two group partners. Choose one of the other tables to sit at. Please be mindful not to disturb the settings of those tables. We will reconvene in fifteen minutes."

Of course, Vigna was not included in these discussions. He retired to a corner of this very large spacious room and sat, curled up, hugging his knees to his chest.

Sir Douglas had found himself a stool and sat up at the bar sipping another whisky. He had withdrawn from this disgusting barbarous endeavor. But he was also now rather drunk. And everyone knew that when he got drunk his moods changed suddenly and dramatically, without any warning. He banged his empty whisky glass on the counter and turned to face the barbarians, as he now called them.

"Your attention, bastards!" he call in his feigned Oxford accent. If you must do this, here is what will happen. Listen up!"

The groups dispersed and everyone turned to face this icon of the cricket establishment. Church attempted to reclaim the attention he deserved from the groups he had created. "We're still deliberating!" he called out in his best commentator voice.

"Excuse the expression, but shut the fuck up!" came Sir Douglas's reply. He would have his way. His upper lip even stiffened just as it was supposed to. "Here is what will happen. First, the leather belt is not a convincing implement. Looks like a schoolboy thing. It will be a leather whip, cut down into nine thin strips at one end, knots tied in the strips at 10 centimeter intervals. A woven handle. There is one in the museum of Australian slavery. There is also a whipping triangle in that museum."

Gasps from the board members followed, all taking big sips of their drinks. Sir Douglas continued:

"Second, eleven strokes of the lash will be administered because there are eleven team members. The team will line up in single file at the end of the cricket pitch. At the other end the triangle will be erected over the stumps. bails removed of course. Vigna will be tied to the triangle accordingly. He will be naked except for his cricketer's helmet to protect him from an errant stroke, and a jock strap for additional protection. The team will form the line according to their standard batting order. Each member will run up to the triangle, where an umpire will hand him the whip. He will step away and have one practice swing. He will then step forward and lay on the lash as hard as he can, aiming for the back. He will then return the whip to the umpire, run back and the next team member will run forward."

"I take it I can video all this with any angle I want?" asked Church.

"As you wish," answered Sir Douglas.

"And I will be there with the umpire, with a hot mike, allowed to speak to any of the participants, including Vigna?" persisted Church.

Cousins interrupted. "Wait a minute! What if my client cries out in pain, or uses an expletive?"

"That will all be caught on live TV," answered Church with much satisfaction.

"You OK with that?" Cousins runs over to Vigna, still crouched in the corner. "Is this all what you want?"

"The more painful, the more dreadful, the better. I must suffer and be seen to suffer," said Vigna, now standing and straightening up.

It looked as though all were agreed. But then a board member raised his hand. "Just one last question," he said, "what if a team member refuses to take part? You know, someone, don't know who, might find whipping against his religion or something."

"There is no religion on earth that is against whipping the guilty. In fact, many require it to be administered to the innocent," came a soft voice,

Who on earth had made such an outrageous statement? They all turned to its source.

It was the bar tender.

*

You may be expecting a deliciously salacious account of the spectacle in the Melbourne Cricket Ground on day one of the Third Test match of Australia against England. Or maybe you are thinking or hoping that it would not occur? But I assure you that the Great Event, as it came to be known, did take place before a record crowd of over 90,000, more than any Australian Football Grand Final crowd. And I would add that you should be ashamed of yourself for eagerly anticipating such a spectacle of one naked former cricket captain whipped by his team mates. guilty or not, before a half-drunken mob that fully appreciated its carnal florescence, and when they woke up from a deep sleep the next morning, they would feel wholly satisfied, just as Peter Vigna hoped.

Peter Vigna survived the ordeal and was appointed captain of the team immediately after the whipping. He accepted the captaincy, still bleeding, and suffering quite a lot from the added pain of the salt poured copiously into the wounds (though, because of the widely varied accuracy or perhaps will of the team members, not many strokes of the lash actually broke the skin; indeed some hardly touched his naked body).

If only the story could end here. It is true that Peter Vigna went on to score huge victories for his team and his fans. He was seemingly fully restored. But, like his historical forebear, Pietro della Vigna, there would be more. Pietro della Vigna fell out of favor with the court of Frederick II and was forced to commit suicide after being falsely accused of what amounted to be treason. In Dante's Hell, he was turned into a tree that could not bear fruit, its leaves blackened. Peter Vigna the cricket hero was destined to live with the original rejection by the cricket establishment played out through the spectators and his followers who would never forget what he did, the spectacle of his punishment only reinforcing their belief in his guilt, even though they saw that his suffering may even have outweighed the severity of his breaking the cardinal rules of cricket.

Every now and again, when Peter Vigna led his team on to

the field, he would hear, or maybe he imagined it, an occasional hiss, boo, or the chant of "cheat!" On the other hand, each time he walked off the field when his team won — and they never lost under his captaincy — the cheers were almost enough to affirm his innocence. Except that, he knew, as does everyone who has lived, affirming innocence does not erase guilt.

Moral: Without punishment, being sorry carries little weight.

14. Disposal

A dysfunctional family meets its logical end.

Here's a question. If a person lives with another all their life — a son with his mother, a wife with her husband, for example, how well do they know each other, really? It is true that people living together in the same house or space will develop various kinds of routines, and by that standard one supposes that they can predict what each of them will do every day.

But suppose that the relationship is abusive, by some count, what then? Perhaps the abuse also becomes routine, so may even not be noticed for what it is?

Right on his forty-fifth birthday, Frederick Baskin broke with routine, but this was not at all easy. He was born of a mother whose marriage lasted just short of two years, and by that time she had been beaten so much about the face and chest that she had aged some twenty years, or more. She had descended into a state of despair, her clothes turned to rags, the pain of her beatings assuaged by brandy, when she could get it. Her only solace was her son whom she tried hopelessly to care for, and to love, who, from the moment he was born cried and screamed pretty much nonstop. Her husband blamed her for this unholy noise, accusing her of not feeding him, and to add to her distress chose to beat her breasts mercilessly, which made it impossible for her to feed little Frederick.

Phyllis was her name, and she was well known locally by the police who answered her frantic calls almost on a weekly basis. They came, they arrested her husband, referred her and her screaming child to the social welfare department, kept her husband in lockup until he faced the family court judge who upbraided him and sentenced him sometimes to a few weeks in lockup. The social worker who came to the house had come to know Phyllis well, and had on many occasions advised her to leave her husband and go to a refuge. But she refused this solution, because, she said, her son needed a father. Yet on some occasions, through the fog of alcohol, she had thought of killing her beast of a husband, but was too frightened to try, as she did not know really, how she could do it. And besides, she did not want her son to grow up with a murderer for a mother.

Then came the one stroke of luck that changed the course of Frederick's life, or to put it in her words, her husband got what was coming to him. Late one night, it was when Frederick was all of three years old, her drunken husband met his end, staggered on to a busy road and was run over. Phyllis celebrated the event by telling Frederick it was his third birthday, and made him a chocolate cake with candles and sang happy birthday to him. It was virtually the only time that Frederick had stopped crying.

*

Imagine living in a small house, on welfare, scrounging for a living, depending on the good will of others to make ends meet, and with a screaming three year old who seemed never to be happy. In truth she was tempted every day to beat the child until he stopped crying. But she knew that this would be self-defeating. She learned, instead, to ignore the screaming, and managed to last it out until the child was exhausted, his screams dying down to a whimper.

The social worker had proclaimed that little Frederick screamed because he wanted attention. So Phyllis had tried giving him lots of attention, playing with him, even taking him out shopping with her, but this turned out to be a disaster when people in the stores gave her disapproving looks, of course, blaming the mother for the child's behavior.

One might say that Phyllis was caught in a situation of her own making, caused by her abusive husband, thank God, now gone. Maybe time would heal. And so she wore ear plugs to dampen the screams and grew to ignore the wails and whimpers. So it was after a year or two, hard to measure time under such uncomfortable circumstances, that Phyllis managed to slowly make headway with her child, and send him even to school, where, needless to say, Frederick did not do well. He was constantly in the principal's office on account of his rowdy screaming and violent tantrums. It was not long until the school informed Phyllis that her child needed special placement because of his behavior problems. The school psychologist recommended him for a special school for disruptive children, but it was located way across town, and Phyllis could not afford to send him there. So instead, she did what any caring mother under those circumstances would do. She decided to home school him.

And so began the long, endless process of Frederick's education and growing up. Unfortunately, though completely understandable, Phyllis had turned to alcohol to help her manage the day, a deep irony that she only occasionally recognized. Much of the time she was in a kind of alcoholic stupor. This took the form of her nagging Frederick to do his lessons, brush his teeth, wash himself, etc., etc. The list of things to nag a growing child is endless.

The morning routine had never changed for some forty years. Phyllis got up and cooked bacon and eggs for Frederick, who sat morosely at the table and pushed them away when served. Instead he looked in the cupboard for his favorite Cheerios breakfast cereal. One would have thought that Phyllis would simply give up on the bacon and eggs, but not at all. Every morning she nagged Frederick to eat a proper breakfast, that it was the most important meal of the day. For his part, Frederick had developed a routine in which he went to the cupboard, complained that they were nearly out of Cheerios, sat down and slurped spoonfuls into his mouth. At which, Phyllis nagged him to eat quietly, didn't he have any manners at all?

And over the years, Phyllis had developed prickly ways of getting at Frederick. He never, after all, went out of the house, or if he did, not for long. So she harped at him to go out and get a job; a lazy slob, that's what he was.

Then there was the TV. He complained that it was old and they needed a new one. She pointed out to him that, if he went out and got a job, maybe they could afford a new TV. Frederick, now a mature adult, never flew into a rage, which would be understandable given the circumstances. After all, it was she who had home-schooled him, so it was her fault if he couldn't get a job. Never mind that he had simply no inkling to go out of the house. He was happy enough in his bedroom, playing video games, reading comic books, and, well, what else can a lonely male do on his own?

But Phyllis would not let him alone. She nagged him day and night. Removed the lock from his bedroom door so it could not be locked shut. She went into his bedroom constantly without knocking, always asking him when he was going to fix the toilet that wouldn't stop running. Surely he could make himself useful? He ought to think himself lucky that she provided him with a roof over his head. And besides, she had told him a thousand times, that she had saved him from his violent drunkard of a father.

*

One cold morning, Phyllis sat at the kitchen table, eating her toast. Frederick slouched in and went immediately to the cupboard to retrieve his Cheerios. He opened the refrigerator and looked for the milk. There was none.

"Eat your breakfast," said Phyllis, her raspy voice now riddled with the smoke of an intake of one or two packets of Craven A's a day.

"Eat your own fucking toast," answered Frederick. He leaned over the table and pushed the eggs and bacon away from his place. He then proceeded to pour out his Cheerios into his bowl, and sat down staring at them. His eyes were narrowed. He was really annoyed. His mom of course noticed, and with some satisfaction. He drummed his fingers on the table, then dipped them into the bowl and started to eat the Cheerios by hand. Phyllis took a bite of her toast and munched it loudly.

"Want milk?" she said with what could only be interpreted as a sneer.

Frederick had had enough. He grabbed her hand across the table and growled, the noise coming from deep inside him, "I've fucking had enough of you."

Phyllis tried to pull her hand away, but his grip was too tight. She was suddenly frightened. It reminded her of her husband — Frederick's rotten abusive father—in the early days, when Frederick screamed incessantly.

"You're just like your pig of a father, you are. You're no good, trash. You can't do anything. You're a useless bag of shit!"

Frederick's grip tightened.

"Go on then," she taunted, "hit me, just like your stinking father did. Hit me! Go on! I'm used to it. I've put up with you for long enough. Get out of the house and don't come back!"

Frederick pulled her across the table, his meaty hands tightening around both her wrists. Now she lay on top of the table, belly down. She kicked her legs but they were well off the floor and went nowhere. He stood back from the table and pulled her up to face him. She found her footing and tried to knee him in the crotch. And she did, but not hard enough. It only served to enrage him even further. Now he let go of her arms and went for her throat, thumbs pressing hard against her voice box.

"You'll never nag me again, you fucking chain-smoking piece of crap." His meaty hands tightened, her eyes bulged, there was no stopping him now. No turning back. No wish to turn back, in fact.

The rest followed logically. She flopped to the floor and lay dead. But just to make sure she could never nag him again, Frederick went to the cutlery draw and drew out a steak knife. And with it he thrust it into her throat and cut out her voice box. "You'll never nag me again," he said with great satisfaction. And with that, he went to the sink and put the voice-box down the garbage disposer. The loud hum of the disposer was music to his ears.

He went to the refrigerator and searched some more for the milk, and sure enough, there it was in a different place, in the back. The bitch had hidden it from him. Well, she had learned her lesson now not to mess with him!

He went to the sink and washed his hands. Then he poured the milk over his Cheerios and sat quietly eating his breakfast.

After he was done, he called the police.

Moral: A matching punishment is driven by revenge.

15. Truth in Sentencing

A Self Inflicted Punishment?

Albany District Court judge Jonathan Tears took his job as seriously as any of those who elected him to that office could hope for. He insisted at dinner parties when asked about his job, that it was not a job at all, but a calling not unlike that of a clergyman or a doctor, one in which he every day displayed his devotion to public service, to serving his fellow man. Justice was what he cared about most of all, justice and in the long run fairness. He was daily faced with choices he had to make, deliberating on the punishment of miscreants who were brought before him. Of course, only the guilty could be punished, and that was what the court that he administered as the sole arbitrator of its functioning, certainly ensured. His juries were carefully selected; the prosecutors and defense attorneys abided by the established procedures of his court and that of the county and State of New York; his clerk of courts observed the proper procedures.

Judge Tears made all his administrative decisions concerning pleas of guilty, plea bargaining and so on, as transparent as possible. As the final arbiter of justice he must be well informed of any attempts to short circuit the system, especially the routine making of bargains, always a little questionable, but without which the work of the court, overburdened by cases, could not be achieved.

Furthermore, he took every case heard before him seriously, whether it was a minor offense or a serious one. And once a verdict of guilt was delivered by the court, it was his prime responsibility to deliver a sentence that served justice, especially with regard to the suffering caused any victims of the crime. He made it a point of having victims contribute to the sentencing, and if at all possible, rendered a sentence that took into account the suffering of the victim.

So it was on the first day of November, just a few weeks

before Thanksgiving, he heard a case that appalled him, almost brought tears to his eyes at particular points, when the victim and the victim's mother displayed their anguish. They had suffered, though the father was noticeably absent from the sentencing hearing. And upon inquiring why the father was not in court for the sentencing hearing, his clerk of courts reported that the father was out of the country but had sent an email to him demanding the severest punishment that matched the horrible details of the crime be administered without mitigation. The offender had to get what was coming to him, that was what the father had said.

Justice Tears noted this input and took it seriously. The trouble was that, if he took it really seriously, it was not at all clear whether he could in fact deliver a just sentence, or to put it more precisely, whether in pronouncing a sentence it would guarantee that the punishment would match the crime.

The evidence of guilt in this case was clear and insurmountable. One Mike Malone, a fifteen year old, had been molested by the local priest on a number of occasions after choir practice. The actions would not have come to light except that Mike's mother caught him masturbating one morning in his bedroom when she went in to clean his room. She scorned him and in his defense he pleaded that he couldn't help it because Father O'Brien had shown him how to do it and so he was practicing. Of course, his mother was appalled, and immediately, perhaps mistakenly she wondered in retrospect, she called the police. She took it upon herself to make that call since her husband, who would have been even more upset, was out of the country on business, and could not be contacted. She had no doubt at all that her husband would have given the boy a good thrashing, then dragged him around to confront Father O'Brien and given him a good thrashing too.

"Albany emergency dispatch," came a monotone voice. "Please state your location and address."

Mrs. Malone almost hung up the phone. She was overcome by embarrassment.

"It's Mrs. Malone at 53 Smith Street. My son Mikey has been molested by Father O'Brien and I don't know what to do."

The well trained emergency dispatch officer responded in her practiced monotone voice. "Is anyone there injured? Who else is in the house?"

"It's just me and my son. I don't think he has been injured," answered Mrs. Malone, on the verge of hysteria.

"Is he able to breathe?"

"Yes, he's fine. I only just found out that it happened."

"Stay calm Mrs. Malone. An emergency unit is on its way."

The juvenile police unit showed up, a specially trained female officer taking charge and interviewing the boy with his mother's permission. Mike, for his part, was a little puzzled, though of course upset that there were police in his house and they even came into his bedroom. His puzzlement was caused by the fact that he actually enjoyed the sexual encounters with Father O'Brien, and had not thought it all that awful. In fact, it made choir practice much more enjoyable. So, when asked for details of his encounters he was very reticent, and essentially clammed up, as is pretty common with teenagers anyway. But in the end, after considerable cajoling by the officer and his mother, he provided a few details, but asked that his mother leave the room while he described them, as it was very embarrassing talking about the details of sex in front of his mom. The worst thing they tried to make him do was reveal the names of any other boys he thought may have been victimized.

By the time all of this made its way into court, the details had been reported in the local newspapers, and this was the worst thing as far as Mike was concerned. He was embarrassed and teased at school by other boys, especially bigger boys. Of course, the papers did not print the names of victims, but that did not stop everyone finding out who they might be.

In any case, we need not go into the details of these shenanigans, except to say that Father O'Brien appeared in court, was found guilty of several charges of indecent assault on under age children. He foolishly in his defense, against the advice of his counsel, the public defender, claimed that the boys liked it and that it was all done with their consent.

Judge Tears was a judge to be reckoned with, so when the public defender Jack Flynn, found that Judge Tears would be presiding over the case, he was none too happy and dutifully conveyed this to his client, Father O'Brien. The public defender, a good catholic himself, had visited Father O'Brien on a number of occasions in preparation for this trial, had even asked the disgraced priest to hear his confession, though Father O'Brien had resisted his request for some time, given the circumstances. Besides, Father O'Brien's superiors had warned him not to do so, and in fact had announced that, should he be found guilty, he would be drummed out of the priesthood. Not that they had the right to do so. Only God and Jesus could do that. And as far as he was concerned, he had done nothing wrong except give his young charges a little pleasure. Brightened up their lives, even.

Public defender Flynn looked over the small crowd in the courtroom. There were a few parents of other boys who had eventually come forward and owned up to being the Father's victims. But it was pretty clear who was the ultimate victim, Mike, who sat his head bowed, too distraught to look up, too embarrassed to look at Father O'Brien, frightened that their eyes might meet, and then he would remember the occasions of his encounters with the terrible Father O'Brien. Having had to describe in detail in front of the jury and the courtroom what they did together was something he would never forget. It was now a nightmare.

Judge Tears entered the courtroom. "All rise!" cried the clerk. All rose then seated once Judge Tears had himself seated and rustled a few papers back and forth, then looked out at his courtroom.

"The defendant will rise," said the judge, looking over his spectacles.

Defender Flynn nudged his client. Father O'Brien rose, his face expressionless, no doubt his entire body was numb, his mind thoroughly overcome with remorse. Or at least, that was what his defender had drummed into him. Remorse! Feel remorse! Say that you are sorry and say it showing that you really mean it! He stood, head bowed, stroking his greying beard. Judge Tears spoke.

"You have been found guilty of despicable deeds, you have heartlessly taken advantage of your innocent charges, broken every rule of decency, and disgraced the great church that you represent. It is a shame that there is no punishment in the law of this state that is equal to the crimes you have committed. You deserve to have done to you what you have done to your young innocent charges. The court can only hope that the punishment that it imposes upon you will come some way to making up for the damage you have done to these young lives."

Father O'Brien stood still, looking down, his balding head seemingly pointed at the judge, a manner not approved of by his defender, who nudged him, trying to get him to look up.

"Mr. O'Brien!" demanded Judge Tears, clearly upset. "Look up when I address you! Acknowledge what you have done!"

Father O'Brien, humiliated, managed to raise his head just a little, and mumbled, "I'm sorry, your honor."

Judge Tears ignored the inaudible remarks. "I hereby sentence you to five years of incarceration in the care of the Correctional Services of the state of New York, and may you receive at the hands of your fellow inmates what you did to your young charges. You raped them, so shall be done to you."

Judge Tears departed, without the slightest look at the criminal O'Brien, nor at the rest of the court. He had delivered his sentence, may God have mercy on his soul.

The officer of the court applied the necessary handcuffs and other procedures of security and marched the criminal from the court, whereupon he would be transported to the place of incarceration where Judge Tears' punishment would be faithfully administered, no doubt. Sex offenders, as everybody knows, are the prime targets of assault in prisons everywhere.

*

It may be safely assumed that Father O'Brien was dealt with according to the insinuations made in Judge Tears' sentence. Mere incarceration was not enough for this crime. The punishment did not match the crime, as one would say, reflecting Judge Tears' frustration that the law did not allow him to sentence

Father O'Brien to be raped, just as he had raped his innocent charges. If he were raped in prison, was this not a proper matching of the punishment to the severity of his crime? This was undoubtedly on Judge Tears' mind when he made his remarks, later to be regretted. Of course, in a civilized society, we do not punish criminals who might even deserve such punishment, in this way at all. They receive a civilized punishment that is prison.

One might leave it there except that the media who were present at the sentencing hearing took careful note of Judge Tears' remarks and dutifully reported on the sentence in full. They immediately saw the great gift of a news headline that Judge Tears had given them: JUDGE SENTENCES RAPIST TO BE RAPED.

The New York Commission on Judicial Conduct reprimanded Judge Tears for this outrageous sentence and ordered him to step down from the bench. Of course, the punishment that Judge Tears had imagined was eventually and frequently carried out, without any judicial intervention. Such punishments were under the purview of the New York State Department of Corrections, which remained "unaware" of such punishments.

Let's not forget the victim. Mike continued to masturbate without any outside assistance, as did all his co-victims. He carried the guilt for the rest of his life, and was reminded of this every time he looked at his mother. He blamed her for going to the police, which further added to his guilt. As for his father. He continued to be preoccupied with his work and never mentioned the incident. It was as though it had never happened.

Moral: The punitive effects of a sentence are immeasurable.

16. Bullies

Like water, punishment finds its way.

In 1948, when Midge (for Midget) was in grade 4, he was easily the smallest kid in the class. The biggest kid was Bomber, a kid who had been kept back a couple of years, so he should have been in grade 6, and even then he would have been the biggest kid in grade 6, he was so big. They called him Bomber because he farted all the time and he smelled and made lots of weird noises.

Mr. Gowt, the teacher, made Bomber sit in the front seat, on his own. He was always calling out, screaming even, and would spend most of his time crawling around under the desk. He couldn't do his work and could hardly read. His workbook was full of drawings he had made then scribbled in heavy pencil all over them. And there were ink blots all over. Every page was disgusting, Mr. Gowt told him almost every day.

Above the usual chatter, Mr. Gowt said in his high-pitched loud voice, "settle down now, children. Sit quietly and pay attention." All responded and the room became silent, except for Bomber who made his usual noises. "Take out your workbooks. You have twenty minutes to finish the sums on the board. First finished and gets them all right will be milk monitor for today."

Milk monitor was a coveted chore, handing out the free milk to all the kids just before morning recess. A wave of excited chatter rippled across the room, and for a moment even Bomber was excited.

Mr. Gowt took out his watch. "Ready! Go!" he called.

Bomber slid beneath his desk, trying to find his workbook that he had dropped on the floor. Mr. Gpwt, a tall thin man who had a broad English accent (one of many Englishmen who migrated to Australia just after the war) wedged himself into the seat beside Bomber. "Now Bomber," he said, "let's see if we can get some of your sums done."

Bomber, greatly surprised, came up from under the desk and

handed Mr. Gowt his workbook.

"We won't need that," said Mr. Gowt. He produced a small box of oblong colored blocks of four different lengths and colors. He sat the longest one on the desk then asked Bomber to pick four short ones of equal size that would make the same length. Bomber was thoroughly bamboozled. He dropped his workbook on the floor and grabbed a handful of blocks, then began to sort them. Mr. Gowt slid out of the desk, looking on with great satisfaction. But Bomber continued to handle the blocks, unable to match four blocks with the long one. Instead, in frustration, he simply built towers, just like he did when he was a toddler, then smashed them down and they all fell to the floor.

Mr. Gowt was incensed. "Bomber! How could you do such a thing? All the trouble I have gone to get these special blocks for you. You are a very naughty boy!"

Bomber slid down under his desk and grunted, a bit like a snorting pig. The rest of the class giggled and rustled. Mr. Gowt looked at his watch. "Time's up!" he announced in his most stern voice, trying to make it as deep as he could. "Pencils down!" He quickly went through each sum and called on different kids for the answers. Midge called out as loudly as he could, and got them all right. "Midge got ten out of ten, anybody else?"

A girl answered in a sweet voice. "I did Mr. Gowt."

The bell went for morning recess.

"Midge and Mary are the milk monitors," announced Mr. Gowt, "the rest of you sit quietly. Midge and Mary came forward and collected the little bottles of milk to pass out to the class. And as Midge passed Bomber's desk, Bomber put out his hand from below and grabbed his ankle, causing him to fall forward and drop two bottles of milk. One bottle broke and splashed milk everywhere. The children gasped.

Midge, shaking the milk off his hands, trying to get up, snarled, "dummy! You can't even count! You're a baby! You should be in kindergarten. Dummy! Look what you've done. Dummy!"

And the rest of the class chimed in, "Dumm-ee! Dumm-ee!"

"That's enough, class!" cried Mr. Gowt. "What Bomber does is none of your business. Now stand quietly and go out for recess. Walk! Don't run!" He turned to Midge. "I know you are upset with Bomber, but one should not speak to another like that. It's not his fault he's like that."

Midge was thinking, "Like what?" but held his breath.

"I'll clean up the mess, Mr. Gowt," said Mary.

"Thank you, Mary, that's very kind of you."

Midge looked at Mary with a smirk of disapproval. She was such a goody-goody. "Can I go wash my hands?" he asked.

"Yes, you may. And take Bomber with you." He grabbed Bomber and pulled him up from under the desk. Mr. Gowt was clearly very angry. "Go with Midge and clean yourself up," he ordered.

The thought of Bomber being clean was such a joke, smiled Midge to himself. But Bomber already had a hold of him and was dragging him out of the classroom and to the tap outside the school where they would wash their hands. Or not quite. Bomber had something else in mind, that is, if he had a mind.

Bomber pulled Midge to the tap and turned it on. He pushed Midge under the tap, head first. Midge screamed, "help! Stop it! You're soaking me! Me mum will yell at me!"

"Too bad!" growled Bomber with a big grin. That's what you get for being a shit. That's what you are. I hate you and all the rest of you smarty-pants shits."

"I'm gunna tell on you. You swore!"

"No kidding? And here's more!"

And just as Bomber pushed Midge's head under the tap, a strong hand gripped him by the scruff of the neck and pushed him away. Midge looked up, shaking the water from his hair. The biggest kid in grade six stood there, holding Bomber by his neck, and his other hand clenched into a fist. "You want a punch in the guts?" he asked with a challenging grin.

"Let me go, you're hurting me!" cried Bomber.

By this time, a gang of kids, all boys, had circled around, watching and cheering. "Grab Bomber's arms and hold him out," ordered the grade 6 kid. Two kids grabbed each of Bomber's arms and pulled them so that Bomber was spread out, trying to kick, but unable to reach anyone.

"I'll get you bastards for this!" shouted Bomber.

The grade sixer walked over to Midge and put his hand on his shoulder. "OK. Now you can hit him back. Make it a good one to teach him a lesson."

"You bastards!" cried Bomber again. "I'll get you all for this. I'll bash every bloody one of you. You wait! You'll see!"

Midge stepped forward and raised his fist. Would he do it? "Bomber deserved it, didn't he?" He asked himself. And he looked around at the gang of kids, egging him on. He had to do it. But who knows what Bomber would do to him afterwards.

"Go on then," taunted Bomber. "Do it, and see what will happen to you."

The grade sixer nudged Midge forward a little. "Don't be scared," he said, " I won't let him beat you up. Go ahead. It's only right. It's not fair that he keeps picking on you. He doesn't pick on his own size."

All of that was true, thought Midge, almost shivering in fear at the thought of Bomber getting at him later on, when there was no one there to save him. He raised his arm again.

"Hit him in the guts!" cried one of the kids.

"Yair, go on. Get on with it. Give it to him. It's time he learned his lesson!"

Out of the corner of his eye, Midge saw Mr. Gowt step out of the school and come towards them. Perhaps he would be saved.

"I'm warning you!" snarled Bomber.

And Midge knew he had to do something. After all the Sixer had done for him, he had to do what he said. He couldn't just walk away. They would all call him a coward, and the Sixer would never save him again. So he got ready to give Bomber a punch in the guts, and swung his arm, fist clenched. But he saw Mr. Gowt now hurrying towards him, and found, to his consternation, that his fist just as it reached Bomber's middle, opened into an open hand and became the slightest of slaps.

"What's going on here?" called Mr. Gowt.

Suddenly, the circle of kids dissolved and there was no one there, except Bomber spitting and snarling, and Midge, standing, arms hanging by his side.

"He's been bullying me, sir," whimpered Midge. "He pushed me under the tap."

"So I see," observed Mr. Gowt. "Bomber, put out your hand!"

Bomber meekly put out his hand. Mr. Gowt put his hand in his pocket and pulled out the leather strap with which all, but especially Bomber, were familiar.

Bomber looked at Midge as if to say, "don't think you won't get yours too," and down came the strap making a loud crack as leather hit the well-worn skin of Bomber's right hand.

"Now the other," said Mr. Gowt as Bomber put out his left hand and received the same, this time hurting a lot more.

The bell rang sounding the end of recess. Midge ran back to class. Bomber followed, plodding slowly .

Mr. Gowt was looking forward to lunch time.

Moral: Fair punishment depends on the hands
that use or abuse it.

17. A Matter of Honor

The reward of punishment.

Honor among thieves is a popular characterization of criminals. But honor is that commodity of men and boys who trade in it, collect it, and treat it as something to put on a shelf to be adored. More importantly, it cannot exist without others who are charged with the power and authority to confer it on the honoree, so that they can then admire it. Honor can easily be lost by one small misstep by the honoree, an ill-advised word spoken in the heat of the moment, or inadvertently, a "Freudian slip" as people of the twentieth century might have said. Then again, one may break the rules of honor if one does not know what the rules are. These are the dangers of the spoken word that becomes an insult to one whose honor has been questioned.

Or, honor may serve to urge those who have mutual interests in their honor as a group: a special ops force, various military units, a football or cricket team, variously called "esprit de corps" thought of as the moral fiber of a team or group that has adopted a particular endeavor or challenge against which they must use all their combined energy. Great military leaders such as Alexander the Great, Julius Caesar, Napoleon, won their battles largely because of the honor they bestowed on their troops, the badges, medals, ceremonies and awards for bravery and courage bestowed on individuals who excelled. Theirs is an honor won in battle or competition. Woe to those who do not take this competition seriously: in games, those who cheat (break the rules) are humiliated and punished (tampering with a football or cricket ball to gain advantage for example). Or dosing one's body with performance enhancing drugs may be enough to drum such person out of the group that bestows the honorifics.

The importance of honor may also depend on where one actually lives and into what geographic or social setting one is born. The upper echelons of society into which one is born usually carry with them particular locations in a city or country in which one lives, as well as the history of honor that is bestowed upon the families who give birth to their children. These are born into honor that must be unquestionably fostered and held high. Such were the gentlemen of the 18th and 19th centuries in much of the Western world, particularly those who for various reasons were on the fringe of such societies and thus had to work harder to demonstrate their devotion to honor and its defense against attacks (insults, slights etc.).

In contrast, poverty stricken areas of large cities, usually contained within specific boundaries in inner city locations or ethnic diaspora in outer fringes of a city, are devoted almost entirely to the pursuit of honor, a commodity not as scarce as the material needs of life. In these places, actual food and material means of living are scarce. In contrast honor does not cost any money and does not require physical or complex infrastructures to exploit or develop, and thus produce sustenance. Rather, honor is something that can be created out of nothing but social relations, and in most cases, this honor is traded, exchanged and maintained by gangs of young men and boys, whose women, such as they are, watch from the sidelines and bear the children who will become future gang members. Many of the occupants of these gangs may lie, cheat, steal and perpetrate violence. And they do it in the name of honor.

But wait. Members of sporting teams and military groups are expected to fight against others who are their designated opponents or enemies. They must abide the rules of engagement, but let there be no doubt, the rules must not be broken and one must give no quarter to one's enemy. In the military, provided the rules are obeyed, killing one's enemies is honorable. So when we say that there is honor among thieves, we acknowledge that this is an admirable trait, confined to thieves who steal from us, yet stealing is surely not an honorable occupation. Aha! But they do not steal from each other — so goes the popular belief.

Most importantly tthe measure of ensuring that the rules of honorable men are enforced, requires that those who break those rules must be punished. Thus we come to our story of an innocent (no such thing) boy who runs afoul of this complicated set-up.

*

On his twelfth birthday, Napoleon was just walking out the front gate, such as it was, one hinge broken, the wood rotting away, only a couple of palings left, when he was accosted by a huge man, or so it seemed to him. At first he thought it was Mike Tyson, but then saw that the man was too skinny, and his arms and fingers too slender. His fist reflexively tightened around the ten dollar bill in his pants pocket. It was a birthday present from his mom. She had given him the choice of the money or the weed, and he chose the money because he knew that if he wanted, he could buy the best weed in town or even something else down by the Crips hangout. Actually, she didn't give it to him, he had taken it from under the sugar tin in the kitchen. She was too high to notice. He was too young to join the gang just yet, but it would not be too long before they let him in. Even so, he did errands for them and generally was tolerated by the others as a kind of mascot.

"Whatever you got, it's mine." growled the man putting on an evil, snarling face.

Napoleon turned to run back inside the house, but the long arm of his father reached out and grabbed a handful of his blue t-shirt, the shirt that one of his Crips friends gave him. It was well worn, a hole here and there, cigarette burns in random places. The shirt tore at the neck, and Napoleon grabbed the man with both hands.

"Let go of me!" he cried, "you're a dead man!"

"You're my kid and what's yours is mine you little fucker!" laughed the man. He stooped to grab the ten dollar bill that fell to the ground. Napoleon seized the chance to run back inside, through the front door and out the back, over the old fence, through the weeds of next door and away to Magic Johnson Park to inform Nod Boddy, the Crips leader, of the shockingly horrible act. Not only had the man, claiming to be his father, robbed him, but he had torn his sacred shirt. It was a crime against the whole Crips gang and could not go unpunished.

*

"Tell you what," said Nod Boddy with a stern face. "You did good, my man! You did good. But now's the time you step up and be a man if you wanna be a Crips boy. That shirt, it's all torn up. You gonna let your ol' man get away with that insult?"

"It's why I ran straight 'ere," panted Napoleon, breathless.

A few other gang members gathered round.

"So what's he look like?" asked one of them.

"Mike Tyson," answered Napoleon.

"Shit, man. You lucky you aint dead!"

Another spoke up. "Nods," he said, "I know the guy. He drinks down at the Tavern on 121st street and deals a bit on and off. He aint no Mike Tyson. He's harmless."

"Not any more, he aint," lectured Nod Boddy. "We'll go down there and find him. And Napoleon, here, can step up and show us if he's ready."

Napoleon's face lit up. "What you want me to do?" he asked. "He ripped my Crips shirt and took my ten dollars!"

"Fuck the ten dollars! He dissed the Crips. If the Bloods hear about that, they'll come after us. We gotta defend our honor! Aint that right boys?"

"We want blood! We want blood!" they cried as one.

Nod Boddy put his arm around Napoleon. "You're about to become a Crip. My man!" He put his hand out and they did the Crips handshake. Napoleon had been practicing it for many months. A complicated series of hand and finger actions. "Look boys! He's gonna be a Crip!"

"Yo! But he's gotta show us what he made of, first!" called one of the gang.

"You got a gun? Who's carry'n?" Nod Boddy looked around his gang. They all looked sideways at each other. Guns were a priceless commodity. Contrary to popular belief that gangs were awash in guns, they were actually scarce because of all the gun laws. So there was some hesitation among the gang members.

"I can get him one. It's stashed down by the old kids playground by Jemison school."

"But that's Bloods territory," murmured one of the gang.

"All the better, then!" announced Nods.

"You ever shot a gun, Napoleon, my boy?"

"There's always a first time," grinned Napoleon.

Nod Boddy stood up on an old tin can. "I hereby proclaim that Napoleon will save the honor of the Crips by dispatching one Mike Tyson look-alike. Go forward, and may the honor of the Great Crips be with you!"

Napoleon had seen the Crips guys handle a gun often enough. But he was surprised when he was handed the gun at how heavy it was. He turned it over in both hands, ran his finger along the barrel. There were specks of rust here and there, He brandished it around, much to the amusement of the gang.

"It's fuckn loaded!" said one with a grin, but none shied away from it scared that they might be shot.

"Are you sure it's loaded?" asked Napoleon. "I don't want to get up close to the big fucker, and the gun doesn't go off."

"We always keep our guns loaded, in case of emergency," observed Nod Boddy. "And this is an emergency!"

Napoleon looked around. He passed the gun from one hand to the other, trying to get used to the weight. "You care where I do it?" he asked.

"It's up to you, big guy! But you gotta get it done before sunset tomorrow. That's the Crips rule. Twenty four hours rule. Offenses against honor have to be corrected within twenty four hours. If you're gonna be a Crip, you gotta learn the rules."

"That fucker won't know what hit him!" said Napoleon, aiming the gun at a crow perched on a wire above.

"So one piece of advice, Naps my man. There's four bullets in the gun. You gotta empty the lot. That's the rule of engagement."

"Got it!"

"And when you're done, stash it somewhere only you will know where it will be, and especially were the cops won't find it."

"I got a great place. I'll put it…"

"Shut up you silly fucker. Keep it to yourself. So you can tell the next one to be blooded."

Napoleon tucked the gun inside the back of his old jeans. He had put on his old Crips shirt backwards, so the rip would show even more. "That fucker Tyson needs to be taught a lesson! No one fucks with the Crips!" he recited to himself as he walked in the direction of Tom's Tavern, a bounce in his steps.

He waited outside, across the street. He dare not look inside the Tavern in case some drunk grabbed him. So he did not know whether Tyson was in there or not. "My fucking father! Who says so? And anyway, after I'm done he won't be anyone's father!" he smiled to himself.

Drunks talking loudly came in and out the tavern. None looked like Mike Tyson. He lingered in the shadows as dusk approached. It was a typical cool late summer evening in Los Angeles, the air still, the sky clear, though Napoleon did not look up. He started to walk back and forth, getting impatient. His father had ten dollars, surely he'd be in the tavern. That's what they said. Then he heard chatter, men arguing. He stepped out of the shadows and looked about. Two large black men came towards him, silhouetted against the fading blue sky. He ran towards them, his hand on the gun behind his back. They ignored him, kept walking and gesticulating, deep in their argument. Now he could make out their features. It was his fucking so-called father all right.

And all of a sudden, there he stood, no more than ten yards from them. He grabbed his gun, its weight causing the barrel to catch on the top of his jeans. He tugged hard and it let go. The two men stopped arguing and stood grinning at this twelve year old kid waving a gun around. His father leaned forward, squinting in the dim light.

"You who I think you are, you little fucker?"

Napoleon pulled the trigger. He was surprised how hard it was to pull. But suddenly the gun went off and the recoil almost caused him to drop it. But he was a determined little bugger, that's what he was. He raised the gun slowly and carefully and this time aimed at his father's chest. He'd heard the Crips boys talk about where you should aim. The chest was the best, the biggest target. He squeezed the trigger not once, but twice. The first seemed to hit the target, as his dad staggered back a little and put his hand to hist chest. His Dad's mate though, leaped forward and grabbed his wrist. "Gimme the fucking gun, you little shit!" he cried.

Napoleon, trying to break loose, pulled the trigger again and the last of the four bullets zoomed straight into the man's face. Blood poured from his jaw and he let go. Napoleon ran, making sure to keep the gun. He'd spent his four bullets and he had to stash the gun. He could hardly wait. He'd be inducted into the gang, for sure.

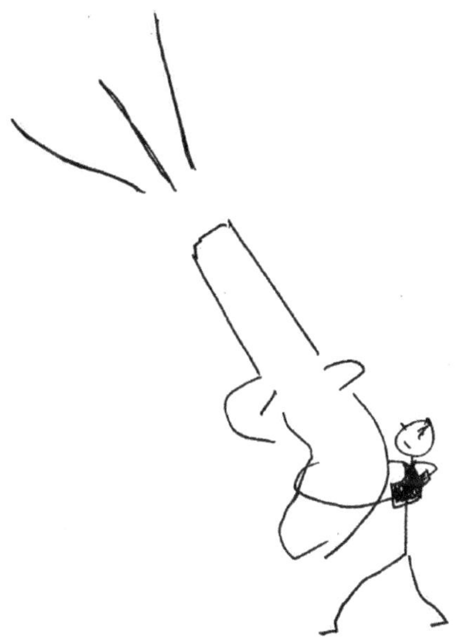

The next day, the Crips gathered and conferred full member-ship on Napoleon. The L.A. Times reported in a small note at the bottom of page two that a man was shot near Jemison school and a ten year old girl had been shot while sitting in the living room watching TV. A stray bullet had entered through the window and killed her instantly.

Moral: The side effects of punishment are incalculable.

18. Finding Fault

The mini monstrosities of a classroom

Gentle reader, before I tell you this story, I must paint for you a little of the physical environment that made it all possible, though I hasten to add that it by no means caused the series of incidents (a considerable understatement) that resulted. After all, it was humans who made this physical environment in the first place, and humans who, once trapped inside of this environment of their own making, made possible the disasters that inevitably occurred.

Before ball point pens were invented, there were ink wells and pens. Moving to pens from pencils for kids in about grade three was a huge coming- of-age graduation. However, fountain pens, those amazing gadgets that had a little rubber tube inside them, into which you sucked up the ink, were not permitted. All kids had to have a simple pen that had a wooden shaft and a metal pointed nib, the design of which was surely one that made sure that a kid's use of pen and ink would not go smoothly. The nibs were a piece of thin pointed metal with a split down the center, and at the back end a small indentation on each side of the nib.

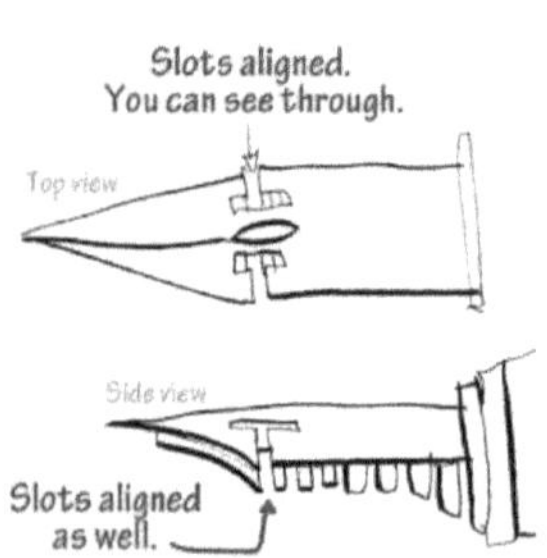

Why that indentation was there is probably the great unanswered question of all time. For it was the source of many embarrassments and of very serious spilled ink disasters. For those who find this difficult to believe, here is a simple drawing of a nib of the 1940s and before.

One might see no special problem with such a pen, but the problem arose when the pen was coupled with its source of ink: the ink well. The cunning design of this well, a thin ceramic or Bakelite container, had a small hole at its top, and a wide lip, so that it dropped nicely into the hole that was bored into the top of the school desk.

To give you a better idea, here is a photo of an old pen and inkwell in a school desktop. You can see signs of use, though the inkwell has been considerably cleaned up.

Every Monday, the boys in grade five vied to be appointed ink monitor (girls not allowed because of its messiness; it was a boy's job). This required the mixing of dark blue ink powder in a large container with a set amount of water. Each inkwell had then to be filled as it sat cradled in its hole on top of the desk, or if the desk was a double, there were two holes, though sometimes only one in the middle which the students shared (made for disaster). It was particularly difficult to pour the ink into the wells when they were seated, so sometimes they had to be lifted out and stood on the desk beside the hole in order to be filled. Or even held up to the pouring device. The temptation, of course, to the boys was to accidentally on purpose spill the ink. This is why the ink monitors had to arrive in the classroom well before the bell rang for start of classes, to fill the wells before the kids came in.

Young Mr. Potts, always dressed in a nice suit, covered by an old grey dust coat to protect it from chalk dust and other smudges of a busy classroom, supervised the two boys this Monday morning. Tich was in his element, and had practiced at home pouring water from a jug into egg cups so he would be sure not to spill any ink on this day that he had looked forward to for a long time. The trouble was that his collaborator, Dog (so called because he spent a lot of his time crawling around under his desk and making barking noises) was not so careful. The rest of the class could not understand why Mr. Potts ever allowed Dog to be monitor, because it seemed that he was forever being growled at and never did his work. But Mr. Potts, fresh out of Teachers' College, was careful not to discriminate against a child simply because he was dumb or otherwise handicapped. All children were able to learn. It was a matter of fairness, as he had been taught in Teachers' College over and over again, that each child was different and each child should be allowed to progress at his or her own pace. Never mind that Dog was not progressing at all, could barely write his name, and was still doing work at a grade one level. This was an embarrassment to young Mr. Potts, especially as the school inspector had visited his classroom the week before and left a caustic note on his report expressing his displeasure at the lack of progress of Dog. Mr. Potts was still suffering from this rebuke, and more importantly, worried that now he would not get his promotion. So he stood at his very carefully arranged desk, so tidy, as he often reminded his pupils, "a place for everything and everything in its place," and looked with some satisfaction at the two boys, carrying out their task, Tich highly skilled, and Dog even doing well under Tich's tutelage. He was hoping that Tich would be a good influence on Dog, maybe even teach him something.

Mr. Potts stood perfectly upright behind his carefully arranged desk as the children marched in, and stood at their desks.

"Good morning children," said Mr. Potts.

"Good morning Mr. Potts," chanted the children.

"Now sit quietly. I have something special to show you all this morning. "

A familiar, even comforting, rustle of the kids' shoes scraping on the wooden floor. An excited murmur. Mr. Potts reached for a large rectangular envelope that sat, perfectly aligned with the edge of the desk on top of the perfectly aligned blotter pad, which was, so far today, spotless, no sign of ink stains. He opened the envelope and peered inside. The children started to chatter.

"Now, children! No chattering. Heads down on your desk, please. That's the way."

The children all, even Dog, put their heads on their desks and covered them with their arms.

"OK. children, You may look now!"

The children looked and gasped, and chattered, and ooed and aared. The girls in the back giggled.

Mr. Potts held the picture high and walked around the room showing it. It was a charcoal portrait of someone who looked like Mr. Potts, but wasn't him. The figure had a big bushy moustache, and Mr. Potts had nothing of the sort. But the eyes were not quite the same, though all the rest was definitely Mr. Potts. Tich raised his hand.

"Yes, Tich?"

"Is it you, Mr. Potts? It sort of looks like you but you're not that old, are you?"

"Very good, Tich. It is not a picture of me, but of my grandfather, drawn when there was no such thing as a camera, there were no photos at all."

The buzz of excitement and the clear display of the children learning made Mr. Potts very happy with the class and with himself. "When you go home tonight, ask your parents if they have drawings of their grandparents. And if you can, bring one in tomorrow."

Dog raised his hand.

"Yes, Dog?"

"I have to go to the toilet."

Mr. Potts looked at him sternly. "First, Dog, you know that our rule is that you cannot go to the toilet before morning recess, and we have only just now started our morning class."

"But sir…"

"No buts. Second, you know that the way you said it was discourteous."

"Dis-what?" responded Dog cheekily.

"You didn't say please," called one of the girls from the back.

Dog stood up and jiggled his legs. "Please, Mr. Potts, I have to go."

"Sit! And mind your manners!" growled Mr. Potts. Dog had ruined the whole lesson.

Mr. Potts addressed the class. "Get out your workbooks and do the arithmetic I have put on the board."

The children responded with mutters, chatter and the banging of desk lids as they were opened and shut. Dog slid down under his desk and started to bark, somewhere in that bark the word toilet could be heard.

Mr. Potts placed the drawing on top of the blotter pad, taking a moment to admire it. He felt very close to his grandfather, even though he was a baby when his grandfather passed away. He then looked up and scanned the class. There was a bit of chatter, mainly from the girls at the back, but all the kids were doing their work, with the exception of Dog, of course.

"Those of you who finish before recess bell may come up and get one of the special comic books I have on my desk, and read until recess. In the meantime, I am going to pass the picture of my grandfather around the class to let you see close up how the charcoal drawing was done. Yes, that's right. The artist used a piece of charcoal to do the drawing."

"Didn't they even have pencils in those days?" asked one of the girls.

"Of course they did. But you know, artists still today like to use charcoal because it has a nice clear black and white effect." He handed the drawing to Tich who sat at the front of the row in his desk that he shared with Dog. "You want to look at it?" he asked Dog.

But Dog barked and scratched around at something on the floor under the desk.

Mr. Potts moved around the class checking the arithmetic, giving help, and praise where deserved. He was half way through, when there was what might be called a quiet shriek from one of the girls.

Mr. Potts looked up. "Now girls, that's enough chatter. What's going on there?"

One of the girls held up the drawing, waving it around. "Now! Please be careful with that drawing, it is a valuable work of art!" ordered Mr. Potts, "and a family heirloom."

"What's that? asked the girl.

"Something very special that is handed down from one generation to another."

"What's a generation?" The girl started to giggle and gave the drawing to one of her friends, who declined to take it. "Oooh! I'm not taking it. You're not going to blame me for it!" she cried.

"What?" asked Mr. Potts, "blame for what?"

The girl held the drawing up to Mr. Potts so he could see it.

A huge splash of ink covered a good part of the drawing. Mr. Potts almost leaped over the desks between him and the drawing. He almost cried, 'O my God," but managed to hold it back. "Give that to me! Who did this?" he demanded.

A deathly silence descended on the class. Even the barking of Dog ceased, though his scraping feet did not.

"Come forward who did this!" he demanded once again.

But not one child came forward. All looked down and sideways at each other, dying to see who had done this terrible thing.

"I will ask one more time. Come forward who did this. Come forward this minute!"

Silence. Now all looked down, none wanting to be seen as either having done it, or knowing who did.

The morning recess bell sounded. The children squirmed in anticipation.

Mr. Potts looked at his watch. "All right, then," he said, "you will all stay in until the person who did this terrible thing owns up."

*

Morning recess came and went, but still the class sat, with no one owning up. Dog put up his hand and asked, "please sir, can I go to the toilet? Please? I couldn't before because we didn't have recess."

Mr. Potts relented. After all, Dog had seemingly learned his lesson and his request was reasonable. Besides, it would give the class a chance to point the finger at Dog who, of course, was the prime suspect.

Dog left for the toilet and soon returned. He had met the principal in the hallway who had asked him where he was going and why didn't his class go out for recess. Dog said he was going to the toilet and didn't know why. The principal shrugged and walked off.

Dog returned to his classroom which was deadly silent. Mr. Potts had ordered the class to sit still and read. And if anyone was tired of doing that he made them do the sums from the board all over again. But still, no one owned up to the terrible deed. Mr.

Potts began to walked backwards and forwards in front of the class, his hands clasped behind his back. Finally, he stopped and faced the class.

"One last time!" he said, clearly on the edge of a breakdown. "If no one owns up, I will have to keep the whole class in as punishment. No lunch time, and at the end of the day, you will be kept in for an extra half hour."

The class stirred, and the noise of shoes scraping the floor rose to a crescendo. There were loud whispers of "that's not fair" and "but I'll miss my bus," but Mr. Potts was adamant.

"I have told you. This picture of my grandfather was extra special. It is a terrible thing for someone to have done. Horrible! Horrible!" There was even a slight trace of water in his eyes. He turned away from the class so that they would not see it. And when he turned back, the class became suddenly silent.

One of the girls from the back had raised her hand. "Sir?" she called out, a very serious look on her face.

"Yes?" answered Mr. Potts, hoping for a resolution. Even he had to admit to himself that the punishment he was dishing out to everyone because of the misbehavior of one individual was certainly unfair.

"We all know who done it, Mr. Potts. It was Dog!"

Other kids eagerly chimed in. "That's right! It's always Dog."

Tich looked down and saw Dog rummaging around under the desk. He had been there most of the time all morning. He doubted if it were him. But he said nothing.

"Dog? Get up from there. Come on! Stand out in the aisle. Let me see you! Come on!"

But Dog remained where he was, emitting his usual barking noises. Tich leaned down to him and whispered, "you better come out! Mr. Potts is mad as hell!"

Dog stayed where he was.

"Dog! Come out!" called Mr. Potts. He was now more certain than ever that it had to be Dog. On the edge of losing it, he darted forward, pushed Tich aside, and grabbed Dog by the arm. "Come on, you little devil! Out you come!" He dragged him out of the desk and to the front of the class. Dog went limp and then when Mr. Potts let him go, he just plopped to the floor and would not get up. Just stayed there rubbing his nose and eyes, red in the face. He had been there many times.

"Did anyone see him do it?" asked Mr. Potts, immediately regretting it.

The class remained silent, each looking at the other. Then a shy girl who sat at the front of the class away from the other girls slowly raised her hand.

"What is it Gladys?" asked Mr. Potts.

"I saw him do it, Mr. Potts."

"Are you certain?" asked Mr. Potts, now the fair and impartial judge.

"I saw him. He was trying to write something in his workbook and he dipped his pen in the inkwell and the nib caught on the lip of the inkwell and it pulled the inkwell out of the hole and the ink went all over the desk."

"Where was the picture?" asked Mr. Potts.

"I was just handing it to Dog," answered the shy girl, glancing around furtively, the rest of the class looking on as though some awful secret was about to be revealed.

Tich stood up, excited. "Sir! I don't think that could be right. There's no ink on our desk."

The shy girl spoke up, certainly with some difficulty. "I cleaned it up while Tich was over in the corner sharpening his pencil."

The waste paper bin was in the corner of the classroom at the back of the class. It was a special pleasure of every kid to go there and sharpen their pencils on the sharpener attached to the wall above.

Mr. Potts, wanted very much to get this behind him. The simplest solution to this nasty situation was to believe what the girl said and get the punishment over with. He walked across to the shy girl and leaned over to look in her eyes. "You're sure of this?"

"Yes Mr. Potts," she whispered, looking down.

He returned to stand beside Dog who was sitting on the

floor, morose, his cheeks puffed up and red, his eyes though, steadfastly fixed on the shy girl.

"Dog, stand up this minute!" demanded Mr. Potts.

Of course, Dog did not comply.

"Come on! Stand up! I've had enough of you!" He walked across to his desk and withdrew his leather strap, which he was proud to say he rarely used. But his time it was absolutely necessary.

A great hush descended on the class. The girls at the back strained their necks as high as they could so that they would see everything.

Mr. Potts stood facing Dog, dangling the strap in front of him. Dog cringed, raising his arm as though he were about to be slapped all over. He did not and would not stand up. He liked being on the floor. There was something comforting about it, though he wished it were under the desk as well. In fact, he started to crawl for his desk.

"Stop right there!" commanded Mr. Potts.

Dog crawled forward, but then Mr. Potts put his foot down, literally, on Dog's fingers as he crawled. Dog stopped. He could no longer move forward.

Now, Mr. Potts was faced with a very difficult and dangerous decision. Dog was stuck in a typical crawling position, his bottom sticking up crying out to be smacked. Mr. Potts, an upstanding gentleman of the community, and accomplished teacher, knew very well that the regulations of the Victorian Education Department allowed the strap to be applied only to the hands and lower legs. And it was limited to six strokes at any one time. He jiggled the strap a little, as though to loosen his wrist. Then with a flick of his wrist, the strap whizzed upwards as he lifted his arm in a swift motion so that the strap, like a writhing snake, leaped up then down, slapping Dog's bottom with a sharp crack.

Dog screamed so loud that it frightened all the kids in the class who looked on dumbfounded.

"Let that be a lesson to you," said grim Mr. Potts, looking around the class, so it was not at all clear whether he was talking just to Dog or to the whole class.

Tich looked on in horror. He glanced across to the shy girl who looked away. He knew that it was she whose pen had caught in the inkwell.

Moral: Punishment is the negation of fairness.

19. Parallel Lives

The monstrosities of mass punishment..

Rose Humphries was just one of many Londoners who bore the brunt of the German Blitz during 1940. Her parents had refused to send her north into the countryside where she would be mostly safe from the bombs. If they were going to die, they should do it together, was her mother's way of thumbing her nose at Hitler. And so, in that year on September, 19 1940, Rose found herself ogling at Winston Churchill who had come down from his perch of government to inspect the ruinous remains of houses on Portman street, just near Marble Arch. The bombing had fortunately not destroyed the apartment building in which she lived with her mother and father (when he was there), and it was obvious that, if it had, and she were inside, it would have been the end of time for her.

Churchill picked his way through mounds of rubble and puffed at his cigar as if to blow away the smoke and dust that rose from the piles of bricks, broken concrete, splintered timber and small fires that still burned in many crevices. Only nine years old at the time, Rose strained to get close to Sir Winston. She had heard so many stories about him. He was fearless, and he had told Hitler to go to hell lots of times. It all seemed like a Fairytale to her. She wanted to touch him as her way to make sure he was real. She imagined him as a kind of giant who would one day crush Hitler. Churchill came near, poking at the rubble with his cane, harumphing and puffing. Her mother held her back. She was, after all, one of many crowding around, hoping to get close to this giant who would eventually save them. That he would, they had no doubt.

Though the numbers would mean little to Rose. Approximately 32,000 civilians were killed during the blitz and 87,000 seriously injured. Some two million houses were destroyed. Churchill was well aware of the dreadful destruction and of what his people were going through. He knew it, and his people knew it. It made it a simple calculation as to what should be done to such people who committed these crimes on innocent people. Unlike World War I, and other wars before it, this was not a war confined to a series of battles between military sides. Rather it was a huge battle in which civilians were the targets and the pawns. It even had a military term: "strategic bombing."

*

Churchill was the only politician in the United Kingdom who saw it all coming. He had pleaded with Chamberlin and many others to prepare the country for war. He was convinced that Hitler would not stop at Poland. That his Third Reich would gobble up all Europe, and as soon as that was accomplished, turn his eyes to the United Kingdom.

It was not so much the battles. Churchill had grown up with them throughout his childhood playing out all the great battles of history with his toy soldier collection. It would be reasonable to say that he was obsessed with war. He did not go to university, which no doubt he could have done, Oxford surely, given his father's high positions in politics. Rather, he wanted to be a soldier, and that is what he became, fighting in British India, the Anglo-Sudan war, the second Boer War and other skirmishes. He became a famous war correspondent, and eventually joined politics, following in his (disapproving) father's footsteps. As First Lord of the Admiralty, he oversaw the disastrous campaign in Gallipoli, noting that "the price to be paid in taking Gallipoli would no doubt be heavy." A drastic understatement: 250,000 casualties, 46,000 allied forces dead, and the enemy (the Turks) the same number of casualties with 65,000 dead. And then there was World War II. In evaluating Churchill's handling of both wars, it is hard to get out of one's mind his toy soldiers all lined up, kept as they were as a child well into adulthood. All of the great battles of western history he played over and over again.

But the enemy, whoever it was, had to be fought, and when overcome, punished severely for their crimes. When it came to World War II, it was a simple matter to Churchill, though not to many of his peace-loving opponents. Hitler was an insane evil figure, bent on the destruction of the western world as it was, his aim to establish a master race that would bring in a new world of prosperity and great accomplishments. Like Churchill, he had a dream, and it would cost many lives. Only Churchill's dream was the defense and preservation of the established social structure of western society and politics. He saw Hitler clearly as the great destroyer of civilization. Not only had he to be defeated for what he would do and had already done, but also for who and what he was. A tyrant and the arch enemy of civilization, as were all his followers.

Thus arose the Allied version of strategic bombing.

*

Gert Mueller lived with his mom and dad just around the corner from the Waldorf Astoria on Joachimsthaller Street. His dad was a mechanic who took care of all the plumbing and electrical and other essentials that kept the famous hotel running smoothly. On any ordinary day there were always important problems to fix, but on August 26, 1940, the first major bombing of Berlin occurred, signaling to Gert's dad that he was destined to have his hands full keeping the hotel running. As it turned out, though, the first bombing caused young Gert, all of twelve years old, to cry, when he learned that the enormous explosion he heard on that day was a bomb falling on the Berlin Zoo, very close to the hotel and his home. Worse, his favorite elephant was killed in the attack. And much worse, after this very poor start of the bombing by the allies, their attacks were to become more and more lethal, resulting in around half of all buildings in Berlin destroyed, some 50,000 people killed, and hundreds of thousands made homeless. Gert's father would lose his life while attending to his job, a massive wall of brick and stone collapsing on him as he walked to the hotel early one morning to inspect the damage of the night's air raid. By the end of the war, and much of the year following it, Gert and his mom survived by some means unfathomable. Gert had little memory of that time. It remained a mystery to him how his mom kept him alive.

*

From 1940 through the end of the war in 1945 Churchill saw

to it that bombing raids were relentlessly directed at a number of German cities (Dresden perhaps the most infamous) to destroy infrastructure, but most important of all, to kill as many Germans as possible and destroy as many homes as possible, especially when assisted towards the end of the war by the U.S. Air force. As Churchill's head of Bomber Command Sir Arthur "Bomber" Harris said: "We can wreck Berlin from end to end if the U.S. Air Force comes with us. It will only cost us between 400 and 500 aircraft but it will cost Germany the war." This was great sounding talk, much of it bravado, though, since about half way through the war, Hitler's Luftwaffe was holding its own, not to mention that the Germans had invented the self-driven V2 rockets that gradually could be aimed with more and more precision as the technology improved.

One could argue, though, that it was not the Americans who would turn the war around in the Allies' favor, but in fact the Russians, thanks to Hitler's fatal error of double-crossing the Russians and attacking them on June 22, 1941. It was to become a battle that would repeat the fatal error made by Napoleon a century before. Russia turned both battles into a war of attrition, sacrificing its own military, but especially its civilians, who were starved and sacrificed by a frozen earth policy to draw the German troops well into Russia, until the unrelenting winter destroyed the German military, along with a great many Russians, military and civilian.

By the time the Americans joined the war after the attack on Pearl Harbor on December 7, 1941, the stubborn British led by their stubborn Prime Minister, were gritting their teeth, the air force suffering what seemed like unsustainable casualties. And eventually, these numbers would become appalling on all sides, even when compared to those lost as a result of the USA dropping two atomic bombs on the Japanese. The USSR lost 12 million military and 15 million civilians in World War II, by far the most of any of the allied countries. And Japan lost 1.5 million military and half a million civilians. The U.K. Lost 403,000 military and 92,700 civilians; the USA lost 6,000 civilians and 407,000 military.

*

The winning of wars is commonly attributed by historians to the great leadership of famous leaders or generals: Alexander the Great, Julius Caesar, the Duke of Marlborough, Napoleon, Wellington, Bolivar, Churchill, and yes, Hitler (at first a spectacular winner). Yet all these great leaders also lost particular battles, and an analysis of the battles over which they presided shows that there was much luck or good fortune attached to the events (commonly attributed to the "fog of war") and that includes the weather and various other unforeseen events. What a great irony it is, then, that the moral certitude that follows victory is displayed with such flourish. The morally upright are the victors, and the losers vanquished and humiliated, their leaders seen as the most evil of doers. The winners build monuments and worship their heroes of past wars--the losers forever disappearing into the moral depravities of history.

Well, not quite so. For later generations, unscathed by the personal sufferings and losses of distant forebears, assiduously ferret out details of the shocking depravities of war, and reveal to the innocence of modernity, that the heroes of past wars, the proclaimed winners, also committed atrocities in battles and aftermaths of battles. From which the distasteful conclusion follows: the winners are reduced to the same level or morality as the losers.

*

It is much easier to weigh up the degrees of evil of particular persons and their actions, than it is to weigh up the degrees of good overall. For evil flaunts itself, and invokes in its finders, an outrage easily justified. The outrage clearly showing itself to be pure and good: the opposite of evil.

For this reason, the Nuremberg and Tokyo trials were held in order to demonstrate to the world (but really to the allies themselves) the justice and moral superiority of the victors over the vanquished. These trials were, in their own way, world shattering events of moral turpitude. The losers of the Great War and their respective countries (mainly Germany) were humiliated by having to sign away large portions of their territories, including those not taken by them in the war. They were stripped of their economies, (forced into impossible debt) largely sentenced to poverty and humiliating subservience to the victors. Churchill, to become the hero of World War II, strongly opposed the Treaty of Versailles, because it had deeply humiliated the enemy, thereby, he argued, guaranteeing that they will remain the enemy and guaranteeing another war. None believed him. Churchill had a kind of gentlemen's morality: we have a fair fight, then we shake hands and respect each other and continue on our way, all the time respecting our enemy that was.

But the Nuremberg and Tokyo trials changed all that. The confused and ambivalent morality that lay buried beneath the trials was well demonstrated by the case of Alfred Jodi, who signed orders for the summary execution of Allied commandos and Soviet commissars as well as the instruments of surrender on 7 May 1945 in Reims. He was hanged 16 October 1946 and post-humously rehabilitated in 1953, which was later reversed. Never-theless, these trials of the justice of war did not stop the victors from using prisoners of war as forced labor for a few years after the armistice was signed. But in the grand scheme of morality, forced labor and other reparations (Germany had to give up some territory to Russia and Poland), took the back seat to the grand show of the Nuremberg and Tokyo trials.

But what of the insignificant individuals whose lives were disrupted by these moralities of war and justice?

Rose Humphries lived to tell the story of the blitz to her children and grandchildren. Her mother, laid ill from malnutrition and other maladies of poverty caused by war, died at a young age of 42, leaving Rose alone with her father who returned from the war early in 1946, repatriated from an Italian prisoner of war camp. Great Britain, though the victors, was great no more, and it took several years for her dad to find permanent work, which he did, naturally, in the building industry. For her part, Rose took it all in her stride, and when the U.K. Joined the European Union in 1973, she was an eager young woman who quickly ran to Europe to see what all the fuss had been about, and especially to discover Italy and the Italians who, strangely, her father spoke of as great friends and who knew how to enjoy the small things (eating) in life, even though in the aftermath of the war, eating had become a necessity for survival, not a means of daily pleasure. In fact, it was in post war Rome that Rose met a fine young Italian man from Trieste. They married and lived in Rome ever after. One can only marvel at the resilience of humanity!

Gert Mueller was a teenager by the time Berlin was under reconstruction, and the schools were back in operation. His mother wanted him to become a mechanic like his dad, and perhaps had history been kind to him, and his dad survived, he would have. But in the absence of his father, it was necessary for him to find work— and there was lots of it rebuilding Berlin — to help restore their own house and lives, especially that of his mother who had given all to keep them alive, during the ghastly few years of reconstruction in Berlin. But Berlin was their home, and his mother would not budge from their old apartment. And once the schools got under way, he was able to go to night school to make sure he could get an education and make a life for himself. That was what his mother (and his father if alive also) harped on every day and night. It would be understandable if he resented it. But he did not, for he saw that it was the only sure way forward, and that it would take great effort and perseverance. He was not to know, of course, that he would meet a glamorous American young woman a nurse who worked for the Red Cross. They became friends, he began to help her on her many forays into homes that suffered far more than his own. She told him of the marvels of the United States. He was enthralled. They married and he went with her to New York, a city far greater than Berlin ever was, where he would go to school and eventually become a law professor specializing in European and International law. His mother remained in their Berlin apartment where she died in 1980. just as the question of German reparations to Poland was raised again. Gert hurried home to his mother's funeral, sold their apartment, and would never return again to Berlin. Living in New York with his own family, he had managed easily enough to forget those dark days after the war. Why go back?

These parallel lives were simply two of many, many more

life courses, after the war, repeated over and over to an infinite degree, a remonstrance to every one of them, of their refusal to give in to the tyranny of moral turpitude. That is, of immoral morality; of good and evil intertwined and unwound by trials of justice and punishment. Could those trials truly identify who were specifically responsible for all those millions of deaths? Hitler and Churchill perhaps? And add to that maybe Roosevelt, Eisenhower and Truman, not to mention Hirohito and his great generals?

Or, the easiest, blame it all on Hitler, and the actions of his opponents pardoned because they were forced to do what they did in order to win— and therefore assume ownership of morality and its definition.

In sum, a just punishment for genocide and its correlatives (unnecessary wars for example) is an impossibility because there is no punishment that is sufficiently severe—unless, of course, genocide were the punishment. But this would erase the distinction between crime and punishment, would it not?

Moral: The morality of heroes feeds off the suffering of others, whether winners or losers .

20. Pardon my President

Why JFK was assassinated.

Everyone knows how President Kennedy's presidency ended. But few know the real truth of why it came to be. There are plenty of theories and accounts of how the assassination happened, who did it, how many shots were fired and the rest. But none have even speculated as to why it happened. This story, based on true events, drawing on hitherto hidden documents found in the crypt of the Roman Catholic church of the Resurrection in Chicago, explains the deeply troubling events that led up to the assassination. Of course, we all know the shock of the event. Anyone who lived through it will tell you exactly where they were and what they were doing at the time of the killing. Just as all those who lived through the nine eleven attack, the Kennedy killing delivered a psychological shock of the same intensity, even though it was just one person who was killed, compared to the two thousand or more who died in the World Trade Center attack. Why is this?

In 1960, the musical Camelot, written by famed composers Lerner and Loewe appeared on Broadway and swept New York audiences off their feet. Based on the myth of King Arthur and the round table, the musical drew heavily on T. H. White's *The Once and Future King*. It contained all the necessary ingredients of a love story and politics: Love, faith and faithlessness, disloyalty, trysts and love triangles (an understatement), not to mention various wars. All of this, though, done with great gallantry, virtuosity, honor and flare. Possibly the idea of the "perfect gentleman" grew from these dim beginnings of Englishness. After a *Life Magazine* article suggested that Jackie was JFK's "Genevere" the media ran with the idea creating the fabulous image of the Camelot presidency. Never mind that the myth was all about Kings, royalty supposedly anathema to American democracy. JFK and his handlers fully embraced the myth. It so happened that JFK was at Harvard together with Lerner who sent him advanced recordings of the major songs. JFK's favorite lines appeared in the final number in which Arthur knights a young boy, telling him to pass on the story of Camelot to the next generation. To reproduce the lines here would cost a ton in royalties. Suffice it to say that there were three portentous words included in the four lines "brief," "shining," and "moment."

*

David Powerhouse was proud of being JFK's personal assistant. Without JFK, where would he be? He treasured the memory of PT 109, the dangerous but raucous days of navy service. Little did he realize then that he would one day end up in the Whitehouse. His friends always asked him what was his job of personal assistant? It sounded like some kind of servant. As far as he was concerned, it was fine for people to think that. He was proud to serve. But in fact, he had two important tasks. First, to keep all negative press coverage to a minimum. Everything that was said to the press had to go through him, except, of course, the president himself, who had a small team of expert writers to help him. And second, to make sure any threats to his well-being were dealt with accordingly. And by the summer of 1963 the FBI was reporting worrying threats almost daily. In fact, things got so bad that Powerhouse insisted on going over to the FBI every day for a briefing, rather than have the FBI visit the Whitehouse every day, an event that would trigger nosey reporters into asking embarrassing questions, or worse, inventing stories of presidential assassination threats.

The trouble was, his boss knew something was going on. "Err, P-H," he said, "you got some sweet thing over there with J. Edgar?"

"Mr. President, no sir!" laughed Powerhouse. "I was going to tell you though. We're very worried."

"Err, why is that, P-H?"

"Threats, sir. They're coming in all over. You're not safe, sir. We need to double or triple your security detail, especially when you go out on campaign."

"Now, you know P-H, I don't scare easily. Any pattern?

Nothing coordinated, I hope?"

"No, sir. Don't think so. At least that's what the FBI says. Just a lot of chatter and daily threats coming in by phone and letter. They follow them all up of course."

JFK sat back in his chair and surveyed the oval office. Then he stood and walked over to the south windows. Powerhouse joined him. "What is it, sir? Is there something I can do?"

The president turned and faced him, then put one hand on his shoulder. "You know, P-H, there's a lot of steamy material out there that could harm me, not so much me, the presidency. You know what I mean?"

Powerhouse looked away, a little embarrassed. "I'm not sure what you're getting at, Mr. President."

"Of course you are. I'm sure everyone talks about my, shall we say, adventures. Thank goodness the press treats them as part of the Camelot musical. Fantasies that never happened."

"Sir?"

"Not a word to anyone about this. I'm scheduled to visit Martha's Vineyard August 30, right?"

"I'd have to check the schedule, just a moment." Powerhouse ran out to his desk.

"It's the Chappaquiddick Beach Club Labor Day celebration," the President called after him.

Breathless, Powerhouse returned to his boss. "Yes, that's right. You'll be there a couple of days."

"Then I want you to do something for me. This is top secret, No one, and I mean no one, must know."

"OK."

"There's a very old friend, you have probably met him from time to time, the Monsignor D'Andrea, priest at the Resurrection Catholic Church of Chicago. I want you to go there and accompany him to the compound at the Cape."

"How do you want me to travel?"

"Rent a Beechcraft Bonanza. It will be able to land at the Cape Airport. And will not attract the attention that a US air force plane would."

"How long a stay? We'll have to get the Monsignor back, of

course," mused Powehouse.

"A couple of days, max, I should say."

*

Monsignor Anthony D'Andrea leaned back in the plush leather seat of the Lincoln Continental that purred off down West Nelson street. He turned to take one last look at Resurrection Catholic Church of Chicago a place he thought of as his home. It was an exciting time, a day that would be remembered forever by every American. John F. Kennedy Junior had been elected President of the United States on this day, Tuesday, November 8, 1960. The stout Monsignor expected to be offered the White-house chaplaincy. But he would decline. One should not move so fast, he would advise the president. JFK was the very first Roman Catholic to be elected President. That was enough. Little did he know, however, that JFK did not have such an appointment in mind. Not at all.

The limousine drove straight on to the tarmac at Midway airport and up to the waiting Beechcraft Bonanza. Powerhouse stood at the bottom of the stairway to welcome him. "Thank you for coming at such short notice," he said as they shook hands. The Monsignor detected a slightly lilting Irish tone.

"I am honored that the President has thought of me after so many years. It is probably ten years since I last met with him."

"He speaks of you often. He took his first communion with you, I think, back in 1940, I believe," said Powerhouse.

"That is probably right. You are very well informed, young man!"

"It's my job."

"Perhaps. But in this case it is your destiny and clearly one of devotion," the Monsignor said with an air of authority.

"Besides, I've known him a long time. I served under him on PT-109 during the war," added Powerhouse.

"Then may I ask why he has sent for me?"

"That I do not know, Monsignor. He has not offered me a reason. He has, however, insisted that this visit be kept secret and away from the public and other prying eyes," answered Power-house, displaying his own air of authority. In fact, he did not especially like the Monsignor. Powerhouse was a protestant after all, a fact that the Monsignor with his sensitive religious antenna had already detected, in spite of the slight Irish twang that at first threw him off.

"I see," the Monsignor replied unnecessarily, "now you have me wondering and worrying"

"You don't need to worry, Monsignor. He's fully charged, fit and well."

*

They arrived at the Kennedy compound late on the evening of August 30. The Monsignor was made comfortable in the guest house, bid good night and left to sleep, for which he was grateful.

The next morning he was awakened by a light knock. Monsignor called "enter," and in came JFK carrying a tray of coffee, toast and jam, followed closely by a servant carrying a newspaper, looking a little embarrassed.

"Your breakfast," smiled the President. "I think I remember that you like a large breakfast to start the day?"

The Monsignor struggled to get out of bed, but JFK put down the tray, took him by his shoulders and said, "stay there my good friend. Relax and enjoy your breakfast. Can we meet in the garden at say 10.00 am?"

"The garden?"

"Yes. We can talk there without any interruption. And there is a gentle breeze. Perfect for a morning walk."

The President turned and left, not waiting for an answer. The Monsignor set to on his very large breakfast. And in no time he had showered and walked out in the direction of what looked like the garden.

JFK met him half way. "Thank you for coming. I hope you had a nice trip?"

"I am honored to be here with the thirty fifth president of the United States," said Monsignor with a little hint of a bow. Now what is your pleasure?"

"Well that's partly what I want to talk about, Father."

"I am all ears, though pleasure is not usually my business, if you see what I mean," Monsignor answered with a big Irish smile.

"Exactly. I've had some dalliances…"

"Oh now I see. You want to make a confession?" The Monsignor stopped and turned to face the President.

"I think so."

"Well it's about time, isn't it? When did you last make one?"

"Not for many years. In fact I can't really remember," said the President looking the Monsignor squarely in the eye.

"Now I know why you did not take on a Catholic for the Whitehouse chaplain."

"Come on Tony," said JFK, "let's not be disingenuous."

"Apologies, dear boy, I have sinned too," quipped Monsignor.

"You don't mind 'Tony'? It's what we called you back in my Chicago days."

"Of course not. And your confession?"

"As I've said, I've had some dalliances…"

"Why now?"

"Tony. You know what it's like in the rough world of Chicago and gangsterdom. I know you could get dispatched any time. The same applies to me," said JFK with a deep frown.

"You've been threatened? I'm appalled to hear that," cried Monsignor.

"It's not unusual. But I have good intelligence that the threat level is unusually high."

"And so you want to make things right with Saint Peter," asked Monsignor half joking.

"Something like that," JFK answered a little sheepishly.

"Then let's get started," said the Monsignor with a little too much enthusiasm. He pointed to a seat by a small fountain. "Shall we sit?"

"Not sure where to start," mumbled the President as they sat down together.

"Well, you might start by crossing yourself and saying what everyone else says, 'bless me father for I have sinned.' You need not kneel. We can just sit here and talk."

"Thank you Tony. "Bless me Father for I have sinned…"

The Monsignor interrupted. "Here is where, after extensive

self-examination you recount all your sins. In your case, since you have not confessed for a long time, you need to take the time to remember and recount them all. If you like we could stop and when you've done that—it's called contrition by the way—we can get started."

JFK felt around in his hip pocket. "I've made a kind of rough list. I've probably missed some. You want the list?"

"No my son. You must recount them to me. It's part of your contrition. You must own up to having done all these things, and that they were sinful."

"OK Tony, here goes. I'll try to do them in order. The one I regret most was bedding my father's call girl, Marlene Dietrich, probably in 1962. I felt kind of like a double-crosser doing it…"

"That was not the real sin, was it?" pressed the Monsignor.

"What do you mean?"

"The tenth commandment. Thou shalt not covet thy neighbor's wife."

"Oh, right. I guess that applies to nearly all my dalliances."

"And not to mention the sixth commandment that forbids adultery," added the Monsignor with a touch of sarcasm.

"Tony, for Christ's sake! Take it easy. I'm doing this because I want to."

"You're doing it for your own sake, not Christ's. But we will discuss that issue after you've recounted your many sins. Please continue."

JFK turned to look the Monsignor in the eye. "Then there was Judith Exner, you probably know her," he said with a grin. "She was a mob moll."

The Monsignor stared back, expressionless. "You're not taking this seriously," he said sternly. Unless you do, this confession will be a waste of time." He looked up. "It's not me. It's the big man upstairs."

"Sorry, Tony. It's just me. I can't help seeing the funny side of things. It's my Irish upbringing."

"The Irish only see the funny side of things when they're drunk, and even then they're maudlin. You have not taken anything this morning?"

JFK was about to respond, when Powerhouse came running up. "Mr. President, Bobby's on the phone. Says he can't make it this weekend."

"Tell him fine. I'll call him back later today."

"You don't want to talk to him? He's excited about his investigation of the mafia," queried Powerhouse.

"Not now, David. I'm busy with the Monsignor here."

Powerhouse ran off and JFK turned back to his confessor. "Then there was Inga Binga the supposed Russian spy, and another spy, I think, Ellen Rometsch I think her name was. The State Department expelled her earlier this year, I believe. And then there was Mimi Alford the Whitehouse intern. She was easily the best, I'd say, but none of the glamor of the other high flyers, if you get what I mean. I encouraged her to do a job on Powerhouse. Well, she didn't need much encouragement. And there were quite a few others. Two Whitehouse secretaries that we called Fiddle and Faddle. Jackie knew all about them, so they say. She never said anything to me. And a few more. Can't remember their names. "

"What about Marilyn Monroe?"

"Oh of course. How could I forget her? She wasn't much in bed, to tell the truth. Great to take to a party though."

The Monsignor stirred uncomfortably, clearly annoyed. "Mr. President, I must tell you again. Making a confession is a serious undertaking. You must not make light of it."

"I think I better get back to the house. I'm a little worried about Bobby. He's like a bull in a china shop sometimes. He needs to be careful with the Mafia. I guess you would know all about that, wouldn't you Monsignor?"

"The rate we are going, this will take all day and much of night," complained the Monsignor.

"So be it. I am prepared to do what it takes. But I have a country to run, Tony. You'll have to fit in with my schedule. Unless of course, Chicago cannot do without you?"

"I am here at your pleasure, I mean, as is needed," Mr. President. "I too want to serve my country in the best way I can."

JFK got up to leave, took a few steps then looked back. "Oh,

I forgot one more. Mary Meyer. An FBI agent's wife, I think."
As he turned towards the house, the Monsignor called after him.

"When we resume, I am going to ask you to kneel before me
and say you are sorry for your sins. It must be sincere and convincing, you understand?"

JFK walked hurriedly away.

The Monsignor, brooding and trying not to be annoyed with
the most powerful man in the world, went walking around the
Kennedy estate, admiring the beautiful gardens, finely clipped
lawns, and of course the wonderful views of the ocean. He
plodded over the sand dunes and stood looking up at the almost
blue sky, a haze of salt air creating a mist between him and the
Heaven to which he had prayed so often. He stayed there, lost in
time, perhaps praying, his mind a little foggy. He was lost in the
Holy Spirit. Then he heard a faint voice calling him.

"Monsignor! Tony!"

He turned to see that the President had returned. Shadowy
figures inhabited the dunes around him.

"You are not alone?" asked the Monsignor.

"Sorry Tony. The Secret Service guys. They insist on keeping
watch over me when I'm in such a dangerous place as the seaside."

"Come to me, my son, and kneel before me!" commanded
his confessor. The Monsignor stood facing the ocean. JFK
walked first down the beach to the edge of the water, then back
to his confessor and kneeled before him. The Monsignor placed
his hands on JFK's head. "My son. Please tell me, Jesus's messenger on earth, that you are sorry for all the sins you have
recounted."

JFK wanted to looked up but the heavy hands of the Monsignor made that difficult. "Not sure how to say this and how I
can convince you that I'm really sorry," he said in that well
known thick Bostonian accent.

"Just repeat after me, then, my son, and do so with a heavy
heart:

"My God, I am sorry for my sins with all my heart. In
choosing to do wrong, and failing to do good, I have sinned
against you, whom I should love above all things."

JFK complied, but added, "I am trying to do good. I am trying to make everyone equal, and ensure that the blacks and former slaves among us are treated equally and with humanity." And as he said this, the Monsignor lifted his hands from JFK's head who now looked up. The Monsignor saw tears in his eyes. Christ had heard his plea. The President truly cared. He was sorry. He put out his hand and JFK took it in both hands. "Rise my son, you have confessed your many sins and now must take full responsibility for their correction."

JFK looked up. "What does that mean?" he asked. "I'm doing good every minute I am President. Doesn't that make up for the sins I have committed?"

"Maybe. But we are not quite there yet," answered the Monsignor.

And at that moment, as if on cue, Powerhouse appeared from the dunes.

Powerhouse stopped dead in his tracks. This had to be a first. The world's most powerful man, on his knees in front of a priest, who, in his own opinion, was of dubious character. Although the media had not got a hold of it, he knew from his daily briefings with his FBI contacts that the Chicago Mafia was involved in all kinds of plots, especially in Cuba, and although he had no direct evidence, he assumed that the Monsignor must be involved, given the reach that the Chicago mob had all over Chicago, and even other major cities, especially Las Vegas.

The Monsignor stared his most penetrating stare at Powerhouse. "Mr. Powerhouse," he said, "this is not a good time."

"Asshole," Powerhouse muttered to himself, "who does he think he is?"

The President grabbed the Monsignor's hands and pulled himself up. "It's all right, D-P. We're done here for the moment. What is it?"

"The First Lady will be arriving tonight with the kids. She wants to know if you will be here. She wants you to call her before she leaves."

The President looked at the Monsignor. "Well, Tony, looks like we will have to break it off again."

"We need just another half hour, I think. We made excellent progress this morning," persisted the Monsignor.

A gust of wind blew a little sand past JFK's lined face. He called out, "tell Jackie that I'll call her in a half hour."

Powerhouse backed up over the dunes, yelling over his shoulder, "in half an hour, then, Mr. President."

The Monsignor persisted yet again. "Now, Mr. President, we have reached the third and probably most important phase of the confession."

"Yes, Tony. And what's that?"

"Repeat after me:

I firmly intend, with your help,

to do penance,

to sin no more,

and to avoid whatever leads me to sin."

Reluctantly, JFK complied.

"You have to really mean it, my son. I sense an element of reluctance," frowned the Monsignor.

"Well, it's impossible, isn't it? You know me. You know my family. How can I make up for all the sins of my past and even harder, to promise to sin no more. In this complicated world and especially in politics, it's impossible not to sin. It's an occupational hazard, don't you think?"

"My son, you are of course right. That is why you, along with all other good Catholics, must make confession often, preferably on a daily basis, but surely at least once a month, for a man of your standing."

"And while we're at it. What about the sins of my father?" countered the President. "They were legion. Am I responsible for them as well?"

"You should take on all the guilt you can, and in that way lead a good life that tries very hard to assuage the guilt of the past."

"I'm responsible for the sins of my father and everyone else?" asked JFK incredulously.

"You're President of the United States. It's only to be expected," answered the Monsignor with an air of false dignity.

"I am President, Tony, not Christ Himself!"

"Mr. President. This is just banter and delaying tactics. Face up to your sins. Convince me—seriously, for Christ's sake—that you are sorry for your sins. And once we are there, I can then take you to the next step."

"Which is?"

"Absolution."

"You mean, Tony, you can absolve me of all my sins?" asked JFK, full of hope and doubt.

"That's right, so long as you do penance and make up for the sins you have committed and the evil you have done to others," came the sacred reply.

"What penance do I have to do, then? It must be an awful lot, given the heavy baggage of my past sins, let alone those I might have to commit in the future."

"In a nutshell, you must give your life up to Christ," announced the Monsignor.

JFK replied quickly. "I have already. I am doing the ultimate in public service. And the enlightened legislation I have put forward—the great leap forward— I will save the lives of millions, enrich families everywhere, let alone help spread the message of democracy all over the world. I am in a place where I can make the lives of the poor better, even bearable. Who could do more?"

"All of that is commendable. But I caution you that life cannot be evaluated according to riches or poverty. Of course, we must help the poor. But we must not become rich on their backs. Do you follow me?" The Monsignor's authority competed with that of the President.

"You sound like Castro, Tony. I don't know if we must go that far," JFK grinned.

The Monsignor looked at him sternly. "You have steered us away from our immediate concern. You must dedicate yourself to correcting your sins. You might start with your own family." The Monsignor almost bit his tongue as he said that. He even blushed a little.

"How would you know, Tony? You have no family," said JFK, pushing back.

"Must I remind you again, my son, this confession is not about me, but you. Face up to it please! You must if you want redemption!" lectured the Monsignor.

JFK laughed. "Now you're sounding like Billy Graham."

"I will ignore that remark, obviously designed to deflect once again away from your responsibility for your own sins," said the Monsignor haughtily.

A silence overtook them. The soft crashing of the ocean took hold. A sudden gust of wind whirled though the dunes.

"Well, I've done that, haven't I? I've told you of my dalliances," said JFK quietly.

The Monsignor ignored this further, very annoying, expression of this man's superficiality. "Maybe you could begin by coming clean with Jackie and apologizing to her," he said with an unfortunate touch of sarcasm.

JFK returned a look of incredulity. "You've got to be joking!"

"No, I'm not. If you are serious about making up for your sins, you might start with those whom you have hurt most," he said with a deep frown, trying to hold back a smile.

"Anyway, she knows already. She even hinted to a group of tourists she was showing over the Whitehouse, that I screwed one if the secretaries."

"She is the closest to you. She and your children. If you did that, it would demonstrate to me—but more importantly to yourself—that you are truly sorry for your sins and have acknowledged them."

JFK sighed. "All right Tony, I will do it. Not today though. It will have to be after the Texas trip coming up in November. You are a hard man of the church."

"I take that as a compliment, Mr. President."

"So are we done?" asked JFK putting his hand on the Monsignor's shoulder.

"Not quite, my son. It remains now for me to formally acknowledge that you have fulfilled the requirements of contrition and penance, and now we reach the stage of forgiveness. Please kneel again, so I can dutifully carry out this task."

JFK looked around to see if there were any Secret Service looking on. He could see none. They always kept themselves well hidden. But he sensed their presence none the less. He knelt down, feeling the coolness of the sand on his knees. The Monsignor placed his hand on the President's bowed head and recited:

"God, the Father of mercies, through the death and resurrection of his Son has reconciled the world to himself and sent the Holy Spirit among us for the forgiveness of sins; through the ministry of the Church may God give you pardon and peace, and I absolve you from your sins in the name of the Father, and of the Son, and of the Holy Spirit. Amen."

The Monsignor removed his hand and said, "you may rise, now, Mr. President. The process of absolution has been completed. So long as you carry out your serious promise of avoiding sin and making reparations when you can, you will be right until your next confession."

"Thanks Tony. You're the one! Now I must hurry back and call Jackie. Don't worry. I promise I will carry out the tasks I have committed to this morning."

"See that you do."

"Are you staying over tonight? It would be wonderful if you could spend time with Jackie and the kids."

"Thank you, but I have pressing duties back at the parish. There is one last thing I'd like to know, though. How come you chose me as your confessor. You must have many options to draw on, your family priest which I assume you have?"

"You came highly recommended."

"Oh? Who by?"

"Al Capone."

Moral: An insincere confession invites dire consequences.

21. Unforgiven

Donald Trump wins by losing, maybe.

It is the year 2022, June 21. Eighteen months after the somber swearing in of the 45th president of the United States, twelve months after Facebook and Twitter restored Donald Trump's accounts, though Trump had not posted anything on the accounts until this day. One year after Congress voted to impeach Trump for his role in the riot that broke into the Capitol and dared to vandalize its sacred precincts. Politicians both left and right breathed a collective sigh of relief that at last, the blunt needle in their side had been eliminated. Even though the Senate once again, narrowly failed to find him guilty, it was enough to assure Trump's many enemies, that as a politician, he was done for.

Trump's new post to his restored Twitter account stunned the world. Everyone thought he had gone away, probably playing golf at one of his resorts, and good riddance. The post said: NEW RALLY—BUY YOUR TICKETS NOW! And the link went to Trump's new web site that immediately opened up with a pulsating image of a MAGA hat that was inscribed: TRUMP LOVES YOU. Tickets were $400 each at the Ohio Stadium, or $50 streamed to your living room. The rally would be on April 15, Good Friday. He had considered seriously scheduling the rally on President's Day, but finally decided against it. Good Friday made much more sense, as his forthcoming YouTube video would reveal. This would be a rally like no other, details to be announced within a few weeks.

The details that emerged over the next couple of days were vague, sketchy and tantalizing. Members of Congress and the Senate from both sides of the aisle would probably be participating, along with personalities from the dreaded main stream media. Maybe Trump was going to do what the media had harped on ever since his impeachment. Start his own political party, just like Berlusconi did in Italy back in 2007.

The stadium tickets sold out within a week, all 102,000 of them. Streaming tickets were a little slower on the uptake, until the announcement came with further details of the show. There was much puzzlement. What was the point of a rally if he could not be elected to any office because of his impeachments? Though technically, not found guilty by the senate, nevertheless every poll showed belief in his guilt was overwhelming.

On March 31, Trump appeared on a new YouTube video. It was brief, and created an uproar. The video opens with a long shot down a red carpeted aisle of Trump kneeling facing an altar, bedecked with photographs of his family surrounded by lush flowers from Florida, looking up at an ornate gold ceiling and glistening organ pipes. He then stands, turns, and we see that he is dressed in something like a choir boy's robe. His hair is all ruffled, looking a bit like that of his former counterpart in the United Kingdom, Boris Johnson. His face and expression is something to behold. It is long, corners of his mouth turned down, jowls of his cheeks prominent, pale, even pallid. Although the robe covers his body, there is a sense that it is much larger than it used to be, rotund perhaps. And then he speaks in that very familiar voice, the almost hidden New York accent:

"The last time I spoke to you was on that awful day when some of you, well meaning, but nevertheless foolish, broke into our sacred Capitol, the heart of our government. I said then that 'we (not 'I' but of course I do) love you, go home in peace.' I am here today to acknowledge that, buried in my accomplishments as your president, I did many wrong things and said many hurtful things to and about many people. And after my impeachment, I now know that I did not do enough to prevent the attack on the Capitol. And the impeachment has at last revealed to me that those who oppose me do so because I am a horrible person, not because of my politics."

Trump turns to the altar again and looks up. The organ quietly plays the hymn "Forgive me my Lord."

He then turns back to face the camera, drops to his knees and raises his hands up high, looks up at the gold embossed ceiling and then looks right in the camera and recites along with the music, "Forgive me, forgive me, O my Lord; I slipped and sinned, and in wickedness; Fooled and erred, I await Your mercies."

He stands again and clasps his hands together, then speaks into the camera, his mouth in its characteristic expression, the corners dipping down, but his cheeks trying to raise a smile. Or so it seems. Then the words came out, words than people did not expect, though they anticipated something that would disturb and shock. They were not disappointed. Trump said, almost wistfully:

"I know many of you will not believe me when I say I am so sorry for everything that has happened. I bear full responsibility for who I am and what I've done. But I also know that just saying I am sorry is not enough to satisfy all of you, and I mean all of you. I have therefore decided, after much deliberation and seeking the advice of God, to undergo a time honored way of making amends for my sins, to be whipped until my blood runs, and to undergo this well-deserved punishment before a capacity crowd in the Ohio stadium and streamed online. During that whipping I will also pledge that I will never commit these sins again, never use the term 'fake news', and never ever say hurtful things to anyone. There will be much more that I will promise. I only hope that after my punishment, you will all be able truly to forgive me."

The media and political reaction to this speech was predictable. Extremists of either party called it deplorable or pathetic, but others in the center saw it as a positive step. The many Christians, who would make up a sizable part of the audience, understood immediately what was happening. It was Trump's first shaky step to rehabilitation, redemption, then love, true love—messianic love, that is. The media, as usual, was unable to figure out what was happening. They had, after all, ferociously fed on all his past sins, so their automatic reaction was to accept this latest spectacle as more of the same, as another of his sins, so called. As far as the media were concerned it mattered not a bit whether Trump was sincere or not, truly sorry or not. It was spectacular news. And that meant money. So Trump's announcement achieved already an important win over the media, its cynical approach to everything, exposed by the very object it derided.

However, the greatest challenge to the politicians and their handlers on either side of the aisle was to figure out, once they had posted their various one line responses to the video, how or whether to react to this incredible event. The sensible among them counseled a wait and see approach. But the vast majority of them were so used to reacting in hateful ways, that they simply went along with the ebb and flow of Twitter announcements. The careful handlers pointed out to their bosses that for now it was probably best to say nothing; after all, Trump was no longer president. But even though they were all greatly relieved that he had been replaced for over a year now, the tendency was to forget that he was no longer president and to react accordingly. This was Trump's terrible legacy. Nobody would ever forget his presidency. Generations to come would all hear the stories; though it would be centuries until historians were able to sit back and evaluate his achievements and their positive or negative characteristics.

Of course, they did not have to wait long. Just two weeks.

*

Trump's handler, Steve Canon, now restored to the level of handler and friend once again, was charged with working over selected members of congress and the senate. Since the Democrats owned both houses, he first approached Sticky Shoemaker, leader of the senate, who initially refused to meet with him, having one of his subordinates respond. "Mr. Shoemaker has made it clear that he wants no part of this and considers it yet another foul attack on his own religious affiliation and the Jewish people. Everyone knows," said the handler, "that the Jewish people do not whip sinners. They stone them."

Canon, not one to give up easily in the face of aggression replied, "of course, you are right, but we cannot allow stoning, because it might kill President Trump."

Shoemaker's subordinate quickly replied, "he is no longer president, please do not call him that."

Canon considered arguing that everyone still referred to Clinton, Bush and Obama as presidents, but decided it was not worth it. He turned to move on to his next interview but he had no sooner left, than was called back to Shoemaker's office.

"Senator Shoemaker will see you now, but make it brief," said the handler.

Canon entered the office to see Shoemaker leaning back in his chair, his feet on the desk, hands behind his head. Canon nodded and took a seat without being asked.

"Steve, so pleased to see you out and about, and not in jail," said Shoemaker with a big smile, the big smirky smile his opponents detested. "We have some early results on public reaction to Trump's pathetic video."

"No kidding?" answered Canon.

"I will participate in the following way. Although I do disapprove of the dreadful actions of the impeachable Mr. Trump, I am prepared to participate so as not to insult our good Christian Democrats. Jews and Christians are united against Trump." Shoemaker took his legs off his desk, leaned forward in his chair and said with deliberate pomposity, "our religious differences are slight," and quickly added, "that's not for publication."

"So?" asked Canon.

"I will, that is as leader of the Senate, select and supply the whip."

"O.K. But we already have one that we borrowed from the Museum of Torture," said Canon with a straight face.

"Frankly, Steve, we do not trust Trump, for good reasons. Having been fired once by him yourself, I'm sure you can understand. Besides, we want to make a clear statement, show bipartisan collegiality in the face of this ghastly man who will not go away. We see this as an opportunity to at last put him behind us."

Canon shrugged. "O.K."

Shoemaker continued. "I have already set up a Forgiveness Committee to decide on what kind of whip and how many strokes we will administer, and breaking from tradition, I have appointed a Republican to chair that committee."

"Who?"

"It is not official yet, but it will be former leader of the Senate, Mitch Deadpan."

"Fine. I'm sure my boss will approve of that. However, we

had thought that Speaker Felosi might want to decide how many strokes of the whip would be applied."

"I will convey that to the committee. I doubt that they would object to that," said Shoemaker with his characteristic smirk.

Canon stood up to go. "Excellent. I'm on my way to meet with Speaker Felosi now."

"Just one thing, Steve."

"Yes, senator?"

"I do not think we can deliver the choice of whip before April 15. It's a very complicated undertaking, as has been pointed out to me from some preliminary information I have received from CIA operatives, who know most about these things."

"That's fine. Unless of course, your chosen whipmaster wants a rehearsal."

Shoemaker did not respond. He was already looking down at his desk and writing.

Canon was shown the door by a subordinate, and handed over to yet another intern, who ushered him through the various passageways to Speaker Felosi's office. There, he was introduced to one of the interns who inhabited the busy area outside the entrance of Felosi's office. The intern knocked lightly on the door.

"Come!" came the voice familiar to all.

"Sit, Mr. Canon. Or stand if you want. I just spoke with Mr, Shoemaker. Assuming a knotted whip, four half-inch leather strands, five feet long, and two foot handle, the number of strokes will be fifteen."

Canon remained standing and said, "OK" and turned to leave.

"Of course," she added, "depending on the skill and strength of the person who does the whipping, the number may have to be adjusted."

"Agreed. We already have a nomination for the whipper."

"Who? A Democrat, I hope?"

"We thought that it would be better to have a Republican, so the Democrats can keep, shall we say, clean hands of the whole affair."

"Who is it, may I ask?"

"Arnold Schwarzenegger." Canon could not hold back a slight grin.

Felosi's face erupted into a great smile, to the extent that it was possible.

"An excellent choice Mr. Canon! I am beginning to think that we have turned the corner on Trump."

Canon was not quite sure what that meant. "Does that affect how many strokes?" He asked.

"What do you think, Steve? It seems about right to me." Felosi grinned yet again.

"Fine with me. I'll have to mention it to the Donald, but I know that he has given iron clad assurances that he will accept anything that either side of the aisle proposes."

"And Schwarzenegger has agreed?"

"Yes. As you saw, he was really upset when he delivered that video on Kristallnacht and the Capitol riot. He is waiting for the Senate Committee on Punishment and Forgiveness to deliver the chosen whip to him so that he can practice the strokes."

"Thank you Steve. And you have my best wishes for a successful event."

Canon held back yet another grin. Trump had done it again. "Don't these guys know what they are agreeing to?" he thought. But then he thought again. He admitted to himself that he had no idea what the outcome of this outrageous spectacle would be. Especially as Trump had been impeached not once, but twice. Was Trump, his former and current boss, angling to get Congress to annul the impeachments? Could President Biden issue a pardon? That not likely either.

Trump's YouTube video went viral of course. Many millions all around the world viewed and commented. Some expressed their disgust. Others asked cynically, what was he up to? Others, and these were the majority, could hardly wait for it to happen. Some posted suggestions as to what kind of whip would be desirable, and others made what they thought were jokes, that Shoemaker should wield the whip and Felosi stand there counting the number of strokes. And maybe President Sage Bush could be the one to tie Trump to the rack or whatever would be used to hold him still, and Hillary Clinton could rip the shirt off his back. And the former First Lady Michele Obama could apply salves to the wound, perhaps the first small sign of salvation, give him his ray of hope.

The most amazing thing of all was the worldwide clamor for tickets to attend the event. Not even Canon had foreseen this outpouring of—no, not sympathy, one hesitates to give it a name—prurient concern, let's say agogness, an appropriately ugly neologism. Both houses of Congress passed resolutions demanding that a special section of the stadium be set aside for members, and both bills had tacked on to them a demand that the Royal Family of the United Kingdom be given pride of place even though Prince Charles had recently called for the United States to pay reparations to the Royal Family for their own insurrections against them in 1776 or thereabouts.

The day came, the stadium packed to capacity. Interviews with those in attendance revealed an amazing fact: there were equal numbers of Trump lovers and Trump haters. At last the great division that had overtaken the people of the United States of America had been healed! And it was the promise of Trump's punishment, his public humiliation and suffering that had brought the people of the USA together. Unity at last! And who should they thank for this amazing accomplishment? After all, President Biden had campaigned on bringing the people together, unity not division. But it could not have happened without someone to punish, and Trump, willingly so it seemed, had offered himself.

And here is where the first step back to divisiveness raised its ugly head. The New York Philharmonic, arranged on a stage in the center of the arena, played the hymn "Forgive Me Oh Lord" as a solemn procession entered the stadium. Cardinal Bell led the way, carrying the whip placed on a large satin cushion in front of him. He was accompanied by Mayor Charlatan, arm in arm with his new wife Bwana Brawley, followed by a score of altar boys singing the hymn. Then followed Trump himself, stripped down to tight fitting jeans and bare torso, the front end of the large wooden cross resting on his shoulder, the rest of the cross supported by the shoulders of significant members of the golfing fraternity, all of whom at some time or other had accused Trump of cheating at golf (perhaps the worst sin of all).

Naturally the social and formerly secular media erupted with outrage that Trump would mock Jesus in this way, and this on God Friday of all days. A flutter of gasps and giggles of surprise rose from the audience. But after the initial reaction, the usual boos, hisses, and streams of abuse echoed around the stadium, followed by the old Trump chant of "four more years" then overcome by the detractors with a boisterous "lock him up."

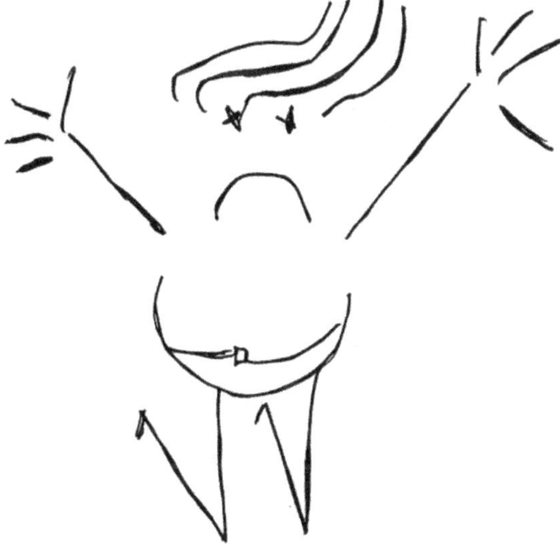

After a circuit of the arena, pausing twelve times at which Trump dropped to his knees and struggled to rise up each time, the procession halted in the center of the arena. Trump climbed the steps of the stage and sat on a huge chair, obviously designed to look very much like the electric chair that was first used in New York. Then a nervous, hurried voice blurted over the very effective PA system. "Quiet Please! Quiet Please!"

It was the voice of NBC's almost equally disgraced Chris Duomo. "People of diversity!" he called, and half the crowd responded with cheers of approval. "I first apologize for having accepted the doubtful honor of compering this awful event. But quite frankly, even though this disgusting personality has been impeached twice over, it is my less than humble opinion that impeaching is not enough, given the terrible damage this idiot has done to our great country and to the world order." Duomo pranced around the stage like a rock star, lapping up the cheers of approval. He even took off his loose jacket and showed off his bare arms and tight muscles.

The crowd responded by chanting: "Whip! Whip! Whip!"

To which Duomo responded, "patience! We will get to that! But first, I want to call upon none other than Samantha Showers, former Ambassador to the United Nations, who will perform the first act of punishment, a time honored practice originating in France after World War two."

The crowd reacted with deep murmurs, an immediate symptom of on-coming boredom. Samantha Showers took the mike from the reluctant Duomo.

"I'll be brief," she said, to which the crowd clapped and cheered. "During the German occupation of France in World War Two, I am ashamed to say that many women gave themselves over to the Nazis. When the war ended these women were appropriately punished for sleeping with the enemy."

More murmurs of boredom. "Lock him up," came the cry rippling around the stadium.

Showers continued. "Their punishment was to have their hair shaved off. And that is what we will now do to the twice impeached president."

Duomo darted across the stage to retrieve the mike, and handed Showers the electric shaver. She immediately strutted across the stage, her long blond hair waving in the breeze. Trump sat, tied into the chair, face expressionless. With big sweeps of the shears she shaved off the dyed, lifeless locks that had been such a point of derision from his detractors.

"Traitor! Traitor!" came the chant from half the crowd.

"Stand tall! Stand tall!" chanted the other half."

Showers stepped away and took a small bow. The job was done, and Trump sat still, looking vacantly ahead.

Suddenly the crowd went quiet. Would he really do it? Let

himself be whipped? Surely that was going through the minds of all the spectators. There sat Trump stripped down to the waist, his distended belly drooping over tight jeans, and his shoulders drooping even more than was his usual poor posture; his bald head seeming too small for such a large body. There was something pathetic about the whole scene. Tears of anticipation formed in the eyes of both his detractors and loyal supporters. But it was time. Trump had promised it and as his supporters knew, he always did what he said he would do. He kept his promises. He was loyal to them as they were loyal to him.

Duomo beckoned to Schwarzenegger, who came forward looking slender in tight jeans and a Never Trump T-shirt that accentuated his well-known muscles. Cardinal Bell presented him with the whip, which he took and held high for the crowd to see, then examined it carefully, running the knotted strands through his very large hands. Duomo ordered Showers to untie Trump's arms and legs and the chair was moved to the center of the New York Philharmonic Orchestra for the conductor's stand as he conducted the next piece which was, again, "Forgive Me Oh Lord."

They set up an A-frame and tied Trump to it as though he were an Australian convict of a couple of centuries ago. It had been Trump's outlandish intention to have himself whipped on the cross that he had born upon entrance to the stadium, but the social media had erupted with such vitriol, damning Trump for portraying himself as the second Christ, that Canon quickly dismembered it and hid the bits under the stage. Schwarzenegger positioned himself before the A-frame and swung his whipping arm a little. He paced out how far away from Trump he should stand in order to lay on an efficient and effective stroke.

The crowd stirred, anxious and impatient. It wanted action. There was jostling in parts of the stadium because some wanted a position where they could see Trump's face, others wanted to see the bloody lines on Trump's back where the lash broke the skin. The crowd became even more restless when it realized that the A-Frame had been set up to face the large box of the official party of esteemed leaders of the USA, indeed, the world. In fact it resembled a crowd that had been imported from England's Royal Ascot. Front and foremost of this elegant gathering sat Prime Ministers Trudeau and Johnson, Prince Charles, and wedged in between them President Biden and their several female attendants, including Vice President Kamala Harris, though she had initially refused to attend because, she said, it reminded her of the savagery that her ancestors suffered at the hands of Britain's imperial rule. No representatives of Islamic countries attended, seeing nothing special in the event, all expressing satisfaction that the West had at last followed the example of the Middle East. Behind these elegantly dressed important people were various members of the British parliament, shabbily dressed, as were those from the lower house of the Congress, with the exception of Speaker Felosi who outshone them all in her pink satin and lace dress with a fancy collar reminiscent of Queen Elizabeth I. Behind them all were the US senators, a mixed bunch if ever there was one, led of course by Shoemaker in his twenty year old suit. Many of this crowd sat low in their eats, frequently sneaking out to the concession stands. It was as though they were embarrassed to be there, or thought that maybe they shouldn't be there but couldn't resist going, didn't want to miss the spectacle.

The security guards dotted all around the arena were getting a little nervous. They sensed the growing restlessness of the crowd. They worried that a far right or left supremacist might do something violent. To make things worse, there was a short delay when Duomo resisted giving up the microphone so it could be attached to the A-Frame near Trump's mouth in order to catch his cries and howls of pain. In place of his microphone, Duomo now held a stack of very large poster-size cards. Stepping forward, he held the first card above his head and pranced around the stage as though announcing the round number of a boxing match. It was the number "one."

The crowd erupted in an applause that quickly died down. Schwarzenegger raised his arm and brought down the whip with an audible "swish." Trump's body stiffened, and he yelled out in pain, the words just discernible, "Forgive me! I am so sorry! Oh Please!" The crowd erupted into cheers and applause. Many called out: "Give it to him Arnold! Give it to him!" These were probably mostly Trump's detractors. Others cried (actually cried): "We love you! Love you!"

Schwarzenegger did a round of the stage, showing the whip and brandishing it a little. Duomo raised the next card. Trump called out, More! Give me more! All that I deserve!"

But then an ominous sign emerged on the arena. An ambulance quietly rolled out and did a slow lap then parked next to the stage. A medic emerged dressed in full biosecurity regalia. The crowd gasped. The figure looked like an alien from somewhere. And suddenly a thin voice wafted from one of the children present, "ET go home!" The crowd broke into laughter as the chant gradually took hold: "Trump go home! Trump go home!"

Trump strained at his bonds and waggled his head, trying to get Duomo's attention. Samantha Showers saw it and tugged at Duomo's arm.

"The mike, the mike! Give the medic the mike!" called Trump. The medic stepped up on to the stage and removed his mask and helmet. It was Doctor Ben Parson. Duomo held the microphone to Parson's face.

"I am here to administer any necessary emergency assistance to the President, I mean former President, I mean Mr. Trump. After each stroke of the lash I will check his heart and, if the skin is broken, at his request and against my advice, pour salt on the wounds." A buzz of excitement filled the arena and Parson replaced his helmet. Showers pulled the microphone from Duomo and placed it back on the A-frame. Parson placed his stethoscope on Trump's chest and after a moment nodded to Schwarzenegger.

Schwarzenegger took his place and lashed out, this time with what was clearly a harsh, stinging stroke that broke the skin of Trump's back in several places. Blood ran down his back and on to his jeans. Those able to see his front saw trickles of blood find their way over his bulging stomach. Parson stepped forward, checked his heart and sprinkled salt on the open wounds.

"I am so, so sorry! I am so, so sorry!" cried Trump, the audience very used to his habit of repeating everything he said several times over, all throughout his presidency, especially at his rallies. But this was not a rally.

Or was it?

It seemed not, especially as people from both opposing factions made up the crowd. Yet it was surely concerning to the political pundits in attendance (they were watching on television in the bars and rooms that surrounded the stadium with no direct view of the arena, relegated there by Trump who said that it was all they deserved), that the crowd was really into it. They seemed to "get it." And Trump was truly "getting it." Getting what he deserved and, paradoxically, "loving it." The talk show creatures would later call this "narcissistic masochism," in a feeble attempt to deny the truth of his suffering. Was he not sincerely asking for forgiveness? Was he not sincerely sorry for all that he had done? If this could not convince the onlookers who had unwittingly become part of the punishment, that Trump was truly sorry for his sins and crimes and the hurt he inflicted on friends and foes alike, what would?

Must we continue through all fifteen of the strokes? In fact, once four strokes had been administered, responded to by the pleas for forgiveness and cries of pain exuding from Mr. Trump, the crowd became gradually silent. One could put this down to sheer boredom, as happens in a cheap movie that relies only on violence to entertain. Or a growing callousness of the onlookers, unmoved by the pain inflicted, an adaptation to the evil that confronted them. Surely intentionally inflicting such pain on any individual guilty or innocent, and participating in the enjoyment (is that the right word?) or satisfaction of inflicting the punishment, is surely an evil in itself. Even if the one punished clearly deserves it? One wonders whether many in the crowd were asking themselves the same questions. The strange thing was that after the first four or five strokes, the crowd started to dwindle. And by the time the fifteenth stroke was applied, close to half the stadium was emptied. The block reserved for the esteemed persons remained a block. They would see it through to the end.

As the number of strokes neared fifteen, and the cries from Trump became more and more feeble, the crowd came close to silent. Trump's supporters, of course, were mesmerized by his devotion, and what they took to be his forthright honesty. Of course, quite a few of them thought he had done nothing that required forgiveness, and many thought that his positive achievements counterbalanced his faults. The detractors were, however, the most perplexed. They had indulged themselves in a kind of distasteful revelry, seduced as they were by the Trump public and open plea for forgiveness, and, they had to admit, the violent way in which he suffered and pleaded for forgiveness. Surely his plea for forgiveness, as sincere as it might be, was nevertheless something that they could not forgive? Were the Never-Trumpers also Never-Forgivers? For many, they came to realized that they were locked into a kind of circular logic that they vaguely sensed had become a compulsive ritual. And so they had become silent, or they left.

It would be more accurate to define this incredible display of openness on Trump's part and his begging for forgiveness as something simpler. He was, after all, a simple man. Was that not the main characteristic that his supporters loved? This contrasted with his detractors taking his simplicity as idiocy. And the simple answer to the very difficult moral questions thrown up by his amazing foray into punishment, its deserts and forgiveness, is that this was simply another way for Trump to overcome his detractors. Impeached or not, he would win in the end, no matter the personal costs. Trump did not like losers, but loved winners. He could not be a loser. This was his last ditch effort to erase that loss. He would push his opponents further into the moral confusion that had become, in the 21st century, the obvious lead weight that drove both their rhetoric and legislative agendas. Surely the media had understood that Trump would never go away, impeached or not. Indeed, it was good for them if he remained actively in the limelight. This spectacle showed them that he did not need to be elected to any office to win over the public. The question is, having won them over, what next? Or is winning simply satisfying for its own sake?

The Great Men of history, all of whom liked winning and despised losing, in different ways (mostly by risking their lives on behalf of their followers) posed these moral questions to their populace, supporters or detractors. In most cases, these moral problems were eventually solved by getting rid of the Great Man, whether by killing him (Julius Caesar) or by exile (Napoleon) so that the puzzling moralities inextricably mixed with politics as we have seen with Trump, can be glossed over, with the pretense of their solution. It is not until another "Great Man" arises that humankind will be confronted with these impossible moral logics. Take note, though, and this is advice for Mr. Trump. The exploits of all such Great Men are recounted over and over again in histories, plays and movies. Such an attractive thought for one who seeks to join the immortals! However, it is also very clear that this fact of never forgetting the Great Man lies at the heart of never forgiving. No matter to what lengths Trump goes to be forgiven for his sins, they will never be forgotten. The only sure way to forgive is to forget.

Moral: Accepting punishment, deserved or undeserved,
never guarantees forgiveness.

22. Greatness

Of winners and losers.

It is difficult to avoid the impression that there is something terribly wrong with the history of western civilization when the exploits and achievements of its greatest men are constantly recounted. These begin with Alexander the Great, responsible for at least 3.5 million deaths of soldiers and civilians (a rough guess) resulting from his constant wars and pillage; Julius Caesar, so forgiving, but responsible for around 3.5 million deaths (another rough guess) resulting from his battles, not to mention cutting off the hands of all men and boys in a village that refused to acknowledge his supremacy; Napoleon Bonaparte, around 3.5 million including 1 million French civilians, plus the deaths of his enemies in battle and massacre of civilians.

The numbers, of course, do not carry much weight in and of themselves. We are numbed by their abstraction. Besides, they have been disputed many times over by various historians and other experts. But what is not disputed is that the Great Men, all to a man, obviously loved war. They reported, or more accurately bragged, of their exploits, the battles they won, the territories they acquired, and especially Napoleon who worshipped both Caesar and Alexander. They publicized and basked in the glory of winning. One can only assume that Napoleon actually believed the numbers Caesar reported (many unbelievable), though, one must also acknowledge that Napoleon, like Caesar, was a master of propaganda and communications. He established his own magazine, or one might say today a Twitter account, and relentlessly pounded his adoring French citizens with a recounting of his amazing exploits, full of incredible numbers of the vanquished, and the heroic exploits fashioned and made possible by him, the Great Leader. This was a man who was not even French (a kind of Sardinian Corsican), who had sided with the revolutionary movements against royalty that led to the French

Revolution of 1789 and eventually the beheading of King Louis XVI in 1793. Yet in the aftermath of the bloody revolution, in 1795 a National Convention was held in which a five member directorate was appointed by parliament to govern France. It had as its direct governing tool, an effective army to suppress any dissent from those (Jacobins and Royalists) who objected to the Directorate. The army was commanded by General Napoleon Bonaparte, who ruthlessly put down any insurrections or even public demonstrations of dissent.

In 1799, amidst financial crises and other objections to the government of the Directorate, Bonaparte staged a *coup d'état*, appointed himself "first consul," mimicking the first Emperor of Rome, Augustus, who insisted on being called first citizen, "Princeps" rather than "Emperor." On the gold coin Napoleon had struck to commemorate this big event, his depiction as "first consul" looks very much like that of Julius Caesar on his various coins. It wasn't long, though, before Bonaparte called himself Emperor, established a dynasty and obsessed with producing progeny so that the accession to the throne of France would be inherited by his offspring.

And for a while it worked. But as is well known, after his having fought many battles, broken many peace treaties, conquered almost all of Europe, he did what all Great Men are supposed not to do. He lost a decisive battle, the Battle of Leipzig that alone cost some 90,000 casualties. He was thus eventually deposed from the throne by the *Sénat conservateur*, and as part of the peace Treaty of Fontainebleau between France and the Allies (the rest of Europe fighting against Napoleon), exiled to the Isle of Elba.

The story could end there, but we all know, it did not. Yet we should pause for a moment and reflect on what made this man so great. His failures up to this point were few, if we think of success and failure as being winning or losing battles. But historians have nevertheless sung praises to him for his great accomplishments in other fields of governing: he completely reorganized the decrepit bureaucracies that governed France, invented an acclaimed legal code that remains dominant to this day, introduced a centralized system of education for all citizens, a model that influenced much of Europe, enhanced and supported the sciences and the arts, set the bases for introduction of the metric system throughout Europe, and much more.

All these accomplishments must be measured against the violence and destruction he reaped, driven by his obvious love of war. Would not many of these accomplishments of science, education and law have occurred without his interventions? Were so many wars and killings really necessary to introduce a new education system throughout Europe, for example? This is, of course, a silly "what if" notion. But surely humans, civilized humans, are capable of improvement in their ways of doing things (education, law, governance) without such carnage? Is carnage a necessary requirement for progress?

Putting silly questions aside, what we are concerned with in this small essay is to answer the more serious and human question: did Napoleon get (deserve) what was coming to him? His love of war killed and maimed countless people. Should he not pay a price for this? Any ordinary person who did one tiny inkling of what he did, would surely be punished for it.

No doubt you are already answering my question. He met his Waterloo.

It is by their actions that individuals define what punishment they deserve, or will be visited upon them. The means of this carriage of punishment is expressed in the common observation, "he brought it on himself." Does this apply to Napoleon, the Great Man of history?

Keeping in mind his love of war and conquest (of quite a few women as well), let us look at how he fared after failure. One of the perplexing and really annoying things about Great Men who reap terrible devastation is that, even when, on the rare occasions they lose a battle (easily the worst disaster they can imagine), their followers nevertheless rally around, and cling to them, through much of this death and destruction. Their loyalty is buttressed by certain rules of war that help a great man overcome his losses in battle. Those of the military who see the loss coming, and desert, are often punished severely, often by execution. They are cowards. Those remaining loyal are heroes. This rule serves well to deflect responsibility for any defeat away from the Great Leader, on to the pathetic, cowardly men under his command. The great general is depicted as having empathy for his troops, he eats and sleeps in the same quarters as do they (Julius Caesar, or so he wrote, supposedly also Alexander the Great, probably not Hitler though he was once a common soldier). Churchill, another great man was also a great lover of war and glory. He lived it as an officer in the Boer war and World War I and wrote about it as a war correspondent. He also worshiped Napoleon.

But back to Napoleon. Although he was forced to abdicate, and as his punishment he was sent to the Isle of Elba where, incredibly, he was given sovereignty over the island of 12,000 people and allowed to retain the title of Emperor. Thereupon he supposedly started a revision of its governmental structure, introduced modern education and health systems, and much more. It is hard to see this exile as anything other than a cynical joke. Especially, as the promised income was not forthcoming, and it was the British of the allies who were administering his exile. So it was that on 26 February 1815 with 700 men, Napoleon escaped in the brig of a ship disguised as British, while his British overseer was away in Italy visiting his doctor. (Though there may have been a woman involved). Thenceforth, with his small band he landed at Golfe-Juan and made his way north to Paris. Contrary to the expectations of the powers that controlled France from Paris, and totally unforeseen by the allies, most or many of the troops of the standing French army went over to Napoleon, so that by the time Napoleon arrived in Paris, he was once again Emperor and commander of a large, though eventually not large enough, army. King Louis XVIII fled to Belgium. On 13 March the Congress of Vienna declared Napoleon an outlaw and the allies, Great Britain, Russia, Austria, and Prussia pledged to raise 100,000 men to oppose him. Through what might have been, in retrospect, an unpopular move, Napoleon introduced conscription and managed to expand his army to 200,000 men.

The die was cast. Napoleon, as usual, decided to go on the

offensive, and having studied carefully the locations of the allied forces, chose a strategy that had worked well for him in the past: divide and conquer. He planned to make sure the two enemy forces that sat in quite different locations were kept apart. He would keep them divided, attack and destroy the British force commanded by the Duke of Wellington, and then turn his army against the Austrian force commanded by Prince Blücher. These two battles came to be known as the Battle of Waterloo that began on 18 June 1815. Incredibly, Wellington had ignored the warnings of his spies that Napoleon was approaching. He even attended a ball the night before the battle, a great social event attended by all his top generals and senior officers. Such was the attitude of the allies who simply could not believe that Napoleon was any immediate threat. Most had also believed that the French standing army would not go over to him.

Much has been written about these events, Wellington's attendance and approval of the ball seen as some kind of dereliction of duty. Wellington did, however, since all his top officers were in attendance at the ball, give instructions and orders to his officers while at the ball, so that eventually the army was ready to respond to what would be a tough onslaught by Napoleon's forces. Wellington had also, days before the ball, reconnoitered the expected battlefield, so knew the terrain and the advantages and disadvantages it would present for his army.

How battles proceed, the thrusts and counter-thrusts, the movement of troops, the delivery or confused delivery of orders and commands, the importance of the terrain at particular points of battle, and probably the most important of all, the morale of the troops, are of great fascination to students of warfare and those whose job it is to do battle. And in this case, certainly in the early stages, Wellington's apparent inadequate preparation for the battle, augured well for yet another amazing victory by the little genius Napoleon. After all, Wellington when asked what he thought of Napoleon, replied that Napoleon's presence on the battlefield was equivalent to 40,000 men.

In any case, we do not need to concern ourselves with the intricacies of battles, the outcomes of which, in most if not all cases, are largely determined by unforeseen events, including the weather, that is, luck. By far the most important event is the outcome, because we know that the winner is always a hero of great character, and the loser is the one now deserving of punishment. In sum, Napoleon was vanquished. Wellington was the heroic victor, Napoleon the loser. He met his Waterloo.

But of course, losing is not really a punishment in itself, is it? For Napoleon it almost was because he was not used to losing, though he had lost big the first time round, resulting in his exile to Elba. This time, the powers of Paris and the allies were bent on a more serious punishment. And certainly, given the deaths caused by Napoleon's provoking the Battle of Waterloo he deserved considerable punishment, don't you think? Although battle statistics are notoriously unreliable, the rough numbers are 41,000 casualties on Napoleon's side (no figure on how many of these were deaths), and 24,000 (4,700 killed) of the allies.

Sit back and ask yourself. What punishment do you think Napoleon deserved for this dreadful loss? How does one match the destruction and damage of the war to the punishment of one man, the instigator of the war? Is the humiliation of the loss a sufficient punishment?

This time, the allies took no chances. The punishment would be exile to the island of St. Helena, way too far from any large land mass, no people for Napoleon to govern. He was essentially a captive kept in a reasonably equipped house, but far from the palatial trappings he had during his stay at Elba. Though, given the death and destruction of the Battle of Waterloo, one could surely think of apt punishments that would match at least a little of the violence and carnage that resulted from Napoleon's battles and his obvious thirst for war.

Execution, perhaps? He showed no hesitation in executing Jacobins and others he deemed were a threat to his rise and reign. Not to mention the carnage, destruction, and plunder— which he took to a whole new level, just visit the Louvre to see a fraction of the spoils. The Prussians pressed Wellington to have Napoleon executed. Given the dreadful violence, maiming of his soldiers, blood and body parts strewn over a huge area, bodies piled on top of each other. Surely an execution would at least play a small part in matching Napoleon's crimes? But Wellington refused, telling the Prussians that, if they wanted Napoleon executed, let them do it. He would not, even though he had Napoleon in custody. And what of Napoleon's collaborators? Should they not also bear some of the blame for his love of war? Perhaps the practice in Roman times, to sell off the losers of a war or battle, into slavery? Especially as Bonaparte reintroduced slavery into French colonies.

One could go on. But it rapidly becomes clear that matching a punishment to crimes of such magnitude is an impossibility. Because Napoleon "met his Waterloo" he got what he deserved, that is, he lost. And this, perhaps was the worst punishment of all, given how much he loved war and winning. Yet he was surely rewarded by historians of the future (his future that is). There are monuments throughout France and elsewhere to his fame and glory, to his non-military achievements (the Napoleonic legal code, education and agricultural reform etc.). Do all such achievements neutralize the terrible massacres of millions of lives caused by his wars?

His actual punishment, exile to British-held St. Helena on October 1815, was still a far more mild non-capital punishment than what he might have received if sent to one of the many horrible prisons of the period (they are not much better today). There he remained, eventually dying of a stomach ailment, probably cancer, on May 5, 1821. He had expressed his wish to have his remains buried "on the banks of the Seine, among the French people I have loved so much." This was denied to him. Excepting that, in 1840 his remains were removed to a crypt at Les Invalides in Paris, in the dead company of other French military leaders.

And so in the end, Napoleon won perhaps the greatest battle of all, the battle of posterity. He left huge accomplishments behind him that outstripped the destruction of his wars, and for this we have to blame all subsequent historians, even those critical of his reign and exploits, for having recognized them as such. He was clearly not punished enough in posterity to make up for the "rewards" (benefits to civilization) of his non-military accomplishments.

Should the monuments that neutralize his bloodthirsty love of war be torn down? Should his punishment be ignominy, relegated to the dustbin of history? We are often told that these monuments are also a reminder of what happened in the past. That we should never forget them or else we may repeat them. Is this but a fanciful wish that humanity were something else? We should not forget that it was the "people" after all who made Napoleon possible. As far as punishment is concerned, maybe they also got what they deserved.

In sum. Winners are punished by losing, for which they are forgiven. Losers are killed or enslaved, and rarely forgiven.

Moral: Winning in war is the moral justification for punishing the losers.

23. A Notice of Infraction

The punishments of everyday life.

Robert Smith, better known as "Smithy" to his mates (few of them left) lived quietly in his small unit on Walker street in a small seaside village called Anglesea. Not the one in England, the one in Victoria, Australia. He was a widower of twenty years and counting, and had come to enjoy in a quiet way his solitary life, his two bedroom apartment with small kitchen and open living room spacious for his meager needs. His period hi-fi set was the largest piece of furniture in the apartment, which he enjoyed daily listening to tapes and old LP records of his favorite musical shows, especially those of Rogers and Hammerstein. Even better, he had hooked up his vintage color TV to the hi-fi set so he could watch his videos of the musicals. He rarely watched ordinary TV, though, because he found most of it, especially the news, to be from another world, one he had no knowledge of, nor interest in. Inside his unit he had constructed his own world where everything was predictable, and every day would be like every other day. A perfect environment for an admittedly old man, though he would be offended if someone referred to him as such.

His daily routine consisted of waking at 8 am. on the dot, no alarm necessary. To the bathroom for ablutions in the following strict order: toilet (standing not sitting), shave with electric shaver (rotary only), then shower, no shampoo (waste of money). Drying quickly in front of the space heater that he had connected to a timer (a tinkerer, he was always handy with mechanical things, having once been a mechanic), powder all bodily crevices, (he did not believe in deodorant), check for ear wax with a match stick (forbidden by doctors), combing hair of which he still had a reasonable amount for a man of ninety, applying a little hair oil. Switch on the electric jug, return to the bedroom to dress, then to the kitchen where the jug has finished boiling. Pour a little hot water into the little brown two-cup teapot, rinse and tip out, then add a spoonful of tea, fill pot to the top, replace the lid, cover with the tea cozy (rather stained after years of use). Pour a little milk into the waiting teacup, then pour the tea through a tea strainer. Sip the tea and take his daily aspirin, then pour hot water into the bowl into which the night before he had tipped half a cup of Uncle Toby's oats. Stir then sprinkle a little salt and sugar, and add a little milk.

By the time he finished his oats and drank his tea and washed the breakfast bowl it was 9.30 am. Back to the bedroom for his wallet that he kept beside his bed, then his hat hanging up behind the bedroom door. Time to walk to the local store to get the daily paper. Step out of his apartment, lock both the regular door and the screen door, place the keys under the third rock from the edge in the cactus rockery, walk out to the street, check the mail box for junk mail, then on to the shops, cross Walker street at the driveway to avoid stepping off the curb, walk on the shops side of Walker street on the grassy strip, to the corner at Camp road, then down the hill keeping to the left of the footpath, past the Post Office (a quick wave to the post lady), past the Chemist, to the News Agent for the paper. Then a careful retracing of his steps back to Walker Street and his welcoming home. All the while he walked, back straight (required constant effort) head up, and hat pulled well down over his forehead. Should anyone he knew say hello, he would tip his hat and say g'day, but never stop. There was a time when he would stop and chat, which was when he played bowls with the local club for several years. But he had quit a few years ago when he was dropped from one of the pennant teams because, they said, he was too old. This daily routine Smithy repeated every day except Sundays when there was no paper. His paper, *The Geelong Advertiser,* was not printed on Sundays. There were Sunday papers, *The Age* and *The Australian,* neither paper did he find at all relevant to his life. In truth, the only pages of the Addy he read were the births and deaths, mainly the deaths.

On this particular day, January 15 2015, Smithy was returning from the News Agent and had just turned the corner where the mobile library often set up shop, when a group of three teen-age boys, late teens he guessed, jostled past him, full of laughter and banter, each carrying armfuls of soda and fast food. One had taken a red shopping basket from the local IGA supermarket full of chips and soda. For some reason, still inexplicable to Smithy, he found himself staring at the young lout with the basket, certainly not minding his own business as he always did. The lout grinned at him, but really, took little notice of his glare, and a glare it was. The young bugger was blatantly stealing the basket. And before he knew it, he heard himself saying, "I hope you are going to return that basket."

The three boys laughed and one of them said, "what's it to you, you old fart!"

Smithy was shaken to the core. His day had been disturbed as though lightening had struck the tree next to him. He looked the other way, quickly turned the corner and hurried as fast as he could walk back to his haven on Walker Street.

The boys kept walking as though little had happened. The boy with the basket had, in fact, intended to return the basket after they had carried their groceries to their house. They had just borrowed it without asking for permission. In any case, the brief encounter with Smithy was enough to invoke the obstreperous inclinations of teenagers, to do the very thing that Smithy had accused them of. Once at home, they had no use for the basket, and the boy who took it mentioned that he might get around some day to returning it.

This encounter weighed heavily on Smithy. It had disturbed the order of his day and, after a couple of days brooding, he decided to phone the supermarket and report the incident. The manager of the supermarket was very courteous and thanked him several times for reporting the theft. Smithy gave a reasonable descrip-ttion of the three boys, and the one who carried off the basket. The manager said he thought he knew who they were and would have his security people look into it.

As luck would have it, the boys did get around to returning the basket, though no one at the supermarket noticed, and in fact there were no "security people" employed at the super market. It was too small a market to employ separate security. So there the matter lay, the theft eradicated by time and circumstance.

The next day was the day on which every month, Smithy drove into Geelong to do his grocery shopping. He had done this for years because he thought that the prices were lower in Geelong. This presumption was doubtful, given that he had to pay top dollar for the petrol that ran his 1988 BMW. In any case, he drove, being careful to obey all speed limit signs, to the supermarket some twenty six kilometers from Anglesea. There he stocked up on all his groceries for the month, including litres of milk that he would keep in his freezer and use as needed. And lots more. He had a strict routine of supermarket shopping. It would take many pages to outline the routines. Suffice it to say that this was a typical monthly supermarket day in which nothing out of the ordinary happened. He arrived home after a regular uneventful drive to Anglesea, unloaded his car, all the chilled or frozen things first, placed in their appropriate places in his refrigerator. Satisfied, he made a cup of tea and sat down at his kitchen table and played his usual game of poker (playing both sides) in which of course one of him had to win!

Two weeks went by until the order of his day was once more disturbed by an unexpected and shocking event. He collected his mail and found a letter from the Victoria Police. What on earth could it be? And when he opened the machine-folded and printed letter, he gasped in horror. It was an infringement notice for driving four km. per hour over the speed limit of seventy, the exact location listed in the machine printed notice, Princes Highway in Waurn Ponds, just after the turn-off to Epworth Hospital. But there was more. Apart from the fine of $207, there was also a requirement that he report to VicRoads and do a driving test. The notice sternly informed him that this contravention had automatically tripped a requirement that drivers over the age of ninety who broke any traffic law, be required to undergo medical and driver examination to determine whether it was safe for them to drive. His license had therefore been suspended until he fulfilled the requirements.

This was too much for Smithy. How could this be resolved?

How could he get to VicRoads without a car? He became dizzy and plonked down in his armchair. What are these people doing to him, spying on him with cameras? What right do they have? It seemed like every right. And how could he fight this false charge? And false it was. He had a very carefully worked out routine for driving into Geelong to the supermarket. He drove very carefully, kept to the speed limit exactly, never deviated.

The next day he phoned up the VicRoads who were very nice to him, once he managed to talk to someone. They told him to read the back of the notice where it said how to appeal the fine. He had done that. It looked impossible. And besides, it still meant that he could not drive his car anywhere until the appeal was processed. And what chance was there of winning? Zero.

*

There were two weeks until his next trip to Geelong was due. He then took what for him was a momentous decision. He would pay the fine and drive in there anyway and be damned about the license. So he paid the fine online following exactly the directions printed on the infringement notice. He found this all very unsettling. He was a dutiful law abiding citizen. He had never knowingly broken any law or even rule for that matter. He absolutely never, ever walked on the grass even when there was no sign that he should not.

As the day for his drive to Geelong drew nearer, he became extremely nervous. His hand shook when he poured his tea in the mornings. He even forgot to pour the milk into the cup first, before pouring the tea. Nevertheless he was so upset with the government for torturing him in this way that he held fast, though he did stop taking his daily aspirin, thinking that maybe it was the aspirin that was making him jittery. Of course, this was simply silly. He had taken aspirin daily for twenty years or more, ever since they had said it thinned your blood and prevented heart attacks.

The trouble was, though, that when he stopped taking the aspirin he began to notice that his short term memory was not quite so good. It had never been too good for many years, but now he seemed to be forgetting silly little things, like not putting the milk in his tea, or putting it in again forgetting that he had already done it. So a few days before the big trip, he started taking the aspirin again and by the time the day of his trip arrived, he had more or less calmed down.

He was about to step out of his apartment and into his car when the phone rang, a most infrequent event in itself, as he had only one relative, a son who lived in New York, and rarely called. He almost did not answer it, but finally turned back and took the call. And very lucky that he did. It was a call from VicRoads saying that there had been a mistake and that his license had not been suspended and that he did not need to submit to another driving test, though the nice lady added that for a person his age it was strongly recommended that he visit his GP and get tested. She also thanked him for his payment of the fine, and no, it was not a mistake. Smithy said no word at all, until the lady had finished talking. He then said "thank you" and banged down the receiver. He was very angry, even red in the face. He went out to his car slamming the door behind him.

Strangely, though perhaps not that strange, sitting in his car in the garage, all silent, no light on, he felt secure and cared for. This old car had done sterling service. It was like an old friend.. He even talked to it when he was stressed out over something. He started the car, then switched it off, and sat silently, thinking some more. "That's the way old girl," he muttered to his car. That's the way." He took out his handkerchief and wiped a little dust from the dashboard. Then he backed the car out. He was a man of resolve. The cameras had picked on him. He would take steps to even up the score.

So far, you could be forgiven for assuming that Smithy was a silly old man whose life was stuck somewhere in the 1970s. But that would be a mistake. He had always been a tinkerer of mechanical things. When radios first appeared, he tinkered with those and could fix any radio there was. The same with clocks, the same with cameras, still and movie. Anything that was mechanical. So it was a logical step when he bought a computer as soon as they appeared on the market, and upgraded his computers frequently to keep up with the amazingly rapid development. And the appearance of the Internet also piqued his natural curiosity.

He started watching YouTube videos that taught how to repair computers, how to manipulate and exploit the huge potential of the Internet. He became something of an expert, and no one knew it.

As he backed the car out of the garage, still deep in thought, he backed into the fence that separated his drive from the next door neighbor. He got out to look at it, and was pleased to see that the damage was slight, although the fence had been pushed over a little. A voice called out from his neighbor on the other side of the fence. "That was close, mate! You should get a rear camera for that old jalopy of yours!"

Smithy occasionally chatted with his neighbor, though he truly found any such conversations stressful. He was courteous, but really much preferred his own company. "Maybe you're right," he answered. And as he drove out the driveway, he headed straight for the auto store and bought a rear view camera, which he would install himself. And on his way into Geelong and back, he carefully noted where all the speed and red light cameras were. There were so many! How could you avoid becoming one of their digital victims? And with some, admittedly twisted satisfaction, he made a point of driving everywhere at exactly the speed limit indicated, and just to make sure, he drove at five Ks below that limit. After all, the rules stated that these were speed limits, so you could drive at any speed under the limit specified, was that not correct?

But now, his compulsive nature was slowly taking a new turn, or perhaps one should call it adaptation. The cameras fascinated him. He watched videos on the internet that explained how they were controlled. He joined so-called "dark web" groups to discover how to hack into wireless devices. It turned out to be not so difficult. All one needed were the right devices and a little tweaking of them if one knew how to do it. And probably the most sure thing he learned from these dark web sources was that the majority of installations of camera and other surveillance devices, some security systems and the like, were relatively easy to hack, that those manning them tended to not really believe that someone wanted to hack into their systems. The passwords were therefore easy to crack, if you had the persistence and the right tools and a little information about the target.

Some of Smithy's routines had to give a little. His afternoon poker games stopped. He no longer walked down to the news agent. He stopped reading the daily paper. Instead, he spent all his time huddled in a corner of his garage, a bright light shining over his shoulder, tinkering away, finding his way through the labyrinths of the Internet, until after many weeks, perhaps several months, he sat back with a sigh of great satisfaction. He had completed his task. It was now time to test it.

*

In Smithy's opinion the trouble with speed cameras was that they only caught speeding infractions. But few such catches were related to any serious car accidents. Red light cameras were a little better, but the trouble with them was that they too often snared drivers who were caught half way through an orange light. The nearly innocent were therefore treated the same as the clearly guilty. That contravened Smithy's refined sense of justice. There was not a lot he could do about that, but there was plenty he could do now that he could hack into the speed cameras. It was, however, going to take up a great deal of his time. He was sorely tempted to simply sit at his computer in the garage and randomly pick innocent victims by sending the image of their license plate along with a speed that he made up, to the Victoria Police computer that received all the wireless infractions. But of course, he did not yield to such a temptation. He was a rules man, through and through. No, he would drive slowly to Geelong and all about Geelong and watch for what he considered louts driving dangerously. And there were always plenty of them. He was of the opinion that speeding was not necessarily in itself dangerous.

So, he would station himself in the vicinity of a camera, hack into its operation, wait for a dangerous driver, then transmit the license plate number and an outrageous speed to the Victoria Police. That would ensure that the offender received a truly heavy fine. Over the weeks and months that followed he developed an extensive list of types of dangerous driving and the appropriate illegal speeds he would submit. And then he had an even better idea. Why limit himself to speeding infractions?

Smithy guessed that he had probably made an error or two in his little game with Victoria Police. He had awaited with eager anticipation for a knock on his door, or more likely an infraction notice in the mail, to appear at the police station to answer for all the speeding reports he was sending to them via their cameras. Several months went by, and nothing happened. He had foolishly assumed that the computerized bureaucracy that received the speeding data and spewed out the infraction notices would sooner or later send someone an error message. Nothing of the sort happened. In fact, one had to assume that all the infraction notices that Smithy had caused to be sent out must have been either not paid by the offenders, or more likely paid without any appeal, eager as such offenders would be to get rid of the threats delivered by those infraction notices. So they would, in effect, plead "guilty" even though they were innocent of the specific infraction listed in the notice.

And so Smithy returned to his daily routine, all except his poker games in the afternoon. Instead he would park himself anywhere near a camera and send infraction notices to all kinds of drivers whose behavior he disapproved. All he needed to do that was the license plate number. So, he enjoyed sending notices to those who parked in no parking zones, those who parked in spots reserved for disabled, if in his opinion the driver was not disabled. Then he spread his reach to those individuals who behaved rudely to him anywhere, in the supermarket, or even in the street. He would follow them to their cars, note the license number, and shazam! Case closed!

Unfortunately, after some months, Smithy began to realize that he was not getting as much fun or satisfaction out of these mischievous punishments that he was delivering to unsuspecting persons. In fact, it was not long until he started playing his poker games in the afternoon, just could not be bothered getting into the car and driving somewhere where there was a camera. There was no fun in it any more. Why was this? He looked back to the days of labor he put into developing his hacking skills, what joy it was the first time he sent a fake infraction notice! But then it slowly sank into him that he was not enjoying his delivery of punishments by notice because there had been no response from the Victoria Police bureaucracy at all! He then realized that the true satisfaction of punishment was to see the offender actually punished. In this technological infraction bureaucracy the punishment remained hidden. There was nothing to see. The notice arrived in the mail. The recipients swore and complained to themselves. But then paid the fine. He now saw that he had unwittingly contributed to this enormous hidden machine of punishment that wasn't. He had become a cog in the machine of big brother.

Moral: Punishment hidden is punishment denied.

24. Felony Media

A new off-the-wall TV series breaks all records.

In Safar, 1442 A.H. a ground-breaking late night talk show was aired on Ozone TV, the new network experts predict will overtake the slowly dying cable and satellite networks of the world. The new technology is far superior to satellite because it can bounce signals back to earth by navigating them via the ozone layer around the earth so that they can be retrieved from any place in real time, rather like the monkey king who hitched a ride on earth's clouds. Even more important, the Ozone layer is there to stay, not like satellites that eventually fall to earth and these days can be shot down at any time. Our TV-Internet combination offers customers a simple, basic service, with just the one channel, the Felony Channel, the most popular channel in all TV ever, and the fastest Internet service. The Internet service comes free with a subscription to the Felony Channel. This makes it far cheaper than any of the competition. It also makes the channel accessible and affordable to the poorest customers anywhere around the world.

By far the most popular show is the Tommie Felon show that premiered in Safar, 1442 A.H. (I repeat myself, a habit of all TV personalities whether in front or behind the scenes). The first episode turned out to be so popular, its viewing surpassed many of the top You Tube videos. When one considers that the Tommie Felon show runs for approximately 20 minutes, including commercials, it makes You Tube, and other competitors look pretty limited. The naysayers had warned us that our viewers would not have the attention span to stay with a twenty-minute show. How wrong they were!

We are currently in negotiations with UAE TV to release the franchise to them with the hope that they will begin broadcasting the show sometime in the autumn of 1448 A.H. As part of our promotional literature for distributing the franchise of the show, we have prepared this brief account of the first record-breaking show and a little background on its basic premise. The season premiere was such an important event that we reproduce here a small piece of the transcript, slightly revised and edited.

The set for this show is modelled on the prison cells of the notorious Kilmainham Gaol in Dublin, Ireland, a classic 19th century multi-level prison, each level lined with bars of cells and railings, iron steps running up and down in the center of the prison, and catwalks connecting each side, seemingly suspended in space. The show opens with the camera panning first with a wide angle to take in the expanse of the prison, then takes us on a quick tour of the cells while the credits appear, finally entering the cell where the moderator sits dressed in a stylized prison guard uniform, her figure accentuated just a little too much, although these days it's difficult to reach any higher level of excess. Let us just say that her appearance is one of voluptuousness, admittedly an ugly word, if it is a word, but seems to us to be quite appropriate. No doubt the producers and directors of the show spent a lot of time coming up with the costume, especially the bright green of the uniform contrasting with the dull surroundings of the prison cells, the black bars, grey blankets, and beds of galvanized iron anchored to the floor. Of course, this set is not in Ireland but constructed in the Felony Channel studio in space leased from the new Freedom Tower in New York City, on the hundredth floor.

The moderator sits at a small round table with polished chrome legs and glass top. The chairs are of black finely wrought iron, nicely crafted curves, no cushions, rather like high-class outdoor furniture. There are strict rules of conduct for the interviews. (Of course, the rules are made to be broken). There must be no touching; in fact, the guests and moderator must maintain a distance from each other of at least one foot. The guest, if a felon and currently serving time, must be shackled at all times to his or her chair and is transported from whatever prison in a high-security van, clear windows all around, a little bit like a squat version of the old Pope-mobile.

Before we proceed with the edited transcript of the first

show, a word about our famous moderator is necessary in order to dispel any misunderstandings or misconceptions about what the show's basic premise is all about. We wanted a moderator who could connect easily with all classes of people (we do not use "class" in the Marxist sense but in the scientific sense), who could convey with ease an air of deep understanding of her guests and of the topics discussed. Naturally, the title of the show conveys to the audience that this is a show about criminals, what they do to their victims, and what is and should be done to them once they are caught. As even the least informed members of our audience know, Tommie Felon has been convicted on several occasions (one of them a cause célèbre when found naked except for a G-string in the President's office —we do not need to say which president—of course, this was not a crime at the time) and another was falsifying the forms required to qualify for health insurance so as to get maximum coverage to pay for a novel kind of sex change operation. Tommie received two years in prison for that felony, sentence suspended, and there have been a string of events in which she allegedly violated her probation by soliciting sex from various politicians who sent her revealing photographs of themselves, mistakenly thinking she was a prostitute. We assure you that we conducted an extensive background check (in fact we had the FBI do it for us under contract) and can say that Tommie has never prostituted herself. We admit that there must be one qualification to this postulation, which will become clear when we describe the structure of the show and its now well-known daily schedule.

The Tommie Felon show is aired Monday through Saturday at 8.00 pm. E.S.T. On Mondays, Wednesdays, and Fridays, Tommie is dressed out as herself, a voluptuous female, as we described above. On Tuesdays, Thursdays, and Saturdays, Tommie is dressed as himself, a straight, slim, mildly muscled-up male, his correction officer's jacket short sleeved to show off his upper arms, and his correction officer's pants, a slim modern cut of shorts, styled after those worn by Australian Rules Footballers, showing his lower thighs, shapely knees, and curvaceous calves. In sum, Tommie Felon is a transgendered individual who we are totally convinced is able to connect with the amazingly diverse range of people making up our audiences all around the world. So long as anyone watches the show two nights in succession, the intrinsic conflict built into the show is overwhelming. What more basic, anatomical conflict between humans can there be but that between male and female, yet how dependent each is on the other? The premise is established unequivocally right from the start. And so it easily leads to the conflict of another kind, between good and evil, captor and criminal.

It is a simple logic of the show's premise, therefore, that the moderator, she or he, conflicted with him- or her-self, sits at the center of the table, flanked on one side by the captor and the other side by the criminal.

Now that we have provided the *raison d'être* of the show we may continue to the edited highlights of the very first show that broke all records for a pilot. It was a Monday show, so Tommie was dressed as a female as we have already described. The guest felon was a serial murderer and rapist who, as the media promoted and we were happy to confirm, made Hannibal the cannibal seem pretty tame, and as well was way smarter than was Hannibal (who was a fictitious character anyway). This guy was real. (We use the past tense because he was killed under suspicious circumstances when he escaped from the Pope-mobile look-alike and was run down by a hit and run driver, an old guy driving a vintage K-car, according to witnesses.) The following is an abridged version of the original transcript, reproduced using the exact script format.

Series 1: The Tommie Felon Show
Episode 1. The Sado-Rapist

Directed by Quince Titillatio
Produced by Ozone TV in collaboration with
the Felony Foundation
The advice and assistance of the society of felons is gratefully
acknowledged

TOMMIE prances on to the set and advances to the front of the stage. She wears a bright, iridescent green cloak that she hugs with both arms across her bosom. With a wonderful flourish, she opens the cloak and stands tall, her arms extended up, holding her cloak as though she were Batman. She flings the cloak to the audience, and there are squeals and screams as those in the front seats fight to claim it. Her cloaks, made of recycled and sustainable tissue and colored with the slime of the slugs who inhabit the Olympic Peninsula, have become a valued collector's item. She blows kisses to the audience, steps down to the front few rows and kisses her fingers, then touches them on the heads of worshipping admirers. She returns to the stage, her back to the audience, then suddenly swivels around, her head buried in her hands, lily-white elbows pointing to the floor. It is the cue for the audience to go quiet. She raises her head slowly from her hands, her face showing pain, her eyes tearing, painted eyebrows slanting inwards.

TOMMIE

Oh, my Dears! What a show we have for you tonight! An evil thoroughly despicable killer and rapist who has done terrible things to his victims, things that even you, my dears, could not imagine!

AUDIENCE

(chanting)

Tommie dearest! Tommie dearest!

TOMMIE

Yes, my dears. I do this for you! Only you! But can you bear it? Do you really want him? He is so terrible, so frightening, so horrible!

AUDIENCE

Bring him on! Bring him on!

TOMMIE

Then I present to you, our felon of the day, killer, rapist and vivisector, a man whose name we refuse to speak, the felon himself!

A security guard drags the criminal on stage, as he staggers under his chains that clank loudly nearly pulling him to the floor. CRIMINAL swears at his attendants and makes obscene gestures at the audience to the extent that his chains allow. The guard roughly pushes CRIMINAL forward and on to the chair. TOMMIE prances to the CRIMINAL and gracefully places herself on his lap, leans back, kicking her leg closest to the audience out in a wonderful ballet pose. CRIMINAL tries to grope her bosom, snarls, and drools, but TOMMIE quickly slides off and takes her seat at the table, sitting up straight and formal. She speaks directly into the TV camera.

TOMMIE

And now I present to you our felon's accuser, tormentor, or is he also his excuser?

TOMMIE looks slyly at the audience.

AUDIENCE (chanting)

Scuser! Scuser! Scuser!

TOMMIE

Yes, yes, yes! I present to you our world famous excuser of criminals, Dr. Fallatious Hood, the greatest Hoodie I know!

AUDIENCE (chanting)

Hood-EE! Hood-EE!

HOOD, the accuser, and tormentor, a lofty forensic psychiatrist, quietly slips on to the set, seeming to appear from behind our transgendered moderator. TOMMIE extends her hand briefly to HOOD but retrieves it quickly after their eyes meet for an instant. She immediately turns to the CRIMINAL, licks her bright red lips in a tantalizing manner, and grasps his chained hand tightly in hers. She stands and raises the CRIMINAL'S hand with hers.

TOMMIE

My dear friends. I present to you, on my left, evil!

AUDIENCE

Eee-vil! Eee-vil!

CRIMINAL scowls right on cue. TOMMIE stretches for HOOD's hand and raises it too.

TOMMIE

My dear friends. I present to you, on my right, good!
AUDIENCE
Boo-oo, good! Boo-oo good!
HOOD pulls his hand away and leans forward, staring into criminal's eyes.
TOMMIE
Dr. Hood. You first. The good must lead the way! Ask the question that everyone wants to be answered!
HOOD
That's easy. Everyone wants to know why you do it.
CRIMINAL
Do what?
HOOD
Don't play cute with me, you filthy scum. Vicious, sadistic rape and murder of course.
TOMMIE
Doctor! Doctor! Tut! Tut!
AUDIENCE
Tut! Tut! -- Tut! Tut!
CRIMINAL
I enjoy it, that's why I do it. I would have thought it was obvious.
HOOD
Enjoy?
TOMMIE sighs and looks bored. She puts on her headset and sways rhythmically as she listens to Iz Mer, Turkish rap star, currently her favourite.
CRIMINAL
Yes, rape and killing. It's very pleasurable.
HOOD
Pleasurable?
TOMMIE rolls her eyes and signals to the audience to don their headsets.
CRIMINAL
Well, no—more than that!
HOOD
How many have you—?

CRIMINAL

Oh! Who can say? There's been so many—

HOOD

And what methods do you use?

TOMMIE removes her headset and leans over to CRIM-
INAL, beckons to audience

TOMMIE

Ooooooh! Aaaaaah!!

AUDIENCE

Oooooh! Aaaaah!

CRIMINAL

Well, I prefer to use instruments that happen to be around at
the time. A kind of situational ethics, if you see what I mean.
There's a symmetry about it. Strangle her with her own stocking,
put out her eyes with her own lip-stick case. Or shoes—shoes are
really good. You can do a lot with shoes—

CRIMINAL'S voice trails away.

HOOD

Anything else?

CRIMINAL

Well, I couldn't describe them all. Take too long. I suppose
you'd say it's the blood that's the best part.

AUDIENCE (Conducted by Tommie)

Tell us! (clapping) Tell us! (clapping)

HOOD

And, er—the other part?

CRIMINAL

You mean rape?

AUDIENCE

Ooooh!

TOMMIE puts her hand to her ear, leans over to the
criminal.

HOOD

Ahem, er, yes.

CRIMINAL

Of course, that's a good part of it too. I couldn't describe
them all.

HOOD
Well, just some of the better ones—
CRIMINAL
The better ones you wouldn't exactly define as er—
HOOD
What do you mean?
CRIMINAL
Well, because I don't do it in the er—
HOOD
Oh, you mean anal intercourse?
TOMMIE rolls her eyes, dons headset
CRIMINAL
Oh no! That's nothing!
HOOD
Then?
CRIMINAL
No, well, I —
TOMMIE removes headset, beckons audience.
HOOD
Go on.
CRIMINAL
No, I'm not going there. Let's just say that I do whatever I must to maximize my pleasure.

TOMMIE jumps up from her seat and runs to the front of the table. She conducts the audience in exaggerated gestures.

AUDIENCE
(chants, clapping)
Tell us! Tell us! Tell us!
CRIMINAL (flattered by audience attention)
Have you ever read American Psycho?
HOOD
I wouldn't waste my time with such trash.
TOMMIE (chanting)
Yes, we have! Yes, we have!
TOMMIE rushes to the front of the stage, waving her arms.
AUDIENCE (chanting)
Yes, we have! Yes, we have!

CRIMINAL

Then you're ignorant. I've gone well beyond that smart ass from the Hamptons. Drills, saws, rats. I've done way better than that.

HOOD leans forward, aggressively, stares at CRIMINAL

HOOD

Why do you do it?

CRIMINAL

I just answered that, didn't I?

HOOD

Not really.

CRIMINAL

What do you mean, then?

HOOD

The killing and the rape, why?

TOMMIE waves to the audience again.

TOMMIE AND AUDIENCE (chanting)

Bor-ing! Bor-ing!

CRIMINAL

I remember there was one time when I felt I would never find one to satisfy me. I'd just finished my finals and was watching a football game in a run-down bar. This raunchiness hit me. I just had to find the hottest, roughest one—

TOMMIE rushes back to her seat, and with an exaggerated flourish sits then leans over to the criminal, hand to ear

HOOD

But why?

CRIMINAL

Why what? I just told you, didn't I?

HOOD

Why kill them?

CRIMINAL

Before or after?

HOOD leans back, exasperated. TOMMIE pivots to him and gives him an exaggerated hug, and looks deep into the camera.

TOMMIE

My poor dear! It must be so hard for you.

AUDIENCE (sighs and swoons).

HOOD

Either.

CRIMINAL

Well, I mean they're not much use afterward, are they? Besides, they might remember what I looked like.

HOOD

Aha! So you're afraid of being caught!

CRIMINAL

Well of course! Wouldn't anyone?

TOMMIE leaps up and runs to the front, laughing hysterically, the audience joins in.

HOOD

But you're not just anyone--

CRIMINAL

What do you mean?

TOMMIE returns to her seat and with her chin in her chest, croons to the camera

TOMMIE

Oooh! Dark! Oooh, spooky!

AUDIENCE

Spooooky!

HOOD

Well, you're different.

CRIMINAL

What?

HOOD

Different. You know. I mean not everyone goes around killing and raping.

CRIMINAL

Yes, the pathetic fools! If only they could!

HOOD

Again. Why are you frightened of getting caught?

CRIMINAL

That's a really stupid question—

AUDIENCE

Stu-pid! Stu-pid!

CRIMINAL

As I said before, who wouldn't be?

HOOD

But you keep doing it, you must have realized you'd get caught sooner or later. Surely—

CRIMINAL

So?

TOMMIE (leaning into HOOD'S face)

Yes, so?

HOOD

So, why keep doing it?

CRIMINAL

Because it makes life bearable if I assume I'll never be caught.

HOOD

But you have been!

CRIMINAL

So that's life. You've probably got terminal cancer.

CRIMINAL chuckles, looks to audience for approval.

TOMMIE laughs raucously. Audience joins in.

HOOD (very serious)

We're going round in circles.

TOMMIE puts her finger to her lips and raises her hand to the audience. Silence ensues.

HOOD

Let me start again. Why do you kill people?

CRIMINAL

I just do it. It's who I am. It's my life. I love my life. Who doesn't?

HOOD

Don't you care for other people?

TOMMIE AND AUDIENCE (chanting)

Doesn't care! Doesn't care!

CRIMINAL (outraged)

What?

HOOD

I said, don't you care for other people?

CRIMINAL

Of course, I do. What sort of a question is that ?

HOOD

Then why do you do it?

CRIMINAL

What?

HOOD

Why? Why?

HOOD leans across the table and grabs the criminal by the throat.

AUDIENCE (chanting)

Why! Why!

CRIMINAL tries to push back but his chains will not let him. TOMMIE stands back, hands on hips.

TOMMIE

Go Doc! Go Doc!

AUDIENCE

Go doc! Go doc!

HOOD

Tell me! Tell me!

CRIMINAL

You're hurting me!

CRIMINAL stands pulling his restraining chains tight, catching TOMMIE'S extended arm, ensnaring HOOD'S hand as well. They all struggle and fall in a heap behind the table.

TOMMIE

Oh, Doctor! Oh, Doctor! Save me!

TOMMIE flings herself back, legs flying up in a classic V position, kicking the table over. Members of the audience run up to save her, but they are restrained by security guards.

HOOD

Oh! Sorry! I, I didn't mean to—

CRIMINAL

That's what they all say.

TOMMIE crawls, half drags herself to the front of the stage. Her contortions are Shakespearian.

TOMMIE

Oh my dear, dear friends! I thank you with all my heart. Why does the doctor behave so badly?

HOOD (contrite)

All I asked was why he does it.

HOOD stands as if to leave.

CRIMINAL

You must know why. You're the psychiatrist after all!

HOOD (glaring at Tommie)

You are a despicable, evil person—

TOMMIE (shocked)

Who, me?

TOMMIE points at her breast with both hands. She looks at the audience seeking approval.

AUDIENCE

Yes, you! Yes, You!

TOMMIE feigns horror, runs to the doctor and hugs him.

TOMMIE

Please stay doctor. We all need you! You're the only doctor we have!

HOOD

There's no point continuing this interview.

CRIMINAL untangles his chains and gets back to his seat.

CRIMINAL

Oh! But I thought you wanted to find out all about my crimes?

HOOD

I did—I do!

TOMMIE

Oh, thank you, doctor! Thank you!

TOMMIE kisses the psychiatrist full on the lips then waltzes down to the front row of the audience and brings up an overweight man in his thirties to help right the table. TOMMIE kisses him too, on the cheek, then dismisses him to the care of a security guard.

CRIMINAL

All right then, ask me some questions.

HOOD

I have, and you won't answer them.

CRIMINAL

You haven't given me a chance.

HOOD

I've pleaded with you.

CRIMINAL

I've tried to answer you, honestly.

HOOD (despondent)

It's no use.

TOMMIE

There, there Doctor. I'm sure he doesn't mean it, do you Mr. Criminal?

AUDIENCE (chanting)

Mean it! Mean it!

CRIMINAL

Why don't you ask me about my childhood? Everybody else does.

HOOD (fed up).

All right then. What about your childhood?

CRIMINAL

Well, I mean, you'll have to be a bit more specific.

HOOD (disinterested).

Yes, I suppose so. You were an illegitimate, only child, I suppose?

CRIMINAL

No, certainly not. I have two elder brothers and two younger sisters. Our family is very close.

HOOD

Your father left home when you were five or six, having beaten you mercilessly since birth?

CRIMINAL

No! Good heavens, you must have had a terrible childhood!

TOMMIE stands, signals to the audience, and conducts as if they were a choir.

TOMMIE AND AUDIENCE

The doctor was abused! The doctor was abused!

HOOD

Well, it wasn't the happiest, but—
CRIMINAL
Were you close to your parents? I was. All us kids were. We
were a very close family. Loved each other. The usual arguments
occasionally, but generally a wonderful family.
HOOD (slyly)
And your mother. Why haven't you mentioned your mother?
CRIMINAL
You didn't ask me. Besides, it's implied when I say 'family.'
HOOD
You mean your mother was nothing special?
CRIMINAL
That's not what I said!
HOOD writes down notes.
HOOD
I see.
CRIMINAL
Are you really taking that down?
HOOD
Of course.
CRIMINAL
But you've invented it. That's not what I said at all. That's
dishonest.
HOOD
Nonsense! Let's get on with the questions. Your mother—
CRIMINAL
You can't justify it. You're dishonest.
HOOD
Your mother—
CRIMINAL jumps up, one of the chains pulling free. A
security guard rushes forward to restrain him.
CRIMINAL
You're nothing but a faker, a quack!
TOMMIE'S eyes light up. She signals to the audience once
more, though it needs no asking.
AUDIENCE
Quack! Quack!

HOOD

It's not dishonest. It's a matter of interpretation. I've studied criminals for years. It's my expert opinion.

CRIMINAL

Expert dishonesty.

HOOD

I'm a very experienced forensic psychiatrist. I make careful scientific impartial judgments.

AUDIENCE

Lies! Lies! — Lies! Lies!

CRIMINAL looks to the audience with approval. Blows them a kiss, but gets an unexpected response.

AUDIENCE

Kill the quack! Kill the quack!

CRIMINAL (enraged)

Barbarians! I don't kill just anyone!!

TOMMIE

Now! Now! Mr. Criminal. Remember, they will vote for your release as will our viewers!

CRIMINAL

Where's the pleasure in killing the quack? Now if they wanted me to kill you—

HOOD

Mr. Felon! Look Out!

TOMMIE

It's not Mister, and you know it, you insensitive brute!

HOOD

Miss, Mrs., then. Whatever. You're in danger! Get away quickly!

TOMMIE

It's Madam, if you don't mind!

AUDIENCE

Look out! Look out! Madam, look out!

CRIMINAL wrenches himself up off his seat and thrusts his body and chains with all his might towards TOMMIE who puts both hands to her throat and tries to slide under the table out of the way. HOOD pushes his chair back, watches, and takes notes.

TOMMIE

Help me! Help me, my God help me!

Security guards rush forward, but it's too late. CRIMINAL slipped under the table and has wrapped Tommie in his chains. He bites off her ear lobe and spits it out at the audience.

CRIMINAL

Fellow barbarians! I give you blood!

AUDIENCE

Blood! Blood! He gave us blood!

HOOD scurries off the set, walking backward, half bent over and hoping not to be noticed. TOMMIE swoons and licks her own blood as it trickles down her face. CRIMINAL follows her example and licks the blood off her cheek.

TOMMIE

Oh! Mr. Criminal! Why me? Why me?

TOMMIE becomes listless and floppy, as though in a drunken stupor. CRIMINAL looks out at the audience.

CRIMINAL

Neck or nose? Neck or nose?

AUDIENCE

Neck! Neck! — Neck! Neck!

CRIMINAL bares his teeth like a snarling dog. But a young security guard, pretending to participate in the blood-licking, has crawled under the table and, after one lick, lifts a leg and fiercely rams it into CRIMINAL'S chin, causing him to bite off his own tongue. The guard unravels the chains from TOMMIE and pulls her free. She envelops him in her not so floppy arms and guides him to the front of the stage as they stagger together. There is blood on both their faces. The audience stands and jumps and screams in ecstasy.

AUDIENCE

Kiss! Kiss!—Kiss! Kiss!

As the ecstatic couple complies all too well with the audience demands, other guards have not managed to unravel CRIMINAL'S chains from the table and chairs, so they drag him off the set along with the table and a chair. CRIMINAL gasps, chokes, face turning blue, blood pours from his mouth. TOMMIE and the security guard come out of their embrace. Tommie swoons again and waves to the audience.

TOMMIE

My dears! My dears! You have saved me! I owe you my love and my life!

TOMMIE falls back into the security guard's arms.

TOMMIE

Take me! Take me!

Security guard lifts TOMMIE off her feet and carries her off the set while she blows kisses to the audience.

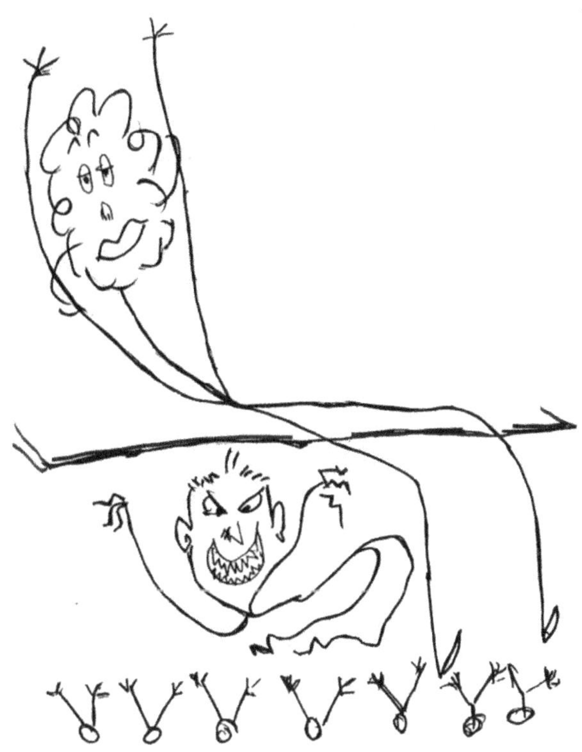

And there we have it. This was the most highly rated season premiere ever of a talk show (to repeat, repetition is good in our business). For your curiosity, the studio audience voted to parole the criminal immediately, but the viewing audience did not agree. It voted overwhelmingly for a continued sentence of life in prison without parole, with a sizable portion of respondents urging that the original death sentence, which was commuted by then Governor Bunyon, be restored. (As an aside, a sizable minority also urged that the psychiatrist's license be revoked).

Please be aware that Tommie is well and her ear lobe has been reattached successfully. However, the security guard was fired for the liberties he took in saving her, specifically licking the blood from her face, which, the gender harassment board in its review, rated as an unnecessary invasion of Tommie's privacy and was, in fact, a sexually tinged touching. As for the criminal, the prison surgeon was unable to reattach the pieces of his tongue since it seems that he chewed them up thinking that they were pieces of Tommie's ear. In fact, the surgeon had to remove additional parts of the tongue because of the danger that rough edges in the mouth may turn cancerous. The criminal launched proceedings against Ozone TV claiming several million dollars in damages, but the judge threw out the case because (1) the damage was self-inflicted and (2) the contract the criminal signed with Ozone TV clearly specified that we would not be held liable for any damages that resulted from the criminal's actions. Clearly, all the unfortunate spilling of blood was his doing, not ours. His lawyer claimed that we should have foreseen the events and chained the criminal down more securely, but our consideration, in this case, was that we did not want to treat the criminal in an inhumane manner. As it was, we received a considerable amount of mail from viewers, and media pundits that we had, in fact, weighed the criminal down with so many chains that he was treated like a beast of burden. The criminal has appealed the case to the U.S. district court, but we are confident that the court will not hear the case.

Clearly, we are breaking new ground with this show. This is real time television, in no way edited or scripted. In fact, as can be seen from this "ad hoc" script, if one were to actually write such a script and expect players to act (no, be) the part, we could not write in the actual spilling of blood as occurred in this episode. Of course, we could have people act the parts out and have special effects make the spilling of blood seem real, but that is not our idea of reality TV. There is no script. We do create an environment with participants we have carefully chosen, and we do, of course, employ a moderator who is incredibly talented. Tommie's behavior we can more or less predict, and the same goes for the audience. However, we cannot predict precisely what the guests will do. This is what makes The Tommie Felon Show so exciting and why people all over the world tune into it with high expectations that we try not to disappoint.

We are confident that the proposed franchise of the show to the new and exciting Lor-Renz Arabia TV network will be equally successful. We are working with them right now to develop the set, which will be based on the notorious Abu Ghraib prison, in fact, may even be shot on site (pun intended!). Guests will include high ranking Al Qaeda or ISIS operatives, one in particular who has perfected the skill of beheading hostages, and others including dedicated suicide bombers of various sizes and ages and genders, and on the contra side, prosecutors and inter-rogators who have perfected the procedures for extracting the truth from their quarry, including the efficient means of punish-ment for the convicted such as beheading and cutting off other limbs with one stroke of the sword, and the use of hot water boarding.

Speaking of which, we have engaged the services of a well-known Hollywood head hunting team to find the very best moderator for the show. Naturally, we are not looking for a transgendered person, but rather for a terrorist with a strong history of violence who is also a doctor and pacifist, thus providing the standard premise of the show: a balance between prosecutors and defenders, violence and peace, good and evil.

Moral: Being part of the punishment is part of the problem.

25. Felony Media Episode 2

Audience participation at its Best.

Before I reveal the guts of Episode Two I would like to begin with a small apology, small because I am not really apologetic for having stretched the actual facts in my review of the pilot of this series—dare I say truth, which we all know exists only in the mind of the main stream media that claims to own the truth, a big lie in itself—I could go on.

To get back to it. I apologize for having twisted a few small details. The Criminal was not killed, or if he was, he was brought back to life for this the second episode, the one that should have been full center of the pilot, in my unhumble opinion. You will see why shortly when I provide a blow by blow account of the second episode, which was shot in our Australian studio, because we had a contract with the major manufacturer of cricket balls in Australia to provide us with several hundred balls for the sole use in the show. Related companies also provided us with a score of cricket bats made of pure and resilient British willow, and dense plastic-like stumps that bounced when hit, and generally behaved in ways that wooden stumps would not. Their very sharp bottom metal-capped tips, however, proved to be of great stabbing potential, a detail that many discerning members of our studio audience will no doubt appreciate.

Because of the potential for misuse of these cricket paraphernalia, we found it necessary to vet our studio audience carefully. Each person was asked a series of questions to determine their suitability to be part of the audience participation. I say participation, this also is an understatement. We planned to engage the audience *en masse,* to give them a huge opportunity to (1) express their views of the overall presentation of the show and (2) take part in the actual interrogation or should we say, post interrogation part of the show when it became time to decide on the appropriate punishment for the criminal, and once decided, to apply the punishment.

Those who tuned into the pilot of the Tommie Felon Show already had the chance to assess the extent of guilt or innocence that applied to the criminal. And surely, his outrageous behavior towards our host and disrespect to our audience, contributed to his guilt. Indeed, the more he professed his innocence, the more guilty he became. I'm sure that those of you who tuned into the pilot or streamed it later on NetStyx would agree with that.

The vetting questions we asked our potential audience attendees were:

1. Are you black? (Yes, back row).

2. Are you a Christian? (Yes, disallowed entry)

3. Are you a Muslim? (Yes, back row with Blacks).

4. Have you ever killed someone? (Yes, special front row seat regardless of race or religion, given complimentary cricket bat).

5. How many people have you raped in the past ten years? (one or more, second row seat, regardless of race or religion, given complimentary cricket stump.)

6. Can you throw a cricket ball? (No, refused admittance.)

7. Have you ever had sex in public? (Yes, seated on the knees of front and second row attendees.

8. What does LGBTQ stand for? Must get four out of five letters right, otherwise denied entry.

Perhaps you are wondering whether I am on the level about our choice of Australia for the second episode. It's a long way from the cradle of civilization, and besides there is much more cricket paraphernalia available in India. The fact is, we chose Australia for entirely different reasons. Cricket was just a coincidental attraction. It came down to either New Zealand or Australia, so now I have given it away. We came to the conclusion that the Australians, specifically the Victorians were much more likely to appreciate our bombastic and freedom loving show, since the Victorians were well used to doing what they were told by their Premier during the corona virus lockdown of 2020, so we thought we could control our audience more easily. As well, there are plenty of terrorist-like refugees in Australia, living quietly in the suburbs, if not imprisoned on some island in the pacific or somewhere else in the middle of the Australian desert. It was our considered assessment that if we could include as many of these individuals in our audience as we could, their pent-up violence would burst forth, if only given the opportunity by the outrageous behaviors of our star performers.

Finally, you may wonder what became of Tommie Felon, our great performer of the pilot episode. You will be shocked and excited to see him (this is not a typo) in his (not a typo) new role as terrorist par excellence, masquerading as a Yemeni refugee. He will preside over the entire show, the perfect character to sentence the guilty to their punishments, to prescribe the punishments deserved by the criminals who are lined up ready for our show as I speak.

And now to the show!

Well, not just yet. There is one more issue that I need to reveal. While we do like to surprise our audiences, we do not want to disappoint them. The criminals we have lined up for you are not your usual criminals. No, I take that back. They are common, everyday criminals, many of whom you will immediately recognize as people who might have been your neighbors. But be assured we have worked closely with the Victorian government officials to locate only those who were absolutely and beyond any measure of a doubt, guilty of their crimes and infractions. It will not be your role (if you are lucky enough to be in the studio audience) to pronounce guilt or innocence of the accused. That has already been decided by the legal apparatus of the Victorian Government. It is your role to decide on the punishment and once done, to see that it is carried out. To be clear. We fully agree with the Victorian Government that there is no relationship between the finding of guilt and the administration of punishment The inherent truth of this claim is demonstrated by the following digression—no, not a digression, a necessary case study that clearly illustrates the Victorian Government's absolute devotion to good punishment.

Young entrepreneur (actually, not an entrepreneur, but a Melbourne university student from Guandong province working his way through university), was convinced that in fact the evidence collected by surveillance companies was all that was needed to convict the criminal! As he liked to recite to his potential customers, "seeing is believing" (said with a distinctive and exaggerated Chinese accent so as to encourage his customers to correct his pronunciation and therefore feel superior to him), he would run through the many examples of drivers and pedestrians alike ignoring red lights, the technologies of face recognition and license plate recognition combined when needed, to identify within seconds, the name and address of the perpetrator.

"There, you see?" Ling Song would say with a big smile. "Absolute proof of guilt! You can catch these criminals and give them the punishment they deserve!"

At first his customers were a little doubtful. It seemed a little too close to home for some of them. For they too knew full well that they had probably run through a red light, or certainly an orange light, not to mention exceeded the speed limits (hidden and unhidden) at some time or other in their past.

Ling Song pushed his iPhone in front of his customer's face. "You have big fines for these criminals?" he would ask with his big smile.

"We do. We rake in a lot of money," would be the answer, said rather sheepishly. "That's the trouble. We get criticized for not being serious about it. That all we are doing is making money and we don't really care about the infraction itself."

"Why not other punishment then?" asks Ling Song.

"It costs money to punish criminals," comes the answer.

"Why not punish the worst offenders with something else?"

"Like what?"

Ling Song always shrugs and says, "I don't know. I only sell cameras. You big boss, why not make up your own punishments?"

"Like what?"

Ling Song smiles and shrugs. "You like the cameras? We give you special price and free installation. Charge only for data link to facial recognition and licensing."

"And how much would that be?"

"Only one cent per infraction. Very cheap! And with your money you buy more punishments to use for serial offenders."

The deal was struck and the Victorian Department of Health and Criminal Justice Services (the two ministries of Health and Criminal Justice had been amalgamated into one during the Corona Virus pandemic) signed a contract with Healthy Cameras Pty. Ltd. to install cameras on every corner of every city, town and village in Victoria, and in addition, after considerable cajoling from the talented Ling Song, installation along all border entry points from its neighboring states New South Wales and South Australia. They were, of course, installed in every conceivable location in airports and train stations, as well as beaches around Victoria to ensure that people swam between the flags. Thus, punishment was inevitable.

Now, back to the show.

Entrance to the show facility was set up like a turnstile entrance to a cricket match at the Melbourne Cricket Ground. The answers to the vetting questions were fed into a computer and immediately the green light that said "RIGHT" flashed if the participant was designated a criminal, and a red light that said "LEFT" if the participant was designated a punisher. Because the computer assumed that everyone had committed an offence at some time or other, the splitting of criminal from non-criminal was done randomly. Of course the participants did not know this, so some were very surprised to find themselves back stage where the criminals were caged. Others, especially those who had answered in the affirmative that they had killed or raped someone were greatly surprised to find themselves in the front rows of the auditorium. Mind you, as I am sure you, my cynical reader have already surmised, it is very likely that some if not most respondents lied to the vetting questions. That is why the idea to randomly sort the participants to guilty (backstage) or not guilty (audience) made much more sense.

Once the audience was seated, the free popcorn distributed, and the criminals backstage sorted into dangerous and not dangerous, a final sorting of the audience was conducted. This was not so much sorting but organizing the audience into an effective and efficient assault force, to borrow a military expression. Our audience coach, a leading player in the AFLW (Australian Football Women's League), dressed in the tight shorts of a male footballer, called for silence and easily gained the rapt audience attention.

"Welcome all!" she cries with a big smile, mesmerizing all with her bright overpainted red lips, "my name is Dolly and welcome, all, to this our second exciting episode of THE FELONY MEDIA SHOW EPISODE 2, or possibly renamed, depending on what you, the all-important audience, wants, PUNISH OR BE PUNISHED!

[Screams of approval]

"We have now just one small matter to attend to before the great show begins. Thank you all for responding to our pre-show questionnaire. We now would like to know if there is anyone in the audience who has played cricket professionally or at the state or commonwealth level. Show of hands please!"

Three hands raised. The rest of the audience murmured their excited approval.

"Thank you," says Dolly, "please come up to the front so I can give you your badges that mark you as leaders of your team, captains, let's say, and give you the key to your store of balls, bats and stumps."

The proud men came forward, shook hands with Dolly and received their keys.

"You may now select your team members," says Dolly. Immediately, audience members call out, wave their hands, "Me! Me! Pick me!" they shout.

"You may give your team member whatever implement you think he or she or it can wield," says Dolly in the loudest of voices.

Team members from the front two rows began to argue.

Clearly the cricket bat was the favorite.

"All the weapons, I mean tools of punishment, are equally effective!" yells Dolly. "It's a matter of how you use them!"

The captains issue the tools. The killers get cricket bats, the rapists get metal-tipped stumps, and the rest get cricket balls, as many as they can carry or pocket. Each captain, without any provocation by Dolly, begins to berate each other's team. The competition is going to be fierce.

Back stage there is an unwelcome silence. To seasoned show business people, silence is not golden, when it comes to performance in an auditorium. It conveys an air of uncertainty, of dissolution, of incompetence. Dead air, as they say in the live radio business. People began to whisper. Some were puzzled as to why they were sent back stage. They thought they were there to watch a show, to be in the audience. Not to be herded into small cage-like structures, basically cages on wheels. And upon being pushed into the cage, each participant was given a small card on which was inscribed their crime or crimes. It was when each criminal saw what they were charged with, that the silence gradually broke into low muttering, and then finally, nervous crying, some angrily denying their crime, others pleading to be forgiven, that they didn't mean to do it, and others flat out admitting guilt and saying "so what?" as if they had a right to commit a crime, to break the law. Of course, all, no matter what their first reaction to the crime of which they had been found guilty, complained that this was not fair, that many others, perhaps everyone, had committed the crime for which each was charged, so why weren't they here in the cages as well? How could any government claim that justice was done when it sorts people into guilty and not guilty on some unknown criterion, but that seemed to be random?

Now bedlam. People rattled the cages, screamed, sobbed, expressed their anger and guilt in all manner of ways. Some even stripped off all their clothes in defiance. Of course, to the producers of the show, this only served to make things even more entertaining. This episode would be a blockbuster, its streaming to be universally proclaimed, money would accumulate. What a winner!

Stage hands lined up the cages ready to wheel on stage.

And now the star of the show, Tommie Felon herself (it was a Monday) emerged from her dressing room. She was naked under the black flowing gown of a high court judge. No one would know that, of course, unless she for some reason, perhaps a spur of the moment act, had an urge to reveal her sensational body, scars and all.

You may remember that the criminal who featured in the pilot, and whom Tommie defended against all kinds of wrath and anger, was dragged off the stage in chains, never to be heard of again. You may wonder why he disappeared from the public consciousness. The answer is very simple. He was paroled and became an ignominious nobody living under an assumed name in a back street of North Philadelphia where he was the victim of a gang shooting, when an errant bullet entered his small one room apartment and lodged in his temple behind the right eye. He lapses in and out of a coma where he resides in Temple University Hospital. Efforts were made to transport him to Australia for the special Australian episode, but the Victorian Department of Health and Criminal Justice Services required that he spend one year in quarantine, the explanation being that the Victorian government, indeed the Australian government, were not prepared to risk the importation of criminality into Australia which, as of this date, had the lowest criminality rate of any advanced country (and would be even lower were it not that the Australian government had allowed New Zealanders to migrate *en masse* without any vetting procedures at all). Besides, Australia had a very nasty history of criminal importation, indeed embarrassed that it owed its very existence to it.

I know I said that the notorious criminal of our first show would be in attendance, even a star of the show. But I said that just to get your attention. He definitely will not be in the show, thanks to the Australian government strict immigration policies. Besides, Tommie Felon threatened to quit if she had to perform on stage with that criminal again. She had enough scars on her body to last a lifetime. And there was a limit to which she could cover the scars with tattoos.

I could here revert to the script presentation of the show as it unfolded, but to be honest (if you can believe it) I thought, in retrospect, that the clumsy layout of the text in the script style I presented in the pilot episode detracted from the story I wanted to tell. It is easier and simpler to just tell you what happened. I was there (well, actually I wasn't, technically, I was safely viewing the show from the production booth across the street). But I didn't miss anything, in fact saw much more than if I had been there. We have cameras installed everywhere as you can guess. And when I say everywhere, I mean everywhere. Backstage, dressing rooms, all toilets, under audience seats, attached to participants' ID cards pinned to their lapels and other garments. Even the cricket paraphernalia have cameras attached to them in certain places.

I admit, though, that there is nothing like "being there" as they say. I miss being on the spot, issuing commands to Tommie, taking her by the hand, giving her s slap on the bottom to hurry her along. You know what I mean? When I'm there, she can't ignore my commands. In fact, she typically discards the ear phones through which I convey my commands.

Here she comes. She's hidden in one of the cages that the stage hands are pushing on to the stage. There's a rustle of excitement in the audience. The captains must stand, cricket bats at the ready, and face their teams to keep them calm. It's too soon to let them have it. If punishment is to be effective, timing is all important.

Tommie pushes open a door in her cage and jumps out. The criminals behind her try to follow, but she slams it shut, with the help of a burly stage hand. She gathers her judge's robe around her body, sticks out one naked leg. There's a huge audience applause and yells of excitement. The captains stand uncomfortably, shifting their weight from one leg to the other. They can't hold their teams down much longer. Someone cries out,

"Criminals! Filth! You're going to get it!"

Tommie prances across the stage, all smiles. Then she tightens the robe around her, so tight her shapely form appears, exaggerated. Hisses and boos respond. They want action. They want all revealed. The captains frown. They raise their bats, now holding them over their shoulders.

The criminals rattle their cages. Stage hands appear from all over and hand them cricket balls. Tommie turns to face the cages.

"You have the right of a defense, do you not?" she asks everyone.

"Let them have it! Let them have it!" screams the angry audience.

One of the criminals manages to throw a cricket ball and it hits a captain on the back of his shoulder. He turns to face the stage. "Who did that?" he asks, deeply offended.

"What do you care?" calls Tommie, now prancing across the stage, leaning forward to the captain, extending her tattooed arm.

The captain takes the bait. He takes her hand in his and tries to climb up on the stage to join her. A security officer runs over and tries to grab him before he can climb up. "No audience on the stage!" he cries.

But it's too late. The captain's team is outraged that he has joined the other side. They begin to pelt the stage with cricket balls and stumps, and a couple with cricket bats rush forward and manage to bash his legs. Tommie pulls her hand away. Her work is done here!

"The innocent must have their say!" she cries, as though she were Moses with the tablets in hand.

The criminals rattle their cages again. They are flimsy cages. It will not be long before they can break out. Those who have cricket balls throw them. Their anger spreads like a huge tsunami throughout the entire auditorium.

The audience of innocents is now well organized. The errant captain has returned to his team and they have forgiven him for his misjudgment. He is easily the best bowler among them, and a pretty good batsman as well. They line up to take it in turns throwing their missiles. The captain points to vulnerable targets. But the other teams will have none of it. They are totally undisciplined. Throwing cricket balls, stumps all over the stage at no particular target, simply causing bedlam and fear on the stage. Tommie tries to fend off the balls, but it's no use. A flying stump hits her right in the shoulder and stays lodged there, the metal tip stuck in her chest just above where one of her breasts used to be. The enraged criminals in their cages rattle them more, the violence sure to break them open. But they are hindered by the stump missiles that have turned out to be much more lethal than the hard cricket balls.

The third team under the leadership of their popular captain,

follows him as he rushes forward with his cricket bat. He bashes the security guard who tries to stop him from climbing on the stage. He gets there easily and then turns to his team, "up boys and girls or whatevers! Let's get them and finish the job! They'll be all out before they know it!"

Tommie rushes forward, trying to pull out the stump embedded in her chest. The esteemed captain grabs her by the stump and with the other hand gives her a good bashing over the head with his bat. "Stop!" she pleads, "stop! I am innocent. I am just a media personality. I am innocent, I say."

"You're as guilty as the rest of them, and now you have to pay for it!" cries the captain of team three. "I'm more famous than you are anyway!"

His team is now on stage as is most of the audience. They rush this way and that, throwing balls and stumps, and the better cricketers swish their bats, pretending they are hitting fours and sixes. At last, one of the criminals manages to break out of a cage, and this is followed by screams of delight and delirium as other cages burst open.

Tommie manages to climb up on one of the empty cages and stands tall, She now has at least four stumps embedded in her body. She is pale and bleeding. She has touched her wounds with her fingers and painted her face with blood. It's like her lipstick, always bright red. She raises her hands and calls out in a feeble, dying voice, "those who punish shall be punished! The innocent shall be guilty!"

None of what I have reported here is true. Here I sit serving my sentence of one year in quarantine because the Department of Health and Criminal Services of Victoria accused me of conspiracy to break COVID lockdown rules. They stopped me at the Tullamarine airport as I deplaned from the only Virgin flight into Melbourne from the UAE where I had been negotiating the season adoption of the Tommie Felon Show by the Lor-Renz Arabia TV network. I lied to the entry officials and said I hadn't been to London. I don't know how they found out. I am serving my sentence in an open cage put up in Melbourne's Federation

Square. There is a sign attached to the cage that reads "I broke the lockdown rules." Every night on the network news, the Premier of Victoria delivers the verdict and shows me crouched in a corner of the cage. "I know this is painful for you all," says the Premier, "but we can't allow the lockdown to be broken. It takes just one who does not do the right thing, and the rest of us suffer."

Moral: Fairness and punishment are evil twins.

26. The Hungry Priest

A hermit feeds on the sins of others.

In the small town of Castrovillari at the foot of the Calabrian mountains, there lived a former hermit, who called himself Vashpa, now a priest. He serviced the beautiful (to its inhabitants) church of San Giuliano.

In his days as a hermit, living in a cave in the mountains, he had learned to live off the land, had meager needs, a few morsels to chew on every other day, and water from the streams that trickled down from the mountains. He spent his time meditating, sitting on his haunches, chanting chants that he made up as he went along, and reading ancient scriptures that were supposedly unearthed in the desert of Sinai. Actually, they were dried up and shriveled pages from a discarded copy of *Il Messaggero* that had washed down from one of the streams.

How many years had passed he had no idea. Certainly, his gaunt, unshaven figure looked the ideal picture of a hermit and a very wise old man, though he was not that old, he just looked like it. Yet his asceticism had not impressed the powers of above and below, for a drought descended upon all of Calabria, a place where there was never all that much rain anyway, and his source of water dried up. Hardly able to rise up from his haunches, he staggered down the foothills and emerged in the town of Castrovillari. And as it so happened, he staggered into the one tiny convent there, inhabited by sisters of the order of Mother Teresa.

The sisters were over-joyed to take him in, and in so doing, spoiled him like an only child, which he was—sort of. They told him of the abstemious ways of Mother Teresa, she gave or herself to many, a true saint. The least the sisters of the convent of Mother Teresa could do was to take him in and to set him on the same path as their unofficial (because she was Irish) patron saint, Íte. They marveled at his asceticism, indeed thought it a small miracle for one to have become an ascetic without the aid or even knowledge of the Christian faith.

More importantly for him, though, were the catechisms, biblical studies and readings, hymnals, and all the other paraphernalia of the catholic church. For ascetics of all religions, time, as we common people understand it, stands still. In fact, it might well not exist, for each day is like every other day. Of course, here is where appearances can be very misleading. Time does not stand still at all, it relentlessly pushes forward. But for an ascetic such as Vashpa, it appears so. Without full understanding of his existence in time, therefore, he was about to ignore his body and devote himself entirely to the Scriptures and rituals of the catholic days.

He showed such devotion, and acquired so much knowledge, that the sisters petitioned Bishop Giuseppe Fiorini Morosini to ordain him upon their recommendation, without his having to attend school in the Vatican. In their application they listed over one hundred pages of his studies, exceptional grades earned when they examined him, his dedication to the church and especially his renowned asceticism. This request was so unusual that the Bishop immediately forwarded it to the Vatican for His Holiness the Pope to examine and offer his guidance.

Meanwhile, the sisters, feeling that they had reached the pinnacle of what they could do with their adopted neophyte, broke with past practice and took it in turns of chaperoning him to attend mass at the local church of La Madonna del Castello. Here he learned to take communion (not officially of course, the wine he took was non-alcoholic), and to mingle with other worshippers, who, however, were puzzled at the sudden emergence of this hermit, whose fabled existence had been the talk of the town before he emerged as a real person. They knew him as Vashpa and asked the sisters of the convent who was this person and why did he have a strange name. There were many rumors about him, as naturally happens when a person lives as a hermit and never communicates with the outside world. In the absence of information, people will invent it, if they must have it.

And so it was that the sisters of Mother Teresa decided that they must approach their apprentice and ask him where he got his name, and more importantly insist that he take on a real name, that is, an Italian name.

The trouble was that Vashpa liked his name, and he was very used to using it. He had many conversations with himself when he was a hermit, and always addressed himself as Vashpa. He could not imagine calling himself any other name. When asked where did he get the name, he replied that he did not know. It must have been the name given him at birth. Of which he, of course, had no memory. Did he not have parents? Did he not have a childhood? Where did he grow up? To these mundane, though obviously crucial questions about his existence and identity and who he really was, he answered he had no memory. In fact, he became very agitated when constantly asked his true name. He would reply Vashpa. And who were his parents? And he would answer with a shrug, "Mother Nature." This, the sisters took as near blasphemy, and they spent much time making confession to Jesus for their punitive thoughts and their unkind demands upon their charge. Fortunately, Time, a concept unknown to dedicated ascetics as we have noted, does not stand still but moves forward, relentlessly. And such a notion makes it possible for resentment to be overcome and for the healing of fissures by Time. Thus Vashpa learned from the sisters that "time heals all."

Had he still been an ascetic he would have responded with "it is healing that demands time, not the other way round." Such utterances befuddled and frustrated the sisters of Mother Teresa. Their outstanding pupil had become an obstreperous and heartless critic of their own existence and their lives. Yet they had devoted themselves to him, gave him everything he needed to become a saint. He appeared not to appreciate their good will. Such thoughts only made things worse, because they knew that it was a sin to expect gratitude from others.

Finally, Vashpa could stand the stress no more. And at breakfast (dry toast and sparkling water from the local spring) he announced that he would adopt a name well known to the church. The sisters became excited, and much relieved. Each of them looked up to heaven, crossed themselves and silently said, "thank you Jesus."

"And what name have you chosen?" asked the Mother Superior.

"Íte," replied Vashpa as he munched his toast.

One could feel the air sucked out of the sparsely furnished room as each of the sisters put their hands to their mouth and looked up once again to Heaven.

"But that's a girl's name!" exclaimed Mother Superior.

"No. It's a Saint's name. Is not gender irrelevant to sainthood?" replied Vashpa once again noisily chewing his toast, then sipping water.

"But you are not a saint," countered Mother Superior, unable to hide the venom in her voice.

Silence reigned. The sisters looked down at their empty plates.

Vashpa was tempted to say, "but I will be," but knew that it was a sin to want anything too much, let alone sainthood. Besides, he had to admit that he had done nothing of good will at all that would qualify him for sainthood.

Mother Superior broke the silence. "God will be the final judge. Sisters, from now on we will call our wonderful neophyte, Íte. She is, after all, our patron saint." She turned to him and said with a smile, such as it was, covered by her habit, "we are most honored, Íte, to have you among us, for you have allowed us to be part of your life. May the riches of God, Jesus and Mary lead you to a Heavenly place."

All the sisters wriggled a little in their seats. They were not quite sure whether to clap or not. Íte was himself overcome. With teary eyes he said, almost sobbed, "I am overjoyed sisters, my holy family."

But then, a terrible, portentous thing happened. His tummy gurgled and he reached for another piece of toast. Right then he knew there was something wrong. He felt hungry, and had not felt hunger over his many years of fasting. Worse, it was the last piece on the plate and there was another sister still to come. It should be left for her.

Mother Superior blinked her eyes and looked down. "I think, you must make confession. I will accompany you to the church of San Giuliano. It is a dear little church, and it has a dear little confessional.

*

It was a typical hot and dusty day in Castrovillari, as they walked together through the small vineyard where sisters were already snipping and tending the vines, then stepped on to Via Giudeca. Mother Superior walked briskly, causing Íte to stumble a little to keep up. He was not used to such physical exertion. And his tummy gurgled some more. They walked in silence, broken only by the crunching of gravel under their feet. Íte felt the need to make conversation. This also came as a shock to him, another sign that there was something wrong. He had preferred silence for so long, and had broken it among the sisters when he conducted his studies and ask the sisters questions to explain this or that about catholic rituals, masses, catechisms and other ways of the church. He had never made small talk, as people call it.

Yet it was Mother Superior who broke the silence. "I will go as far as the door of the church. Father Bruno will be expecting you."

They turned a corner into Largo Giuliano. Íte stopped briefly to take in the most typical scene of southern Italy: the historic, mildly ornate stone church, at the far end of the largo that was more or less rectangular, not a soul (literally) in sight, the hot wind blowing billows of dust around the square, a wall to his right plastered with the latest political posters and the occasional death notices. Mother superior led the way to the steps at the front of the church. Her well-worn heavy black shoes scraped on the cobblestones as they stepped up to the old wooden door.

"I will leave you here," she said, "and may Jesus and Mary be with you." She turned and left.

Íte struggled to open the heavy wooden door, painted an ugly dark green. And upon entering he immediately crossed himself as taught by the sisters. There were two confession boxes one on each side of the main altar that was painted white and edged with gold, surrounded by many trinkets, relics, and ornate cups and boxes on show. Both confessionals were located at the back of the altar, appearing as though they were actually doors to the rear. The question was, which one to enter? Íte walked silently forward, admiring the slender silvery organ pipes that rose up from the altar on both sides. Of course, the entire altar was constructed around the magnificent display, if rather small, of the depiction of San Giuliano himself. He approached the altar, kneeled and crossed himself again. He then thought he heard a slight cough from the altar on the right. So he approached, and entered through the red drapes.

Unfortunately, the door was simply an entry to the various small chapels that were on show behind the altar. He quickly withdrew and came back to the main church and then spied the confessional in the apse, off to the side almost hidden behind a white column. He knocked lightly and heard the cough again. He opened the simple plain walnut door, and there found himself in what looked like a typical old fashioned telephone booth, only with a seat.

He sat and looked at the ornate grate that separated him from his confessor, who moved and shuffled a little.

"Bless me father for I have sinned," mumbled Íte.

We need not recount all the sins he confessed. It is enough to say that he had not all that many to confess, since he had spent the last many years in silence alone with himself and his cave. So there were few opportunities to do anything bad, except of course, those things that had to do with himself and only himself.

What is most important however, is what came out of it. Íte left the confessional a changed person, or so he thought. A weight had been lifted from his shoulders, and each time he said a Hail Mary, according to the priest's orders, the weight lifted some more. He was so happy with this first experience of confession that he hummed a hymn all the way back to the convent. And by the time he reached the convent he had a plan. A magnificent plan.

But it was interrupted.

Íte walked quickly through the vineyard nodding to the sisters as they worked. One looked up and informed him that the Mother Superior had asked that he go straight to her as she had important news from Bishop Morosini

"You are to be ordained by Bishop Morosini this coming Saturday at Holy Mass in the Church of San Giuliano. This is a great honor! No bishop has come to Castrovillari for at least seven years! You must have truly impressed the Vatican. And to do that without having to set a foot in Rome. All of it virtual! We at the convent are so proud of you!"

Íte was overjoyed, another sin to reckon with.

Íte was duly ordained and informed by Bishop Morosini that he would be contacted soon with his orders, the diocese to which he would be allocated. Newly ordained priests were usually sent off to distant parts of the world, or tiny places in Italy, such as where Íte was already stationed, with his sisters in the convent. He almost requested that he be allowed to stay at the convent, but thought better of it. The Bishop might wonder what he was up to. His hope was that the sisters and especially Mother Superior would speak up for him and make such a request. For he could see that they very much needed him. There they were stuck in their little convent, with nobody to confess to. How could the church overlook such a serious need? His grand plan was to build a confession box, and then hear their confessions daily or as often as needed. They must have many, many sins all bottled up. He would free them from their sins! What better way to thank them for all they had done for him!

The wheels of the Vatican turn slowly. No letter of placement came. Íte was therefore free to pursue his grand design. He made the treck into Castrovillari and checked out the confession box in the church of San Giuliano. He took a photo and made drawings. He would make a replica for the convent. Where it would be placed, he worried a little, because the tiny chapel in the convent may not have room.

And so it was done. The confession box, the "dark box" as those who envied it (ex-catholics and non-catholics) called it, was placed just outside his own room at the end of the hallway. He had to modify the priest's cubicle a little so that it could fit into the hallway space. The sisters were so excited when he invited them to come see his handiwork! They came, touched its freshly polished walnut exterior, took just a tiny peak at the confessor's booth, not of course the supplicant's booth.

The next morning at breakfast, Íte declined to take toast, had just a little sparkling water. Once all the sisters were at the table, he stood and announced, "The confessional will be open for business this morning and will remain open until all confessions are heard."

Mother Superior spoke, her face beaming, looking around the table. "Sisters, remember your chores and duties. Though confession is of course the most important part of a good Christian's life, it must not be undertaken without due consideration of your other responsibilities."

"Would you like to be first?" asked Íte, turning to the Mother Superior.

"I would be most honored," she whispered.

Íte excused himself from the table, and Mother Superior followed him to the hallway. Íte squeezed himself into the priest's cubicle, and Mother slipped superior into hers. He made a small welcoming cough, and Mother Superior settled down to a long confession.

"Bless me father for I have sinned," she began.

When Mother Superior stepped out of the confessional, she was shocked to see all the sisters lined up down the hallway, awaiting their turn.

"Now sisters, go off and attend to your duties. There is no telling how long each confession will last. We must rely on each sister, once she has confessed, to report to me, and I will send in the next. I will make up a roster. Of course, if you have something very urgent to confess, we can let you jump the queue."

The Mother Superior was so happy that the sisters in her charge were able to confess daily, if they wanted or found it necessary. But she failed to notice that the confessional had become the central organizing feature of the convent. Nor did she, or anyone else notice that Íte did not show up for breakfast. He was, in fact, always available, always in the confessional.

Íte for his part felt no hunger for food. He was used, after all, to fasting from his previous life as an expert hermit and ascetic. He had arranged for one of the sisters to slip him a small glass of sparkling water each morning before he began the morning sessions. And each time at the end of the day when he went to bed, he took a small glass of sparkling water. That was all.

Yet over the days and weeks that followed, he began to notice that, contrary to what happened to his body when he was a hermit, he was getting fatter, and fatter. None of the sisters noticed this because they never even caught a glimpse of him these days. He was entirely in the confessional or in his room. Nor did they notice that he ate nothing. All he took was a little sparkling water each day and that was brought to him by his first and last confessors respectively.

It took the sensitive and perceptive Mother Superior to suspect that something was amiss. She began to realize that when she did her own confession, Íte did not want to let her go. He kept pressing her to confess more and more, to the point that she began to make up sins in order to please his appetite that seemed to be insatiable. But she said nothing, until one day she heard a cry from the confessional, from the last confesser of the day. She hurried to the confessional and found Íte, his face twisted in pain, wedged in the doorway of his cubicle. He had become so fat that he could no longer fit through.

"Father!" Cried Mother Superior. "What have you become?" And immediately she fell to her knees and asked for forgiveness for having asked such a prying question, lacking in empathy.

"Oh! I knew I should have made the doorway wider. But it would not have fitted in the hallway," answered Íte. "Just push me back in, and I'll be fine. I can sleep here for the night."

"But you can't do that. What will you do if you…" Mother Superior's voice trailed off, embarrassed.

"I have no need. It's a kind of miracle, I suppose," he said with a saintly smile. "Now off you go, get your sleep. I will be here waiting for you in the morning, and come as early as you want." The earlier the better, he thought to himself. For he had a great hunger. Not for food. But for confessions. He gobbled up all their sins, and with each confession, he became fatter and fatter.

It finally dawned on Mother Superior that Íte had gone through some kind of conversion. His extreme asceticism had become its opposite. He grew fat on all their sins. She pictured him vomiting up all their confessions, the sins coming out of his mouth like the words in a 16th century bible illustration. What was the equivalent to putting a finger down his throat? Or maybe it was too late for that. Maybe what was needed was an enema?

The next morning, Mother Superior brought Íte his sparkling water. In it she had mixed a triple dose of Epsom salts. She forbade any of the sisters to attend confessional until further notice. She went back to bed and dreamed of Íte whose likeness had taken on the shape of the devil itself, gobbling up the sinners in his huge mouth, spewing out the sinners from his anus, just like she had seen in a Bosch painting.

Moral: Punishment is the insatiable tie that binds . .

27. The Punishment Game

A law professor is convicted of evil intent.

In a regular card game, the dealer deals the cards to the players and each player gets an equal number of cards. The dealer, depending on the game, mostly places the remaining cards in the middle from which each player according to rules, draws a card and or deposits a card. Generally, in any game that requires a dealer, the role of dealer is rotated to each player in turn, to neutralize any advantage that the dealer might have.

One could say that a card game represents the ideal of the distribution of benefits and losses for each player. It is a game of chance, though there are some card games that mix together chance and manipulation, such as poker, or bridge. But even in these games, the attempts to overcome chance by cunning are considerably challenging, depending on the skill of the player, especially the ability to calculate the possibilities of how the cards will fall, whether these are guessing how an opponent will play their card, or calculating (usually card counting) what cards they hold.

In an effort to counteract the intrusion of chance into a game, there are, of course, rules. It is the rules that maketh the game, someone said (maybe not). And it is the ability of each player or team of players to overcome the oppression of these rules that makes for a winner. However, in the wider field of life, the "game of life" one might say, we should understand one very important truism: that rules are made to be broken. The logic of this frustratingly true statement is unassailable. There would be no point having a rule if there were not the expectation of it being broken. There are two ways to think about this conundrum. People do things that others do not like, say for example, defecating in public. "There ought to be a law against that," exclaims an outraged citizen. And so a rule is made that prescribes a punishment for that act. Note here that the act preceded the punishment. But there is another way of looking at it. I am a lawmaker (member of parliament, city council, senator etc.). We have decided that in order to prevent the spread of a pandemic there will be a curfew that forbids anyone in the streets after 9.00 pm, anyone who does to be fined $10,000 plus six months jail time. This is a case where the rule precedes the crime. It is enacted in order to punish. Traffic laws are a prime example of this.

In any game though, whether football, cricket, basketball, cards or a board game, losing is equated with punishment. Consider how we routinely deal with little toddlers who love to play games. Until they get older, we "let them win," knowing full well that losing will result in tears, often very loud. The losing response is built in. People hate to lose. And top athletes unabashedly say, when interviewed and asked what motivates them to become the best, they universally reply: "I hate to lose."

Those who lose in the game of life are, without any compassion or hesitancy, referred to as "losers." The hidden assumption is that they are losers because it is their fault, when it is quite obvious that this is a great example of Freud's notion of projection. We project on to others that which we deny in ourselves. Few can stand losing, though because of life's vicissitudes, we lose in one way or another, every day. Those who die, of course, are the ultimate losers, in spite of the considerable human ingenuity to deny this awful fact.

Society's iconic losers are of course its criminals, especially repeat offenders, who are ingested through the turnstile of the criminal justice system, found guilty and punished. This story is about one such person, one of many, one, though, who is always not far away from the "law abiding." In fact we are all a hair's breadth away from criminality as this story, based on true events (aren't they all?) shows.

*

Before we begin the story there is one more complication that hinges on the manipulation of the rules by those who are subjected to them. Here, the best example is in the very competitive game basketball, though it applies to probably all sports, especially contact sports. There are so many refined rules in basketball that some players have become adept at rule following and rule breaking by "drawing a foul." Or, in criminal justice terminology, victim-precipitated homicide (or whatever else). This story reveals a complicated web of precipitation, intrigue, trickery, moral superiority, a winning hand, and of course, the loser.

*

John Jones was a law professor at Temple University, Philadelphia. He commuted each day from his home in center city at 12th and Pine. His two kids, Peter 12, and Mary 10 attended the local school on 5th street, where his wife Laura taught school. Each morning they would all walk to the school together, then John would say his good-byes and take the bus to Temple. On this day, it was spring break, so there was not a lot of pressing work to do, no classes at least, so John went straight to his office and closed the door intending to catch up on a lot of old correspondence, especially email, that he had put aside during the busy teaching of the past several weeks. He opened up his email and skimmed through the list. There were a few from friends and colleagues to which he quickly replied, then one email that he was about to delete, but then, on a whim opened it. The email subject heading was simply, "please help me."

Now, he knew all about phishing and what not. But every now and again, curiosity or whatever else, caused him to open an email or click on a link that he knew he should not. The email said:

"Dear Professor. I am a teenager and lost my way. Can you help me please? I don't know what to do."

John immediately thought it may be a possible suicide and clicked on the reply button.

"How old are you and what kind of help do you need?"

The answer came. "My name is Caroline. I am 15. Home from school because they bully me."

"I could arrange for you to get help. There's a suicide hot line."

"I don't think I need that. I just need someone to talk to. I'm all alone. My dad left, and my mom, well she's an addict."

"You are on your own, then?"

We need not go into the series of emails that occurred over the next few hours. Eventually, it ended up with John agreeing to go to her house to help her, though she had made it fairly clear that the kind of help she had in mind was not life threatening. In fact she sent him a series of photos of her, each one successively revealing more bare skin. She was very beautiful, looked much older than 15. John, still convincing himself that he was doing good, agreed to come to her house, and see what he could do. He had thought of calling the police and reporting the problem, but knowing the police in North Philadelphia as he did, he doubted that they were the answer. Besides he did not know the address. He then thought of notifying the social welfare department, so emailed the girl asking for her address. The email came back immediately with an address not far from Temple. In fact, when he looked it up, it was only a couple of blocks down Broad Street.

Another email showed up. "Are you coming soon? I don't think I can stand this much longer."

John called up the social welfare department of Philadelphia. It had a branch in North Philadelphia, he thought. Unfortunately, he got a recorded message saying that because of COVID, they were overloaded with cases. He left details and Caroline's address. Then tried to get back to work. But it was no use. He could not concentrate. He tried not opening up his email. But in the end, gave in. It was just ten minutes since her last email with the address asking what time he was coming.

Finally, he gave in and said he would be there in fifteen minutes.

It was a bright and sunny spring day, A strong cool wind blew right down busy Broad street. The buses left clouds of blue smoke as they accelerated between stops and cars competed with each other to overtake them. John walked the two blocks, then stopped at the lights at the corner of Montgomery Avenue, crossed Broad and walked two blocks to Sydenham street. The corner house, she had said.

He rang the bell, no answer. Knocked loudly on the door. No answer. He turned to leave, then suddenly the door opened. A man dressed in an old crumpled suit answered.

"What you want?"

"I'm here for Caroline. She said she was in some kind of trouble."

"Who are you?"

"John Smith, I'm a professor at Temple University Law School. Is she OK?"

"Come right in. You were expected. This the girl you came to see?"

The man showed him one of the photographs showing a lot of bare skin. In fact she was naked.

"That's her. But why are you here? She said she had no father. May I see her, please?"

"OK. That's it," called the man raising his voice.

Suddenly police in uniform appeared from the adjoining room, one quickly darted forward and stood behind him.

"I am detective Swanson. You are under arrest for soliciting sex with a minor. Cuff him officer!"

John was dumbfounded. He looked around as the officer roughly grabbed his arms and handcuffed him. Another patted him down and removed his cell phone and wallet. "But, but, I came here to help her…"

"Yeh, that's what they all say," sneered the detective.

"But it's true! Please! I am a lawyer. You can't do this! Ask the girl, I had no intentions to do anything with her."

"I asked the girl and she said you did."

"Where is she? Bring her out! She'll tell you," cried John, now so weak at the knees he was on the verge of collapse.

"I am that girl," said detective Swanson, grinning proudly.

"You, you…" John managed to hold back the expletives that sat on his tongue ready to be spat out. "It's a trap!"

"That's right, and you helped us spring it."

They marched John out of the house, down the steps to Sydenham street, then to West Montgomery Avenue where the police wagon stood waiting. And from there, a quick trip to the local holding center of Police Headquarters. The officials finger printed him, booked him, photographed him, signed for his personal items, one of them his phone which he managed to use to send a quick text to his colleague and friend, a trial lawyer. He was led to a holding cell, there to wait. He looked down the row of cells. The depressing look of the place was already unbearable. What would prison be like? He looked around the cell. At least there were no others. Though, he was not sure whether right now his own company was good company. He sat on the bench his head in his hands and asked himself. Was he guilty? Had the thought entered his mind? The naked picture. Was he not like the former President Carter who famously admitted a feeling of lust from time to time? Did this make him innocent? Or guilty?

*

John's trial lawyer promised him an excellent, though standard entrapment defense, but warned that the jury would probably not buy it, even though it had a lot going for it. It was the police who had invented this crime and invented the victim, in fact there was no victim. If it was a crime it was they who committed it, not John, and so on. He knew the statistics. Over ninety percent of entrapment defenses failed in court, especially if the prosecution had video, which they did. They had video of John entering the building, seeming to thirst for the nude teenager, or at least that was how the prosecutor would make it look. It would not matter how many character witnesses he brought on, juries were tough on sex offenders. They loved to find them guilty. His lawyer therefore urged John to take a plea. It was like a game of poker, he explained to John, except that he had a pretty poor hand. You try to plea down to maybe a misdemeanor, though with sex offenses it was very hard to do. On the other hand, if found guilty of the major charge against him, attempted rape of a minor, he guessed it would be, then he could get many years in prison if found guilty.

"But I didn't do anything!" John pleaded over and over again. The more he pleaded, the more he appeared guilty.

The reasons for pleading guilty to a minor offense were overwhelming. Not only might he avoid prison time, his wife and children would be saved the embarrassment of publicity that follows a trial in open court. And it would save the humiliation of his wife having to get up in court and testify as to his upright and moral character. And if he could plead down to a misdemeanor, then he might be able to keep his law license.

John sat in jail all this time. Bail was refused, as it often is for sex offenses, especially with a minor. How could he face his children? What would happen to them at school, once it got out that they had a sex offender for a father? And everyone would know because even for the most minor of sex offenses, he would be placed on the sex offender registry, available for all to peruse on the registry web site.

After many, many sleepless nights, John, his legal mind running through all the logical parameters of his guilt and or innocence, the possible ramifications after conviction and punishment, he came to the conclusion that the logical solution that caused least humiliation to those he loved was to confine the punishment to himself, to him alone. He had imagined all the humiliations and bullying his kids would get, but also thought of the opportunities that might arise for his loving wife to start anew, not having to be reminded of her sex offender husband who sat in jail or whatever. Certainly, even if he pleaded to a minor offense, his university would without doubt fire him. So she would have to become the breadwinner for the family, though he had managed to put away a reasonable amount into a retirement account. It would be a struggle, but manageable.

She could continue living with the kids without too many hardships, without him.

Moral: Guilty or innocent, the losers are always punished.

28. Punishment Therapy

A restauranteur seeks counsel during COVID lockdown.

It takes a long time to qualify as a psychotherapist. Matilda White after graduating with a Ph. D. in psychology from Melbourne University, obtained additional certifications in Rogerian and Pavlovian therapy when she served as an intern at New York's Bellevue Hospital. She then returned to Melbourne and served another four years as psychotherapist at the University of Melbourne Hospital Parkville clinic for mental health, tucked away in one of the fancy row houses on Royal Parade. Now, thirty four years old and unmarried, she at last settled into a private practice. She had no time for a personal relationship. All her time was spent on relationships with clients.

For many years, her various colleagues who took it upon themselves to give her advice, informed her, often intrusively, that she was too devoted to her work, that she should "get a life," that it was unhealthy to work such long ours to the exclusion of all else. She couldn't count the times that she had been lectured with the old saying: "All work and no play makes Jack a dull boy." Putting aside the sexist connotations of that outdated saying, she often wanted to say back to her well-meaning colleagues that devotion to work was the healthiest thing that anyone could do. And besides she had many relationships, all with her clients. She valued such relationships above everything else. By serving her clients she was serving herself. That's right. It was healthy, she was convinced, that she be dependent on her clients just as her clients were dependent on her. It seemed just. It ensured that each did not take undue advantage of the other. How many relationships had she noticed among her friends and colleagues where the stronger exploited the other? It was an occupational hazard of therapists that they might lapse into exploiting their clients. The pressure of time (as more or less assured by the ways in which Medicare reimbursements worked and the ceaseless demands of insurance companies) constantly weighed on the shoulders of all practitioners who dealt with clients.

*

It takes a long time to become a patient of psychotherapy. There are a lot of factors involved. Of course the main one is the process of denial, the natural tendency of humans to deny problems that face them, their infinite capacity for self-deception. This is followed by the terrible fear that one's colleagues or friends or relatives may find out that you are seeing a therapist. "What on earth can be wrong with them?" Or, alternatively, "it's about time. There's something really wrong with them."

John Paolo was such a person, like any other hard working person, or so it appeared. He owned a very successful Italian restaurant and pastry shop on Lygon Street, Carlton, a chic suburb of Melbourne that served the many professors and students of Melbourne University. He worked long hours, chatted with his regular customers, supervised his young staff (usually students) and worked as a barista as well at busy times. What would such a successful, congenial person like John Paolo need from a psychotherapist?

First of all, you may have noticed from his name that John was Italian, of course. He was raised in a loving Italian family (could there be a family that was not loving?) that migrated to Australia two generations ago. The trouble was, though, that he took a disliking to the Roman Catholic church and the demands it made on his family's lives, not to mention money. Worse, his loving and doting mother had him pegged to go into the priest-hood. The day she pestered him to do so was the day he graduated from high school and immediately got a job as a barista in one of the few coffee shops then in Carlton. She hugged him and said, "I'm so proud that now you're ready to become a priest." He lost his temper, raised his voice and in anger, told her to mind her own business and to shut up!

He had felt really bad after that, and of course he apologized. He even went to confession and confessed to the priest, whoever he was, and received platitudes and useless demands of whatever number of Hail Marys to repeat. John Paolo on that day, as he left the church lost his faith and never returned to it except for special occasions when relatives got married, or christenings. As the years went by and he threw himself into his work, and got his own coffee shop and later a restaurant up and running, he had no time for anything else. You might say his work was his faith. And to see the customers come in, the money mount up, what more could one want?

Unfortunately, the year was 2020, the year of the corona virus. All Victoria, especially Melbourne, was locked down, his restaurant and bar closed. His life's work, not so much ruined, he had enough money tucked away to withstand a year or so of income loss. Initially, it did not bother him. But after a couple of months, there were fewer and fewer things for him to attend to with his business. He had way too much time on his hands. Without work. What was there? He began waking up in the middle of the night, thoughts running through his head. Always bad thoughts. Memories of things he had done wrong. Little things and big things. They came to him every night. Perhaps the worst, his yelling at his mother about her wanting him to join the priesthood. It became so bad, he made a list of things he had done wrong, then screwed it up and threw it away. He tried repeating prayers he had learned in chapel when a choir boy, and that worked a bit, but the bad memories, especially those that he had tried to forget, many to do with sexual relationships tormented him. He had been a bit rough on occasions. Said some things too. Why must these memories come to haunt him every night?

He tried sleeping pills. But soon realized that they were addictive and blunted his mind, a condition that he could not withstand. He again thought of going back to the church and confessing to a priest. He got as far as the church door, but turned back. He had lost his faith when a teenager and it would never come back to him, he was sure. The trouble was he had too much idle time on his hands. Spent all the time thinking about himself. He needed someone to talk to. And that was when, as he was walking aimlessly around the neighborhood, he passed the mental health clinic in Parkville. The thought that he might be mentally ill, of course, shocked him. But in the end, the sleepless nights, the uncontrollable bad memories, forced him to the edge, and finally on one of his walks, he stepped into the Melbourne University Hospital Clinic for Mental Health.

*

"Your problem is that you have way too much guilt, John," announced Doctor White. She sat across from her client, John Paolo, on a faux suede couch, her legs together and knees slanting to the side, small dainty feet, and toes, the nails painted in deep purple, peeping out from elegant Italian sandals.

In contrast, John Paolo sat stiffly on a wooden chair with a woven wicker seat, no cushion. "I don't need a therapist to tell me that," he said, trying to keep his very strong feelings of aggression bottled up. "That's what I've been telling you the last couple of sessions. That's why I'm here."

"Yes, indeed. I was just summing up," smiled Dr. White, unruffled. "The long list of bad memories of past, shall we call them events, is certainly overwhelming. And of course, I'm sure you know that it's not unusual. In fact, if any person sat down to make a list of all the bad things they had done, they would probably equal or surpass yours."

"OK, so guilt is normal. Is that what you're saying? That there's nothing wrong with me?"

"No, I'm not saying that. The fact that you have come to me, says that for you, it is not normal, that you are unable to live with the guilt. People deal with their guilt in many different ways. That it's bothering you, causing you continuous sleepless nights, is not normal. And we need to do something about it."

Paolo leaned forward, waving his hand as though to gear himself up. "So we've had four sessions and I don't feel any better. What do you recommend? And don't say medication. I want my mind to be clear, not half there, if you see what I mean."

Dr. White stood up from the sofa, leaving her notebook and pencil behind. She came up to him, then suddenly clapped her hands loudly at his ear, stamped her foot, and screamed "Aahhh!"

John was stunned and jumped up from his chair. "What the…!"

Dr. White returned to her sofa and sat. She smiled kindly.

John noticed the kindness. But he also noticed her slightly purple lipstick. Her mouth was, well, enticing. It was at that moment that more guilt readied itself to descend upon him. He could easily jump up and ravish this woman. He tried to put it out of his mind, more so, out of his body. But the more he tried, the more impossible it became. He remained speechless, crossed and uncrossed his legs.

"I startled you," purred the therapist. "That was a simple example of fright therapy, or to put it in official terms, the first Pavlovian administration of pain therapy."

"It wasn't painful. I mean…"

"I know. The guilt, it leaped on you, first into your head, then right down to your toes." She wasn't sure why she said the last part, about the toes. She frowned slightly and made a mental note of her lapse, as she called such occurrences. She could see, however, that her client had been put off guard, placing him in a vulnerable, or should one say, ready state, to receive her therapeutic schedule, one that would drive the guilt out of his head. Pain therapy would do it.

John looked at the floor then up and into his therapist's eyes. He had to remind himself that she was his therapist, not a potential partner. She scared him. But she enticed him.

Dr. White stood up. "Well, our time's up. We've made good progress today. Same time next week?"

"Thanks Dr. White. Yes, I'll be back."

*

Now, there is pain, and there's pain. Tearing off the fingernails is pain. It is excruciating. Slapping you on the buttocks is painful too. But it is a different kind of pain. Certainly not excruciating. However, when the therapeutic schedule requires that one administer pain to one's client, slapping the buttocks is a little too close to other parts of the body that may react differently. That is, those parts may be stimulated in ways that make the pain pleasurable. It seems like a contradiction. But then whoever designed our bodies had quite a sense of humor. Our bodies and the minds that accompany them are full of contradictions. There is an old saying, "she is her own worst enemy." It sums up the angst in which we all live.

"Welcome John. Let's get down to business. Please take your place on the chair. But first remove your shirt, so I can get a look at your bare back.

John did as he was told. He had thought of little else all week except imagining her in the nude and on the couch. His bad memories had receded. Her therapy was working! He sat on the chair, but then Dr. White gently touched his elbow and said, please sit astride the chair, facing the back of the chair."

Again, he did as he was told. The therapist went to her desk and retrieved from the drawer a small whip, a little over one meter long, three thin strands of leather attached to a leather bound handle. She held it in front of his disbelieving eyes. She herself was a little worried because she had inadvertently touch his elbow, which broke the therapist-client rules, that there must be no direct touching of bodies.

John did all he could to hold back a gasp. He gripped the back of the chair until his knuckles were white. And before he could say anything at all, the therapist lashed his back with a stroke of the whip. He wanted to scream, but held it in. She said nothing. She gave him two more strokes. Red welts appeared on his back. A nice smooth live back, observed Matilda. Actually, a gorgeous back. She stepped back, upset that she had thoughts or were they feelings that she should not have as a therapist? "That will be all for today. How was your guilt last week? On a scale of one to ten, ten being the worst, how would you rate it?

"Can I turn around now?" asked John.

"Yes of course." Dr. White had returned to the couch and sat writing notes. She did not look up, because she was worried if she saw his naked front, she might make further mistakes.

"I'd say about seven since last week. It's helping, doctor. Amazing."

"Excellent. Then same time next week? It will be a double session, as there will be a lot more to do."

"A lot more of what?" He tried to feel his back. It felt extremely sensitive to touch. Burned a little. But his body felt very much alive, as though he had had a couple of stiff shots of espresso.

"It depends on what you report to me next week. Oh and by the way, please do not try applying a whip or anything to yourself. It must be done under strict clinical control."

"Of course. I'm a lapsed Catholic. I don't do that sort of stuff," John replied with a grin.

Doctor White gave him a clinical look. "If you don't mind, Mr. Paolo, we will keep religion out of your treatment. As a matter of fact, I take back my advice about doing it at home. I'll write you a prescription that will allow you to purchase a do-it-at home whip. These are a smaller version of the one I used, and there are no knots in the leather strands. "

"Really?" asked John in disbelief.

"Yes. Medicare classes it as a prosthesis class B. The pharmacy on Grattan Street has it."

She handed him the prescription. "See you next week, John," she said with a clinical smile.

*

John could hardly wait for his next appointment with Dr. White. His sleeplessness had gone away, that is, after he had finished imagining what his therapist might do with him next time.

Pain therapy schedules are not widely acknowledged to be effective in treating guilt. In truth there have been no peer reviewed studies of its effectiveness. And it should be acknowledged that Dr. White was trying this therapy after having been disillusioned by the several other talking therapies, none of which worked, in her opinion, especially did not work on eradicating or even alleviating guilt. Some research had suggested that Pavlovian conditioning, applying a painful stimulus to a person to remove an annoying habit or other aspect of behavior, had been affirmed by many peer reviewed studies. It was a time honored method of behavioral therapy. What she was doing was simply an extension of Pavlov and his dogs.

It had been argued by modernists that Pavlov used rewards to get his dogs to salivate at the sound of a bell. But rewards, it had been found time and again, simply made the subjects soft and pliable so that they would do anything to get the reward. Witness the dogs who will go half crazy to get a tiny morsel as a reward for doing some silly antic. They do not go crazy when they are taught discipline using pain as the stimulus. It is like everything else. Too much of a good thing, whether reward or punishment is not recommended. Moderation is the rule. However, the trouble with any kind of conditioning (rewards and punishments) is that there is the constant temptation to keep increasing either the rewards or punishments. That is, the danger of the slippery slope.

And so, in the double session, there is a hint that the temptation had already begun, as far as the therapist was concerned. She, or course, is nor aware of this. Rather, she sees it as a scientific step in a carefully arranged schedule of punishments. The ultimate reward being the eradication of her patient's guilt.

John arrived a little late for his appointment. Dr. White was a little annoyed, but tried not to be. She did not want to waste the double appointment.

"Hell, Mr. Paolo. You may lay flat on the couch, and take off your top clothes first to show your back. It has no scars I take it?" She examined his smooth olive back. Not a scratch or mark. She donned a pair of surgical gloves and rubbed her fingers over where she had lashed him. All fine and smooth. Without another word, she lashed him three times on the back with her whip. John yelped a little, but then smiled, then gritted his teeth awaiting the next stroke. Instead. He felt his therapist's hand (fully gloved) on his shoulder.

"How would you rate your sense of guilt this week, Mr. Paolo?"

"You can call me John. I'd say a four or five."

"Then we are making excellent progress. Now slide down your pants to bare your buttocks." She turned away while he did it.

He heard the rustling of the leather strands as she raised the whip above her head, then brought it down in a fast lash, but the stroke just grazed his well curved buttocks, so tight for a fifty year old Italian male, she thought. The client grunted.

Matilda gripped the whip tightly and then brought it down with a fierce lash and it connected across both buttocks, eliciting a yell from the client.

"Did that hurt you badly?" she asked, "there's no skin broken, if that's what you are concerned about."

John was amazed to hear himself say, "Oh no! It was great! I mean, wasn't too bad." Lying on his stomach caused other parts of his body to react to the lash as well. It was a well-known autonomic reaction. His face became flushed.

"The schedule calls for several more to the buttocks and back. Shall I stop? You look a little distraught."

"Oh no, doctor White. It's all good," John mumbled into the arm of the couch.

Doctor White stopped to make some notes. She then set her timer and returned to the schedule. It recommended a pause of one minute between applications.

Very quickly, the double session (a total of thirty minutes) was up. John, embarrassed turned away as he pulled up his pants and buttoned his shirt. He rubbed his very sensitive buttocks and tried to place himself in front of the couch so that the stains would not be noticeable.

Dr. White, now at her desk, said without looking up, "single session next week, Mr. Paolo. You did well today. Let's get the guilt down to two or three next week."

"Thank you doctor." John hurried away.

*

She's on the couch. John had thought of little else since their last session. It took an herculean effort to control himself. He had not expected to be assigned the chair with the wicker seat. She sat with her knees together on the edge of the couch, legs bent at the knees, slanted, her sweet toenails painted in that very light purple, peeping at him through her white sandals. He sat in the chair and shifted it a little to face her, his hands clasped tightly in front of his belly. The edge of the whip peeped out from under her bottom. She must have sat on it without knowing, absorbed as she was reading the notes she had taken last week. John wriggled in his chair and moved it a little forward scraping it on the wood floor. He coughed a tiny cough. She looked up and smiled.

"So how is your guilt index today?" she asked.

"It's a four," I think. Not all that much progress from last week, I'm afraid. He was lying, of course, hoping for more of last week, and if she gave it, he would take it to another level.

"Well, I'll soon see to that. But just to make sure, you should come here and sit by me. "

John of course couldn't wait to get on the couch. "You're sitting on the whip," he said as he sat down beside her. He looked for last week's stains and saw none. She might be sitting on them too. He managed to place his bottom tightly against hers and the whip dug into him.

"Oh, just a minute," said Dr. White. She felt for the whip and her notebook dropped on to the floor. John leaned over to get it.

"Leave it," she said, "you need to get naked today." He needed no second asking. He stood up, and in a flash everything was off.

"On to the couch," she ordered as she stood up beside him and raised the whip.

John was half out of his mind. He grabbed the whip out of her hand and gave her a light belt on her shapely bottom.

"Ouch! Mr. Paolo. That's not what you should be doing. Now, give me the whip this minute!"

But he held the whip tightly and stood back, hands on hips. "What's your guilt rating, doctor?" he asked with a devilish grin. "Maybe we should attend to that. You know, transference and all that."

"You've been reading up on psychotherapy, I see," smiled Dr. White.

But John was not listening. He grabbed her lightly buttoned thin cotton shirt and pulled it open. It was not enough. He dropped and used both hands to carefully remove her clothes. She did not resist. But she did lean down to pick up the whip, then quickly turned to him and gave him a lash across the front of his legs. The little leather strands found their mark. And indeed over the next few minutes that seemed like a lifetime, they left their marks in every imaginable place.

"Your guilt index?" John asked as they fell on to the couch together.

"Ten, she said, "and yours now?"

"Ten!"

They took it in turns to use the whip on each other. They found themselves on the couch, then on the hard wooden floor, standing or prostrate, it didn't matter. And by the time the buzzer on Doctor White's timer went off signaling the end of the session, they were both exhausted.

"Session is over, Mr. Paolo. Please get dressed and we will continue this therapy session next week."

"But what about my guilt?"

"Do you feel any? I don't. I feel liberated."

"Exactly how I feel. Then that means I'm cured?"

"Unfortunately, that's not likely. But we will review your progress at our next session. Please keep a record of your daily guilt level. Take a rating morning and night."

"Thank you doctor. You've done wonders for me."

Doctor White was at her desk again. "Good-bye," she said without looking up.

*

John returned to his empty restaurant and made himself an espresso, double shot. The past hour had turned into a fog, a blur. His body tingled to the point that it hurt, especially from the red marks of the welts doctor White had laid on him. What had happened to him? It was the most amazing thing. But had he done it or had she? He was reminded of when he was a little kid and his mom yelled at him, he would always say, "it wasn't me, he did it," blaming his older brother.

He went upstairs and showered. There was no one he could talk to about this. If he did, they would tell him that he just raped his doctor. And that wasn't what happened, was it? If you went back to the very first session, it was she who started it all. And now, in the frightening carnal fog that had descended upon him after this session he did not know who was to blame.

And there it was. That word had nosed its way into his thoughts. It signaled that horrible word. Guilt. He walked around his vacant restaurant, polishing tables, cleaning cutlery. The fact was, he could not wait for the week to go by so he could face off in another therapy session. Maybe it was all part of the therapy. After all, it had begun to work. The whipping, that is.

So John Paolo continued to show up for his weekly sessions, and each session repeated the last, except that the ferocity of the exchanges with the whip gradually tempered, and his guilt level remained at five. He began to think that his therapist was no longer interested in his problem. That it wasn't therapy at all. But just sex.

*

At last the COVID lockdown had been lifted and his restaurant was almost back to what might be a new normal. A limited number of customers dining in his spacious restaurant. Friends to say hello to, regular customers calling to make reservations. Most of his staff had returned, happy to have work to do, as was he. Nothing like constant work to keep a man happy, distracting him from the carnal fog. He gradually began to miss a session or two, or three. And in the end he quit going. On quiet days in the restaurant he tended to think back to the first sessions with Dr. White. My God! How could he have done it, and worse, actually loved it? But then, the early sessions had really saved his life, mental life that is. They were like a gift from Heaven, though re-living them now was like going into the depths of Hell. He yearned to do it all over again, but with someone else. Because he had to face it, the doctor now disgusted him. He had done a one eighty.

And so, at the end of a very good day at the restaurant, after he closed up, he had made an appointment to see a priest at the church in which he had been christened. He had not been to church for many years. Too busy with his business, was his excuse to the local priest who pestered him from time to time, and treated him well none the less, each time John treated him to a free lunch.

The confession got off on the wrong foot. John didn't want to confess all his sins at once and have them absolved. He wanted just to tell someone about his adventure with his doctor and ask whether it was his or her fault. The memory of those intense exchanges with the doctor dominated his mind night and day, but especially at night when he had no distractions. Working seemed to be the best antidote. Thank goodness the lockdown had ended, otherwise he would have gone crazy, he said to himself many times over.

In the end, after an acrimonious start, the priest agreed to have lunch with him at his restaurant at which John could reveal everything. And he did tell all, and watched as the priest's face reddened during the more lurid accounts. The priest gobbled up everything that was put in front of him. John had simply a Campari soda. And when he finished he looked the priest in the eye and asked, "well?"

The priest, youngish and with a typically well-scrubbed appearance, looked up. "These are shocking things you have told me," he said quietly and with a very faint Italian accent. "Now I see why you have come to me. The church has had its problems with sex abuse, as you know."

"Father, I don't care about the church's problems. It's my problem that I care about. If we have another lockdown, I don't know what I will do. I'm scared I'll go back to her."

"Either you should do that right away and continue your therapy, since it got you through the terrible lockdown, or…"

"Or what Father? Go back? How could you countenance that?"

"One question at a time, John. As I was saying, or you should report her for unprofessional conduct and sexual abuse of you, her patient."

"But if I do that, the press, it will go crazy with it. I can't!"

"Then there is a third option," the priest said with a faint smile, perhaps a little patronizing.

"And what is that?"

"You can come back to the church and make regular confessions and receive absolution for all your sins. There is no therapy on earth that can do that, talking or non-talking cure." The priest took the last spoonful of panna cotta and sat back most satisfied. He put out his hands, palms facing up, inviting John to take them. "In us there is hope. In earthly therapy, there are only false promises, or worse as you have discovered, debased trickery."

They both sat in silence. The priest's hands still open. John stirred uncomfortably in his seat. It did seem to be his only way out. But he couldn't just blurt out that he didn't believe the church either. They had told so many lies in their sex abuse scandals. "Is there no other way?"

The priest, wily as many are, answered, "well there is a fourth way that could be chosen along with our way."

"And what is that, father?" John reached out one hand only and clasped the open hand of the priest.

"You could get a lawyer and sue for damages, just like they have done against our church."

As the routines of his restaurant slowly returned to pre COVID levels, John's spirits revived somewhat. He did go to church and did begin to make regular confessions. Whether these were to that same priest he did not know, though he thought he recognized the voice a couple of times. He consulted with a lawyer who had successfully brought a number of cases of sexual abuse against the Roman Catholic church and other churches as well, but it quickly became apparent that such a course of action would only lead to money received or spent, and would not relieve his guilt level one bit. He had come to the conclusion after his many confessions that one cannot buy off guilt. On the other hand, he tried his hardest to remember the wonderful feelings of ecstasy he had experienced in therapy with Dr. White, and that managed to assuage his guilt at least down to a level of about 4. So that was not too bad. In fact, it inspired him to go back to her non-talking cure.

It had been a year since he was last in Dr. White's office. She was just the same, and dressed in just the same clothes, the light cotton shirt, tight business dress, white sandals, light purple lipstick and painted toenails.

She smiled at him as he made himself comfortable on the couch.

"Please sit on the chair for today's session," she said, very businesslike, as though they were meeting for the first time.

"I brought something for you," said John, reaching into a shopping bag.

"Oh! Thank you. But our professional rules of conduct do not allow us to accept gifts from our clients," she said with a serious look.

"It's not really a gift. More like something I hope will aid in my therapy."

"Oh, well, Perhaps that's OK. Let me see it?"

There was a loud rattle and John produced a set of handcuffs that he dropped on her desk. Dr. White leaned forward and picked them up, a serious look on her face.

"Stand and face the wall, hands behind you," she ordered.

Moral: Guilt, the God of Life

29. Discipline

Parallel fathers discipline their sons.

Around 353 BCE, there was a Roman consul Titus Manlius, famed in battle and the most upright and respected politician in Rome. He was also a stickler for discipline, possibly one of the founders of the military discipline and martial laws of modern times. Orders from above had to obeyed no matter what. There was no leniency, the orders had to be obeyed to the letter.

So it was in one of the perennial battles Rome waged, this time with the Samnites against the Latins, Manlius and his co-consul Publius Decius were convinced that military discipline had become too lax and that it needed to be reasserted. Manlius therefore called his legions together and made a moving speech reminding them of the importance of discipline and that orders must be obeyed absolutely. And he restated his long held views on morality, pointing out his own virtue and total devotion to a moral life. He also recounted how important it was for Roman soldiers to work together as teams, immediately follow orders when formations had to be changed. Legions had to be deployed according to the battle conditions, such as the phalanx, the tortoise and others. It was the brilliance of Roman discipline to deploy their formations quickly that made the Roman military the great fighting force it was. Their methods dominated the battlefields of Europe for centuries, certainly to the 19th century, ending with Napoleon.

After his moving speech, and cheers of "Manlius! Manlius!" by the legions, Manlius, sent them into battle. He was particularly proud on this day because his son, Sextus, was a Centurion, commander of eighty men. Eager to make a name for himself and to please his father, Sextus, instead of maintaining the formation he had been ordered to do, saw an opportunity to overcome several groups of Latin skirmishers, so led his men into battle, breaking formation. He and his men crushed the enemy and returned to base victorious.

When the entire battle was over and Manlius had won yet another battle, he called the legions together.

"Fellow soldiers! You are bathed in glory today, having shown courage and devotion that has no equal. I am so humbled by your great bravery."

The legions cheered, "Manlius! Manlius!"

Manlius raised his hand to indicate silence. The troops stirred a little as they calmed down. Then Manlius spoke in a stern and solemn voice.

"Sextus Manlius, my son. Step forward!"

Sextus stepped forward, beaming, proud of having led his men to victory.

Manlius spoke again. "Soldiers all! Witness this Centurion, who disobeyed my clear order to remain in formation until the order is given to do otherwise. He broke formation and led his century into battle, and although victorious, it clearly defied my order. The punishment in the military for disobeying an order is death."

The legions stirred, but of course said nothing, not even a whisper.

Manlius continued. "It is therefore my moral duty, according to military law, to sentence you to be beheaded. This punishment to be carried out immediately!"

Sextus dropped to his knees, tears in his eyes, but also accepting his fate. He knew it was deserved. The camp Prefect stepped forward, raised his sword and delivered the blow.

*

In the 20th century, Freddy lived in a modest house in a distant suburb of Geelong called Norlane. His dad worked at the local Ford Motor company. He had built their house and planted the garden and was very proud of it. Freddy, being just ten years old took it all for granted, of course. He often played in the front yard on the grass and mowed the lawn when his dad asked him to. His mum stayed inside most of the time, cooking and sewing, and knitting. One of the things that his dad was very proud of, though complained all the time about it, was the golden privet hedge that ran across the entire front of the garden. It had become so high that Freddy could hardly see over it. He had to stand on tip toes to watch the cars go back and forth on the Melbourne Road.

On this day, having mowed the lawn, Freddy decided that he would do something special for his dad. He would trim the hedge to save him the bother. He went into the garage to retrieve the clippers, had a bit of practice opening and closing them. They didn't seem too hard to use, though his dad had told him on a number of occasions that they were too dangerous for him to use and that he was not to touch them. But his dad complained so much when he trimmed the hedge, Freddy he was sure he would be really surprised and happy when he came home and it was all done.

And so Freddy set to work. It took him much longer than he expected, and his arms got really tired. As well, he had to stand on a box to be able to reach the top. Clipping the sides, his dad had always said, was the easiest. It was the top that was hard, and now Freddy understood why. He sat down to rest for a while, and noticed his mum peaking at him through the front window. But she didn't come out, although she knew he shouldn't touch the clippers.

He had just finished the job and stepped back to admire his handiwork, when his dad arrived home in their old A model Ford. He pulled into the drive and hurried over to Freddy.

"Freddy," he said, "What have you done?"

"I thought I'd do the hedge to save you having to do it," said Freddy proudly.

"But look at the top of it," complained dad, "it's not straight. It has to be perfectly straight, not wobbly and all over the place. Besides, I told you never to touch the clippers."

His dad was angry. Not what Freddy had expected. And he was annoyed with himself that it had not occurred to him that the top of the hedge should be straight. Of course it should! But he had been too engrossed in cutting it, he took no notice of whether he was cutting straight or not.

"Gee, I'm sorry dad. I thought…"

"That's the trouble with you, you don't think. Think before you act! Aren't I always telling you that?"

Freddy knew he was too old to cry, but he was now on the brink of tears. "Gees dad," was all he could think of to say.

His dad looked at him, and then looked at the lawn. "The lawn looks good. Here's your pocket money. I ought not give it to you."

"Thanks dad." Freddy was puzzled and disappointed. He didn't expect to be paid for the hedge. He did it to please his dad. It was the same for the lawn, really.

"But you disobeyed me," said his dad with a frown. "I don't know what mum has cooked for dinner, but you will not be getting any. It will be straight to bed for you."

"But dad!"

"No buts."

Moral: Discipline gained, empathy lost.

THE END

FICTION

9/11/TWO
By Colin Heston

This gripping novel offers a glimpse into the real world of counter terrorism, hints at why 9/11 was allowed to happen and warns us that it could easily happen again. It's politics as usual in New York City when Larry MacIver, world renowned criminologist, is tapped by NYC Mayor Ruth Newberg to save NYC from a second 9/11 attack. Will it be nuclear? Will it be bio? MacIver and his geeky assistant Manish Das must overcome FBI ineptitude, CIA intrigue and, most of all, the evil and ruthless Iranian terrorist Shalah Muhammud, to save the city. Will it be a drone next time? Will New York politics doom the city's defences? Written before drones were widely in use, the novel seems prescient of much that has happened (should and should not have happened) in the world of counter terrorism.

Miscarriages
By Colin Heston

Teen Chooka grows up in the weird world of 1950s Aussie pub life. When his alcoholic dad dies, he searches for his identity, and that of his shadowy underage girlfriend, Iris. Captivated by the pub's many crazy customers and their raucous stories, Chooka becomes a boozer just like them. But Iris, after a miscarriage, disappears and Chooka sets out on a search that takes him to foreign places including Melbourne university and Vietnam. The search ends in a Melbourne pub, where they start over, but this time there's a different ending.

"…a brilliant, unforgettable book about real people…a sensitive, touching and poignant story." - *Reader's Favourite.*

Ferry to Williamstown
By Colin Heston

In this raucous Aussie story, corpses pop up in the Yarra river while Lizzie entertains her powerful and kinky clients in her Winnebago, parked on the ferry to Williamstown. Tightly bound Detective Striker, confronted by the mob of Catholics, wharfies and communists who rule Williamstown, struggles to solve the mystery. Lizzie gets engaged to her uncle Bobby, the lame ferry driver, and her mum, Babs, spellbound by the strange Father Zappia, tries to solve her own mystery of St. Robert's toe. She throws a raucous send-off party for Lizzie, and out of the chaos emerge many truths.

Holy Water
By Colin Heston

In this very naughty, hilariously irreverent farce, Alphonso, a Mexican drug lord, captures the market in Holy Water, acquires a university for his LGBTQ daughter, and makes an Australian cardinal the pope. "The worlds of gender, religion, and university life will never be the same again. Whoever wrote this book should be locked up with the outrageous characters s/he invented!" (*Chronicle of Lower Education*).

NONFICTION

The Art of Punishment. 2 Volumes. by Graeme R. Newman
A Walk in the Park by Robin. V. Clarke.
A Primer in Private Security by Mahesh Nalla and Graeme
    Newman.
A Primer in the Psychology of Crime by Mark Seis and Shlomo
    Shoham.
A Primer in the Sociology of Crime by John P. Hoffmann and
    Shlomo Shoham.
Close Control: Managing a Maximum Security Prison by
    Nathan Kantrowitz.

Corporate Crime, Corporate Violence by Michael J. Lynch.
Crime and Social Deviation by Shlomo Shoham.
Discovering Criminology from W. Byron Groves edited by
    Graeme R. Newman, Michael J. Lynch.
From Gangs to Gangsters by Marylee Reynolds.
God as the Shadow of Man by S. Giora Shoham
Justice with Prejudice by .Michael J. Lynch
Just and Painful 2nd Edition. by Graeme R. Newman
Migration, Culture Conflict, and Crime edited by Joshua D.
    Freilich, Graeme R. Newman, S. Giora Shoham, Moshe
    Addad.
Personality and Deviance by S.Giora Shoham.
Punishment and Privilege 2nd edition edited by Graeme R.
    Newman.
Race and Criminal Justice edited by Michael J. Lynch and E.
    Britt Patterson
Representing O.J.- Murder, Criminal Justice and Mass Culture
    by Gregg Barak
Salvation through the Gutters by S. Giora Shoham
Sex as Bait by S.Giora Shoham
The Mark of Cain by S. Giora Shoham
Valhalla, Calvary and Auschwitz by S. Giora Shoham
Vendetta (Italian) by Graeme R. Newman and Pietro Marongiu.
Vengeance: The Fight against Injustice by Pietro Marongiu and
    Graeme R. Newman. 2nd edition .
Who Pays? Casino Gambling and Organized Crime by Craig A.
    Zendzian.

PLUS
Just about every book written by Sir Arthur Conan Doyle,
Charles Dickens, and many hundreds of other classics
many recent, of fiction and nonfiction.

READ-ME.ORG INC.
OPEN ACCESS PUBLISHERS AND FREE LIBRARY

Australia, New York & Philadelphia

www.ingramcontent.com/pod-product-compliance
Lightning Source LLC
Chambersburg PA
CBHW061118100726
47911CB00013B/585